THE
KENNETH
ANDERSON
OMNIBUS

Kenneth Anderson (1910–74) was a hunter, nature enthusiast and an adventure-seeker. His love for the denizens of the jungle led to some of the best literature on wildlife and his books are acclaimed as classics. He has written approximately eight books and sixty short stories which recount many of his real-life adventures and hunting exploits in the jungles of South India. Anderson belonged to a Scottish family settled in India for six generations. He spent most of his life in Bengaluru, where he was employed with an aeronautics company. His invaluable contribution to the shikar literature in India continues to inspire scores of wildlife lovers.

THE
KENNETH
ANDERSON
OMNIBUS

VOL. III

SELECTED STORIES FROM

THE TIGER ROARS
AND
JUNGLES LONG AGO

RUPA

Published by
Rupa Publications India Pvt. Ltd 2014, 2025
161-B/4, Gulmohar House,
Yusuf Sarai Community Centre,
New Delhi 110049

Sales centres:
Bengaluru Chennai
Hyderabad Kolkata Mumbai

P-ISBN: 978-81-291-3272-7
E-ISBN: 978-81-291-4146-0

Eleventh impression 2025

15 14 13 12 11

Printed in India

Contents

The Tiger Roars

1

The Novice of Manchi

The narrow trail wound in and out between clumps of giant bamboo that rose on every side, the tall graceful fronds arching like huge bouquets of elegant, feathery blooms. It was the time when the bamboo tree was seeding, when each length of cane was crowded at its tip with tufts consisting of thousands of tiny seeds. These seeds look like ripe grains of wheat but are smaller; yet the weight of thousands of them was enough to bend each frond low to the earth, creaking and groaning under its burden as it moved with the gentle breezes passing along the jungle aisles.

The seeds fell in showers, carpeting the earth and the narrow path with a thick layer that mostly decayed, but here and there showed signs of sprouting into tiny dark green seedlings. This carpet felt like sawdust and had a springy consistency: it deadened the sound of anything moving over it, and of the killer that now stalked from bamboo clump to bamboo clump in search of a meal. Overhead, thousands of parakeets screeched as they hung by their feet, head downwards above the twisting trail, pecking the seeds with their razor-sharp curved beaks, deftly severing the husk from the kernel, which they crushed to a fine powder before swallowing. They were small compared with other members of the parrot family, being about twice the size of the domesticated budgerigar, but they were of many hues, ranging from emerald green to peacock blue, some with pale yellow wing-feathers and heads of rose pink or deep purple, and others of a uniform green, ringed around the neck with a narrow collar of red and black.

A lone traveller, walking cautiously along the jungle trail, did not heed the parakeets nor the thousands of other birds, including wild pigeons and doves, that fed on the seeds of the bamboos. He gazed intently ahead and glanced furtively to either side, slowing down and even halting now and then to study a particularly dense clump of bamboo before drawing level with it. His sharp, restless eyes tried to penetrate the thick growth to see if anything was hidden there. His ears, too, were alert for sounds far different from and far more arresting than the raucous, strident screech of the parakeets. The sounds he was listening for, and dreading to hear, were the sharp crack of a bamboo branch being broken, or the deep rumble of contented feeding, or the swishing sweep of ponderous feet brushing through the carpet of seeds and decaying leaves.

The man was afraid of meeting a wild elephant or a herd of them, for there were many in this area, especially at this time of the year. But his hearing was not attuned to the approach of the killer, who first sensed and then saw him. The killer made no sound whatever, unlike the screaming, fluttering birds above or the ponderous elephants beneath, engrossed in their search for vegetable food. This killer was by no means harmless, nor was he a vegetarian. He dealt death swiftly and surely and he was at this moment very hungry indeed.

The man was a poojaree, a member of an aboriginal jungle tribe that inhabits the forests of the Salem district in southern India, and the trail he was following was the footpath that led through the forest from the hamlet of Aiyur, southwards for about ten miles to the still smaller hamlet of Manchi, nestling on the slopes of a great range of hills. The *path* ran down a valley, as also did a rocky stream, the two crossing and recrossing frequently, and sometimes running parallel to each other, while the hills towered on both sides, to east and west, in an unbroken chain of jungle. The narrow *path* was visible now and again, but disappeared as suddenly beneath the tall, bending, swaying bamboos as they moved to the gentle currents of the forest breeze.

Fine webs, almost invisible, frequently caught and tickled the face of the poojaree whose attention was wholly concentrated on the possible presence of the elephants. He brushed them off angrily with both hands, much to the annoyance of the large, long-legged, yellow-and-black-and-red spiders, six inches and more across, whose webs extended from tree to tree, secured by gossamer-like threads that were unbelievably strong, supporting a central area of a web eight or ten feet in diameter and of an intricate, finely-woven pattern. The dew had condensed on these webs and drops of moisture glistened in the sunlight that filtered through the bamboo fronds. All was still, all was peaceful, except for the din of the feeding birds.

Keera, the poojaree, passed a dense clump of bamboo after making certain no elephant sheltered behind, but failed to see the killer in its black and rusty coat that crouched low to the earth and stared at him with malevolent, unblinking eyes.

The man heard a coughing roar twice: 'Aa-arrgh! Aa-arrgh!' Then the tiger charged.

Keera whirled around as a great shape with widely-extended jaws engulfed him. The poojaree screamed but once: 'Aiyooo-oo-oo!' He screamed no more. The birds that had ceased chattering for the moment, when the tragedy was enacted, started to screech again and from the side of the pathway came the crunch and crack of bones as the tiger began his meal.

Away on the hillside a troop of langur-monkeys had been feeding joyously, their cries of 'Whoomp! Whoomp, Whoomp!' echoing across the narrow valley. Then the sharp hearing of the langur-watchman caught the distant sound of the tiger's roars and the fainter, futile, agonized human scream. He knew that the tiger had made his kill and the hoarse, guttural, langur alarm-cry issued from his lips as he stood on his hind legs high up on a branch to discover if possible in which direction the killer was moving.

'Ha-aah! Harr! Harr!' called the watchman, over and over again. The langurs ceased playing and scampered in terror, to huddle in families on the tree-tops; while the deer and other creatures on the floor of the jungle, whose sharp ears had detected the sounds of death and the alarm of the monkeys, raced uphill and away from that valley of doom.

Time passed, and the life of the forest resumed its normal course. The birds forgot the tragedy in a matter of seconds; the monkeys and the other animals took perhaps an hour to calm down; while the poojarees in the distant hamlet of Manchi would undoubtedly have forgotten the death of their clansman Keera in a month or two had not another of them been killed a fortnight later; and, ten days after that, a third.

These things the poojarees could not forget. A dreadful fear overshadowed them. A scourge lay upon their tiny village; a man-eater had come to stay!

These people belong to a tribe that lives on the produce of the forest. They gather wild honey from giant combs built on high rocks and trees; they catch the iguana-lizard which they eat or sell for the aphrodisiac properties said to exist in its tail; they pick medicinal herbs and roots and berries which are traded as medicine; and they cut and collect bamboos, grass and the pods of the tamarind fruit, according to the season of the year. All for a pittance, less than an ordinary person living in Europe or America would spend on feeding his pet dog. Their work, their very existence depends upon the forest, and into that jungle a fearful menace had now come. No man who left his miserable grass hut in the morning knew whether he would return that night. No woman or child was safe; for the second and third victims had been, respectively, a young girl of nine years and a pregnant bride of fourteen!

None of them did anything about it except one man, and that was my old friend and instructor in jungle-lore, Byra the Poojaree. Once before had he summoned me, in the case of the 'Marauder of Kempekarai,' about which I have written elsewhere,* and once again he asked me to come to the help of the people of Manchi.

This time Byra arrived in person rather than convey the message through another. He walked ten miles or more from Manchi to

---

*See *Man-Eaters and Jungle Killers*, Chapter 1

Aiyur village, and thence nine miles to Denkanikota town, whence a bus brought him to Bangalore.

From the story he told me it was clear that the three killings had taken place in comparatively quick succession, within a total of twenty-four days and all within a radius of four miles from Manchi, in the vicinity of the track leading from Aiyur to Kempekarai along the deep valley that I have elsewhere referred to as 'Spider Valley,' because of the large spiders to be found there.

These killings indicated that the perpetrator was a comparative novice so far as man-eaters go. Either he was a young animal that had, for some reason or the other, just launched out on a career of man-eating; or he was a wounded tiger that had been almost incapacitated and was desperately hungry; or perhaps a tigress, killing merely to feed her cubs. This third alternative was extremely unlikely, as there was still a fair amount of game on the surrounding hills, while cattle were plentiful around the villages of Aiyur, Gulhatti and Bettamugalam.

The facts pointed more to his being a beginner. No experienced man-eater would have killed in such quick succession or almost in the same place, as had this tiger. Veterans are far too cunning to do that. They follow a circuitous beat of many miles, covering a large tract of land, and slay at sudden and infrequent intervals, all of which habits combine to make them extremely difficult to shoot.

The course for me to follow would be to strike quickly and bag this beast before he began to learn from experience and became more cautious and adept. That caution would come as soon as the villagers tried to retaliate by shooting him or by some other means. He would be frightened then; or perhaps he would be wounded. That would make him a wiser and far more dangerous antagonist.

I knew the terrain well. For many years I had tramped that dense bamboo jungle in the deep, narrow valley flanked by the two parallel ranges of towering hills, running north and south, closely bordering the banks of the narrow stream that also flowed southwards to merge finally into the Chinar river at a place called

Sopathy. The eastern range was the loftier of the two, culminating in a high peak named Gutherayan, near which was a picturesque forest bungalow known as the Kodekarai Forest Lodge. Kempekarai hamlet lay on the slopes of the other and western range, a short distance above the little stream.

The locale was almost the same as in my earlier adventure, except that the 'Marauder of Kempekarai' had been a more experienced man-eater, hunting in an area west and south of the little hamlet of that name. The present animal had so far confined his activities to the north of the settlement of Manchi and near to the Aiyur track, as I have just told you. For this reason he should be a comparatively easy proposition to bag.

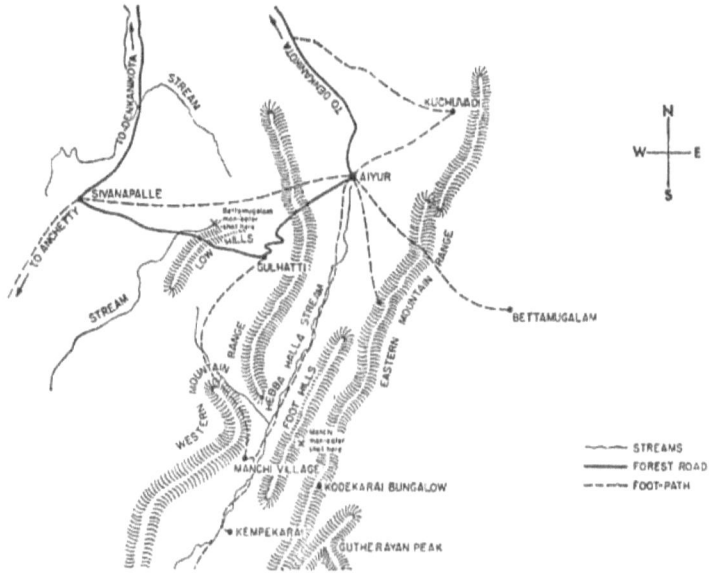

Bundling Byra and my camp kit into the Studebaker, with food to last for about a week in the form of flour for *chappaties*, bread, butter, vegetables—especially potatoes—and of course tea, coffee and sugar, together with my little tent and bedroll, we set out for Denkanikota and Aiyur. From the latter place we would have to walk to Manchi and that would mean that Byra and I must carry the load for upwards of ten miles. Fortunately, it would be downhill for most of the way going, but uphill coming back.

As far as possible, I avoid tinned foods on these excursions. I grant that they are convenient to transport. But like the villagers of India I like my food fresh and simple. Thereby I have contrived to avoid much indigestion and the other stomach troubles that appear to afflict half the sophisticated people of the world, Indians and Europeans alike.

I put my tent on Byra's head, slung the bedroll on to my back, piled the kitbag with the flour and vegetables on his, and carried the rest of the things, including the rifles, myself. I can assure you we were well weighed down, but Byra seemed to feel no inconvenience as he strode rapidly along in front of me.

The valley was hot and humid and I was bathed in perspiration. While my companion was exposed to greater risk from a wild elephant by walking in front, I was in more danger from the tiger, as man-eaters invariably attack the last person on the trail. In both cases, heavily burdened as we were, neither of us would have been able to do much about it. But I don't think we thought about elephants or tigers, being more bent upon reaching the journey's end as quickly as possible and ridding ourselves of our abominable loads.

We arrived at last, and with a sigh of relief I threw down the things I was carrying (except the rifle) just beyond the little pool of drinking water that was to figure so prominently in this adventure. The first requirement was tea—gallons of it—and I asked Byra to fill the kettle from the pool and light a fire quickly. Very soon we were pouring scalding tea down our throats and life seemed to be rosy once more.

By this time some of Byra's friends from the hamlet had gathered around us. They were all poojarees—an underfed, skinny and scantily-clad group—but all as tough as nails. The men wore little *moochas* and nothing else; the women were bare-breasted, the rest covered by threadbare saris that hung in shreds and hid nothing; the children, both boys and girls, were completely naked.

There were the usual greetings, whereupon Byra launched into a prolonged account of how he had travelled to Bangalore to bring his *dorai*, who had immediately come to their help. There was a murmur of amazement and, being of a practical turn of mind, I took advantage of the situation to despatch some of the elder boys to gather firewood from the brambles growing around the pool, and one of the men to lay in a store of water in the aluminium carrier and the water-bottle I had brought with me. These mundane but essential matters attended to, I set about munching the roasted meat, jam and buttered bread brought from home, while I asked my companions to tell me all they knew about the tiger.

I acquired little information other than the bare facts that Byra had already recounted, but there was one new item. Byra had set forth for Bangalore the previous morning. In the early afternoon of the same day, as nobody would go near the pool later than three o'clock for fear of the man-eater, four of the women had gone for water together. They had kept close to one another, relying on their numbers for safety.

The women had finished the task and were turning away when the eldest noticed a slight movement under one of the bushes bordering the jungle some fifty yards away. She looked closer. Her companions, noticing her staring at something, had all looked the same way. On the ground under that bush was the head of an enormous tiger. It was glaring at them hungrily and snarling! With screams they threw down their water-pots and bolted for the hamlet, less than 200 yards away. This time the tiger did not attack and they all got back in safety.

Two of those four women were among the group around me. One described the tiger's head as 'that big,' indicating a distance of a yard between outstretched hands. The other, who was a very matter-of-fact and comely young girl, and somewhat of a wit to boot, said it was big enough to eat all four of them and me as well. Her subtle smile after this statement was perhaps a hint that, after it was all over, I would at least be in good company inside the tiger's belly!

The news gladdened me and I noticed the gleam of satisfaction that sprang into Byra's eyes. Old hunter that he was, he knew that things would be easier for us now. If the tiger was there yesterday evening, as likely as not it would come again this evening. For all we knew, it might be watching us at that very moment.

This fresh development made me change my mind about pitching my tent near the pool. It would not fit into the plan that now came to my mind. To make camp within the hamlet itself was a far from attractive proposition, as the poojarees, who have many good attributes, do not count cleanliness among them. So I got some of the men to carry my things a little beyond the village, to where a wild jack-fruit tree was growing. Beneath its shade I pitched the small tent and put my belongings inside.

The plan that had come to me connected the tiger with the pool. Strange, indeed, that a situation of this nature should be twice destined to arise in waiting for a man-eater. In that earlier adventure at Kempekarai, just a few miles away but many years ago, I had waited all night long at a well for the 'marauder' to make an attempt to kill me. But I had waited in vain. Perhaps this tiger, which was certainly not such an experienced animal, would be more obliging and I was glad I had not made the mistake of pitching my tent, that was. more or less white in colour, within sight of the pool. Whereas the 'marauder' of years ago might have been tempted to attack the occupant, this recruit among man-eaters would surely be frightened away. Or so I reasoned, and Byra agreed with me. Events that night were to prove both of us quite wrong.

At sunset I ate an early supper, finishing the last of the roast I had brought. This time I made no tea and drank hardly any water, for experience had taught me that imbibing liquids does not help when a nightlong vigil for a man-eater is contemplated. Nature cannot be diverted from her normal practices, and the slightest fidgeting or movement on the part of the hunter will betray his presence to the tiger when he comes.

The night would be dark, for which reason I did not follow

quite the same plan as I had with the 'marauder.' That had been a moonlit night and I had deliberately advertised my presence at the well by working the squeaking pulley and pretending to draw water in order to attract the tiger. But this night would be totally dark and it would be foolish to show myself openly. He would hear and see me all right; the only trouble being that I certainly would not be able to see him, and might not be able to hear him either till it was too late!

So I decided to modify the scheme a little by sitting with my back against the *babul* tree some twenty feet from the water and facing the jungle. I would sit quite still and with no movement whatever. The man-eater could hardly attack from the rear. He would have to come from in front or from either side and sitting motionless would not only help me to hear him but it would puzzle him also. He might not notice me at all; or if he did, as a novice he would be perplexed at my immobility and decide to investigate. I hoped he would make some sound in the process.

When Byra heard my plan, he told me that it was a very stupid one. The tiger might attack without making any preliminary sound. He might come from behind. I would hear nothing and see nothing in that darkness; but the man-eater would certainly see me, while he (Byra) would never see me again. For that matter, the tiger might not come this way at all. Why should he be snooping around a pool of water at dead of night? The beast knew very well that people drew water from it—but during the hours of daylight and not at night.

While he was speaking, Byra looked at me significantly, and the meaning of his glance became quite apparent. He was trying to put me off.

'I know all that,' I interrupted testily, 'but it's the only way.' The old fellow was bent upon complicating the situation.

'I never meant that you should not sit for the tiger.' he said aggressively. 'What I meant was that you should be beside me. We should await his return together.'

'Idiot,' I interrupted, being as rude as I could, 'you have not the brains of a flea! In what way will your presence lessen the darkness? Keep out of this and let me try the plan I have in mind, at least for tonight. Tomorrow you may tell me a better one if you can think of one.'

'If you are here to listen,' he concluded pointedly.

And so, an hour before sunset, I took up my position near the little pool, my back to the *babul* tree and facing the jungle, the small stream beyond and the pathway along which we had come that morning. Inwardly, I hoped that the tiger would arrive early and see me and that in turn he would show himself as he had to the four girls, so that the episode might be closed before darkness fell. Unfortunately, the man-eater did not oblige.

The poojarees in the hamlet drew great clumps of thorns, which they had cut earlier, around the low entrances to their wattle huts, stepped gingerly between them and slipped inside. I could hear the thatched doors of the huts being barricaded from within with large stones, gathered from the stream for the purpose. These people believed in self-help, and it was evident they did not have much confidence in my ability to save them from the killer that now threatened their lives.

The sun had sunk behind the range of hills to the west, outlining their heights against a background of blue, which turned to pink and then to orange. As I was facing northeast, I could just catch brief glimpses of the beauties of this sunset. The orange deepened to blood-red, and then to crimson, green and yellow and violet and purple. An instant later it was quite dark.

While I had been watching the sunset abstractly, I had been listening to the sounds of the jungle which at all times are pleasant music to my ears, particularly at the close of the day and again at dawn. Two families of langur-monkeys, one on each of the slopes of the opposing ranges of hills, called to each other across the narrow, deep valley. 'Whoomp! Whoomp! Whoomp!' cried the males of one batch as they leapt from branch to branch, and back came the joyous notes from the other group on the hill slopes across the stream: 'Whoomp! Whoomp! Whoomp!' and 'Cheek! Cheek!' from the females and young.

Then the sounds of pleasure suddenly turned to those of fear and danger as the monkey-watchman of the more distant clan issued his staccato barking alarm cry: 'Ha-aah! Harr! Harr!' which he continued to repeat at short intervals.

The group nearer to me and on the same side of the valley fell silent, while their watchman in turn took up the note of warning, answering the more distant calls of his colleague: 'Haaah! Harr! Harr!' The two monkey sentinels kept answering one another and my nerves tingled pleasantly in expectation.

To one accustomed to such sounds there was a wealth of difference in the timbre of the calls. The voice of the distant watchman was filled with great fear and apprehension, and it was evident that he could see the source of danger. The watchman on this side of the valley, although sounding the alarm also, was merely doing his duty to alert his tribe. His notes were flat and matter of fact. This could be detected by the fact that he called each time immediately after the other watchman, like an echo.

The calls of the two monkeys were becoming less frequent when a junglecock, somewhere on the stream, screamed suddenly in fright: 'Kuck! Kuck! Kuck!' The hen with him, hearing the cries of fright made by her mate, flew quickly away crying: 'Krr-r-r-r! Keek! Keek! Keek!' Silence and a great stillness enveloped the jungle. Then a peacock gave sign of nervousness; 'Quank! Quank! Quank!' His metallic notes broke the stillness and a moment later I could hear the distant heavy flapping of wings as he launched his weighty body into the air to reach a place of greater safety.

I knew the tiger was afoot! He had descended the opposite range of hills and been discovered by the distant langur-watchman. He had crossed the stream and disturbed the jungle fowls and the peacock. He was now coming straight towards the pool and the spot where I was seated.

It was growing darker with the passing of each minute. Would the keen eyes of the nearer langur-watchman detect him? Although the monkey had the advantage of elevation, he was comparatively far away, and no tiger—not even a beginner among man-eaters—will betray his presence unnecessarily. My doubt was settled the next instant when the watchman on the hillside to my left broke forth hysterically, fearfully: 'Ha-aah! Harr! Harr!' His cries were quick now, and independent of his distant colleague, who was still calling, but at long intervals. The note of fear was there this time—of danger and sudden death. He had seen the man-eater. And it was much closer to me than I had thought.

But of the tiger itself I could see or hear nothing. It was growing darker all the time. The bushes at the edge of the jungle before me had lost their individual outlines. They appeared as grey masses against a background of deep chocolate, turning rapidly black. A frightened hush fell over the forest, permeating it, enveloping it. The further langur-watchman had stopped calling altogether, and the nearer one barked only intermittently. He could see the tiger no longer and, having fulfilled his duty by alarming his tribe, was wondering what next to do about it.

The summits of the ranges of hills to my right and left showed themselves as ragged lines of intense blackness against a background of lesser darkness, studded by myriads of stars, flashing and blazing in a distant glory all their own. I concentrated upon one of them. It seemed to change its colours constantly, like a heavenly gem.

While staring into the blackness before me I glanced alternatively from right to left. I slowed my breathing, even tried to hold my breath altogether, in an effort to hear the very faintest of sounds. But I saw and heard nothing.

Then, with nerve-shattering abruptness, a sambar belled in the thickets just the other side of the pool: 'Dhank! Oonk! Oonk!'

The brambles crackled to his departure as he crashed his way through. The sounds of his running were lost in a few seconds, but he continued to call with alarm as he rattled over the pebbles in the stream and scrambled up the slopes of the opposing range of hills, 'Oonk! Oonk! Oonk!' came his cries as they grew fainter with the ever-increasing distance.

Grateful, indeed, was I for the warnings of my jungle friends, for they told me as unmistakably as if I had seen him with my own eyes that the tiger was within a few yards of where I was sitting. The questions were: Had he seen me? Would he see me?

I know the value of stillness in the jungle, and so I sat absolutely motionless, hardly daring to breathe. That was my only hope of escaping the tiger's immediate attention.

The seconds ticked interminably by. They appeared to pass into minutes and then into hours, though I knew that they were only seconds. Then I heard a gentle rustle to my right: the faintest of sounds, as of a leaf being turned over, and it came from a direction in line with the pool. Not a breath of air passed which could have caused that dry leaf to be moved and I knew that the author of the sound was moving through the undergrowth, hidden from my sight, and passing the pool at that moment, and that in a few moments more he would have passed behind me.

Holding my breath I listened intently, but I heard no further sound. Every instinct warned me that the tiger had now passed and was somewhere behind the bushes on the other side of the *babul* tree against which I was leaning. I was filled with an urge to turn around and face the danger, but I knew that if I did so I would certainly make some faint noise. However slight it might be, the tiger would hear it and in all probability would turn to investigate. So I overcame the urge, but turned my head around to see if the beast was creeping upon me from the rear. All I could see was the trunk of the *babul* tree only a few inches away, and beyond that darkness.

I do not know for how long I endured this suspense, but suddenly the silence was shattered by the high-pitched, fear-laden yelping bark of a village dog in the poojaree hamlet so close behind me. The tension was relieved for the moment and I breathed more easily. Two things were evident to me now. The tiger had passed the well without detecting my presence, and had gone towards the wattle huts, obviously in search of human prey. Secondly, and beyond any doubt, it was the man-eater, as no ordinary tiger would deliberately wander near human habitation.

At that moment a perfectly silly notion entered my head. I reasoned that I could achieve no useful purpose by remaining where I was. Assuming that the man-eater did not succeed in finding a human victim, there was little chance that he would retrace his steps and pass the pool again. He might wander away in any direction, while if he did return, he would come upon me from the rear and this time he might not fail to detect my presence.

I cannot tell you, however, why I did not think of doing the most obvious thing; just sit where I was, but facing the hamlet. Instead, I made up my mind to go towards the hamlet myself, shine my torch when I came close enough, and pick up the glare of the tiger's eyes in its beam. That should afford me an easy shot.

This was a silly thing to do. Had I remained where I was, the tiger might have returned to drink at the pool, while I would have been in a fair position, behind the stem of the *babul* tree, for an easy shot. Instead, I got stealthily to my feet, and in a half-crouching position, started advancing towards the hamlet which, as I have already told you, was hardly 200 yards away.

Within a few steps I realized my foolishness, for although there was a well-defined pathway leading from the huts to the pool, in the intense darkness I could not see it and began stumbling among the bushes, making enough noise to scare away the man-eater or urge him to attack. I then thought of going back to the friendly *babul*, but again decided to advance, this time with the full knowledge that the man-eater might be five yards away, behind any bush, and I would not be able to see it.

The hysterical barking of the cur was taken up by others of its kind, and by now some half-dozen village dogs were yowling their heads off in a perfect frenzy, making enough noise to unnerve the boldest of man-eaters. It was extremely doubtful that the tiger would pursue his original intentions in the face of this din; he would either slink off or turn back. And if he did turn back, he would run into me, face to face, at any moment.

With this thought in mind, I made the second mistake of the evening. I switched on my torch—far too soon, as it turned out! As the bright beam cut through the darkness the tiger, of which I did not catch a glimpse, true to the cowardly code of most man-eaters, roared shatteringly from somewhere in front, and I could hear him crashing into the dry scrub beyond.

There was no point in further caution. My quarry had fled and I followed the torch-beam dejectedly towards the *poojarees'* wattle huts while cursing myself repeatedly for the idiot I had been. Upon reaching the hamlet, I called softly to Byra, who emerged from one of the huts. He had been awake and had listened to the alarm-cries of the langurs at sunset, followed by those other sounds. The barking of the dogs had mystified him till the tiger had roared. Only then had he realized that the man-eater was in the village itself. He was even more surprised at finding me there also.

Quickly I related what had happened and was not comforted with Byra's brief comment, heavy with sarcasm. 'Did the *dorai* think he was following a rabbit? Perhaps the years have affected his wisdom!'

It was now just after eight o'clock, and with nothing better to do, I walked to my tent, which you will remember I had pitched under the jack-fruit tree beyond the village, lit the small hurricane lantern hanging from the ventral pole, and made myself a pot of tea. That done, I closed and fastened the flap of the tent, spread my bedding on the ground, not having burdened myself with the weight of a camp cot, extinguished the lantern because I do not like sleeping with a light burning, and was soon fast asleep.

Something awakened me with a start. In the jungle one does not wake as city folk usually do from the snug warmth of a comfortable bed, to yawn and stretch in luxury and maybe spend another five minutes contemplating with dismay the tasks that have to be performed. The forest teaches its inhabitants to sleep alert. When they awaken, they are keyed to instant action, for a second's delay may be their last.

When I opened my eyes, the vague feeling of danger that filled my mind synchronized with my groping hand and outstretched fingers as they fumbled for the rifle I had placed loaded on the ground beside me. Its comforting hardness brought assurance as I sat up to discover what had awakened me with that urgent, oppressive sense of peril.

For a second I could hear nothing, and then came the faintest of scratching sounds, which stopped and started again after a moment or two—scrape, scrape—stop—scratch, scratch—silence, and then once more. The side of the tent moved slightly and something entered from underneath; something that groped about here and there with a sinister purpose. Was it a snake?

That something encountered the edge of my bedding as it lay on the ground to my left barely a foot away, became entangled with it, and pulled away sharply, wrenching canvas and groundsheet with a sharp, tearing noise. Claws! The man-eater was outside!

He had sensed the presence of a human being within the tent, but fortunately, with no knowledge of its flimsy structure, had tried to feel with his paw under the canvas and along the ground in the hope of reaching his prey, whom he would drag out before the victim was aware of what was happening.

A neat little plan, indeed; the only fault being that the victim was myself! Fortunate, indeed, that a premonition of terrible danger had awakened me in time.

I quickly pulled the rifle across my body as I lay on the ground, pointing the muzzle towards where I knew the tiger must be, and slid my right hand towards the trigger.

Remember, it was pitch-dark in the tent when this happened and I did not know exactly where, and in what position the tiger was standing outside. I waited for the next movement and it came again as the groping paw wrenched once more at the bedroll.

Then I pressed the trigger!

There was a deafening explosion and I scrambled to my feet, working the underlever of the .405 Winchester feverishly to fire two more shots blindly through the canvas side of my tent.

There was no sound from the tiger. Was it dead? Even so, it should have uttered a last gasp or gurgle. Was it wounded? Then surely it would have roared with pain. Had it got away? I must have missed. That could be the only explanation for the unaccountable silence.

Like a fool I had once again made an inexcusable mistake. My torch was clamped to the rifle. Why had I not switched it on for a brief moment before firing? A second or two of torchlight would have sufficed to indicate the direction from which that groping paw was coming and where the tiger was standing outside the tent. Instead I had pressed the trigger blindly in total darkness; three times, moreover, hoping to hit an animal whose whereabouts I did not know.

With torch alight, I hastily opened the tapes closing the entrance to the tent and stepped forth cautiously, to direct the torchbeam in every direction. As I had already guessed, the man-eater had escaped, nor was there the slightest sound to indicate in which direction he had fled.

My three shots had awakened the poojarees in Manchi hamlet. I could hear the voices of Byra and some others calling anxiously, inquiring if all was well. Knowing that if I did not go to them soon, the poor fellows would brave the darkness and come to find out what had happened, I walked the short distance to the huts by torchlight and told a huddled, frightened group of little jungle men just what had taken place.

They insisted on coming back with me right away to see the three bullet holes in the canvas of my tent for themselves, and the ragged edges in my bedding made by the tiger's claws. They called loudly upon God in thanks for protecting me. Then I had to leave them back at the hamlet, where Byra implored me to share the hut in which he slept for the rest of the night and not risk going back to my tent.

But this invitation I declined and marched back once again,

and lay down to continue a much disturbed sleep this time with the hurricane lantern brightly burning. Sheer disgust with myself and things in general caused me to awaken long after sunrise. Voices outside greeted me, and opening the tent-flap I found all the poojarees from the hamlet squatting around in a semicircle.

The reason for their visit was a simple one. My foolish actions of the previous evening and night, and the misses I had made with the three shots I had fired, was to be explained in just two words, both of them very simple: black magic! Someone had cast a spell upon me and my rifle, so that I and the weapon did not act in coordination. Who had done it? Why? When? How? The spell would have to be removed if I hoped to kill the man-eater.

Superstition of this sort is rife amongst the simple people of the Indian forests, and large numbers of townsfolk as well. I knew that no amount of reasoning, persuasion or argument would make the poojarees think otherwise. If I ignored their belief, they would just cease cooperating with me, and then blame my failure on the spell that had been cast on me and my weapon. The shortest and easiest way was to agree.

I said, 'Yes; some misbegotten son of a ... has cast a spell without doubt. Will you please remove it, if you can?'

In turn, the eldest among them replied, 'Yes, but it will cost five rupees to do this,' going on to explain that this sum covered the cost of a fowl that had to be sacrificed, and various other articles, together with the fee for performing the *pooja*.

I agreed again, paid the five rupees, and went inside the tent to snatch another hour of sleep. But disgust with myself prevented me from sleeping and I fell to thinking about the man-eater. The raucous screeching of an unfortunate chicken having its throat cut, followed by the acrid smell of smoke and incense, announced that *pooja* was being performed.

In due course Byra's voice called to me from without: '*Dorai! Dorai!* Wake up and come out. The spell is broken. Let us search for the tiger now. We will surely find him, and this time he will fall to your rifle with a single shot, for the weapon will obey your command.'

The *pooja* was not quite complete, however. The grey-beard, who was also the sorcerer of the hamlet, asked for my rifle. Laying it on the ground he made various marks in red and white, using *konkam* powder and lime (*chunam*) respectively, on both sides of the stock. The entrails of the chicken were next looped into a circle and passed up and down the length of the barrel half-a-dozen times to the accompaniment of muttered mantras and some more incense smoke. Finally he scattered the fire in four directions, calling loudly to the tiger to come forth and be shot.

The sun was high in the sky by the time all this was over. Byra and a poojaree lad of about twenty years of age, who turned out to be the grandson of the old man who had conducted the *pooja*, then invited me to accompany them into the forest in search of the man-eater. As everybody knows, to look for a tiger in any jungle, especially a man-eater, by walking about in broad daylight is not only hopeless but foolish and a waste of time. My regard for Byra's junglecraft was boundless, but that a hunter of his experience could lend himself to this sort of foolishness surprised me.

My looks must have shown my disapproval, but Byra and the lad together urged me to waste no further time in idle talk. Evidently they had implicit faith in their sorcerer. We started, Byra leading, then me and next the boy, but as soon as we were out of sight of the hamlet I insisted on altering this marching order and exchanged places with Muthu, for that was the lad's name. If the man-eater did see us, regardless of all the hocus-pocus that had just been performed, the chances were that, like all man-eaters, this one would decide to attack the last individual in the line of march, and the unarmed youngster would not have a chance.

We walked downhill to the streambed where we cast around in the loose, dry sand for recent tracks. Difficult as it always is in such terrain to differentiate between fresh and old spoors, the two poojarees were not long in finding the tiger's tracks where he had approached the pool, with me sitting near it, the previous night a little later, and nearly a furlong away, they found his trail again, this time leading away from the village. Whether this was the spoor left by the tiger when my light near the hamlet had alarmed him, or later on after I had fired my three shots through the tent, was settled by the fact that the scooping out of the grains of sand at the toe portions of the tracks, and the marks of all four feet separately on the ground, showed that our quarry was moving very fast when he made them, with no attempt at concealment or caution. Evidently he was hurrying away after being badly frightened and this appeared to indicate we were following the trail left by the man-eater after I had fired those foolish shots. The absence of blood anywhere confirmed that he was uninjured.

We had not gone far when the trail veered abruptly to the right and led straight up the hillside on the eastern bank of the stream. I remembered that this was the direction from which the monkey-watchman of the first batch of langurs had voiced his alarm the evening before, when the tiger was descending the hill. Now the tiger had returned the same way. Very probably his lair was in a cave somewhere higher up that hill, or perhaps some distance further away, on the slopes of the Gutherayan mountain.

With this discovery came difficulties. The ground became hard and stony once we had traversed the low-lying belt of bamboos. Clumps of spear-grass grew in between rocks and small boulders and all signs of pug-marks vanished entirely.

The two poojarees, experts though they were in woodcraft, were soon at a complete loss. They moved around in small circles, trying to pick up the trail. At times Byra, and then his young companion, would come upon a broken stem of grass or an overturned stone that showed the way the tiger had gone. But this was not for long and very soon they were forced to a halt. Beyond knowing that the tiger had gone up the hill, we had no further indication of his whereabouts.

We discussed the matter in whispers and decided to climb the hill ourselves in the vague hope of coming upon a cave of some sort in which the man-eater might be hiding. To proceed in single file meant covering only a single line of advance, so we decided to fan out slightly in order to search a wider area. Byra went about a hundred yards to my right but remained within sight, while Muthu moved off about the same distance to my left. Then the three of us started to advance cautiously.

The ground became more stony and the boulders increased in size and number, but we came across no signs of a lair. The hillock we were climbing might have been about 500 feet high, but in due course we reached the top and were able to look down the other side. Here the ground dropped sharply to a lush valley, thickly covered with bamboo, before it started to climb the next foothill. Above that hill rose the peak of the Gutherayan mountain.

At a signal from me, and maintaining the same distance apart, the three of us began the steep descent. On this side the hillock was more fertile. There were fewer rocks and boulders, larger and taller clumps of grass, and even bushes and stunted trees that increased in number till we had reached the region of bamboos, where we found ourselves in a green twilit valley beneath the towering fronds. Now we could no longer see each other, and very soon I felt that my companions, unarmed as they were, had exposed themselves to terrible risk, for I could not help them should the tiger decide to attack. The bamboos and heavy jungle afforded ample cover and even the keen eyes of the two aborigines could not possibly penetrate the green wall that enveloped the three of us.

It was as if this thought gave rise to action, for just then I heard a shrill scream of terror from the poojaree boy, who was about a hundred yards to my left. This was followed by short, sharp 'woofs' as the tiger charged him. The roars ended abruptly when Byra, to my right, gave voice to a volley of shouts. Knowing he was doing this in an attempt to frighten off the attacker I added my yells to his as I turned and crashed towards the spot from which the scream and the roars had come.

Short as the distance was, Byra had caught up with me before we found the lad. He was lying on his face just beyond a pile of boulders and long grass, the back of his skull crushed in, while deep fang marks at the base of the neck and over the right shoulder showed where the tiger had first bitten him before smashing his skull with a stroke of the paw. Possibly the man-eater had been seized by a mixture of fear and rage at hearing our shouts, intended, as I have told you, to save the boy's life. But in this instance they had sealed his fate, for the tiger had killed him.

The flattened grass on the opposite side of the pile of boulders showed where the man-eater had been hiding, waiting till the lad had passed before pouncing upon him from behind. We turned the young poojaree over and were confronted by a ghastly spectacle. The force of the blow upon the back of his head had caused the eyeballs to protrude, while the boy had bitten through his own tongue so that the end hung loosely from his mouth, held by a shred of flesh. Blood seeped into the sand where it was forming a little pool.

Shaken and feeling sick, I turned to my companion. His jet-black face had turned to an ashen hue and his features worked violently with emotion. But not a word did he say. Nor did I. What was there to say? We—and most certainly I—could only blame ourselves for our carelessness and for exposing this unarmed youth to the fiendish cunningness of the tiger.

My watch showed it was just eleven o'clock and the sun beat mercilessly down upon the scene.

It took some minutes to recover from the shock.

Then I said, 'You were so sure that we would kill the tiger after that silly *pooja*. Instead, he has slain one of us!'

Byra did not answer at once. When he spoke there was resentment in his tone. 'The sorcerer should have sacrificed a cock. Instead, he slew a hen, for the hen cost him a rupee less. But it has cost his grandson his life!'

I was scarcely listening. An idea had flashed into my mind. I walked through the long grass to the boulders, stepped on one, and looked back at the body. Barely ten yards! The distance was almost too close. There were only four boulders lying haphazardly together, and the largest of them, the one on which I stood, was about three feet high. The others were much smaller.

The idea then became a definite plan. Since there were already some stones on the spot, would the tiger notice if a few more were added? Perhaps not, provided the extra stones were so placed as not to give rise to undue suspicion.

I turned to Byra and said, 'The night will be dark and this will tempt the devil we are after to return to his kill early, provided we leave the body where it is. For he is hungry, remember. He was hungry last night. That was why he went so boldly to the huts at Manchi. And he has not eaten since then. Tonight he will be very hungry indeed. So we will bring some more boulders to add to these four and make a hide in which I will sit. At this close range, when my torchlight falls upon him, I cannot miss.'

'*Dorai* you're completely mad,' commented the old hunter. 'As soon as he sees the hide he'll suspect something. Perhaps he may go away. Maybe not! If he should spring over the boulders, he will be on top of you before you know where you are.'

'Besides,' he continued, 'it's our duty to return to Manchi and tell that rascally grandfather what has happened to the poor boy. Then the men from the village will come and bear his body away and burn it tonight. Thus his soul will gain peace. If we leave his remains here to be eaten by the tiger, and not burn them, the soul will wander in these jungles and torment us for failing to do our duty.'

'The tiger will not eat them,' I cut in sharply, 'for I will be among the boulders to prevent him. That I promise you. Is this not a good chance to be avenged upon this devil? If I succeed in slaying him tonight, will I not save many lives, perhaps your own among them? As a hunter yourself, don't you agree it would be foolish for us to lose such a golden opportunity?'

Byra did not reply. I could feel him weakening. Finally he looked at me and there was complete innocence in his expression.

'We've searched everywhere and cannot find the body, *dorai*. Let's go back now and inform the others. Tomorrow morning we will search again. Tonight you will sit at the side of some jungle *path* to await the tiger, should he pass by, while I will perch like a monkey on a tree, out of sight but not out of hearing, in case you should need my help.'

Thus Byra settled the issue with his conscience and we got to work in right earnest.

In order not to arouse the tiger's suspicion, we moved quite 200 yards away to another area strewn with boulders, big and small. Together we carried half a dozen of the larger ones, one at a time, and placed them in a rough circle with the four boulders that were already there. On this foundation we placed smaller stones, so that in time we had built a circular wall maybe three feet high. I realized it would not do to make this wall any higher, for the additional safety thus gained would be of no avail should the tiger become suspicious on seeing a construction before him that had not been there on his last visit.

Next, into crevices between the stones we stuck handfuls of the tough grass which we tore from tufts and clumps growing some distance away. All this took a long time and was strenuous work, for you must realize the sun beat down on us mercilessly, and the stones and the grass had to be brought from a distance to avoid creating suspicion.

When we left Manchi that morning, boosted by the sorcerer's confidence that we would kill the tiger, I had brought only my rifle and no torch or water-bottle. It would be dangerous to send Byra back alone to fetch these things. Either we would both have to go back, or I could go myself and leave the poojaree up a tree, and if I did that there was always the chance that the tiger might return during my absence and carry away the cadaver of the. unfortunate boy to some more remote spot where it would be difficult for us to find it again.

After considering all these factors in whispers, we decided that we had no choice but to take up our positions straight away. I within the small three-foot fort we had constructed and Byra on some tree within hearing distance, and remain in our places till next morning, in the hope that the man-eater would remember his human victim and come back for a meal. We could only hope that the tiger had not been in hiding within hearing distance all this while, for then our movements during the past three hours would undoubtedly have alarmed him and he would have moved off long ago, not to return. Our only chance of success lay in the hope that he might have gone higher up the hill in search of water and had not heard us. It was most unlikely that he had returned to the stream in the valley for, as I have told you, it was quite dry at this time of the year.

We cast around in a wide circle for a suitable tree for Byra, and came upon one about half-a-furlong away, slightly lower down the hill from the spot where the boy had been killed. This was a fairly large tamarind and offered ample scope for the old poojaree to shelter in comfortably till I called him next morning.

It was two-fifteen in the afternoon, perhaps the hottest time of day, when Byra climbed the tamarind after earnestly advising me to be careful and not fall asleep at any cost. Leaving him there, I returned to my little fort, scrambled over the scorching stones we had placed there to form the wall, and tried to settle down inside. I at once encountered the first difficulty. The ground was so hot that I could not sit on it, but had to remain crouched on my haunches. Apart from being a painful and uncomfortable posture, the wall was not high enough for it. My head showed above the top and would be easily seen from outside, so I had to sit with head bowed to try to conceal myself.

It did not take me long to realize that such a position was absurd and dangerous, for I would not be able to see the tiger should he creep upon me.

I got out of the hide then, walked some distance away, and plucked several handfuls of tough grass stems which I stuck very closely together into the *pugaree* of my 'Gurkha' hat. This took a little time, but I was satisfied with the task eventually. When seen from a distance, there was no hat to be seen, only another clump of grass.

Donning the hat, I returned within my fort of stones, crouched once more on my haunches and attempted to remain motionless. I was just able to look over the rim of the rocks in a half-circle, before and to both sides of me, and by turning my head ever so slowly to right and left, I could even see behind. This movement would not be very noticeable, I felt, as the whole 'clump' of grass on my hat would turn with it and might be mistaken by the tiger for the effect of the hot breeze that was blowing from the valley and the streambed towards the hill-tops and was rippling the bowed heads of the dried grass in waves from time to time.

I soon found that I could not remain still in that crouching posture for very long. My ankles became painful and the calves of my legs became numb. I had to move this way and that, slowly and a little at a time, till after four o'clock, when the earth cooled sufficiently to allow me to sit down.

Up to this time the surroundings had been abnormally silent. Not an animal or bird had indicated its presence by sight or sound. All creation—and no doubt the tiger, too—was sheltering from the devastating heat. Only twice had I seen movement, firstly when a giant iguana lizard attempted to cross, caught sight of Muthu's body on the ground, turned abruptly and scrambled away, and later, when a small python, hanging unnoticed head downwards from a low tree, had dropped upon a passing ground squirrel to crush it to death. I had seen the squirrel, but had not noticed the snake till I saw the python's coils squirming in the grass and heard the squeaks of the victim being crushed to death.

There was a marked cooling of the air by five o'clock and this reminded me that I had drunk no water since morning. There was not a drop to drink anyhow, and worst of all, I would have to remain thirsty till I returned to Manchi the following morning—a truly formidable thought!

A partridge on the hillside to my left broke the long silence at last 'Kee-kok-kik! Kee-kok-kok! Kee-kok-kok!' he called in challenge and within minutes came the acceptance to a fight from another male bird slightly higher up the hill: 'Kee-kok-kok! Kee-kok-kok! Kee-kok-kok!'

The two partridges challenged each other frequently as they drew closer together, hastening to the fray, till finally they met. Then with hysterical cries of 'Kok! Kok! Kok!', the duel started in earnest. Unfortunately I could not see the birds but could picture the battle in my imagination for the ten minutes or so that it lasted, before one of the contestants gave way to the superior prowess and stamina of his adversary. He flew helter-skelter from the scene of battle. I was just able to glimpse his brown form sailing precipitately downhill to safety, while the other bird remained to voice the victory cry 'Kee-kok-kok! Kee-kok-kok! Kee-kok-kik!' once again.

The battle of the partridges had served to while away the time. It was now 5-40 p.m. and the calls of junglecocks from the streambed in the valley rose to announce the advent of eventide. 'Wheew! Kuck-kya-kya-kuckm!' they crowed from down below, to be answered by other cocks on the hillsides in all directions. Occasionally a peafowl voiced its meowing cry, while *bulbuls* in hundreds, on bushes and thickets, joined in the general symphony of calls that remain indelible in the memory of all that have known these beautiful jungles.

But it would not do for me to pay too much heed to these sounds much as I enjoyed hearing them. I would have to remain keenly alert from now onwards, for with nightfall drawing near, the man-eater would remember his victim and might decide to return at any moment. At this time the two tribes of langur-monkeys, one of them on the hilltop above me and the other somewhere on the adjacent hill across the stream, started their eventide gambols, frolicking among themselves and calling boldly to each other across the intervening valley. 'Whoomp! Whoomp! Whoomp!' they screamed as they leaped from branch to branch. I could not see them from where I was sitting, but could hear the bang and thud of their bodies as they landed heavily among the branches of the trees.

I was grateful for the presence of the langur-monkeys. I knew that each tribe would have its own watchman, sitting alert on a tree-top, serious, silent and intently scanning the ground below for movement and danger.

The sun set behind the range of hills at my back and the shades of evening spread rapidly around me. The grasses and bushes and boulders that had been so clear all this while now became hazy and blurred. Distances lost their perspective. In a few moments there was no background to be seen at all; just the few indistinct bushes that grew in my immediate vicinity. All else was a dark-grey void, rapidly turning to chocolate and then to blackness. Muthu's body, only ten yards away, lost its shape and became merely a darker heap upon the rapidly darkening ground.

There was a whirring flutter of movement behind my head that startled me, accompanied by high-pitched, creaking squeaks. The long-eared bat, intent on its search for insects, had thought there might be a few in the clump of grass adorning my hat and had come to investigate. Softly a nightjar fluttered on to one of the stones forming my rampart. It was so close that by stretching out my hand I could have caught it, and I was pleased with myself at having sat so still, for I had even deceived this bird into not noticing my presence. The nightjar snuggled low on the hot rock, puffed out its throat with air, and voiced its usual cry: 'Chuck! Chuck! Chuck! Chuck! Chuckoooooo!'

Then it noticed poor Muthu. Suddenly it took fright, fluttered both its wings like a giant moth, and sailed into the heavy air and out of sight. A little later I could hear it again, this time from far away, where the bird thought it was quite safe, voicing its jerky call.

Now I could no longer see the bushes, the grasses, the stones, nor even poor Muthu. A curtain of blackness closed over me with the falling of night. The stars that to a certain extent illumine the darkness in a jungle were few this night as I raised my eyes heavenwards in search of them. The steely blue-black of the usual night sky was covered by a ruffled blanket of small, broken, cirrocumuli clouds, resembling the ringlets of wool on a sheepskin. They stretched between the two ranges of hills and all but hid the stars from sight.

It was a perfect night for the man-eater to discover my presence and add me to his menu without my ever being aware of his nearness. To see him in such darkness was impossible, and I was entirely at his mercy. Suddenly I became very frightened and began to shiver. Why had I been so foolhardy as to place myself in this predicament by not listening to the old Poojaree's experienced advice? I felt like shouting to Byra. I felt like getting up and dashing away from this horrid place to the faraway tamarind tree in which I knew my friend, the jungle man, was sheltering. A feeling of being closed in, of suffocation, of claustrophobia, gripped me. Panic all but overwhelmed me and the sweat of nervous terror streamed down my face. In the distance, a horned-owl hooted dismally: 'Whoo! Whoooo! Whoo! Whoooo! Whoo! Whoooo!'

At that moment the calm of the night was shattered by the dying scream of a sambar stag from the stream bed down in the valley.

'Aar-aar-aarrhh-aaarrhh!' it shrieked in its agony, and once again 'Aaahhh-gggrrrhhh!' Then there was silence.

I knew the animal that was being done to death at that moment was a stag, for a doe would have uttered a cry of far higher pitch, while the shriek of a spotted deer would have been quite different. Three possible foes could be killing that stag; a pack of wild dogs, a panther or a tiger. I decided against the dogs; a pack would have raised its hunting calls and I would have heard them long ago. Besides, these dogs do not hunt on dark nights. So the slayer was either a large panther of the thendu variety, or a tiger. Nothing else could be killing an animal as big as a sambar stag. Even a thendu would have all its work cut out to bring down a victim of that size.

Very likely the killer was a tiger after all. But was it the man-eater, who was reputed to eat only human flesh? Or was it some ordinary wandering tiger who happened to be in the vicinity too? I knew that the man-eater could not subsist on human flesh alone. His kills were too few and far between. He must be devouring animals as well, and I remembered he was very hungry that night, not having eaten for some time. Very likely it was he who had attacked the stag after all. Perhaps he had been returning for Muthu and had come upon the deer by chance.

The sambar was dead now and all sounds had ceased. The tiger would spend the rest of the night feeding on this new victim and would not come near the body of the poojaree lad. My vigil would have been in vain. The thought was very mortifying indeed.

Mixed feelings of relief from immediate danger, and sheer disgust with myself at my cowardice, set in when I realized that only a few moments earlier I had been trembling, scared out of my wits at nothing but the darkness and the thought of the man-eater's proximity.

I knew that the old poojaree, too, must have heard the sambar's death-scream. Like me, he would wonder if the killer was the man-eater or some other animal. I wondered what conclusion he had reached. The slaying of the sambar had brought to an end the nervous tension under which I had been labouring. I was quite calm now as I wondered over and over again whether the man-eater would return or not.

For the next half-hour or so the forest was hushed and strangely silent. It was as if its denizens were aware that danger lurked by the streambed, and that sudden and violent death awaited any of them who betrayed his presence. I glanced at my watch. It was not yet ten o'clock. I had many hours of tiring vigil before me.

After that the jungle gradually came to life again. I could hear the stealthy nibbling of grass by a barking-deer a few yards to my right. Down below, on the banks of the stream, an elephant was breaking bamboos.

As the heated air from the valley started to rise, the colder air from the hilltops rushed down to take its place. This caused fitful gusts of breeze to blow and carried to the munching barking-deer the smell of Muthu's body that was now beginning to make itself felt. There was a sudden noise as the little animal dashed away for a few yards. Then it came to a halt to voice its barking alarm-cry: 'Kharr! Kharr! Kharr! Kharr!'

The barks came at intervals of a few minutes. It seemed incredible that such a small animal could make such a loud noise. I knew that the call of a barking-deer can be heard for over a mile on a still night.

Shortly afterwards the elephant in the valley, in his hunt for fresh bamboo-shoots, moved upstream. This brought him to the remains of the stag that had been killed a short while earlier. Probably the killer, panther or tiger, was still there, feeding on his prey. Whatever it was, the elephant became excited and began to trumpet repeatedly, the brassy scream of each note disturbing the silence of the forest.

And then I heard it clearly. 'Wr-aagh! Wrr-aagh!'—the roars of an angry tiger coming from the same direction. The elephant screamed again and again, and the tiger roared its defiance in between, answer for answer. I could imagine the scene. The tiger had been feeding, or perhaps just sleeping by the sambar's remains, when the elephant had blundered upon him. Would the encounter develop into a fight, or would one or other of the animals lose its nerve and retreat?

The screams of the elephant began to change in timbre. The high-pitched note of fear gave place to the longer, slightly lower note of anger. I could make out that the animal was a bull. He resented the tiger's presence amongst the bamboos, which he no doubt regarded as his own property, and was rapidly losing his temper.

What would the tiger do? The matter was not left in doubt for long. He suddenly lost his nerve and decided to give way to the irate elephant, even if it meant abandoning his kill. There was sudden silence when the tiger beat a retreat, while the bull elephant, finding his bluster had succeeded in driving away the foe, slowly regained his composure and ceased to trumpet.

Silence once again descended upon the forest. The fleecy clouds that had been hiding the stars since sunset had disappeared about an hour before, and I could now see the dark form that was Muthu, and the nearer bushes and grasses, reasonably clearly in the light of the stars. Now at least I might be able to see the man-eater should he decide to return to Muthu's body. This caused me to wonder again whether the tiger that had just had that altercation with the elephant was the man-eater or not. His display of cowardice tended to offer an affirmative answer.

My thoughts were disturbed at that instant by a growl! I heard it only once and so I could not quite locate the sound or where it had come from, but it was an unmistakable growl. I fancied it had come from somewhere behind me and lower down the hillside, but I was not quite sure.

As quietly as possible, I turned my body a few inches to the left, so as to be able to observe whether anything was approaching from that direction, but I could still see the smudge that was Muthu, by looking to my right.

And then I heard it again: another growl, louder and closer this time. There was now no doubt whatever: the tiger was coming up the hill, he was coming in my direction.

I could not help smiling to myself as I thought of the great service that the elephant had done me in driving the tiger from his kill. The angry tiger had now been forced to remember that he had made another kill, one of those tasty human beings, earlier that afternoon and higher up the hill. So he was returning to it, voicing his anger all the while against the elephant that had disturbed him.

My luck had been stupendous. Not only was the tiger advertising his presence, which was much in my favour on a dark night, but the bad temper he was displaying, and his smouldering resentment against the elephant, would prevent him from being too cautious when he eventually reached poor Muthu. After all, perhaps he would not discover my presence. I was elated at the thought.

Twice more the tiger growled. Then I dimly saw a long, dark ill-defined shape to my left and a little below me. It seemed to move. It disappeared completely. Then it appeared again, this time much closer. It was certainly moving towards me.

The tiger growled again Apparently he was still thinking of the elephant and could not get him out of mind. The throaty, rasping note came from the long, moving object that was rapidly approaching me.

The dark shadow disappeared behind an intervening bush. A few seconds later the slinking shape moved dimly from left to right, and came to a halt over Muthu, just ten yards away. It had not even glanced at the little stone fort that Byra and I had so painstakingly constructed.

The tiger was in such a vile temper that he voiced a series of loud growls when he bit savagely into the poojaree lad's dead body and began to worry the carcase. His recent undignified retreat before the bull elephant, and the fact that he had to abandon his sambar kill, was annoying him intensely. He felt he had to vent his spleen on something.

Only now did I realize how difficult was the task that lay before me. I had to kill the tiger with my first shot, or at least cripple it effectively so that it would not turn upon me. My quarry was a mere ten yards away, but I could just see it as a blur. I had no torch, no nightsight, no white card as an index, that we read about so often, to fit to the sights of a rifle to make night shooting easy. My old .405 did not even have a phosphorescent foresight.

I realized I would have to act quickly while the tiger was still venting its wrath upon poor Muthu's remains. Once it became calmer and settled down to feed, it would notice any slight movement of my rifle and attack me. In fact, if it had eaten enough of the sambar it might just pass on, to return later in the night when it became hungry again, or perhaps not return at all.

Very cautiously I raised the stock of the .405 to my shoulder, taking the greatest care not to knock the barrel against any of the stones we had erected. Holding it firmly, I pointed the barrel as best I could at the front portion of the dark shape that was the tiger.

I knew there was no possibility of picking my shot of firing at some vital place. I would have to take a chance. Perhaps I would miss altogether. Very likely I would just wound the tiger superficially and it would then turn and attack me. There was a hundred-to-one-chance that I would kill it with my first shot.

Steadying my hand and holding my breath, I pressed the trigger. Pandemonium broke loose as the sharp report of the rifle thundered out and echoed against the opposing range of hills. The tiger roared lustily. Fortunately it had been facing away from me when I fired. Not knowing whence the shot had come, it imagined the foe was somewhere in front and sprang upon the nearest bush and began to tear it to shreds. As I feared would happen, I realized I had only wounded the tiger. It had been in a bad temper then. Now it was furious.

And then I made a mistake. Had I done nothing, the tiger would have reduced the bush to nothing and probably have gone away after that, without discovering my presence. But I fired again at its dark shape.

After that the tiger's behaviour was fearsome. Hit a second time, it catapulted itself into the air, fell to earth with a thud, and then began grubbing around in a circle. Evidently the spine was broken, for the animal appeared to be unable to stand upright. But this time it knew where its attacker was concealed, and the grubbing circle it was taking brought it directly down upon me.

Scrambling to my feet, I fired my third shot into its head at a range of scarcely two yards. Then I vaulted over the stone parapet by using my hands and promptly fell down the other side. My feet pricked as if there were a thousand needles in each, for I had been sitting crosslegged for some eleven hours and they were numbed.

Fortunately the tiger remained on the other side of the stones.

A dreadful bubbling, gurgling sound was coming from it, showing that the animal was still alive but grievously hurt and probably dying.

I scrambled to my knees as the blood flowed back to my legs and peeped cautiously over the intervening boulder. The tiger lay on the other side, twitching and gasping and gurgling. My fourth shot ended its suffering.

When the noise died away, I could hear Byra calling to me frantically, asking if all was well. I answered him in the affirmative and told him to come along. A few minutes later my friend appeared out of the darkness and I told him the whole story. On the streambed the elephant trumpeted again.

Unerringly Byra led me through the dark jungle back to Manchi hamlet. There, for the second time, I repeated all that had happened. The inhabitants turned out to the last child, brought lights and returned with us to bring in the bodies of Muthu and the tiger.

My first shot had entered the stomach. My second had smashed the spine high up at the shoulder. It was this second shot that had anchored the tiger and prevented it from escaping. As we had anticipated the man-eater turned out to be a young animal, and this accounted for his inexperienced, erratic ways. The poojarees asked why we had used the body of Muthu as a bait. We asked them why they entertained a sorcerer of such poor calibre in their midst. We also reminded them we had rid them of the man-eater. The end justified the means.

To this they said nothing.

2

The Dumb Man-Eater of Talavadi

I have met many unforgettable characters in my time and most of them have been jungle men; Indian, Anglo-Indian and European. For the forest appears to develop a man's personality. The more time he spends there the clearer his personality becomes. One such character was my friend Hughie Hailstone, who lived in a wonderful home he had built for himself called 'Moyar Valley Ranch,' down at a place named Mudiyanoor, near Talaimalai, in a corner of the North Coimbatore district and not very far away from the Moyar river, which separates North Coimbatore from the Nilgiri forest division.

Now Hughie was a character if ever there was one. He attended the same school as I did, but passed out much earlier. From that time he followed a varied career. But the man had brains. Everything he touched turned to gold. With some of this money he bought a large tract of forest land and on it he built his Moyar Valley Ranch.

Hughie had a fine collection of firearms, the best that money could buy, but among these he had a great fancy for a .023 Mauser rifle with a hexagonal barrel with which, if I remember rightly, he told me he had shot nine elephants and over twenty tigers. Later, Hughie took a great liking to my son Donald and presented him with this very weapon. Donald was, of course, delighted. But what enhanced the value of the gift was the fact that it was Hughie's favourite weapon. Frankly, I do not believe I could ever part with my ancient, but lovable, old .405. It has been my companion and solace for over forty years.

My story begins at a point where in some part of India Hughie either found or heard of a special kind of grass, the stems of which when dry were stronger than the ordinary matchstick, and not so brittle. They would not break easily, and they burned readily. So Hughie conceived the idea of cultivating this grass on a large scale on the lands of his Moyar Valley Ranch with a view to starting a match factory that would turn out a product to be sold at about half the price of those already on the market, and of much higher quality.

He obtained seeds in quantity, ploughed his lands with the first shower of the monsoon rains, and sowed them. Up came the grass in fine style. Acres of it. The land was virgin and the grass grew to five feet and more. I remember watching it as it bent and rippled to the breeze. But before Hughie's grass could be turned into match sticks there came herds of deer, particularly chital, and large sounders of wild pigs. The deer, of course, ate the grass, while the wild pigs made it their home and did considerable damage by digging it up at places, though for the most part they burrowed a maze of low tunnels through it, leading here, there and everywhere. In these tunnels they sheltered and multiplied to the extent that Hughie wondered eventually whether he should persevere with the match factory or run a ham and bacon concern!

Best of all, with deer and the pigs came tigers and panthers to eat them. Rather I should say more tigers than panthers, for the former arrived in such numbers as not only to decimate the deer and pig population, but to kill and eat the panthers too, so that in the course of time the smaller cats learned to give the match-grass a very wide berth.

Now Hughie employed an assistant, a man named Sweza (a corruption of D'Souza), who came from Mangalore on the west coast of India. Sweza was a most versatile individual: he did everything for Hughie, whose problems he not only knew but anticipated.

He once said to me with reference to his employer, 'I don't know why master spend much money to make more money. Master got plenty money to enjoy and enjoy. But no; he want to make matchsticks, tooth powder from *babul* bark, fertilizer from jungle seeds mixed with elephants' dung, invention for finding underground water, digging ground for getting some stones master says got iron, all sort of things. Only spending money. Why for? This very good place. Master should enjoy. Plenty girls got it here. Young girls; not 'nuff husbands here. I tell-it master. He get very angry. He say-it, "Sweza, you bloody rogue you got it one wife and three more women already. I saved you from one more wife. Now you want to put me in the same trouble!"'

But he was a good fellow, this Sweza, game for anything and as keen as mustard. And he ate well! His paunch and his jolly smile showed this.

One Easter, Sweza felt that his master and himself were entitled to roast pork or venison. So he borrowed his master's small-bore rifle after confiding his good intentions to Hughie, and waded into the match-grass, now somewhat withered and thinned down by the summer heat, in search of quarry. Sweza had not gone very far when he saw the snout of a medium-sized wild pig regarding him with grave suspicion from between the stems of the grass. He fired. The pig fell, picked itself up again, and disappeared. Sweza started to follow hard on its trail.

Just then there was a great swishing in the grass where the pig had disappeared, a snarl, and the scream of a dying animal. Sweza beat a hasty retreat and told his master.

Hughie came out with one of his heavy rifles and Sweza led him to the place where he had fired at the pig, pointing out the direction in which it had gone. Hughie went on and Sweza made to follow him from behind, but Hughie very wisely objected to this. He did not want a bullet from Sweza's rifle in his back. So he asked his servant to go back and wait for him in the open.

Hughie came to the spot where the pig had been killed, but there was no trace of its body. The killer had carried it away. Bent and broken stems of dried grass showed the direction he had taken with his burden. Moving cautiously forward, he had gone for quite a hundred yards when suddenly a loud growl from in front told him the killer was feeding somewhere ahead and resented his intrusion. But Hailstone had seen and shot many tigers and was not to be intimidated by a growl. He moved forward stealthily and the tiger growled more loudly. Hughie knew the charge would come at any moment.

A little later the tiger charged. It came in great leaping bounds through the dried match-grass. Hailstone waited till he could see the contorted face clearly, till the final spring would land the beast right on top of him. Then he fired. Thus was born the man-eater of Talavadi! Hughie's bullet struck the tiger full in the face. The impact tended to stop it, but the weight of the body behind still pushed it forward, with the result that the tiger somersaulted just a few yards away. Hughie worked the bolt of his rifle rapidly to get in a second shot. The magazine jammed.

He did the right thing after that. He turned and fled.

Evidently the tiger was temporarily blinded or maybe too hurt to follow. It floundered about in the grass, digging great holes in the earth as, in agony, it bit and tore the ground with its claws and teeth.

Hughie dashed into the bungalow to get another rifle, Sweza running after him and asking what had happened. But by the time Hailstone got to the spot again, advancing one step at a time, the tiger had vanished, while splashes of blood and saliva on the ground made it plain he had received a severe wound in the region of the mouth or throat.

It is a common belief among some hunters that a wounded feline should not be followed up immediately. Sufficient time should be allowed to pass in which the animal might possibly bleed to death. At least, the wounds would stiffen to the extent that the beast would be disinclined to move far, or it might even be incapable of movement. But there is another school of thought which advocates following up at once. The theory in this case is that the wounded animal should not be given time to recover from the shock and pain of its wounds and from its immediate fear. The advocates of this theory feel that, with the passage of time and long hours of pain, the wounded beast becomes vicious and bent upon revenge, whereas immediately after being wounded it seeks only to escape. They also argue that on humanitarian grounds it is very cruel to allow an animal to suffer hours of intense agony with a vital organ shot away.

Now I am not going to give my own judgment on these theories, except to say that both are partly right and partly wrong. Each animal has its individual characteristics and special nature and will react in its own way. Hughie was a firm believer in the second theory and lost no time in following up.

The blood trail through the long match-grass was clear. It left Hughie's land and entered the forest, where things became a little more difficult. Hughie had to rely on his own abilities as Sweza, still trailing behind with the other rifle, was no tracker. They followed it across a dry ravine, where the tiger had lain down and then continued, and across flat country the other side. The fact that the tiger had lain down indicated that it was badly wounded, and as Hughie had followed up at once, the animal could not be very far away. Probably it had heard him and Sweza and was taking cover in the undergrowth. The third item of information was that this animal appeared to be a coward; it should have taken advantage of the terrain and plenty of cover in the ravine to ambush the two men.

By now the bleeding had lessened and after crossing the flat stretch for another furlong the trail began to lead downhill, where the ground became increasingly stony. Hughie had to slow down and keep looking about for the next drop or two of blood. Soon even this ceased and he could go no further. On that hard ground no pug-marks were visible.

For some unaccountable reason the tracts of forest in the Mudiyanoor area are entirely devoid of jungle tribes or aboriginal population. It is believed this has been so since the days when Tippoo Sultan, the Muslim ruler of Mysore, invaded the surrounding country, sweeping all before him. So Hughie had no opportunity to return later and follow the tiger, as there was nobody in all that area who knew anything about tracking.

The village of Talaimalai is about two miles south of Mudiyanoor, where Hughie had his farm. It is a small hamlet surrounded by fertile country. Nearly two months later, one of the villagers from this place bought a tract of land from his neighbour, or rather arranged to buy it, for the sale deed pertaining to this transaction had necessarily to be signed and registered in the office of the sub-registrar and the money paid by the purchaser to the seller in the presence of this august individual whose headquarters were at a larger village named Talavadi, situated seven miles north of Mudiyanoor. So the vendor and the prospective purchaser, the latter carrying the money he was going to pay for the land, which came to Rs 400, including the incidental expenses involved in the sale deed, set forth together on foot to cover the nine miles between Talaimalai and Talavadi.

They had covered two-thirds of this distance when they crossed a stream that had a little water in it. Here they stopped under a large tree to eat the curried balls of ragi flour they had brought with them as a midday meal. The purchaser then went down to the stream to drink and wash while his companion watched him with sleepy eyes.

Suddenly something huge leaped down upon the drinking man from the opposite bank of the stream and back again across the stream to disappear as abruptly as it had come, except that there was no longer any sign of the unfortunate purchaser. He had disappeared, along with that horrible apparition!

The vendor, now fully awake, leaped to his feet and ran as fast as he could towards Talavadi, covering the three miles to that place in record time. There he gasped out his story before the sub-registrar and the clerks sitting in the office. All this being something out of the ordinary, the sub-registrar sent the man to the police station, where the whole tale was repeated.

In the opinion of the constable in charge there was nothing strange about the story. As he reasoned it out, here we have A reporting that he is selling some land to B for Rs 400. A and B set out to register the sale, B carrying Rs 400. On the way, A says that some strange creature appeared out of the jungle and disappeared again, taking B with it. A reports he was more than half-asleep and cannot describe what this strange something was. But the facts remain that B has vanished, the Rs 400 have vanished with him, and the land still belongs to A.

Without further ado, the head constable arrested the unfortunate vendor and locked him in the police station's solitary cell. Then he wrote a lengthy report, stating why he suspected he had caught a murderer. He did not forget to add that the sub-inspector at Satyamangalam, which was the headquarters of the Police and Forest departments and the place to which the prisoner would have to be sent, might please bear in mind when he read the report that it was the humble prayer of the head constable that promotion was long overdue and this brave and dramatic arrest of a dangerous murderer and thief should forthwith clinch matters and lead to the said promotion without delay. He closed the report by saying that he offered daily prayers for the sub-inspector's continued long life and prosperity.

It was not till a week later that the fourth constable attached to the police station at Talavadi returned from leave. The head constable then felt he could manage with two policemen while he sent the other two on escort duty with the prisoner, and his report, to Satyamangalam, where the sub-inspector resided, forty miles away. They should reach there in three days, for they had to walk the whole distance.

Hailstone happened to be standing at the entrance to the grounds of his farm, which abutted on the track leading from Talavadi to Satyamangalam, when he saw the two policemen coming along with a prisoner handcuffed between them. Conversationally he inquired what wrong the man had done and where he was being taken. The constables, glad of the respite, said they were escorting a murderer, while the poor vendor burst into tears, sobbing out his innocence and his story afresh.

Hughie pricked up his ears.

'Stop weeping, you idiot,' he said kindly but firmly. 'If you want me to help you, just answer a simple question. What was this strange something that you say carried away your companion? At least, what did it look like?'

'*Dorai*,' the man replied, striving to control himself, 'I saw my friend stoop to drink water. At that instant I must have fallen asleep. I heard nothing, but seemed to see some huge, long body jump down from the jungle across the stream and jump back again. Then only did I notice the man had gone! I woke up and ran all the way to Talavadi. Now these policemen say I have murdered my friend and taken his money.'

Then he started crying once more at the thought of his plight.

Hughie remembered the tiger he had wounded just two months earlier. He had often thought about it and wondered if the animal had died or had recovered from its wound. And if it had recovered, Hughie knew that sooner or later he would hear about the animal again. Could this be it?

'Did it look like a tiger?' he asked abruptly.

The policemen looked at him stupidly, but the man in handcuffs replied quickly, 'Come to think of it, *dorai*, it might have been a tiger. As I said, I was more than half asleep and the whole thing happened so quickly. But it was nothing in human form that carried away my companion, of that I am certain. It was something long and big.'

'Don't take this poor man to Satyamangalam,' Hughie advised the policemen. 'Save yourself the journey, for he is no murderer. I think I know what really happened.'

But the officers of law and order the world over are dogged in their purposes, especially when they have someone in handcuffs. The policemen continued on their way to Satyamangalam with their captive, while Hughie went in his car to Talavadi. To his mortification, he discovered from the head constable that nobody knew exactly where the incident had taken place except the prisoner himself, as nobody had taken the trouble to investigate the story or make an inspection of the spot.

Hailstone considered telling the head constable about the wounded tiger but decided against it. A man of his temperament, with a one-track mind, might do anything. He might even lock Hailstone up! So he left the police station without further ado and set out for Satyamangalam, overtaking the two policemen and their prisoner some ten miles beyond Mudiyanoor. Glad of the lift, the three men piled into the car and in less than ninety minutes the whole party were with the sub-inspector.

The sub-inspector read the head constable's report and then listened to what Hughie had to say.

'And this man wants a promotion' was his comment after Hughie had told him that the head constable had not even troubled to visit the scene of the tragedy. 'I shall see him reverted! Please take me to Talavadi in your car.'

Back they went, all five of them, to give the head constable at Talavadi the nastiest surprise of his life. Then the vendor took them to the place where the would-be purchaser and his money had vanished. The head constable was made to go too.

Over a week had passed, but when they crawled to the top of the bank they found the pug-marks of a tiger at the spot where it had clambered back with its burden, the unlucky would-be purchaser. Casting around, a little distance away but still to be seen in the sand, were the fainter imprints of the tiger before it had launched its attack.

Hughie had not brought his rifle. The sub-inspector inquired nervously if the tiger might still be there. Hailstone said 'no,' and the six men started searching the immediate surrounding for the remains of the victim. Strangely enough, it was the vendor, now no longer in chains, who stumbled upon the gnawed bones. A few rags and the ten-rupee notes that had been scattered by the breeze in a wide circle in the grass and undergrowth, confirmed that the remains were indeed all that was left of the purchaser. There were only a few, as most of the bones had been removed by the vultures, jackals and hyaenas that had visited the carcase after the tiger had finished.

The man-eater struck a second time scarcely a month later. This was at the village of Nagalur, about halfway between Hughie's place and the Moyar river which bounded the Nilgiri district. The third victim was an old man who was walking behind his two sons on the old Sultan's Battery Road, a couple of miles behind Talaimalai village. This killing took place in broad daylight—at noon, as a matter of fact.

The three men had set out together from Talaimalai to Nagalur, where the second victim had been taken. For some distance their way lay along the old road I have named, a relic of the days of that fierce Muslim conqueror who long ago brought terror to this region. They had not gone far when they came to a mighty wild-mango tree. Monkeys had knocked down some of the ripe fruit and the three men stopped to eat. When they started walking again the father had fallen behind, from where he continued to talk to them about the business that was taking them to Nagalur.

He had reminded them that it was getting late and they had all begun to walk faster, when a sudden choking cry made the two sons turn around to see a huge tiger with its jaws firmly in their father's throat, in the act of springing into the undergrowth that closely bordered the road on both sides.

Where the beast had come from they never knew. It had certainly made no sound whatever, not even a growl or snarl, which was rather unusual, for attacking tigers generally roar or make some sort of noise to inflate their own courage before springing. In this case, all they had heard was their father's last gasp. By this time the attacker had disappeared and the two boys took to their heels, running as fast as they could back to Talaimalai.

Consternation spread among the village folk and the man-eater, as if he knew very well that his name had struck terror in the area, increased the number of his attacks as he began to roam over a wider circle. He killed as far north as the high road connecting Satyamangalam with the large town of Chamrajnagar in Mysore state. He killed to the east as far as Dimbum, a hamlet standing on the escarpment of mountains overlooking the Satyamangalam plain. He crossed the Moyar river and went into the Nilgiri district to the south, and on the west he trespassed into the Bandipur area which lies in Mysore state.

Unfortunately, at just about this time Hughie, who had always been a vigorous man, fell ill. It happened suddenly and unexpectedly. I know he felt deeply about all that had taken place and was happening, for he held himself responsible for starting the tiger on its man-eating career by wounding it, and he chafed at the illness that prevented him from going after it, which he would otherwise have assuredly done. So he wrote to me, and that was what took me in my Studebaker to Moyar Valley Ranch.

Sweza met me at the gate and I found Hughie asleep in a canvas chair on his verandah. He had not heard my car. The change in his appearance since we had last me was almost frightening. A robust man, he had shrunk to half his normal size and looked haggard and very ill. He apologized for dragging me away from home and then, as I sat beside him drinking tea and eating the most delicious mangoes that grew on his land, Hughie told the story as I have told it here, not sparing himself and full of self-recrimination not only for wounding the tiger but for not finishing it off after that.

'These things happen, Hughie,' was all the comfort I could offer. 'You must pull yourself together now and join me in killing it.'

He looked at me wryly and said, 'Kenneth, my hunting days are over. My next *shikar* will be in the happy hunting grounds—if there's such a place!'

Indeed, he never hunted again. Shortly after the end of this episode he went by air to England. He had already bought a house there, a nice place in the country. But he was not to enjoy it, for he had been there only a few days when he slipped and fell down the staircase, injuring himself severely. Soon afterwards he died of a heart attack.

However, we now discussed what should be done. It was clear that it would not be worth my while to visit Nagalur and Talaimalai and other places where the tiger had killed, in order to question the people about the animal's habits and peculiarities. Hughie had already done this before falling ill and told me all he had discovered. To begin with, there was scarcely any doubt that it was the animal he had wounded that had now become a man-eater. The few people who had seen it clearly, particularly the two sons of the old man who had been snatched on the Sultan's Battery Road, affirmed that the glimpse they had got of the tiger's face showed there was something seriously the matter with it. The face had been hideously scarred and contorted. Secondly, the animal's uncanny silence on every occasion when there had been a witness to its attack proved that it was either a very strange animal by nature, or that something was wrong with its vocal chords. Moreover, nobody remembered having ever heard this tiger roar.

Of course, tigers had often roared in the area. This was to be expected, because it was full of tigers. But in no locality where any of the human kills had taken place, or at least not for a few days before or after that killing, had any tiger roared in the forest. For this reason the rumour spread that the man-eater was dumb.

The procedure normally followed in trying to shoot a man-eater is as unexciting as it appears to be self-contradictory. The hunter purchases three or four live baits in the form of buffalo heifers or young bulls and ties them out at pre-selected places where machans have already been put up, in the hope that the tiger may kill one of them. The hunter then sits in the *machan* the following night to shoot the tiger when it returns for a second meal.

Having heard that man-eaters eat men, you may wonder why an animal bait is tied out. Would a man-eater want to kill it? The answer is that man-eaters do not confine themselves to a diet of human flesh. They merely prefer the flesh of men to other meat. Perhaps a man is easier to find. He is certainly easier to stalk and kill. Maybe there is something appetizing about human flesh. But anyway, one cannot very well tie out a human being as bait.

With Hughie's influence and Sweza's help I purchased four

young bulls at Talaimalai village. The two boys whose father had been killed volunteered to help me in tethering the animals and building *machans*, so I recruited them and two more to assist. With Hughie and Sweza we formed a committee of seven persons when we sat down to deliberate on where to tie our baits. Strangely, it has become customary to tether a bait as near as possible to the spot where a kill has already taken place. I do not really know why this is so. It is certainly wrong reasoning to infer that a man-eater, like a murderer, may have a guilty conscience and come back to the scene of his crime. To a man-eater his action is no crime. It is merely his dinner.

I admit I have fallen into the habit myself, but now I come to think of it, the practice follows faulty reasoning. As a matter of fact, a man-eater is more likely to avoid the scene of one of his former kills rather than go there again, because he knows of the publicity it occasioned and the number of people who have visited the spot since the occurrence.

The real thing to do, as I have related in earlier stories, is to try to work out the line of beat the killer has been following by studying a map of the locality and marking on it the places where each human kill occurred and the date of each event. When the tiger is a man-eater of long standing, with many crimes to his discredit, such a study reveals that he has been following a fixed route over and over again, returning to the same localities (but not the exact spot) in which he has killed before, once in so many weeks or months as the case may be. In *shikar* parlance, this habit or practice is known as the 'man-eater's beat.'

I suppose in a way this answers the question posed earlier as to why it has become more or less an accepted practice to tie a bait near the spot where a human kill has already occurred. One hopes it will be on the tiger's beat and that he will come again. But this may not happen for many weeks or even months, for every man-eater does not follow a beat. Most do, but there are exceptions. And in any case such a beat can only be worked out with a man-eater of long standing. The animal I was after had started recently and his killings so far had been haphazard.

All of which brings me back to the fact that it was difficult for us to decide precisely where to tie out and there was much difference of opinion. The two boys advocated trying the Sultan's Battery Road where their father had been killed. The other two men I had recruited to help me said the track leading from Talaimalai to Talavadi would be best, as tiger pug-marks were seen along it nearly every day. Hughie suggested tying the four baits a mile apart from each other and in a straight line, two to three miles south of Talaimalai, where the ground fell away abruptly to the valley of the Moyar river. Sweza suggested tying up somewhere in Hughie's match-grass, where the tiger was first wounded, because he felt it would return there to eat the spotted deer and wild pig that were still abundant.

Of all these suggestions, I decided the last was the least likely to bring success. The man-eater would never return to a place where it had been so badly hurt. So we ruled it out. All the other suggestions were equally good and it appeared to be a matter of luck where and when the tiger would next show up.

Eventually we decided to tether one of the baits on the Sultan's Battery Road, another on the Talaimalai-Talavadi track, and the third and fourth baits at two of the most likely spots along the ridge south of Talaimalai that overlooked the Moyar river, as suggested by Hughie. I felt that the kill, if and when it took place, would be one of these two baits, as tigers passed to and from the Nilgiri forests to the Talaimalai Reserve across this ridge. However, as there was more than one tiger in the area, we would not know whether the man-eater or some quite innocent tiger had made the kill, and the only course open would be to shoot it in the hope that it turned out to be the man-eater. The selection of the exact spot for each tie-up was to be left to me.

I told my four helpers to return at dawn the next day with another eight men, so that there would be a dozen of them altogether, allowing sufficient men for the task of erecting each of the four *machans* that were to be put up before the baits were tied out.

I have found it wise to erect the *machan* first and only afterwards to tie the bait in a suitable line of fire. Then, when a kill occurs, the hunter is ready to take his place. The other way around much disturbance is caused in tying a *machan* after the bait has been killed, and should the tiger be lying in concealment within hearing he generally fails to return.

The *machan* I favoured using at that time, and still think is best, is an ordinary charpoy cot with its four legs cut short. For those of you who don't know what a *charpoy* cot is, I may explain that it consists of a rectangular wooden or bamboo frame of four pieces, about six feet by three. Rope, or wide cotton tape, is laced across this frame, while four legs at each of the four corners complete the cot. Most villagers sleep on the ground, but in certain places unduly infested with snakes and scorpions, *charpoy* cots are the only type that are favoured, for they are made in the villages and cost in the region of five rupees each, including the rope used. Where cotton tape or webbing is employed for more comfort—the price, at the most, is doubled.

My *machan* consisted of a cot of the latter type. Each of the four legs had been shortened to a foot in length, sufficient to provide something by which to tie the cot to the branches of a tree. The cot itself was cut into two and folded on two hinges for convenience of transport. Its advantages are obvious; it provided maximum comfort with minimum weight and noise should I be forced to move about, which, incidentally, is the one thing you should never do in sitting up!

Hughie favoured another type of *machan*, which was nothing more than a folding canvas chair with a footrest to keep your legs from dangling downwards. Sitting in one of these always gave me a sense of insecurity—a feeling that I would either fall out of it, or that the whole structure would collapse at any moment. Of course, this was only prejudice, as in reality there was no real risk either way and I was grateful when Hughie offered to lend me his canvas chair-*machan* to be used in one of the four places we had selected. This meant that the remaining two *machans* would have to be constructed on the spot with bamboos and wood cut in the jungle.

Work began in earnest next day, when the dozen men arrived carrying their sharp knives. Hughie supplied all the rope we would need, so with four of the men leading the bulls I had purchased to serve as bait, we were soon on the Talaimalai-Talavadi road, where we were to tie the first *machan*.

We had gone scarcely a quarter of a mile along this track when we saw, clearly imprinted on the soft earth, the fresh pug-marks of a tiger that had come down the bed of a small *nullah* that crossed the road. The tiger had passed in the early hours of the morning, which was revealed by the fact that the powdery dust bordering the edges of the track had not yet fallen into the depressions made by the tiger's pads. With the passage of a few hours and the action of the wind, this would certainly have happened were the tracks more than six hours old.

Walking up the *nullah*, both to the left and right of where it crossed the road, we saw several older tracks, indicating that this dry streambed was much used either by the tiger whose tracks we had just seen or by other tigers in the locality. Unfortunately, due to their age, these tracks could not be identified for certain with the fresh ones along the road which undoubtedly had been made by an adult male of rather bigger than average size.

A banyan tree grew on the farther bank of the *nullah* just before it crossed the road, and all agreed that this would be the ideal place for the first *machan*. It was an old tree, and many of the roots that had dropped to the earth from the higher branches had in the course of the years, themselves taken root and grown into the thickness of minor tree-trunks. Within this network of the roots and trunks it would be easy for us to put up an inconspicuous *machan*, and I decided to save my *charpoy* and Hughie's chair for one of the other places where natural construction might not be so easy. We completed that *machan* in ninety minutes, and after tying the first bait in a convenient position, set out for our second selection, which you will remember was the Sultan's Battery Road.

The sons of the old man who had been killed showed me where the tragedy had taken place, and within a couple of furlongs of this spot and once again where a *nullah* crossed the road, we erected the second *machan*. This again was constructed on the spot, but took much longer to do, so that it was nearly noon before we set out for the ridge, two miles away, overlooking the Moyar Valley and Nilgiri jungles whence the tigers generally came.

My guides, who had lived in the area all their lives, pointed out first one then a second game trail that led up from the valley to the south of us, down which in the distance flowed the Moyar river, its course easily recognizable by the thick belt of giant trees on its bank. From the height at which we were standing, the Moyar looked like a great green python, writhing its course through the forest.

On convenient trees we tied our remaining *machans*, my *charpoy* first and finally Hughie's canvas chair, while with the tying-up of our fourth unfortunate bull-bait, the work of the day came to an end. The sun was sinking across the jungles of Bandipur to the west when we started on our walk back to Hughie's farm quite five miles away. It had been a long day and we were very tired, but I was very satisfied by the four jobs we had completed. All I had now to do was scour the jungle in other directions by day in the hope of meeting the man-eater accidentally. Meanwhile, I would sleep peacefully at Hughie's place by night till one of my baits was taken.

Little did I know what was going to happen.

The two sons of the old man and the first two men who had volunteered to help me had been instructed to visit the four baits next morning, and every morning thereafter, and to feed and water them, till a kill occurred. They were to begin with the most distant baits, the two animals we had tied on the western ridge, and then work eastwards to the Sultan's Battery Road, and finally to the first bait on the Talaimalai-Talavadi track, which was the closest of the four to Hughie's farm.

It was ten-thirty next morning when I heard them coming up the driveway, talking excitedly, and I knew that a kill had occurred. But the news they brought was surprising—and disconcerting! The last bait we had tied the previous evening—the one under Hughie's canvas-chair *machan*—had been killed and part eaten, and the first animal at the junction of the *nullah* with the Talaimalai-Talavadi road had also been killed and about half devoured.

Two kills on the same night, at points at least five miles apart. This clearly pointed to two tigers. Now which of them was the man-eater and in which of the *machans* should I sit?

Another consultation was held, but this time we were unanimous. The tiger that had killed the first bait—the nearest to the farm—was far more likely to be the man-eater, for its tracks had indicated that it haunted the *nullah*-bed crossing the Talaimalai-Talavadi road on which a human kill had already taken place and which was frequented by human beings. The other kill on the ridge was at a far less frequented spot, where people hardly ever went, but which was used by tigers coming from the Nilgiri district, or returning to it. As such, the tiger that had killed there was in all likelihood not the man-eater. It was therefore decided that I should sit at the *nullah*-crossing that night.

With this settled, the next thing to do was to put in a few hours of sleep.

Hughie called me at one o'clock for a hearty lunch and gave me a parcel of sandwiches for the night, a most acceptable gift. By two-thirty I was on the *machan*, looking down upon the half-eaten young bull as my four assistants removed the branches with which they had covered the carcase that morning to protect it from vultures.

There was silence after their departure and, as was to be expected, no travellers passed along the road, the presence of the man-eater discouraging people, especially towards evening, from using a track on which he had already killed a man. I was surprised, therefore, to hear voices approaching from the Talaimalai village direction some time after five o'clock, and astonished when I recognized the party as my own four attendants, accompanied by Sweza carrying a gun. They came to tell me that the man-eater had killed a woman while she was carrying water from a well near the hamlet of Dimbum, which was seventeen miles away on the Satyamangalam-Chamrajnagar road. Hughie had sent them with the news, as he felt that I might not consider it worthwhile to sit up all night to shoot a tiger which obviously could not be the man-eater. No tiger that had devoured half a bull the previous night would walk a distance of seventeen miles to kill a woman the next morning.

I heartily agreed with the message Hughie had sent and came down from the *machan*. As far as I was concerned the tiger that haunted the *nullah* was welcome to the remaining half of his meal. When I got back, Hughie suggested that I go at once to Dimbum and try to find a place to sit up, either near the well or wherever the woman had been killed. No doubt her family would have removed her remains for cremation, but it was just possible that the man-eater might return to the spot during the night in search of the body of his victim. I agreed and started straight away, taking my four helpers along in case of need.

It was almost dark when we left Talaimalai village and I switched on the headlights of the Studebaker. Just a mile farther on, the road descended steeply to cross the first of several intersecting streams, all dry at this time of the year, and strung out across the road on the opposite bank of this stream, reflecting the beams from my lights, were the eyes of a herd of bison! The herd galloped away, disturbed by the noise when I changed gear to cross the stream— that is, all of them except the herd-bull, which stood squarely in the centre of the road, his head partly lowered and pawning the ground in a attitude obviously nasty and threatening.

Bisons are generally quite harmless animals and run away at the slightest sight or sound of human beings. Here was one of them behaving rather differently. Perhaps he felt I constituted a danger to the herd. More likely he was puzzled by the headlights of the car and never realized that human beings were behind them. In any case, I did not wish to risk the consequences of a charge. It meant shooting the bull—which I had no desire to do—and quickly, for the signs of an impending charge within the next few seconds were unmistakable. If he succeeded, I knew my Studebaker would be a write-off together with some, if not all of us, who were inside. With my own eyes I have seen a loaded trunk overturned by a charging bison on the Tippakadu road in the Nilgiri jungles; the driver had been killed by the truck itself while the bison had disposed of his assistant and the cleaner by goring and trampling them to pulp.

These unpleasant thoughts passed quickly through my mind. There was just one chance left before using my rifle, and I would have to take it at once. That chance lay in the old klaxon horn fixed to the right of me on the wind-shield of the Studebaker. Many an elephant had I scared with this same ancient klaxon! Its blatant, brassy blare had made them flee in abject terror. So I tried it again. I pumped the spring lever of that old horn hard and repeatedly. A ghastly sound rent the jungle silence. The bull raised its lowered head, its eyes dilated by fear of what seemed like all hell let loose, and the next moment it plunged into the bamboo undergrowth and vanished from sight.

After that I saw quite a lot of game, which was rather unusual for so early an hour, and incidentally a 'good omen,' so far as hunting superstition goes. Spotted deer and two sambar crossed individually, a sloth bear was digging by the roadside as my lights disturbed him, and a panther leaped from left to right a furlong after I had passed the Honathetti forest lodge and was negotiating a valley between two hillocks, just seven miles from Dimbum.

We arrived at our destination shortly before 8 p.m., which, all said and done, was excellent going, for the track was not only steep and winding but had been in places completely obliterated by the long grass. Hidden boulders lay in that grass, enough to tear open the bottom of any crankcase or differential that bumped against it. In such spots I had had to slow down to a snail's pace, slowly following two of the men as they walked side by side a few yards ahead to warn me of hidden rocks before one of the front wheels of the car banged against them. Then we would all help to roll them aside, or if they were too big to move I would circumvent them by going off the track.

Dimbum is a hamlet on the main road from Mysore City, past the town of Chamrajnagar, down to another large town in the plains named Satyamangalam, which was the headquarters of the police and forest departments for the area. Fifty miles on lies the city of Coimbatore.

All that Dimbum could boast were a few huts and a teashop owned by a Moplah, a descendant of some Arab trader, who centuries earlier had come to the west coast of India for trade but remained to settle down and marry several Hindu Malayalee women. These men have kept their business acumen through the years and there is hardly any trade in which numbers of them do not excel. The teashop at Dimbum was kept open by the Moplah and his three wives throughout the twenty-four hours of the day. Tired lorry drivers ascending the steep ghat-road from Satyamangalam, sixteen miles away, could count on a large mug of steaming tea or coffee at any time of the day or night, together with a hot meal of curry and rice. There was another essential commodity thrown in with the refreshment, and it was free: cool water for their boiling radiators when their trucks arrived in a cloud of steam after that long ascent.

There is a Rest House for travellers, too, and it is beautifully situated upon the edge of the escarpment that overlooks the valley many thousands of feet below. The nearer part of this valley at the base of the escarpment is heavily forested, but the road can be seen winding through the jungle and finally breaking out into the cultivated lands that stretch away to the horizon. In the middle distance is Satyamangalam, while far away on the skyline to the southwest is Coimbatore.

Those jungles at the foot of the hill recall the escapades of the

tiger I named 'the mauler of Rajnagara,'* for it was there that I
spent some exciting days looking for him without success.

To look upon the plains from this Rest House at nightfall is
like looking down into fairyland. The myriad points of electric light,
frequently interspersed with coloured lights of every hue, stand out
in sharp contrast to the black void. Away to the southwest is an angry
glow upon the horizon: the reflection of the lights of Coimbatore,
too far away to be seen directly, upon the cloud-layered sky.

I drove to the Moplah's teashop, for that I knew would be
the fountainhead of all the information I wanted. Abdulkunni,
the ambitious proprietor, knew me well. In fact, I had dropped
in for a cup of tea at his place on my way to Hughie's farm and
had told him the reason for my visit. He greeted me loudly now
and in his high-pitched, excited voice, began pouring out his news.

'Why do you go to Talaimalai looking for your tiger, *sahib*,
when it's right here? This morning it killed a woman at the well,
just behind this tea shop. A damned nuisance, indeed! We need a
great deal of water here, for making tea and for the radiators of
the hundred or more lorries that need it every day. This requires
many visits to the well and many buckets of water. My three wives
have all refused to go there since they heard the news. Disobedient,
good-for-nothing bitches, all three of them! I have threatened to
kick them out. Even beaten them. But with one accord they told
me to go myself. Cannot somebody rid me of these wenches? Now
I put it to you, *sahib*. Can I possibly leave the teashop? So I have
been compelled to engage a servant on daily wages from today.
This costs money and in any case she is a lazy slut! Look *sahib*, as
a good Mussulman it is not the custom for me to allow strangers
to speak to my womenfolk. But you are a friend, sir. Please talk
to my wives and advise them to fetch the water.'

A difficult assignment indeed! Besides, I had better things to
do than persuade old Abdulkunni's wives to commit suicide. For

---

*See *Man-Eaters and Jungle Killers*, Chapter 8.

that was the fate they would invite by visiting the well with the man-eater about. I could not blame the women for going on strike. Old Abdulkunni thought more of his money than of his wives, but I did not tell him so. It would hurt his feelings.

I said instead, 'I have come to shoot the tiger, Abdulkunni, so if you'll help me, your problem will be solved. Let's not waste time, but tell me exactly how the woman was killed.'

'What is there to say, *sahib*. She went for water. She was returning with it. Then the *shaitan bagh* leapt from the bushes and carried her off into the jungle. She screamed loudly but the tiger only growled. Another woman was going down for water, too, and was but a few yards away when it happened. She heard and saw everything. She ran back to this very place and told us. I had five or six customers here at the time. We bolted and barred the doors and locked ourselves in for nearly two hours. That was another loss of business. It was only when other drivers arrived and banged on the front door that we opened up. Then a large party of us went down to the well. Of the woman there is no sign. Her broken pot remains where it fell from her hands. There is nothing more to tell you.'

'Have there been earlier reports of a tiger in this locality, Abdulkunni? Has anyone else seen it? Did anybody notice anything distinctive about the animal?' I fired the questions rapidly.

But the old man only laughed. 'What can be distinctive about a tiger?' he inquired. 'They all look alike, with a head, four legs and a tail. Besides, why do you ask such silly questions of me? Have I not told you already that nobody except the other woman who was going herself to the well for water saw the tiger? She said it was a huge beast and looked like *shaitan* (the devil) himself.'

One last question I asked, with visions of possibly being able to sit up over the victim's remains of the next day. 'Has the woman's body been found?'

Abdulkunni's derisive grin widened. 'Who is there to search for it, *sahib*? Do you think we are mad? We are alive now. The woman is dead. If we go in search of her body and the tiger finds us, we too will be dead. And that will not help her!'

How often had I not heard those same words before, spoken in so many different languages, when inquiring if a man-eater's victim or the remains, had been found!

It was evident that the Moplah could give me no further help. I would have to do things for myself and think out some plan. So I ordered two mugs of tea for myself, and a mug each for the men I had brought in the car from Talaimalai, and selecting the cornermost table in the grimy tea shop took out my pipe to smoke while considering the best course of action.

The first thing to do was to get rid of Abdulkunni, who had started talking again. Very frankly I asked him to leave me alone as I wanted to think out a plan.

The old man's behaviour was particularly irritating that day. With a wicked smirk, he remarked, 'If you want the tiger, why not call it?' Then he went to serve the tea.

Four tracks join at Dimbum, almost directly in front of the tea shop. Or rather, two of them are tracks, while the other two consist of the main road that passes through the hamlet, leading northwards towards Mysore and southwards to Satyamangalam. I have intentionally counted this one main road as two because, so far as searching for the tiger went, he might cross it to the north of Dimbum, or go down the ghat road as it fell away to the south towards Satyamangalam. The third track was the one I had just travelled, leading from Talavadi and Talaimalai, and the fourth track led into the jungle and was hardly noticeable. It began just behind the Rest House and then wound eastwards through the forest for ten miles or more, keeping more or less to the edge of the continuation of the Dimbum escapement that overlooked the plains as far as the watershed of the Cauvery river, fifty miles to the east.

Being the least used of the four, this last track was the one along which most animals were to be seen, especially bison and sambar. Quite a number of bear came up the escarpment and tigers very often crossed it by steep hidden routes on their long trek of more than fifty miles eastwards, through very dense, jungle and mountain terrain, to the Cauvery river. After about ten miles this track dwindled to a mere footpath that threaded through very heavy bamboo jungles, inhabited more by elephants, bison and sambar than by tigers. For the area is infested by tick, and tigers definitely do not like ticks!

It was pitch-dark outside; an ideal night for using a spotlight in searching for animals.

I could motor up the road towards Mysore for about five miles and then return, shining my spotlight and hoping the man-eater might cross by sheer chance. I could then repeat the performance along the ghat road in the opposite direction. I could even motor along the road I had come from Talaimalai. But motoring along the fourth track to the east would not be advisable. Here I would have to walk. For this track was not only in a very bad state, littered with big stones and full of potholes, but it twisted and turned, and was full of sharp gradients. It entailed far too much gear work and consequent noise, which would drive away the man-eater and any other animal that happened to be near, before I had a chance of seeing them.

Where to begin was anybody's choice and I decided to walk along the eastern track first, while I was still fresh and because it would take the longest time.

Finishing my tea, I paid Abdulkunni and told my four men to catch up with as much sleep as they could while I took a walk up the eastern trail. Not being old acquaintances of mine, they thought I was mad. Abdulkunni, who had overheard the conversation and who had known me for quite a long time, remarked: 'You think he's mad, eh? That's no discovery! I've known him to be mad for a long time.'

For some reason the old rascal was annoying me more and more that evening. I checked the torch in the .405 and the spare five-cell torch that I intended using for the actual reconnaissance, as it would be far too tiresome to keep pointing the barrel of the rifle about so as to use its torch. Then I walked to the Rest House, stood on the verandah plinth for a few minutes to admire once more the twinkling lights of Satyamangalam, and finally started along the eastern track that began behind the bungalow. With the first turn, that came within a few yards, I was shut off from the friendly light of the petromax lantern hanging in front of the teashop and from the sounds that came from within.

The man-eater had disappeared with his victim and there was no knowing where he had taken her. Tigers have been known to carry their kills for a distance of half-a-mile and even more, although generally they don't go so far. He had killed the woman that morning and no doubt had eaten part of her. The rest he would have to come back for after dark to make a second meal. It was now a little after 9.30 p.m., and as the habits of tigers generally go, the man-eater should have returned by now for his second meal and be enjoying it at this moment, or very likely he would have finished it by now. After all, there is not much meat in an already half-eaten human carcase!

If he had eaten his fill, he would next seek water, and I knew there were three possible places for him to do that. The closest was at a water hole that was skirted by the very track I was following and lay hardly a furlong ahead. The second was by a regular stream that crossed the road to Mysore about two miles away. The third was another stream that I had already passed in the car that evening and was about three miles from Dimbum on the Talaimalai road. Apart from the water hole I was approaching, the man-eater could drink at any point throughout the course of the two streams, and the chance of meeting him over water was extremely slim.

I was approaching the water hole with these thoughts still in my mind, and the first signs of its nearness were a row of blue-green lights in pairs, that kept jerking up and down as they stared into the bright beam of my torch. Spotted deer! Here was a herd, either on its way to the water hole or returning from it.

I stopped abruptly and put out the light to allow the deer a chance of going away quietly. If any of them caught the human scent behind my light, if would surely voice an alarm cry to warn its companions. That cry would also alert the tiger if it was in the vicinity, and I did not want that to happen.

The night was pitch-dark and not a sound came to me from the spotted deer. The silence was intense. Not even a cricket chirped. I did not like it at all. It was eerie.

I switched on the torch. The bobbing pinpoints of light had gone. The deer had vanished in complete silence. That was good, for they had raised no alarm. I waited a few minutes longer to allow them to get far enough away, so as not to scent me or see my torch-beam. Then I started moving forward silently along the track. The next turn would bring me to the water hole that lay to the left.

That was when I heard the splashing and gurgling and loud swishing noises. An elephant was at the water hole and enjoying a bath. I stopped again. His presence was a nuisance, for elephants, like most human beings, like their bath. Once they start, they not only gurgle and drink and bathe and gambol, but they lie in the water and play in it, even if all alone, sometimes for an hour at a stretch. I could not waste so much time waiting for the creature to go away of its own accord. On the other hand, if I advanced and it saw or scented me, the chances were that it might trumpet in alarm and that, again, would warn the man-eater, should he be within earshot, that something strange was moving through the forest, something unusual enough to disturb an elephant. For me to make a noise to frighten away the elephant would be folly for the same reason.

Then I had an idea. I pointed the beam of the torch high up to the treetops in the direction of the water hole in the hope that it might be seen by the elephant and cause him to move off. Evidently I was too far away at first, because he did not see the light. Then I advanced till I was almost at the bend of the track before trying again. This time I succeeded. All sounds of that most enjoyable bath ceased abruptly.

There came a great squelching as the elephant lifted his big body out of the mud, followed by a rhythmic plop-plop-plop-plop of heavy footsteps as he plodded slowly through the water to the bank. Then followed repeated hissing sounds as of escaping steam. Although disturbed by my light, the elephant did not intend to deny himself the last luxury of a sand-bath, and that was what he was doing at that moment; he was throwing sand over himself.

I allowed him time, while continuing to flash the torch from treetop to treetop to keep him sufficiently disturbed. The hissing stopped eventually. It was followed in a little while by faint crackling sounds as the beast moved its heavy way through the undergrowth bordering the water hole. Once again came silence. The elephant had moved off and just then the sharp crack of a breaking branch told me that he had stopped for feed, but far enough away not to be alarmed at my passing.

I negotiated the turn in the track and came upon the water hole lying limpid and dark before me, a few wisps of vapour already rising from its warmer surface into the rapidly-cooling night air. Hundreds of pin-points of brilliant red light, like tiny rubies scattered over the water, shone in my torchlight, and from the nearer bank bordering the pool came the chorus of frogs. Alarmed by my approach, they had leaped off the bank in great numbers. With vigorous thrusts of their hind legs they propelled themselves into the centre of the pool, where they whirled around to face me, their tiny eyes glistening and reflecting like a thousand rubies.

I had been to such pains to avoid the elephant raising an alarm at my approach only to meet with a singular defeat at the hands of those most insignificant of creatures—the frogs. The tiger heard them, for he happened to be there, and must have seen me and my light simultaneously.

Fortunately for me, he was on the further bank of the pool, where he must have come to drink, and not on the track, or matters may have turned out differently. Under similar circumstances, any normal tiger would have taken himself off quietly and I would never have known of his presence. But this one growled, and continued to growl, the ominous sound rumbling from the darkness at the other end, across the pool and to me as I came to an abrupt and uncertain halt.

The tiny ruby-red eyes of the frogs floating on the surface disappeared altogether, as if some switch had cut off the power, when they dived beneath the surface to escape that awful sound. On the opposite bank of the pool whence the growling arose there was a great disturbance as the myriad frogs that had been resting on the cool sand by the water's edge threw themselves into the pool for safety and with their tiny legs struck out frantically for the centre.

The growling stopped as abruptly as it had begun. The frogs fell into a hushed silence too. I then directed the beam of my torch around the bushes and undergrowth that grew down to the water's edge at the opposite end. Would I see the tiger's eyes glow in the beam? I saw nothing and heard nothing. My light fell only upon the jungle and a deathly silence covered everything.

The tiger had vanished. Had he made off? A normal tiger would do just that, but no normal tiger would have growled at seeing my torchlight. This beast was far from normal. He was angry, and he was unafraid of the approach of man. Was this the man-eater?

I glanced around nervously. My front was safe. To attack from that direction the tiger would have to charge through water and I knew he was very unlikely to do that. Rather, he would come around the pool and attack me from either flank, or from behind. If he chose a flank attack, he would have to charge along the bank or the track, either from the direction I had just come or from the opposite end where the pathway left the pool. More probably he would attack from the rear, where the jungle bordered the edge of the track and not two yards from where I was standing. Then I would have no chance whatever.

There was but one thing to do and I did it very quickly. I

scrambled down the sloping bank into the water and, feeling the way before me with each footstep, made for the middle of the pool as fast as I could. I knew it was not very deep and there I would be safe from attack from any direction. No tiger—not even a man-eater, at least not in my experience—would attack across water, and even if it did, the tables would be turned entirely in my favour. I would have the tiger in the open and completely at my mercy, long before he could reach me.

The water had reached a little above my knees when the tiger growled again. This time it was a loud growl, almost a roar. And it came from the jungle bordering the track, from the very direction in which I had expected the attack. Had I not sought the safety of the pool just in time, the tiger would have launched itself upon me. He was growling with fury now at finding me beyond reach.

But was I really beyond reach? The next few moments would answer that question. Of one fact I had no doubt whatever: I was dealing with the man-eater and no ordinary tiger. The hate in its behaviour clearly showed that. Hughie's bullet had turned this animal into a fiend.

I waited in vain. The tiger did not emerge. The growling stopped as unexpectedly as it had started, and once again I was plunged into silence with a sea of darkness around me. I played the beams of my torch in every direction as I turned slowly around, hoping to catch a glimpse of the beast's eyes as they reflected the light, or of the striped body slinking from bush to bush. But I saw and heard nothing.

The myriads of frogs that had experienced such a disturbing night, first with the arrival of the elephant, then myself, and finally the tiger, all went below the surface of the water when I waded into it. But they could not remain submerged for long and had to come up for breath. One by one they came to the surface now, soundlessly, to gulp in air, and soon the nearer edge of the wide circle of light thrown by my torch once more revealed hundreds of pairs of tiny red eyes gazing on me in fear.

A long time seemed to have passed since I left the tea shop, but a quick glance at my watch showed it was only 10.30 p.m. How long would I have to wait for the tiger to move, if he moved at all?

I began to get tired of standing in the water. It grew colder and colder and wreaths of vapour arose from the surface of the pool, obscuring the jungle around its edges and making it difficult for the light of my torch to penetrate. At the same time, I realized that if I got back to the pathway I would be at the mercy of the man-eater should he decide to ambush me at any spot along the track. I felt certain he had not gone away but was biding his time till I came out of the water.

Midnight, and it was biting cold! By now I realized I must not shine my torch continuously, for the five cells would run down and under no circumstances could I risk using up the cells of the other torch, clamped to my rifle, for the accuracy of my shooting depended on them. So I extinguished the light and was plunged abruptly into darkness. That was when I noticed that the night was cloudy, with no stars to be seen.

However, there was no danger so long as I remained in the water. My hearing would warn me of the approach of any animal.

Very soon, that was what happened. An elephant came, perhaps the same one I had disturbed earlier. Probably another. I was standing still and he did not hear or see me. The wind was blowing from him to me, so he could not scent me. I felt I was safe, for in any case his sight was too poor to penetrate the mist that had settled over the whole pool like a thick bank of fog, and he would not be able to see me.

I heard the loud 'fooff-foooff-foooff' as he exhaled air though his trunk, and then the sucking noises as he drew in water and splashed it into his mouth and over his body. He drank and he drank, a seemingly endless number of gallons of water.

At last he decided to have a regular bath and I heard the tremendous plop-plop-plop of his great feet approaching me as he waded through the water towards the centre of the pool. This would never do, I thought. So I shone the torch straight into his face.

That night was for me one in which I seemed fated to meet animals of strange behaviour. According to all the rules of the game, the elephant should have turned tail and bolted from my bright light, but he did nothing of the kind. He trumpeted shrilly, coiled up his trunk, and charged me.

Taken aback, instead of putting the five-cell quickly into its pouch at the left side of my belt, so as to leave both my hands free to handle my rifle, I missed the pouch and dropped the torch into the water. Out it went.

There was no time to retrieve it. The charging elephant was dangerously close. I brought the .405 to my shoulder while pressing the button of the smaller torch that was clamped to its barrel with my left thumb. The beam cut through the darkness as I aimed a foot above the head of the elephant and fired in an attempt to halt that charge.

No rogue elephant had been proclaimed by the Forestry Department and so, as far as possible, I should try to avoid killing this animal. I had erred by letting him come too close to me and I should not have shone the torch directly in his face.

As these thoughts rushed through my mind, I awaited the result of that deterring shot. If he still came on, I would be forced to stop him with my next bullet or he would kill me. There was no doubt of that.

Luckily it worked. The great beast braked to a halt by planting all four feet firmly in the mud. The impetus of the rush brought him on, skidding ludicrously in the clay till he ended up sitting on his hindquarters like an elephant at the circus. Encouraged by his failing nerve, I fired a second time, again over his head. The elephant turned and bolted.

When the noise and tumult had died away I felt disgusted, but at the same time relieved. My two shots must have driven away the man-eater. My chance of success was gone. But now I was safe also and could at last get out of the water.

Shivering with the cold, I started my walk back to Dimbum. I knew I had only a short distance to cover, but there was always the danger that the man-eater, driven from the immediate vicinity of the pool by the sound of my shots, might still be lurking somewhere along the pathway and might ambush me.

At last the lights of Satyamangalam, twinkling in the black void of the plains below me, put an end to my tension. I got into the Rest House, took off my wet pants and, as I had brought no change of clothes, went to sleep without them.

A banging on the door awakened me. I had closed all the windows and it was dark inside, but a glance at my watch surprised me. It was 9.30 a.m.

I put on my pants again. They were still wet. The banging on the door was renewed, this time more urgently, and I could hear the murmur of voices on the verandah.

I opened the front door. Confronting me was Abdulkunni himself, his three wives and four or five other people, all in a great state of excitement. Obviously the tea shop had been closed down. Something very serious must have happened.

'Come quickly, sahib,' called the excited Moplah. 'The tiger has just carried away the girl we employed to fetch the water.'

Grabbing my rifle and some cartridges, I hastened with the group to the teashop, while he quickly told the story.

Barely thirty minutes earlier the girl had taken a basket of cooking utensils to wash at the well behind the tea shop. She had decided it would be easier that way than carrying a pitcher or more of water to the building for the purpose. One of the wives had been watching her from the back door to ensure she did not linger unduly over the task. The girl, a maiden of about eighteen years, was bending down, absorbed in her work, when a movement behind her had caught the eye of the watching woman. She had glanced in that direction and was horrified to see a tiger, belly to the ground, sneaking stealthily upon the unsuspecting servant girl from behind. The woman had screeched a warning. The girl heard and jumped to her feet. But the tiger drove home his charge. He had leapt upon his victim and, not waiting to kill her, had taken the unfortunate girl in his mouth and leaped back into the cover of the undergrowth. Terrible screams could be heard long after the tiger and victim had disappeared from sight.

Alarmed by his wife's yells and hearing distant wailing, Abdulkunni and the other members of the household had rushed to the rear door to find out the cause of the disturbance. Then they had come in a body to the Rest House. The man-eater had taken another victim at nine in the morning, and exactly where he had killed only a few hours earlier! This was something unheard of in the annals of man-eaters.

Telling everyone to remain indoors, I hastened to the well. The scattered utensils, some washed and the others not, showed that the girl had been taken by surprise while engrossed in her task, and a single sliding pug-mark indicated where the tiger had stopped his rush to seize his victim and had slipped on the wet earth where the girl had been doing her washing. There were no other marks on the surrounding earth, trampled flat as it was by the feet of the many people who came there all day long to draw water, and baked by the sun's rays. The ground was far too hard to carry pug-marks, while the girl had been grabbed so quickly that there was no blood trail of any kind.

The woman who had witnessed the killing, Abdulkunni's second wife, called to me from the doorway, pointing out the direction in which the man-eater had gone with his victim, and I followed it. The clearing in which the well stood ended abruptly in a wall of lantana bushes that fringed the jungle. No tiger, carrying his prey, would dream of forcing himself through this tangled obstruction. It would be impossible for any beast. There must be some other way and I started to look for it. I found it eventually, a game-*path*, close to the ground, tunnelling at a height of not more than four feet through the lower branches of the lantana. It had been made by wild pigs during the rainy season, when they visited the clearing to root and dig in the swamp which would at that season surround the well. In places the tiger had had to crawl along this tunnel, dragging its victim, and I followed suit, crouching low and at times on hands and knees.

Within a few yards I came upon the first evidence of the tragedy. Some torn shreds of a sari and a quantity of blood on the lantana leaves that littered the game-trail. Probably the victim had been struggling to free herself and this was where the tiger had killed her.

After that there was a regular blood trail, and more shreds of the sari caught on the lantana. There came a bend in the tunnel and here the remains of the girl's clothing had caught on a thorny bush. The man-eater must have become angry and wrenched his victim free, for the scraps of a sari and a skirt had been torn from her body and were hanging on the thorns. With the removal of all her clothing the blood had fallen directly on the ground and leaves, making a ghastly red trail through the tunnel.

I could not know how far the tiger had carried his victim. Probably the screeching and screaming from the tea shop had made him decide to go to a quieter place before commencing his meal. At least, I hoped so. For if he was anywhere near and attacked me from my rear, I was completely at his mercy in this death-trap of a tunnel.

This thought caused me to stop frequently to listen. He might give himself away by growling. Tigers often do that when followed. Partly in anger, partly as a warning, but more often to strengthen their own courage. For all their lives have been spent in pursuing a fleeing prey and it is an unusual and terrifying experience for any tiger to realize he is the object of pursuit himself. Not a sound did I hear. Complete silence filled that twisting tunnel.

At last the lantana began to give way to jungle proper. The tunnel came to an end and I was able to stand upright. There was a grassy glade through which the blood trail led before it merged into a park-like jungle of *babul* and box-flower shrubs with grass between. I judged that I had not far to go now before meeting the tiger, who must have started his meal. That is, provided the man-eater had not heard me and realized he was being followed. If that had happened, he might take himself off altogether or lie in wait for me at some spot close to his kill. He might even creep forward to intercept me, or ambush me from either side or from the rear.

Then I heard a crow cawing some distance away. I listened carefully, and there was no mistaking that persistent cawing. The crow was watching the tiger with his victim and was excitedly calling reinforcements to be ready to enjoy the feast that was soon to follow.

Sounds and the distances from which they emanate are difficult to locate and estimate correctly in the forest. Air currents, the density of tree growth and the terrain all make difficulties. In flat country conditions are not quite so bad, but in hilly areas like this, sounds and distances are often unjudgable.

I reckoned the crow was about sixty to seventy yards away, and slowly, very stealthily, studying the ground before me so as not to tread upon a dried twig or stone and so betray myself, I advanced step by step. I do not know how far I had gone when I heard the first sounds of the feast. The sharp crack of a bone being broken, followed by crunching and tearing.

The crow was still cawing excitedly. I reckoned that I was within thirty yards now, possibly a good deal less. I stopped and began to think.

The crow offered a greater risk at that moment than the tiger. For he was sitting on a tree and had the advantage of height. I knew that if he saw me he would cease cawing at once. He might even fly away. The man-eater, engrossed in his meal, knew that the crow was watching him but had ignored the bird and his cawing as a matter of no consequence. A sudden end to that cawing and the sudden departure of the crow would tell the tiger at once that something had alarmed the bird, that some danger to himself was approaching. For crows fear no other bird and ignore the presence of wild animals. They fear only the human race.

But I had not yet alarmed the crow. At a snail's pace, with infinite caution, I advanced, crouching low, shuffling forward and halting again, watching the ground in front of me before making any movement, glancing to right and left and even looking behind when the tearing and crunching sounds ceased for a moment. For so long as I could hear those sounds I knew the tiger was in front. When they ceased I could no longer know where he was. There lay the greatest danger, for he might creep upon me from behind. Man-eaters generally snatch their victims that way.

Suddenly an uncanny silence fell over everything. At first I could not account for it. Then I knew the cause. The crow had stopped cawing! Undoubtedly something was afoot. Then I saw the crow, but too late. He had seen me first. With what seemed a tremendous fluttering, he flew to another tree.

And I was right: the man-eater had become suspicious. He had started to move. Was he moving away from me or towards me? Was he trying to escape or attack? As these questions raced through my mind, with the corner of my eye I saw the crow rise again. This time he flew out of sight.

I froze in my tracks. But it was too late. The cunning crow flew back to investigate and perched at almost the same spot as the one where I saw him first. He turned his head sideways for a better view of me, cawed and bobbed. Convinced that I was dangerous, he fluttered his wings and then flew to yet another tree to turn around and watch me.

I stopped watching the crow and stared at the bushes all around. And I turned about to watch the bushes behind me. There was a pricking sensation at the back of my neck. Every cell of my body warned me that I was in great danger. I knew that the man-eater was about to pounce.

But I simply could not see him, stare as I might at the undergrowth all around. The jungle was ominously silent. Not a twig cracked, not a leaf stirred. The birds and insects were silent, so too were the bushes and the long grass that grew between the trees. I looked in vain for the stirring of a branch or a blade of grass, the bending of a sapling stem that might betray movement below and the passage of a creeping body.

But there was not a movement anywhere, not a sound. I knew that the tiger was employing all his skill to make his last rush a complete surprise.

And then there came to my mind the scene I had witnessed many years before by moonlight, beside a jungle pool in the heart of a deep forest far away. A sambar hind was approaching the water hole cautiously. All was silent. Suddenly, for no reason whatever, she wheeled noisily and rushed away. The ruse worked then, for the tiger patiently lying in wait to ambush her a few yards further on, now lost his head. He thought his prey was about to escape and he bounded after her. But the hind had too much of a start and got away to safely.

Now I did the same thing. But I did not turn and run back, for something warned me that the man-eater was already there. I stamped noisily and ran forward diagonally, but only for four paces. Then I stopped.

As on that moonlit night so many years before, the simple ruse worked again. The man-eater roared and bounded after me from behind. He took two leaps and then halted in crouching amazement as this strange man before him, instead of continuing to run, turned around and fired rapidly.

The tiger knew no more after that, but I know that if I had not heeded that warning of his very close presence behind me, or if I had run backwards instead of forwards, I would not be here to tell this tale.

3

The Killer of the Wynaad

To the southwest of the city of Mysore lies the heavily forested area of the Kakankote jungles, for centuries the home of many herds of wild elephants that are partial to the kind of jungle that grows in this district. The rainfall is heavy and the vegetation is luxurious. Giant bamboos, rank grass and mighty trees grow together in dense profusion, and a passage through the forest, except for the elephants and the large and harmless bison, is almost impossible. Sambar and barking deer are found in the thinner areas, but as one moves farther southwest and the rainfall and the denseness of the jungle increase in direct ratio to each other, the deer become fewer and fewer, leaving the elephants and bison in almost entire possession of what appears from the narrow road to be primeval, virgin jungle.

Still further on is the Kabini river, one of the natural boundaries between Mysore state to the northeast and Kerala state, in the extreme southwest. In my opinion, the state of Kerala, in the extreme southwest of the Indian peninsula, offers a scenery second only in beauty to that of the Himalayas, though very different. It is a land of dense forests, fertile plantations of tea, coffee, cinnamon, rubber and tapioca, and emerald-green fields in the areas bordering the sea; of gently flowing rivers and waterways without number, along which palm-thatched river boats glide among coconut palms laden with huge bunches of green nuts, and a sea coast without parallel, culminating at the southern tip of the peninsula in the famous beach of Cape Comorin.

The town of Manantoddy, on the Kerala side of the border, stands on the Western Ghats, the range of mountains that run down the west coast of India, almost from Bombay to the far south, at an average elevation of about 4,000 feet above sea level. This district is known as the North Wynaad, to differentiate it from the country a few miles further south, which abuts the Nilgiri Mountain and is known as the South, or Nilgiri, Wynaad. Both areas are extremely fertile, enjoy a heavy rainfall, and are the site of many plantations, producing every conceivable crop.

Pleasant as they are in all other respects, these regions abound in leeches throughout the year, and in the rainy season their numbers are enormous. Moreover, that curse of the drier jungles, the tick, thrives in yet greater comfort than it does in the forests of the interior—both the large crab-tick that gives you tick-fever when it bites you in sufficient numbers, and the microscopic jungle, or grass-tick, smaller than a pin's head, that provokes a small sore wherever it has sucked your blood. Since it bites you all over the body, in hundreds of places, you become a very sore creature indeed, covered with sores that last for many months. You scratch and scratch yourself, night and day, into a mental and physical wreck.

Leeches and ticks suck the blood not only of a human being, but of animals as well. Even the bison suffer, while tigers, panthers and deer become covered with them, especially ticks, so that they hang from the softer portions of these animals' bodies, gorged with blood, like bunches of small grapes.

For this reason, the jungles of the Wynaad hold few carnivorous animals or deer. Now and then a stray animal may roam in during the dry summer months to brave the discomforts, but with the advent of the rains they move to the higher ranges of the Western Ghats, or the drier areas of East Kakankote to escape from the leeches and ticks till the monsoon abates with the approach of winter.

Thus it came about that, when a traveller journeying from Kakankote to Manantoddy was taken by a tiger just within a few hundred yards of the outskirts of the latter, it was regarded as a quite unusual event. Tigers had been seen in these parts but were few in number, and no human had been harmed for as long as anybody could remember. The event was soon forgotten and many months passed.

Then, across the border in the state of Mysore, preparations were started for the next *kheddah* operation, in which many wild elephants were to be caught. Coolies were engaged in hundreds to build the mighty wooden stockade into which they would later drive the elephants before the gate was dropped and the bewildered beasts captured. Much preliminary work was required; timber had to be felled, the forest cleared, bamboos gathered and bound together and then moved to the spot selected for the stockade. This required not only hard work but experienced workers. Men from the jungle tribes, the Karumbas and the Sholagas, provided most of the recruits, for they were experienced not only in tree-felling and bamboo-binding, but in the ways of the elephants, in driving them into the stockade, and in roping and shackling them and taming them afterwards.

That was when the tiger struck, a second and a third time, before people realized that a man-eater was amongst them.

Two Karumbas vanished within three days of each other and the half-eaten remains of the first showed he had been devoured by a tiger.

The body of the second Karumba, like that of the traveller to Manantoddy, was never seen again.

There is another way of getting to Manantoddy from Mysore city, and that is via Coorg, which was for years an independent state but has recently joined Mysore. It is a more circuitous route, but the scenery is even more picturesque. Like the Kakankote road, this route traverses dense jungle inhabited by elephants and bison, where tigers are practically unknown for the reasons already explained.

The Coorgies are a hardy, lively people. In olden days the British conferred a special honour upon them unknown elsewhere in India. Every Coorgie living within the limits of his state was exempted from possessing an arms licence, no matter how many weapons he possessed. This privilege is, I believe, still maintained by the Indian government. It was a laudable gesture but it had one bad result. The Coorgies never abused their privilege by using their weapons against each other or against other people, but they exercised it against the fauna of their beautiful little state to such an extent that the deer have been practically exterminated.

I know a large number of Coorgie families, most of whom are coffee planters, owning wide estates where the coffee berry flourishes to perfection, with oranges as a profitable secondary crop, and I happened to be a guest of one of these families when news of the man-eater trickled through.

The estate where I was staying was situated about midway between the towns of Sidapur and Virajpet, and at a considerable distance from both Manantoddy and Kakankote, where all three killings had occurred. Further, I had not brought my rifle with me from Bangalore, as I knew there was no shooting, at least of the kind in which I was interested, to be had in Coorg. So, when my friend gave me the news one morning over his breakfast table, I listened to it dispassionately, wondering like him as to how a man-eating tiger had found its way into an area so unpropitious, where ordinary tigers and panthers are almost unknown. But my friend waxed enthusiastic and suggested we go after it.

I told him I did not think much of the idea. In my opinion, the animal was not a confirmed man-eater, but was probably a sick or wounded tiger, or perhaps one that had escaped from one of the many miniature circuses that are always touring the country, and had strayed there because of the heavy jungles. I felt that it would either die of its sickness or wounds, or would soon leave these unfavourable haunts and move into normal tiger country, where it could find an abundance of its natural food, when it would stop man-hunting of its own accord. Besides, as I reminded him, I had not brought my rifle.

Timayya, for that was my host's name, offered to bet that I was wrong. The tiger would remain where he was, he affirmed. As for a rifle! He had five, from which I could make my choice.

I reminded my friend that to do so would be illegal. His weapons were unlicensed. It was a part of the stipulation that he, as a Coorgie, was forbidden to lend his unlicensed weapons to a non-Coorgie. And in any case, it was against the rules for anybody, even a licence-holder like myself, to borrow another man's weapon.

Timayya laughed at me, and said, 'What rot!' Then, banteringly, he bet me ten rupees that the tiger would kill again before the week was out. Rather huffed at his words, I took him on.

Timayya won that bet; for on the third day we heard that the tiger had killed again. This time the victim was a woman. She had been washing clothes on the further bank of the Kabini river, just within the limits of Kerala state. And Timayya's free arms permit was not valid in Kerala state.

My friend had set his heart on going after this tiger. I suppose to him, being something unusual, it became a must, and he stated flatly that I was included in the party.

Frankly, I was not keen; but to continue to refuse would have strained our relations. I had known Timayya for a long time, in fact we had been at school together, and stubbornness had always been his failing and his virtue! The estate, when he had bought it cheaply, was considered by the neighbours to be a complete 'write off.' The soil was said to be no good, the variety of coffee that grew there was no good, the shade trees were no good, and so forth! But Timayya was determined to buy. He bought; he worked hard; and he made good.

So I gave in on one condition. I would go back to Bangalore for my .405 and bring along my .450/400 as a spare rifle. He would accompany me. Then we would return to Mysore city from where we would motor directly to Kakankote and the Kerala border. I stressed that I would much rather incur the expense of the additional 240 miles of motoring than be mixed up in arms licence disputes with the police of two states.

Timayya concurred, left his weapons behind and came with me to Bangalore the same night. We spent the next day in buying provisions for a fifteen-day camp in the jungles of the border where we knew no foodstuff, acceptable to our civilized palates, would be available. Timayya bought a jar of some patent cream and a huge tin of D.D.T. as protection against the leeches and ticks. We carried mosquito nets too, along with my small tent, a portable charpoy machan, batteries and torches, and my two rifles. Timayya said he did not want to shoot but would rather watch the fun. Knowing him as I did, I realized this was not strictly true.

We arrived at Kakankote on the afternoon of the second day and then drove to the *kheddah* site to try to pick up what information we could about the tiger. As I anticipated, there was little to learn. So many coolies were about, working on the project, that no one appeared to know exactly when and where the tiger had taken his two victims. But rumour and universal fear were rife. The men had just vanished and their absence had not been noticed for two days or so. Even then it was only by mere chance that, being attracted by the stench of putrefying flesh, some travellers had gone to investigate and found some scanty remains.

Many people had theories to account for the presence of a man-eater in that zone, but not one of them had seen the animal. What they had to say boiled down to the belief that an evil spirit was operating in the forest in the guise of a tiger. This instilled an even greater fear into the coolies, so much so that we knew if another of them was killed, the *kheddah* operation would come to a stop. Such a happening, or even a postponement in the date, would be in the nature of a calamity to the local government, which had invited certain V.I.P.s from abroad as guests at the trapping.

Next morning, we motored the short distance to the Kerala border and came to the hamlet on the further bank of the Kabini river from which the latest victim—the woman who had been washing clothes—had been taken. Once more, nobody had seen the tiger. Only its pug-marks on the river bank, the trail of something that had been dragged away, and a few drops of blood on the leaves and earth had revealed a man-eater's visit.

We went on to Manantoddy and made inquiries at that small town regarding the first victim, the traveller who had been coming from Kakankote. Here again nobody knew anything. A forest guard, returning to his quarters near the Forest Range Office, had come across an odd sandal by the roadside. As it was good sandal, and people do not usually throw their footwear away, he stopped to look at it. That was when he noticed the other sandal lying on the sloping bank of a stream that ran parallel to the road. He walked down to see that too, and found a turban entangled in the bracken that grew by the waterside. Then he looked at the ground and saw the pug-marks of a tiger in the mud. They were deeply embedded in the ooze, indicating that the animal had been carrying additional weight, while a few carmine splashes on the fern leaves revealed the truth.

Blood! The tiger had been carrying away the wearer of the sandals and the turban.

We interviewed this guard and heard the story from his own lips. And that brought us to the end of the trail. There was nothing more we could learn, and we did not know where to make a start. Timayya confessed that he was sorry he had urged me to start upon this wild-goose chase.

Manantoddy is a beautiful place and we spent the night at the inspection bungalow which was fortunately vacant. Unlike most of the bungalows in other states, it is fully furnished with comfortable beds and foam mattresses, has neon lights and electric fans, and stands on a hillside opposite the ruins of an old British dwelling house that had its own private cemetery.

This is the land of fireflies. They come out after dark in their thousands, and the twinkling of their little lights are a fitting background to the chorus of the hundreds of small frogs, known as the 'Wynaad' or 'tok-tok' frog, and the hauntingly-sweet, never-to-forgotten aroma of sprays of the 'Rath-ki-Rani,' the 'Queen of the Night' blooms that open only after dark. We lay in armchairs, smoking tranquilly as we listened to the endless 'tok-tok-tok-tok-tok' of the frogs. Now and again a firefly would find its way into the room through the open window, its little light eclipsed by the brilliance of the neon tube that lit the room.

The next morning we made a leisurely start, our intention being to motor by the direct route to Virajpet in Coorg state, and thence to Timayya's plantation, where I would drop him, stay a day myself, and then go on to Mysore city and back to Bangalore.

We had travelled over ten miles from Manantoddy and were negotiating a stretch of dense forest; mostly of bamboo, on the Kerala bank of the Kabini river, when we saw a party of men approaching us, carrying a litter. And this is where my story really begins, for on the litter was a man, his tattered clothing soaked with his blood.

The bearers told us they were bamboo cutters and had been working on contract by the riverside, just over a mile away, when shortly after dawn that morning and without warning, a tiger had suddenly charged upon two of them, in full view of the others, and struck down one, whom it had grabbed by the shoulder and begun to drag away.

But the two men were brothers, and the one the tiger had ignored was very brave. He had run after the beast with the large curved knife he had been using to cut bamboos.

Seeing he was pursued, the man-eater had started to gallop away, still carrying his victim. The pursuer, realizing he had no hope of catching up with the tiger to save his brother, had then hurled his knife at the departing animal in sheer desperation. Luck favoured him, for the heavy weapon struck the carnivore in its flank. Either in pain, or from fright, the man-eater dropped his victim and bounded into the bamboos.

The hero of this episode, who was one of the men carrying the litter, had then assembled the scattered bamboo cutters and mobilized them into a team to help carry his sorely stricken brother to the nearest hospital, which was at Manantoddy.

There was no time to be lost and we acted quickly. Bundling

the mauled man, with two others to help him, into the Studebaker, I told Timayya to turn around and drive them as fast as he could to the hospital, where he could leave the wounded man. He would then drive back to the bamboo cutters' camp, directed by the two men who were with him, while I went ahead on foot with the rest to see if we could find the tiger.

While Timayya was still turning the car I started at a jog-trot for the camp, the brave brother, whose name I learned was Yega, running beside me while the rest of the party followed behind. There was not a minute to be lost. In all probability the man-eater was miles away by this time, but there was just the slimmest of chances that he might still be lingering in the vicinity.

We reached the encampment in good time, but did not stop till we came to the place where the tiger had dropped his victim. There was a rank undergrowth of weeds covering the ground that showed no pug-marks, but on the bright green leaves were splashes of red—fresh blood that had not yet had time to dry. Whether the blood came from Yega's brother, who had been dropped here, or from a wound made by the knife in the man-eater's flank, we could not at that moment tell.

At this spot I halted the men who had followed and whispered to them to return to their camp. Yega and I would see this thing through together. The presence of many people would frighten the man-eater away, if it happened to be still nearby.

The bent heads of the undergrowth showed the direction in which the man-eater had run after dropping his victim, and I followed Yega, alert for a surprise attack at any moment and from any direction, particularly our rear. He tiptoed in front with bent head, examining the foliage and such glimpses of the dark 'black cotton-soil' type of earth as he could see between the green stems of the crowded plants.

Yega was looking for his knife. We wanted to make sure if his heavy weapon had actually hurt the tiger or not. If it had really done so, we might expect the animal to act quite differently from what he would have done if the blow from the knife had been a glancing one. Most likely, if injured, the tiger would roar and charge us from a fair distance; but if uninjured the man-eater would either attack only when we came fairly close to him, or slink away.

My part of the business now was to watch the jungle more carefully than ever before, ahead on both sides, and also behind, to protect us against a surprise attack. I could not help Yega in his search.

Then we found the knife. Its edge was clean, with no trace of blood. The tiger had not been hurt and the blood we had passed had come from the wounded man.

We crept forward for some distance and stopped. Then Yega shook his head slowly from side to side. The man-eater had stopped running.

We followed for another furlong, when the trail of our quarry petered out. Here the animal had crossed an area of lemon-grass, which is a scented variety with leaves that are largely used for distilling an essential oil. This grass has long, hard tough stems which had bent with the man-eater's passing and then regained their position, so that no trace now remained of the direction in which he had gone. The earth between the large clumps of this lemon grass was a matted carpet of decaying stems and seedlings, showing not the faintest trace of a pug-mark.

Quickening our pace, we cut directly across the lemon grass area, which extended for perhaps a quarter of a mile, to where the jungle began again. But the tiger's trail could not be found again and we were forced to conclude that we had lost him.

Apart from his courage, perseverance was another quality in which this little bamboo cutter was strong. He refused to admit defeat and urged in a whisper that we should go on and on till we eventually found the tiger. Stimulated by his keenness, I entered into the spirit of the chase and we pressed forward for many miles and most of the remaining hours of that day. We passed two herds of bison and a family of wild elephants and it was past 3 p.m., before we finally turned back for the bamboo cutters' camp. This we reached after dark, at 7.30 p.m. I was covered with leech bites and with ticks, and I was unutterably tired, although glad that we had at last come to grips with the man-eater and had such a stout henchman as Yega to assist.

Timayya had returned in the car many hours earlier and was eagerly awaiting our news. Unfortunately, I had none to give him.

We decided to return to the inspection bungalow at Manantoddy, which was only eleven miles away, for the night and to the bamboo cutters' camp the next morning. The prospect of spending the night with them, lying on the ground, with the mosquitoes and what not, was too terrible to contemplate.

That was where I made a big mistake. For when we did arrive the next morning we found the little camp in terrible confusion and all the bamboo cutters huddled together in a single hut. They swarmed out, led by Yega, to report that the man-eater had returned in the dead of the night. He had crept up and snatched one of them from beneath the walls of a hut!

Now you may wonder how a tiger could do that, but the explanation is simple. The huts which the bamboo cutters had constructed were but temporary shelters in the jungle which they would leave as soon as their work was done. They were built of split bamboos and leaves, and the sides of the structures were never allowed to touch the ground. For if they did, the termites—or white ants, as they are better known—would creep up into the walls in a matter of hours and the whole hut would be destroyed in no time. So a gap was left right round the hut, the ends of such bamboos as had necessarily to be embedded in the ground being first defended by a coating of tar.

The man-eater must indeed have been starving. Perhaps being deprived of his victim the previous day had whetted his appetite. He had returned in the early hours of the morning and, emboldened by the silence that reigned over the slumbering camp, had wandered up to the four huts. There, through the gap below the wall of one of them, he had seen the form of a sleeping man. The rest was easy to the hungry, daring beast. He had crept up to the hut and stretched his paw under the gap, fastening his claws into the sleeping man. The man had screamed for help, but no one had had the presence of mind to do anything and the man-eater had dragged his victim out of the hut, tearing down the lower portion of one of the walls in the process.

Unfortunately for the victim, Yega, the one person who might have given help, was not in that hut but in the one furthest away, enabling the tiger to make a clean getaway. The bamboo cutters related in horror that they had had to listen to the poor man's screams for a very long time after the tiger dragged him out of the hut. Strangely, it had not killed him while he yelled and screamed, as man-eaters generally do when their victims make a noise. This animal had carried him away screaming and his comrades had heard his cries grow fainter and fainter as his captor bore him away.

Yega offered to accompany me at once, but the other coolies were utterly demoralized. They remained huddled in a group, calling to God to help them while they rained invectives upon the tiger. There were nine of them, excluding Yega. So I asked Timayya to squeeze them into the Studebaker, even if it came to letting a couple stand on the footboard, and to take them back to Manantoddy and safety without delay. He was then to return to the camp site and wait for me, but while doing so was not to leave the car on any account. In any case, he had my .405/400 with him, so there was no danger of his being unable to protect himself.

Yega and I then took up the trail of the man-eater.

The ground was soft outside the huts and had been cleared of the usual weeds in an effort to keep away the ticks and the leeches. This helped us to find the tiger's footprints, both as he had approached the hut and when he had left, carrying his victim with him. Whatever part of the poor man's anatomy had been grasped by the tiger was clearly not a vital region, for the victim had struggled and kicked the ground, as tell-tale marks revealed.

At one place he had grasped the stem of a sapling and must have held on tenaciously. The tiger had literally torn him free, as could be seen by the particles of skin from the palms of the man's hands that still adhered to the stem and the markedly increased quantity of blood on the ground and leaves at that spot. No doubt this had resulted from an enlargement of the wound as the tiger dragged his victim free.

Now we were able to follow the trail with ease. The poor man had bled terribly and splashes of blood on the weeds, grass and leaves marked the way the tiger had passed. A queer sensation of nausea came over me as I pictured that horrible scene at dead of night in the blackness of the jungle, and the victim's realization that he was to be devoured, that nothing and no one could save him, and that he would never see his wife and children again.

At last we reached the spot where the tiger must have felt he had had enough of his victim's cries and struggles. Here he had laid the man on the ground and, releasing his grip, had bitten him again and again till his wails had been stilled for ever.

All this was written in the marks on the ground and the pool of blood that had streamed from those last fierce and fatal bites. After that the man-eater had continued his journey.

We followed for another furlong, and here at last the tiger had decided to begin his meal. He had left the narrow trail and turned into a small hollow in the ground, sheltered by grass, bushes and bracken, where he had set about devouring the unfortunate bamboo cutter. As we had surmised, the beast must have been hungry, for little remained of the man beyond the usual parts: the head, hands and feet, and a small portion of his chest, with rib bones bereft of flesh. The entrails had been torn out and dragged aside. The meat had been removed from the victim's pelvis, exposing the bone, and the thighs had also been devoured, here again leaving the bare bones in evidence of the great feast.

Far less than a quarter of the poor man remained, but this was enough to make the tiger return that night for a second meal, provided we played our cards cunningly enough and did not arouse his suspicions.

Yega and I looked around and at this point we encountered our first setback. There was no tree within at least eighty yards, a range far too great, as I well knew from past experience, to risk a shot by torchlight at night.

To the uninitiated this may seem an exaggeration. Eighty yards in daylight might appear a mere stone's throw. But those who have sat on *machans* in a jungle at night will know what I mean. Bushes, leaves, blades of grass and rocks all cause obstructions at this distance, and to attempt to cut them away, to ensure a better view when the tiger returned, might arouse his suspicions and prevent him from returning at all. Remember, I could not risk wounding him. I had to shoot to kill.

Tigers and panthers, and man-eaters especially, are very cautious when they come back to their kills. They reconnoitre the approaches to the spot for a long time before they show themselves, and if they feel or sense anything suspicious, if they find any cut branches scattered about, any removal of bushes or undergrowth or rocks, or any addition of leaves or branches that may conceal a hidden enemy, they will give the spot a wide berth and never return. Although he lacks a sense of smell, the tiger makes up for this handicap with an uncanny caution and an ability almost to read the hunter's mind and anticipate his every action.

As if to compensate for the distance of the nearest tree from the remains of the woodsman, a dense patch of tiger-grass bordered the bank of the small depression into which the tiger had taken him before beginning his meal, and this patch was barely fifteen feet away.

If I could hide in that grass without the man-eater becoming aware of my presence he would offer a point-blank target. The moon would rise early, and conditions would be in my favour, always provided the tiger did not become aware of my presence. Would this be possible? For if he did find out, the situation could turn into a most unpleasant one for me.

As I well knew, all tigers and especially man-eaters, which appear to be endowed with a fiendish cunningness, exceeding even the natural caution of their kind, have a habit of taking advantage of every vestige of natural cover when returning to the remains of their victims for a second meal. The clump of tiger grass in which I contemplated concealing myself lay in the direct path of the man-eater's return and so close to his victim that it was more than likely, if not certain, that he would make use of it to conceal his own approach. And however silent I might be, I knew well enough how silent would be his own coming. Should the man-eater discover me before I discovered him, the bamboo cutter's bones would have those of another to keep them company before many hours had passed. It was a gamble, with a heavy stake, that I would have to take.

In order not to disturb the grass by unnecessary trampling, I walked around it while considering the problem in all its aspects. If I hid in that grass, I would have to keep a careful watch in two opposite directions: over the victim's remains and also in the direction by which the man-eater might be expected to make his approach, which would almost certainly be through this patch of grass. This I could not do; I would have at least to turn my head from side to side, even though I kept my body still. That would mean movement, and movement of any sort would be fatal.

One of two things would happen if the tiger became aware of me: he might take fright and disappear, or he would deliberately stalk and leap upon me before I even suspected his presence. Frankly, I funked that terrible alternative.

At this point, Yega came up with a brilliant idea. He and I would sit back to back in the grass, one of us watching the bamboo cutter's remains while the other listened for the rustle that would herald the man-eater's entrance into that same clump of grass, by which time he would not be more than five or six feet away.

What transpired next would have a lot to do with whether I happened to be the one who was watching the victim's remains or the tiger's approach through the grass. If I were watching the remains and Yega the grass, he would have to warn me with a nudge, and I would have to turn around in a second to be in time to shoot. And I would have to shoot accurately. But if I chose to watch the approach through the grass and left Yega to watch over the kill, and the man-eater crept up to the latter from some other direction, I would have to react similarly, except that the situation would not be nearly so dangerous. At least, the tiger would be more than a mere five or six feet away and I should have a better chance to shoot.

I hated to risk Yega's life. And I hated to risk my own. But this was our only chance and I nodded assent.

Strangely enough, in the Wynaad Forest area vultures are not nearly so numerous as in drier jungles of south India. Nevertheless, we took no chances of them discovering the remains and finishing what little flesh remained on the bones. So Yega cut a few small branches from the tree that grew eighty yards away, and these we placed over the bones and entrails of the man to hide them from any chance vulture hovering in the sky above. Then we returned to the deserted encampment.

It took another fifteen minutes for Timayya to come back in the car from Manantoddy. I told him of our discovery and our plan of action. Then occurred one of those awkward situations that sometimes appear between friends. Timayya stated bluntly that he would sit with me in Yega's stead, armed with my spare rifle, but I was not happy about his decision. I did not wish to risk my friend's life for one thing.

Secondly, quite frankly and I suppose selfishly, considering my own life was also at stake, I doubted his ability to keep watch for the tiger as efficiently as Yega would, with his lifetime of jungle experience. As tactfully as possible I put these points to my friend. Timmy became angry—and rude, too.

'Damn it, I'm a planter,' he said, 'not a bloody town-dweller like you. What the hell do you think? If you don't feel like sitting with me, at least lend me the .405/400 and … off back to Manantoddy yourself. I'll do the rest.'

There was a very nasty look in his eye.

I shrugged. 'Okay Timmy, you win,' I said. 'We'll sit together.'

The nasty look faded and a gleam of pleasure and excitement took its place.

When Yega heard the change of plan he was crestfallen. Now it was his turn to look at me reproachfully. I avoided his glance and studied one of the Studebaker's tyres closely.

We returned to Manantoddy for lunch, bringing Yega with us, after which we put in a couple of hours sleep to fortify us for the long, sleepless night vigil ahead. At three o'clock we were ready. Timmy suggested we take tea and sandwiches along with us, to which I assented after reminding him that these refreshments could only be enjoyed the following morning. No sound or movements of the slightest kind could we risk while we awaited the man-eater's return.

We left Yega at Manantoddy, as it would be dangerous for him to accompany us to the spot where we were going to sit and then return alone. Besides, we did not require his services in any way. By half-past three we had reached the woodcutter's deserted encampment. Here we parked the Studebaker close to the huts and before four we were at the patch of tiger-grass.

I removed the small branches with which Yega and I had earlier covered the scattered remains of the bamboo cutter to protect them from vultures, carrying them to a spot quite a distance away. It was a hot and sunny afternoon and what remained of the woodcutter, little enough though it was, had begun to smell, especially the entrails, which the man-eater had dragged to one side. But we dared not remove them for fear of arousing the tiger's suspicions when he returned.

I had already made it a condition with Timmy that I would face the side from which the tiger might be expected to approach through the grass, while he would face in the opposite direction towards the woodcutter's remains. Fortunately, he had not been difficult about this and had acquiesced readily enough. We had brought two of the foam-rubber cushions from the Rest House to sit upon. They would not only provide comfort, but would deaden any sound we might make in movement. Placing these on the ground, we squatted on them back to back and facing in the directions already described. I crossed my legs and settled down to sit in silence, having trained myself to this position after many years of similar experience in the jungle. Timmy whispered that he could not make himself comfortable that way and stretched both his legs out before him. Straightaway a disquieting thought entered my mind: for how long would Timmy be able to sit thus without moving? To me it appeared physically impossible, and I knew he would become fidgety before sundown.

Jungle life in the forests of the Wynaad and the Western Ghats is rather different from that of the drier areas. Animals and reptiles are fewer in number, but bird and insect life is prolific. We quickly became aware of this, for within a few minutes of our arrival and things quietening down, we heard the twittering calls of birds from all directions, accompanied by the chirping of crickets. The cicada of these regions is different from those of the plains: the latter, to which I was accustomed, emits a shrill and continuous high note, but the hill variety, which abounded here, emits a rasping note of fluctuating volume. It almost dies away and then rises to a cadence that jars the nerves, before fading away, only to rise again.

As evening fell, distant junglecocks and spurfowl began to vie with one another in their usual preroosting chorus, to the accompaniment of an occasional, plaintive, brassy cry from a peacock, feeding amidst the fallen seeds of the giant bamboo that grew so prolifically, or grubbing for caterpillars by scratching up the thick carpet of decaying leaves and mould. Around us, from the grass itself came the very faint and indefinable sounds of insects of all kinds on the move: grasshoppers, beetles of countless varieties, and a host of other creatures. A green and slender mantis, that must have been at least eight inches long, appeared just before me, camouflaged so marvellously that I would not have noticed him had he not climbed upon my knee. His body was frail and indefinably delicate, for all the world like a sliver of bamboo and not more than a sixteenth of an inch in thickness, while his wings, of a transparent tissue and veined like leaves, folded across his back to resemble a green sepal of no consequence whatever. So wonderful and impartial is nature's camouflage, that both those that prey upon others by habit, and those that seek to escape from being preyed upon, are equally disguised from one another. This inoffensive-looking mantis, that resembled so closely a slender twig with two green leaves attached, was quite as carnivorous and fierce in its own insect world as the man-eating tiger, whose return we were awaiting, was to the frightened jungle-dwellers.

Darkness came swiftly with the almost instant hushing of the bird-calls. The rustle of activity from the hidden insects in the grass around us increased apace. We felt their movements on all sides, and even upon our bodies. They climbed all over us and got inside our clothing, setting up such an itching that all our self-control was needed to prevent us from moving and scratching ourselves to secure an instant's relief.

I missed my old friends of the jungles of the plains, the nightjars, and thought of them for a few moments. They would be active at this period of twilight, flitting around in their silent, ghost-like fashion, in search of their evening meal, stragglers among the insects of the day that were going to bed late, and early-comers among the insects of the night in search of food.

This diverted my thoughts to the primal instincts of life, the search for food and the urge to procreate that are the two issues that govern all the dwellers of the jungle; to man and his civilization, and the search for wealth, which brings food and power, pleasures and a means of satisfying ourselves in practically any way we desire; and to much similar musing, one idea leading to another. But eventually I pulled myself up with quite a start, discovering that it was now pitch-dark and I had forgotten all about the man-eater and how close to me he might be.

The stench that came to us from the human fragments that had been exposed to the hot sun all day was now quite awful. Myriads of bluebottle flies had settled on them for the night.

The humble bluebottle fly is regarded everywhere as an obnoxious insect, associated only with filth and dirt and carrion. Nevertheless, he can be a great and secret friend to the hunter who watches by night; for the flies in their thousands, when they cover a carcase at night, are alert though resting. Any creature approaching near enough, even if it does not touch the carcase, makes its presence felt to the watchful, restless flies, who rustle in unison. And that rustling can be clearly heard by the watcher in the darkness, provided he is not too far away, is alert enough, has reasonably good hearing, and above all recognizes its significance. The bluebottles were silent now and I was satisfied that neither the tiger, nor anything else for that matter, was anywhere near the carcase.

My friend's back rested against mine tautly, uncomfortably, radiating heat though my sweater. I could sense his nervousness as he strained his eyes into the darkness. This is the most dangerous period for the hunter who risks his life sitting on the ground for a man-eater: the brief fifteen to thirty minutes from twilight till the light of the stars makes itself felt, be it ever so little.

Our greatest danger lay in the direction in which I was facing, the opposite end of the grassy clump in the midst of which we were hiding. If the man-eater approached from there, his keen eyesight, even in that darkness, would enable him to discover our presence while he was yet some distance away. He would not bother to come any closer then. What he would do would depend upon his individual character; he might launch himself from fifteen feet away and be upon us in the fraction of a second, or, if he were a coward, as many man-eaters are, he would just slink noiselessly away.

Then I remembered with considerable trepidation that this tiger could not possibly be called a coward. Barely a few hours ago he had sneaked up to a hut filled with people and dragged a human being away. With tensed nerves and strained ears, I listened for the faintest creak or rustle of grass that might betray the arrival of the man-eater from in front, while hearkening for the buzz of disturbed bluebottles that might herald his advent from behind. There was nothing but complete silence. The immediate danger passed as three things happened almost together. My eyes accustomed themselves to the gloom and I could begin to identify objects around me. The stars came out in their multitude and their gleam seemed to bring back the moments of half-light that had so recently gone. And above all, the fireflies of the Wynaad began their nightly display of living fireworks that would continue till the early hours of the morning, when the mist and the dew would chill the tiny lamp-bearers and force them to seek the shelter of the foliage.

There must have been thousands upon thousands of these little creatures within a few yards of us, winging their way hither and thither in restless flight. The glow of their combined light produced a radiation that dispelled the darkness like a flashlight, then broke again into myriads of individual lights that sparkled through the darkness.

No sounds broke the stillness. The forest seemed strangely devoid of animal life. No friendly calls of sambar or spotted deer could we hear. No cries of the usual birds of the night. There came to us only the undefinable faint movements of the insects in the grass around us. And to the torment caused by the insect marauders on our bodies, the mosquitoes now began to add their torture. They had not worried us unduly until now, perhaps because they had not discovered our presence; but having done so they apparently decided to make the most of their discovery. I did not dare to betray our presence to the tiger which, at that very instant perhaps, might be approaching us. Faintly I could hear Timmy behind me, trying to blow the mosquitoes away.

It was at this instant that there came clearly to my hearing the faint rustling buzz of angry, disturbed bluebottles flies. Something was near the remains of the woodsman. Timmy had heard it too, for I felt him tauten against my back, while he ceased blowing at the mosquitoes. His elbows dug into me in the prearranged signal and remained there as he gripped the .450/400 in his lap.

The flies buzzed again as they rose nervously a few inches above the bones and entrails on which they had been resting. They hummed a while, they resettled themselves and the buzzing stopped. The intruder, whatever it was, had not yet reached the kill or the flies would never have resettled. It was approaching.

Something made the faintest sound from beyond the remains and there came the distant thud of a stone being turned over. Undoubtedly the man-eater had arrived. He was reconnoitring and would presently approach the remains of his feast.

Or was he creeping upon us?

Casting caution to the winds I whisked around, bringing the Winchester to my shoulder and pressing the torch-button, fitted to the barrel, with my left thumb, almost in one movement. The bright beam cut a swathe of light through the blackness and was reflected by two baleful eyes. But they were rather more reddish-white in colour than a brilliant whitish-red. And they were set rather too closely together.

Sitting on his haunches like a dog, the torchlight caught the panther in the act of licking his lips. We could see the red of his tongue sweep across the slightly opened mouth.

Could the man-eater be a panther after all? I dismissed the thought as soon as it crossed my mind, for I had seen the man-eater's pug-marks on the trail we had followed. They had certainly been those of a tiger. Besides, he had been seen by Yega and some of the other woodcutters. This panther was merely there by chance. In passing by, he had stumbled on the kill. He was sitting there in doubt, wondering how it had all come about and if he could take a chance.

At that moment the panther became aware of the torch-beam that was shining straight into his eyes.

He stood up, snarled, turned and walked away. Disgust was

written in his every movement. Clearly he did not wish to involve himself in such a compromising situation. I extinguished the torch as quickly as possible. Was the man-eater nearby? If so, he would certainly have seen my light. That might cause him to run away. Or, having come to know of our presence and whereabouts, he might at that very moment be creeping upon us. But the attitude of the panther soon dispelled this disquietening thought. He seemed absolutely unconcerned. He would hardly be so indifferent if his hereditary and implacable foe, a tiger, were in the vicinity.

The bluebottles settled down and so did we, to a long and uneventful vigil, while the fireflies kept us company to lend enchantment to an otherwise macabre scene. It became cold, and then colder. The insects in the grass around us stopped their restless movements. Perhaps they were feeling the cold too. The mosquitoes grew less active as well and the fireflies began to disappear.

The tiger should have returned long ago. He should have put in an appearance even before the panther. It seemed as if the man-eater did not intend to come back.

Time dragged on. I began to feel sleepy and perhaps I grew a bit careless too. For, although I heard the sound once or twice, it did not register straight away. Then, all of a sudden, I was wide awake and alert.

Something had approached the grass in which we were hiding. Not directly from in front but a little to my left. There had been a faint rustle and then a definite footfall as something heavy had placed its weight upon the grass. There had followed a faint but distinct creaking and cracking of stems.

And that thing, whatever it was, had now stopped.

Had the man-eater discovered our presence, as he must most surely have done? Was he crouching for a final spring? The answer came the very next second when the tiger snarled. He was not more than ten feet away.

I pressed the button of the torch.

The beam lit up a wild scene of violently swaying grass stems. I had a glimpse of something brown that catapulted itself backwards and was gone. Then came a shattering roar from the jungle.

I switched off the torch as the man-eater began to demonstrate by emitting roar after roar. He was very angry; but he was also frightened. I had switched on the torch a fraction too soon. He would otherwise have come on. Perhaps I had done the right thing after all. I might have been too late to stop his charge, once it had been launched.

Timayya had whisked around and, like me, was facing in the direction from which the tiger was now roaring. The beast began to circle us, snarling and roaring horribly as he did so. It was a war of nerves. Either he was trying to work up enough courage to drive home a charge, or he was trying to scare us away. I felt he was following the second plan.

We waited awhile, hoping he would decide to attack; but this he failed to do. The roars now sank to a series of growls, but they came from different directions as the tiger circled. It seemed he was trying to find out how many human beings were hidden in that grass. Was there only one, whom he could easily overwhelm, or were there many?

This went on for another fifteen minutes. But nothing happened. The tiger would not attack, nor did he go away. It was a game of nerves and I am afraid the tiger won.

I decided to draw him out by precipitating an attack. I whispered to Timayya to remain where he was, while I got up and started to walk back towards the encampment, which was only a short distance away. The tiger would probably come after me. On the other hand, he might decide that it would be a better proposition to let the hated man-with-the-light depart while he went back for what was left of the kill. This would give Timmy the chance of a shot.

My friend protested vigorously, whispering 'Don't be a fool!'

But, with restraining hand on his shoulder, I got slowly to my feet, stood there a few seconds to restore my circulation, and then started walking deliberately towards the woodcutter's deserted huts, taking care to make the expected amount of sound a man might make in covering such ground.

The effect on the man-eater was instantaneous. He began to roar again; and then he came after me. You must bear in mind that, except for the starlight, it was quite dark. Purposely, I had kept the torch extinguished so as not to frighten the tiger, but the situation had turned into a most unpleasant one.

I had covered about twenty-five yards when the man-eater screwed up enough courage to charge. I remember thinking to myself that it was fortunate he had chosen to be so noisy about it, rather than make a silent and stealthy rush, when I would not have known from which direction he was coming.

There came the all-too-familiar 'Wroof! Wroof! Wroof! as he launched his attack. I whirled around with the rifle to my shoulder, once again pressing the button of the torch with my left thumb. The bright beam of light cut through the darkness to shine upon the angry eyes of the enraged man-eater, coming towards me in an up-and-down motion as he charged.

It was difficult to hold the eyes in my sights as they moved, and while this thought flashed through my mind, something quite unexpected happened. I was blinded by another blaze of light that obscured the tiger, and indeed everything else from sight, as it shone fully into my eyes! Timayya had switched on his torch and was shinning it directly in my face.

Instinctively, I raised my forearm to cover my eyes and jumped backwards to try to get out of the glare.

The next instant everything was plunged into inky darkness. My finger went off the button and my own torch went out while the beam of light from my friend's torch turned away from me.

It cut through the darkness and on to the tiger, which was crouched on the ground hardly four feet away from me in a ludicrous pose. He looked rather foolish with his head bent low, almost to ground level, front paws outstretched, with his rear up in the air behind him, his curving tail upheld and stiff, brought to a halt by Timmy's light.

It was not an instant too soon, for he had been about to spring upon me when Timmy's unexpected light from behind stopped him.

There came an ear-splitting crash and I saw the crouching tiger literally pushed as if by some invisible force, when the bullet from my .450/400 rifle, fired by Timmy, took him somewhere in the side.

At that instant I stood directly in his path, his nearest enemy, and he came for me with all the hate and speed of which he as capable. My own torch-beam must have completely blinded him when I fired directly into his open mouth, followed by a second shot as he crashed at my feet while I jumped aside.

That was when Timmy fired again. His bullet passed over the tiger and hit the ground almost at my feet, raising a spurt of dust. Everything was over when I found myself running backwards at incredible speed to try to get away from the tiger as he rolled on the ground.

It was Timmy who got the man-eater, for apart from his first shot that had struck the tiger's flank and halted the beast at the instant of springing upon me, he had fired a second which had entered the animal squarely behind the left shoulder. This second shot I had never heard in the confusion. My own bullet had blown out the back of the tiger's head, while my second, also striking his head, had struck the ground near me and had been a complete miss.

Timmy was overwhelmed with delight and executed a war dance around the fallen enemy. Although the skin, and particularly the head, would not make much of a trophy, ruined as they were by the bullets from my two powerful rifles, he kept chanting and repeating over and over again that he had never heard of a man-eater being killed under such unusual conditions.

Needless to say although I was not nearly so exuberant, I fully concurred with Timmy's sentiments. I might not object to having the same experience all over again providing I could be in Timmy's place. But not where I had been!

4

The Man-Hater of Talainovu

In the Kollegal taluk of what was formerly Coimbatore district, part of the Madras Presidency in the days when the British governed India, there is a hamlet called Talainovu. Now the British have gone and with them the Madras Presidency, and Madras state has taken its place; its area is just about half that was covered by the former presidency, for much of the territory has gone to the neighbouring states of Andhra, Mysore and Kerala.

Among these transferred territories is Kollegal taluk, and with it the hamlet of Talainovu. They have now become a part of Mysore state. Cultivation and buildings have spread, and much of the beautiful forest areas that stretched from Talainovu across rugged hills down to the valley of the Cauvery river have been felled ruthlessly, while what is left has been practically denuded of game.

But it will always be easy for me to remember the little village of Talainovu, as I knew it long ago, for two reasons. Firstly, in the Tamil language the word 'talainovu' means 'headache'; secondly, the wily panther that made its abode by the banks of the Cauvery river, in a steep valley some ten miles from the hamlet, gave me a real headache while trying to deal with it.

Man-eating panthers are rare in southern India and have always been so. This panther was never a man-eater in the true sense. Rather, it was a man-hater, filled with deep hostility for the human race, and it treasured this hatred and exacted a toll upon its lifelong enemy until its last day.

To begin at the beginning; a pantheress lived on a forest hilltop, ten miles from the village of Talainovu to the south. Six furlongs away and to the north, lay a deep valley where the hill fell away steeply to the bed of the Cauvery river. To the east the forest stretched for miles upon miles, into and across the boundaries of the Salem district and along the twists and turns of the Cauvery river. But to the west it continued only for about six miles, till it gave way to the low scrub that bordered the main road leading from the town of Kollegal, across a bridge, northwards to Maddur and Bangalore.

This pantheress was a young animal, and when she gave birth to her first cubs, three in number, she was a proud and happy mother, devoted to her offspring and prepared to defend them with her life. According to reports and hearsay, picked up by me at a much later date, some circumstances, we do not know what, induced the pantheress to bring her cubs out of the cave in which they were born much earlier than normal, while they were still too young to move about in safety. Perhaps their father had had designs on their young lives and sought to devour them, as male tigers and panthers frequently do. Perhaps a bear trespassed into their cave. Perhaps food was scarce in that locality.

So the pantheress brought her cubs down the hill and hid them in a bamboo thicket on the banks of the Cauvery river. No doubt this was only a temporary measure till the mother could find a better home for them, perhaps some other cave. But fate decided to be unkind to her that early morning. She had left the cubs in the thicket and had probably been out hunting all the night. The sun had topped the parallel range of hills that marked the course of the big river and was glinting on its tumbling, foaming waters when the pantheress was yet a mile away from the bamboos in which she had concealed her cubs.

And then she stopped in her tracks, for far away she heard a noise, a persistent tap-tap-tap! Humans! And in the very area where she had left her three little cubs unprotected.

The pantheress doubtless broke into a bounding gallop to cover the intervening distance as fast as she could, her only thought for the safety of her offspring. But when she was but a short distance away she must have heard their snarls, and she knew what had happened. The hated humans had discovered her cubs.

The pantheress arrived on the scene to find that half-a-dozen or more almost naked black bodies, glistening with sweat, surrounded her cubs. These were on the ground, back to back, and small as they were they snarled defiance at the intruders. The men jabbered to one another, pointing at the cubs with the sharp, curved knives that they used for cutting the bamboos, an expression of gloating excitement on each countenance, but no sign of pleasure at the three pretty balls of fur that so gamely defied them, nor pity for their helplessness.

Even as she watched, one of the bamboos cutters raised his *koithar* and swiped at the nearest cub. The curved blade bit into the soft body. The cub was flung into the air and fell some feet away, almost cut in two but still living. It groaned faintly as its young blood reddened the grass.

This was the signal for the other bamboo cutters to destroy the remaining two cubs, which they set about doing without further delay. A few slashes of their sharp knives and it was all over. Three mangled scraps of flesh now lay scattered on the ground where previously there had been three living creatures.

Probably an inborn fear of the human to all wild animals, even the worst man-eating tiger and the most ferocious rogue elephant, had held the grief-stricken mother back, but the sight of her dead cubs now drove her crazy. With short, sharp roars, she hurled herself upon the men.

The first man did not know what it was all about for the pantheress tore out his eyes as her raking talons slammed into his face. He fell to the ground, and she leaped over him to bite the second man's chest. He fell, too, his screams joining those of the blinded man who thrashed about on the ground. The remainder, all armed with *koithars*, did not wait. With yells of terror they fled in all directions.

The pantheress made to follow them but then stopped, her attention taken by the two men who writhed upon the ground. With cold fury she set upon the two of them and tore them to shreds.

Then, sniffing at the dead bodies of her three cubs, she picked up the least mangled of them and bore it away in sorrow.

That was how it all began.

When the bamboo cutters returned to their village, they had a harrowing tale to tell of a savage panther of huge dimensions that had attacked them entirely without provocation. They did not mention their part in the incident—at least, not them—and of how they had wantonly destroyed the cubs and infuriated the mother. This admission came later. Naturally, there was a hue and cry. People avoided that part of the jungle where the killings had taken place, or such as had to go there went armed with hatchets and guns, and in groups of as many persons as possible.

The pantheress was not seen or heard of for some weeks after that. People soon forgot the incident, and through apathy or laziness left their weapons behind. The licensed cutters of bamboo and sellers of timber, as well as the poachers, went into the jungle, the former by day to follow their daily routine, and the latter, who lived by stealing and selling the same commodities, renewed their practice of cutting bamboos and wood and floating the stolen material across the river during the bright moonlit nights.

But the vengeful pantheress did not forget. This was her opportunity to strike a second time.

A notorious poacher of sandalwood, whom the people of the forest department and the police knew had been operating for years, but whom they had never succeeded in bringing to book, went into the jungle with his son one moonlit night. They had planned to cut some sandalwood, float it down the river for a mile or so to a spot where the water became calm and there was no undercurrent, and then tow the cut timber across the river to the northern bank which belonged to Mysore state, using the circular coracle made of bamboo and buffalo hide which they kept permanently hidden on the river for this purpose. Once they were on the Mysore side of the river, they knew they would be safe from pursuit by the authorities on the Madras bank and would be asked no awkward questions.

The two thieves began hacking the sandalwood saplings they had marked for this purpose on an earlier visit, and the pantheress heard the hated sound of chopping. As likely as not the noise of wood being cut reminded her, by instinctive association rather than thought, of the day when her cubs had been cut to pieces before her eyes. Hatred must have filled her mind as she started stalking towards the noise with but one thought in her brain—to obliterate those who made it.

The father never knew what happened when the pantheress sprang upon him from behind and fastened her fangs in his throat. He could not even scream for help, but toppled to the ground with the sudden weight upon his back. The son, a lad of eighteen years, saw what was happening, but with thoughts only for his own safety and not for his father's life, dropped his axe and fled precipitately.

It took the pantheress a few seconds to kill the man and that saved the boy from sharing the same fate. Running as fast as he could, he reached the coracle, jumped into it and paddled frantically across the river. When he got back to his hut and burst in upon his mother, it was to tell what had just happened to his father.

The villagers had gone to sleep long ago, but the combined wails of mother and son awoke them. They lit their lights and heard the story, but agreed not to do anything till the next day. After all, everybody knew both father and son were thieves.

The sun was high when a large party of villagers, armed with guns, hatchets, knives and spears and led by the poacher's son, returned to the scene. There they found the old thief lying in a pool of his own blood, his gullet torn out and his whole body badly bitten and lacerated. But it was very noticeable that no flesh had been eaten. The killer could certainly not be called a man-eater. To the men who gazed with horror upon the mangled remains, the attack on the poacher had apparently been for no reason and under no provocation whatever, for at that time few people knew the beginning of the story.

Once again there was an uproar and folk went about only in groups and armed to the teeth. The panic lasted for a longer period on this occasion, but once more time and the usual apathy among the people gradually calmed them down. Eventually, the panther was forgotten again and they carried on in their accustomed ways.

Again weeks passed, and again came the moonlit nights, the period when most of the mischief is done in the jungles of India. For it is during this time that the poachers of game sit over water holes and salt licks to shoot the sambar, spotted deer and other animals that come there to quench their thirst or eagerly to lick the salty earth, while the timber thieves, who steal the sandalwood, teakwood, *muthee*, giant bamboo etc., go into the forest to hack down the trees, cut them to convenient lengths and float the timber down the river or take it stealthily away in bullock carts or, when they are daring enough, by lorry loads.

A third kind of thief also takes advantage of the bright moonlight: the poachers of fish. They do not fish with rods or nets, for the catch would be too small and the work too hard and slow. Instead, in the river pools where they know the large fish congregate at nights to sleep or to feed, according to species, these men explode their home-made bombs, made in secrecy from crude gunpowder and fuses. Floating gently downstream in one of the circular coracles made of a bamboo frame covered with buffalo hide, in common use on the rivers of India, these prowlers visit every pool for a distance of about five miles down the river. The fuse is lit and the bomb is then floated on the water.

While the explosion does no general damage, the concussion in the water stuns the large fish and slaughters thousands of the smaller ones and all the fry for yards around. These casualties rise to the surface, where the larger fish are quickly scooped into the coracle with the help of nets attached to poles. The thousands of smaller dead fish, including the fry, are allowed to go to waste and float downstream to rot and be eaten by other fish and by the crocodiles.

And so the operation is repeated from pool to pool. By this time the poachers have gathered almost more fish into the coracle than it can hold, while the wanton destruction of countless thousands of valuable fry and many species of small fish can be imagined.

Generally a number of men share in the operation, employing two coracles, one from which to launch the bombs, and the other for collecting the catch. The second is often almost at sinking point before the poachers feel they have collected enough. Moreover, there is an unwritten law amongst them that they should not trespass upon the domain of the next batch of poachers, which starts where they leave off, for that would provoke a fight and one or other batch would be bound to sneak to the forest department officials or to the police.

Everyone is happy, the fish are slaughtered, and the local authorities can do nothing about it. Moreover, to make things absolutely safe, each man receives a basketful after every expedition. Should they prove unlucky and they are discovered by some representative of the law, the poachers have but to present half-a-dozen of the largest fish they have caught to the official and all is well again.

The coracle, loaded with fish, is eventually brought ashore at the end of the five-mile stretch. Here the catch is cleaned and gutted and loaded into gunny sacks that the men have brought with them. Every man shoulders a bag, while two men pick up the coracles and carry them upside down over their shoulders. The light flat paddles are taken by one of the others. Now begins the five-mile walk back to the point from which they started, for it is not possible to propel the clumsy, circular craft upstream against the strong river currents. This is the hardest part of the whole business.

The same procedure is followed through the ensuing moonlit nights until the dark nights come again, when the poachers rest and laze it out for a fortnight till moonlight returns.

In very lonely regions where there are no forest guards or other inconvenient persons to interfere, the bombing of the pools is carried on by daylight, although at the period I am writing about there was some restraint, for the forest departments were controlled by British officers. Alas, that restraint has now gone. With Independence, the poachers no longer work by night.

But to return to our story: the moonlit nights came round again and a party of fish poachers systematically bombed pool after pool and netted the stunned fish, filling them into the second coracle, which was propelled by a single man so as to leave more space. They worked steadily until after midnight, when they decided to take time off to go ashore and eat the snacks they had brought with them.

It so happened that the second coracle, the one filled with the catch and paddled by the single boatman, was nearer the shore when his companions called to him:

'Brother, put ashore. We have worked hard and we've caught much. Let's rest for a while and eat the shappad (food) we have brought with us and drink some cold coffee.'

The solitary boatman welcomed the call, for he was lonely. He dug the blade of his paddle into the water, holding the shaft with both hands, first to the right of him and then to the left, with swift, short strokes, to force the clumsy craft across the current which was particularly strong at this place, for not long had passed since the rains had filled the river to overflowing.

Eventually he reached the bank and sprang ashore, carrying in one hand the end of the rope that was attached to the bamboo bottom of the coracle, so as to tie it to the root or trunk of a tree. This he never succeeded in doing. Those of his companions in the other coracle who happened to be watching saw something that looked long and grey spring from behind the *mendhi* (henna) bushes at the water's edge. They heard a rasping roar and saw the black form of their friend go down with a strange grey shape on top of it. They heard his piercing scream and then saw that his coracle, dragging the rope that had fallen from his hands, was rushing downstream on the powerful current.

The boatman who was paddling their craft made a desperate effort to. overtake the runaway coracle. But he was at a disadvantage with the load of men in his own boat. The runaway coracle gained speed as the current, spinning it around and around, drew it towards midstream where the water bubbled and foamed in the bright moonlight over a low cataract formed by a reef of rocks.

The pursuing boatman was almost rash enough to drive his craft into those dangerous waters when his companions restrained him. They watched in dismay as the unmanned coracle lurched heavily against the rocks, tossed wildly from side to side and then capsized, throwing the whole of their catch into the river. Then it was that they turned towards the shore to abuse and beat their comrade for being so stupid as to let the rope slip from his grasp. Why, a large coracle such as the one they had just lost would cost a hundred rupees to make and much more to buy, not to mention the value of the fish that had been lost in the river. Idiot that he was they would thrash him soundly!

But on the bank no one was to be seen. Then they remembered the grey shape in the moonlight, and the roaring they had heard, and how their friend seemed to stumble and fall. They had been so concerned to intercept the runaway coracle that they had ignored their companion's plight.

Some of the men ordered the boatman who wanted to go ashore to investigate, not to do so on any account. Perhaps some evil spirit was lurking there. It had got their friend and might get all of them if they ventured too near. For quite a long time nobody thought of the panther. Then somebody remembered, and reminded the rest. They agreed then that the grey form they had seen had been the lurking beast. It had killed their companion and assuredly was devouring him at that moment.

Using the single paddle, the men took turns to propel their

weighted craft upstream, as they dared not go ashore. They did this for about half a mile and then found they could go no further. So they made for the river bank, where each man exhorted the other to jump ashore first. Finally they did so in a body, relying on the safety of numbers. So as not to be encumbered by the weighty coracle all the way back to their starting point, they drew it some yards up the bank and made for their village as fast as they could in a group, talking at the top of their voices to keep the panther away.

Next day, when the sun was high, the whole village turned out, the men having armed themselves as best as they could, to discover what had happened to the missing man. They found his remains behind the henna bushes. He had been literally torn to bits, but so far as could be seen, none of his flesh had been eaten.

And so it went on, the pantheress attacking and killing where she could, but never eating her victims. Her handiwork was evident by the manner in which each corpse was bitten and clawed savagely, far beyond what was necessary just to kill the victim. She seemed to be taking savage delight in mangling each body almost beyond recognition.

Now, the stretch of river where these events took place was a favourite spot for catching the great *mahseer*, the king of Indian fishes, in spite of all the poaching. But fishing has never held any attraction for me. I have no patience for it. Yet a great many of my friends are devotees and occasionally I took one or other of them to this river for a couple of days.

These visits had to be few and far between, however, because the rough track from Talainovu, through the jungle to the river, is very steep, with abrupt turns that my Studebaker cannot negotiate. Most of my friends owned English cars, and these were equally unsuitable for the purpose. So our visits were limited to those occasions when we could get someone who owned a jeep to come along with us, or to the lucky occasions when we could borrow or hire such a vehicle.

Well, such an opportunity came our way one day, and this

time it seemed to have come to stay. Donald, my son, had bought a jeep! A much-battered vehicle that hailed from Andhra state, painted vivid blue, and with faults in every conceivable part. But Don set to work, and at considerable expense and very great trouble he substituted good parts for bad, so that eventually we possessed a vehicle that would go anywhere.

Then came the day when we set out for the Talainovu fishing grounds, with Donald proudly driving the jeep he had so painstakingly repaired. Next to him sat 'Tiny' Seddon, a great 'mahseer' fisherman, great not only in his fishing potentialities but also in bulk and height. In the back were three of us; an old friend and schoolmate of Donald's, named Merwan Chamar-Baughvala; Thangavelu, who had once been my *shikari* and had found service in our establishment as table-boy, motor-cleaner, the feeder of our domestic creatures and many wild-animal pets, and general jack-of-all-trades, his particular function on this trip being camp cook. Finally, wedged securely and tightly, at an uncomfortable angle that gave little chance to move, was myself.

It is exactly ninety-nine miles from our house in Bangalore to the camping site on the bank of the Cauvery river, some ten miles beyond the village of Talainovu, where we proposed to do our fishing. We left Bangalore rather late, and when the journey ended the sun was setting in flames of red, with a background of orange, vermilion and indigo. We halted a few yards from the river's edge, under the grove of giant *muthee*, tamarind and *jumlum* trees, beneath which we always made our camp.

There were three things to be done at once, and the trained members of the party—Don, Thangavelu and myself—started on them straightaway. Don looked quickly around for fresh elephant tracks, to reassure ourselves that none were in the vicinity to resent our intrusion and come thundering down upon us. Using both feet, I started clearing the ground, in a six or seven yard circle, of all dried leaves, stones and sticks which might shelter scorpions, particularly the small red variety. A sting from such a scorpion is guaranteed to take your mind off all other problems, including the demands of the Income Tax wallahs, for the next eight hours or more. Thangavelu hurried to gather dry logs, a task in which Don soon began to help him, for the camp fire that was to be kept blazing all night in case an elephant came our way while we were asleep.

Tiny Seddon jumped on to a rock half-submerged in the water and gazed pensively at the swirling eddies. No doubt he was seeking inspiration as to where to start fishing the next morning. Merwan Chamar-Baughvala threw himself on the ground I had just cleared and remarked how comfortable it was compared with the jeep.

None of us thought of the panther—because up to this moment none of us knew about it!

The moon would not rise till late. We ate Merwan's contribution of chicken biriyani and pork vindaloo, two very delicious but over-rich dishes, and while Thangavelu was preparing the tea, drank water from the rivet. That is, all of us except Tiny, who was certain the river water contained cholera germs, typhoid germs, and bacteria of every variety. He said he would wait for the tea. Then Thangavelu stroked the camp fire that was to burn all night and we lay back and smoked and told stories, gazing at the starry sky beyond the canopy of leaves above our heads. We counted ourselves fortunate to be able to enjoy such bliss, which so many of our fellow creatures, crowded in stuffy cities all over the world, have never experienced for even a day in all their monotonous lives. And so we fell asleep.

I do not know why it was that I awoke with a start. My watch showed a few minutes past three. The camp fire had died down to a few glowing embers, for Thangavelu, who had undertaken to keep it alive, had long since fallen asleep. Donald, to my left, was snoring loudly. Merwan and Tiny, in that order to my right, had covered their heads with their bedsheets to ward off mosquitoes and the dew, and were sleeping soundlessly.

I wondered what had wakened me so suddenly. Perhaps some jungle noise. Perhaps an elephant breaking branches in order to feed on the higher, more tender leaves. I listened more intently and for a time heard nothing except Don's noisy, rattling snores.

Then I knew what had wakened me, for close at hand I heard a guttural rasping sound: 'Haa-ah! Haa-ah! Haa-ah!' The call of a hungry panther!

Now panthers in the forest are, as a rule, quite harmless animals. Except when they turn man-eaters which is very rarely, or when they are wounded, they are shy, cowardly beasts that avoid the presence of man. No doubt the animal that was now calling, although apparently quite close, had not yet caught sight of the embers of our fire. As soon as it did so, in all probability it would hurry away as fast as it could. Or so I thought as I continued to listen sleepily to the sound.

The call came again, and louder. The hungry panther was certainly quite close. Surely, it must have seen our fire by now? I felt very sleepy indeed and comfortable. Drat the beast, I thought. Why doesn't it let me sleep?

That was when I heard the panther snarl! At last it has seen us, I thought; now it will vanish. But the panther snarled again, long and menacingly.

Strange, I thought, my eyes half-closed with sleep. It is either a very inquisitive or a very angry and daring panther. I mused; but why worry? I was safe in the centre of the party. Tiny was at one end, Don at the other, and Thangavelu by himself not far from the fire.

The panther growled again, low and long, and I sat up abruptly, groping for the torch I had kept near my pillow. Blinking to free myself from sleep, I directed the torch-beam towards the snarling that was growing louder.

It revealed a panther, crouching on the ground a few feet from Thangavelu and evidently preparing to spring upon him. There was no mistaking its posture: I could see its tail lashing to and fro, a sure indication of its malevolent intentions. I felt for my rifle, which I had kept loaded beside me on the ground.

And then Thangavelu ruined everything.

I suppose his jungle instinct was really responsible. It alerted him, but rather late, to the great danger that threatened. He sat up abruptly, and in doing so kicked over the degchie containing the water he had boiled for Tiny to drink. Perhaps the clatter it made, or Thangavelu's movement, or more likely my torch-beam, convinced the panther that its presence had been discovered, and before I could do anything with the rifle, handicapped as I was with the torch in my right hand, the brute leaped aside and disappeared behind the nearest bush.

All this time Thangavelu had been blissfully unaware of any danger. Still half asleep, he had not heard or seen the panther. I awoke the others and told them what had happened.

They were surprised at first. Then Don said, 'Dad, you've had a nightmare. Merwan's chicken biriyani and pork vindaloo are the cause of it. I haven't heard a sound all night and I doubt if there's a panther within miles.'

The others laughed and I was a bit huffed. How could Don say he had not heard a sound when he had been snoring all night? I clambered to my feet, still holding the torch and rifle?

'Come and see this,' I invited, shining my torch on the ground and walking towards the spot where the panther had been lying. But the earth there was hard and nothing could be seen.

'See what' asked Don, sarcastically, while Merwan wailed, 'Why did you wake me up for nothing?'

They all went back to their places and fell asleep again, including Thangavelu. Nobody had believed me. But I knew that the danger that had threatened us, and particularly the servant, had been very real and not part of a dream or my imagination.

I rekindled the fire with the wood that Thangavelu had gathered the evening before. Then with my rifle and torch at hand, I remained awake for the rest of the night with my back propped against my bedroll. I was convinced the panther I had seen had been a man-eater and that Thangavelu had been saved in the nick of time.

The calls that had awakened me showed that it was hungry. The chances were it might return.

An hour later a sambar started calling on the hillside half a mile away. It called for some time before the spotted deer scented or saw the source of the danger. Then they started calling too. Clearly the panther was retreating across the hillside.

By this time a crescent moon had arisen, outlining the immediate neighbourhood. The water in the river gurgled monotonously as it flowed over the rocks and I felt very sleepy. At last the dawn came, when Tiny was the first to awake. He saw me.

'Don't say you've been sitting up all night?' he asked.

'Wake Thangavelu and tell him to make some tea', was all the reply I gave. Then I went to sleep before the water could boil.

Tiny fished all day. He caught a ten-pound *mahseer*, a couple of seven-pounders and some smaller fish. Don tried his hand, but like me he is impatient and caught nothing. Merwan said he wanted to have a bath, and so as not to disturb the fishing, started to wander downstream with his towel across his shoulders. I thought of the man-eater which no one believed I had seen; and called after him, 'Wait a minute, I'll join you.' Picking up my rifle and swinging a towel, I followed him.

That afternoon we all felt sleepy, particularly myself, and the camp was once again hushed in slumber. But not for long. We heard a series of hollow sounds drawing nearer gradually, 'Boomp! Boomp! Boomp!'

Poachers! They were bombing the river and operating in broad daylight, too, evidently without fear of being caught. Soon, around the bend in the river appeared the usual two coracles, the first loaded with men and the other with fish. Catching sight of our party, they paddled frantically against the current to try to reach the other side.

This move incited us to act though. Don fired a shot into the air. Then he called out, 'Come here, or the next shot will be at you.'

The paddling stopped and the two coracles started drifting downstream. It was evident the men inside were debating whether to surrender or make a dash for it. Then Merwan shouted in English, which of course they did not understand. 'Come here, you bastards, or as sure as eggs we'll sink you.'

Slowly the men started paddling the coracles towards us, but stopped when they were a few yards offshore. From our slightly elevated position on the bank, we could look down on the hundreds of fish lying in the second coracle.

Then began a harangue which was as needless as it was foolish. Don threatened and admonished them alternately, for their wrongful activity. The men replied that they saw nothing wrong in it. The fish belonged to nobody in particular. Then why should the government frame rules or demand fishing licences? And who were we to interfere? And so on, and so on.

Thangavelu, being about the wisest in our party at the time, said, 'Give us a couple of your best and largest fish. Then, go and blow yourselves up for all we care!'

In the midst of all this I asked, 'Look, is there a man-eating panther in these parts?'

There was a hushed silence. Then one of the men replied in a low tone, as if he did not wish to be overheard, 'Indeed, *dorai*, there is. It has killed many, many people. Only a few days ago it killed one of our own comrades, whose name was Balu. That's why we are now catching fish by daylight. Normally, we would only do this on moonlit nights, but not a soul will stir out after sunset now.'

So I was right after all!

Don was excited. 'Come here. Come ashore,' he invited. 'Damn the fish. We'll not harm you. I want to know more about this panther. We're *shikaris*. We're interested and will try to shoot it.'

A chord having been established, the fishermen brought their coracles to the bank and tied them with ropes to the roots of trees. Then they stepped ashore and sat around us in a group.

Don and I plied them with questions, and from their answers pieced together the story which I have already related. The men admitted the panther was not a man-eater in the strict sense. So far, it had not actually eaten any of its victims, but had contented itself with mauling and mutilating them hideously. Obviously the animal was female, possessed of unusual sagacity and with a quite abnormal memory, for most wild animals generally forget the past very quickly. This pantheress evidently remembered the slaying of her cubs and her feeling of hatred for the human race seemed as fresh now as on that day. After hearing the story, our sympathies were with the aggrieved animal.

Eventually the boatmen asked to take leave of us. The sun would grow hot and the fish could not be bombed so easily, for they would swim into deeper waters. Disgustedly, we told them to get the hell out of it, but not before Thangavelu had remembered to pick out two of the largest and best fish for us.

'So you see, chaps, I was not dreaming after all,' was my first comment as the two coracles began to draw away. Tiny was the only one to think any more about fishing that day. The rest of us, Thangavelu included, went into close conference as to how to shoot this panther. Don and Merwan were particularly keen. For myself, I was of the opinion that the panther had a case.

From the start, the others felt we had a difficult problem in not having a regular man-eater to deal with. Here I disagreed. In my opinion, given the time, this pantheress would be far easier to come to grips with, because, filled with hatred for humans, she would go out of her way to try and attack us. As I saw the situation, we should operate individually in trying to find her. That would give us four chances to one. Correspondingly, the pantheress would most certainly come for any one of us whom she might see alone, although, according to the fishermen, she had not hesitated to attack a whole group of persons. This plan appeared to me to offer a much greater chance of success than the one proposed by Thangavelu, which was to go to Talainovu in the jeep and purchase two young bulls or buffaloes as bait. For these would then have to be driven on foot to the camp site and suitable spots selected before they were tied out. All this I knew would take considerable time and, as matters stood, there was far less chance of the panther attacking either of the baits than one of us.

Fortunately, Don had brought his .423 Mauser rifle along with his .12 bore shotgun, while I had my .405 and my .12 bore too. This made two rifles and two shotguns, enough to arm all four of us.

We decided to have an early lunch, after which Tiny, with my shotgun loaded with lethal shell, would walk downstream along the river bank for two hours or so, and then turn and come back. Merwan would do the same upstream, using Donald's gun. Don and I, armed with our rifles, would search the jungle separately and in different directions. Thangavelu would climb up a tree somewhere close by and await our return, while keeping an eye on the jeep and our camp kit which was lying scattered around. It was agreed that everyone should get back to camp by 5 p.m. at the latest.

We did this and, with parting admonitions to each other to keep a sharp lookout against surprise attack, scattered according to plan each hoping to be the lucky individual to come across the panther. I do not think any one of us quite realized till he was all alone that what he had set out to do, and was doing in fact, was to offer himself for the next four hours or more as a bait to a most dangerous wild animal that had all the advantages of ground and cover in its favour.

I had decided to go in the direction in which I had heard the sambar calling the previous night. Perhaps this led towards some cave and would afford a better chance of success than just roaming aimlessly in the jungle. A few minutes from the river I picked up a game-trail that led up the northeastern slope of the same hill down which the jeep had travelled from Talainovu. It was a well-defined track, used by sambar and other animals in coming to water at the river during the summer months, and recent marks of deer and bear revealed the presence of a fair amount of game, despite the comparative silence of the previous night.

The path wound diagonally uphill, skirting boulders and heavy cover at a safe distance, as game-trails made by the members of the deer family usually do, for fear of some carnivore lying in hiding behind a rock or bush. This was in my favour, although I knew that a panther was able to conceal itself behind cover of any sort. My thoughts were uneasy and after a while I became anxious about Don and our other two friends. I hoped they were being as careful as I was.

It was too late and too hot for the birds to be calling, and so I proceeded in uncomfortable silence, keeping a sharp lookout to right and left while studying every bit of cover in front of me before I drew abreast of it. The real danger lay from behind, as I knew, since panthers and nearly all tigers for that matter, even when they have made a practice of attacking human beings, never completely lose their fear of man and in most cases spring upon their victims from behind.

And so I halted frequently to look behind me, trying to catch the least movement of leaf or blade of grass that might betray the pantheress as she prepared to pounce. As was to be expected, there were a number of false alarms. My searching eyes detected a twig shaking suspiciously, or a blade of grass springing suddenly upright from where it had been held down by the weight of some hidden presence. Sometimes I heard a rustle, or the distinct crack of a dried twig, often behind me and many times in other directions. Then I froze, half raised the .405, and stared intently towards the sound, expecting at any moment to see the spotted form come hurtling down upon me. Nothing happened. The rustling or the snapping of the twig was not repeated, and the forest remained uncannily silent. Or the twig that shook did so again, or the blade of grass continued to wave in the breeze. Then tension died within me, the hair at the back of my neck relaxed, and I realized there was nothing to fear. Thus I proceeded for some distance till some other movement frightened me once more.

This sort of thing went on for some time, till I realized my nerves were playing havoc with me and that I was behaving like a greenhorn. As likely as not, the pantheress was miles away. As I walked along, thinking my own thoughts, fits of alertness alternated with periods of carelessness and indifference. Time passed uneventfully, and I began to feel things were not as bad as they had been painted by the poachers. No doubt, like all villagers, they had exaggerated the matter grossly.

I reached the shoulder of the hill and began to descend the other side into a lush valley of heavy bamboos. A faint rustle and swish of leaves, then the sharp crack of a frond betokened only one thing. An elephant!

I stopped and gazed at the spot whence the sound had come. Much depended upon whether it was a solitary animal or one of a herd. If solitary, I might expect trouble should I go too close. If I had stumbled upon a herd, it was almost certain that, upon discovering my presence, they would take themselves off. The game-trail I was following led directly towards the origin of the sound. If I now abandoned the trail to avoid the elephant, I knew I would not be able to go far, for very soon I would be foundering in thickets of bamboo and thorn, no place in which to meet an angry panther or an equally angry elephant. So I made up my mind to stick to the trail.

The breeze blew strongly from behind and there were no further sounds from among the bamboos in front. I waited awhile, but the silence continued. This indicated that the elephant had become aware of my presence, having scented me. Either he had moved away, or he was waiting for me to come closer.

No, had he moved away I would in all probability have heard him, for although these giant creatures can walk almost soundlessly, in that heavy undergrowth there would have been at least some faint sounds of his passage. I therefore concluded that he was waiting for me to approach. I delayed for another ten minutes, hoping the elephant would change his mind and avoid an encounter. He did not move. Perhaps he was thinking the same thing.

I should have waited longer, but I became impatient and decided to oust the beast. It was a wrong move, and one that nearly ended disastrously.

Thinking that a nonchalant approach on my part would frighten him off, I began to whistle loudly and advanced boldly along the game-trail. The result was immediate. The elephant charged. He screamed in the way of all elephants when attacking, partly to inflate their own courage and partly to strike terror into their victims, and came crashing through the bamboos straight towards me. The green undergrowth parted violently to reveal a monstrous head with gleaming tusks, a trunk coiled inwards between them, and ears laid tightly back against the skull.

I thought quickly. No rogue elephant had been proclaimed in this area. Therefore, to shoot this monster would mean endless trouble for me with the people of the Forest department. To run away would invite being chased and caught within a short distance. To try to stop him by wounding him, in the knee if possible, would be cruel and cause him endless suffering.

There was but one possibility. A very slight one, but I took it. Shouting loudly, I aimed the rifle over his head and fired a round into the air. If this did not stop him, I knew the next round would have to be at the elephant, if I intended to remain alive.

It worked! The giant animal braked hard by planting all four feet into the ground. There was a cloud of dust and fallen leaves as he slithered to a halt. Knowing his courage had failed him, I seized the advantage by running three or four steps forward and firing a second round into the air.

The huge beast turned about. The note of anger had died out of his scream when he trumpeted shrilly again, this time with a note of fear as he swayed in indecision and then bolted; the short tail which had been stuck out behind in the manner of all charging elephants was now between his hind legs like that of a whipped cur. The noise of his departure died away and I sat down disconsolately upon a nearby stone.

I was glad I had not been compelled to fire at the elephant, but I was disgusted at myself for not having exercised more patience by sitting it out rather than by advancing and so precipitating a charge. For my rifle shots, among those hills, had made a terrific racket. The hope I had entertained of the pantheress showing herself, or attacking me, was now gone. Only half-an-hour had passed since leaving camp. Would it be worth my while to carry on along the track I had been following for the remaining ninety minutes before turning back to the river as arranged?

A few moments' thought made me realize the futility of crying over spilt milk. So I stood up and continued along the trail. There was little danger from the pantheress for the next ten minutes or so. The noise of the rifle shots would have frightened her. The elephant, and any others like him, would now be far away. I made rapid progress through the bamboos, which eventually thinned out as the ground rose gradually higher from the basin of the Cauvery river. The vegetation changed slightly and I came upon a parkland of *babul, boram* and dwarf tamarind trees interspersed with areas of long grass, and here the friendly game-trail I had been following all the way from the big river gave out. Rather, it became lost among innumerable other *paths* that crisscrossed this parkland, which was obviously a favourite grazing ground for deer.

Little pellets of dung lay everywhere, the larger ones made by sambar and the smaller by spotted deer. To my right was quite a mound of tiny pellets underneath a fig tree, now laden with a rich red harvest fruit. Thousands of these figs had fallen to the ground, knocked down by monkeys and all manner of birds by day, and the huge fruit-bats, called 'flying fox' in India, by night. The maker of the large heap of tiny dung-pellets was a jungle-sheep, which we call 'kakar' or 'muntjac.'

These pretty animals, which reach the height of a small sheep and are coloured a uniform reddishbrown, are very gracefully shaped, the males having short, bifurcated horns. They love figs and other wild fruit. The stags, particularly, have the habit of coming all the way back to a chosen spot to pass their dung on alternate days. All hunters, human and animal, know this habit, and so all they have to do when they come across such a spot is to conceal themselves adequately and wait long enough for the return.

Carnivores are well versed in the habits and movements of the deer family and all the lesser animals that form their prey. They have to be, if they would eat. So this lovely parkland, filled as it was with deer, would be a very likely place in which to come across the pantheress and I redoubled my efforts to look for her.

I had gone some distance when, from a direction a little to the right and before me, I heard a series of bird-like calls. The cries grew louder as they approached rapidly. Wild dogs! A pack of them was hunting down a quarry and the chase was coming in my direction. I stepped quickly behind the sheltering trunk of a nearby tamarind tree.

The wild dog of the Indian forest is the cleverest of all hunters and the implacable foe of every living creature. Once a pack of these creatures scents or sees a deer and gives chase, its fate is sealed. They hunt it down mercilessly and intelligently. The main body of dogs run behind their quarry, giving voice to a hunting cry that resembles the high-pitched call of a bird more than anything else, while a few dogs gallop ahead at terrific speed and on both flanks of the quarry. These flankers then ambush the victim and worry it, if they are unable to bring it down themselves, till the main body catches up and completes the job. I have seen a sambar doe, worried by these flankers, cross a dry riverbed with her entrails trailing in the sand for yards behind her, both eyes bitten out, and dogs hanging by their teeth to her throat and flanks.

I heard the clashing sound of horns against wood and a splendid sambar stag appeared. Foam flecked his mouth and sprayed backwards to his neck and shoulders, and his eyes were wide with terror as he galloped in headlong flight. The next instant there was a terrific roar and a mighty striped form launched itself through the air and directly on to the sambar's back.

My earlier thoughts had proved correct. A tiger had been patrolling the parkland in search of a meal. He had heard the wild dogs approach and knew they were pursuing a quarry that was coming his way. Ordinarily, tigers avoid wild dogs and fear them for their reckless bravery, their intelligence and their numbers. Probably this tiger would have avoided them too but for the chance that the hunted animal and his pursuers happened to be coming in his direction. So before he quite realized what he should do about it, he took the decisive step.

For this same reason, the tiger had not discovered my own approach from behind him. His keener hearing had appraised him of the wild dog's hunting cries before I had heard them and he had been listening intently in that direction and had not caught the faint sounds I may have made.

The sambar's back bent to the sudden weight of the tiger and he let out a hoarse bellow of terror. Their tightly entangled bodies sank from view into the long grass. I heard the sharp crack of bone as the vertebral column was broken skilfully by the tiger, and the drumming of the stag's hooves upon the earth as the twitching muscles and nerves of his four legs continued to respond to the last message to flee. Upon this scene, the next instant, burst the pack of baying snarling wild dogs!

Recovering from their momentary surprise at seeing themselves forestalled, they quickly rallied. In a flash they surrounded the tiger and the body of the quarry they regarded as their own. I counted nine of them.

The bird-like hunting call that had been coming from the pack only a moment earlier changed abruptly to a series of long and plaintive notes. I had heard these cries on an earlier occasion, many years before, in the far-distant jungles of the Chamala Valley. There a pack of wild dogs had been chasing a tiger and this queer new cry was the same those dogs had made on that occasion. They were summoning reinforcements. Every wild dog within miles would hasten to their aid.

It appeared to be an unwritten law of the species that no member dared disobey.

The tiger rose to his feet threateningly and I could see him clearly. His body turned slowly to enable him to see how many enemies beset him. His face, was contorted hideously as he snarled and roared with all the strength of his lungs, and his tail twitched from side to side spasmodically, a visible indication of nervous tension, rage, doubt and an unaccountable fear of these unruffled, implacable and cruelly clever foes.

The circle of dogs stood fast, legs firmly yet slightly outspread, each member of the pack now making that loud, shrill summons for help. The roars of the tiger and the yelping call of the nine wild dogs were pandemonium. The jungle echoed and re-echoed with the din.

The tiger realized that every second lost now counted in favour of his foes. In two bounds he charged the dog directly in his *path*. The dog skipped nimbly aside, while those behind leaped forward to attack from the rear. The tiger sensed this and whirled around, flaying wildly to right and left with his two forepaws. The dogs within reach of those mighty paws fell back helter-skelter, but one was too slow. The raking talons struck the dog's hindquarters, his body was thrown into the air with one leg almost torn off, and the dogs behind the tiger leaped forward to bite off chunks of flesh from his sides. Once more the tiger whirled around, once again his enemies scattered before him, while those at the back and on both sides raced forward to bite him where they could.

The tiger feinted and made a double-turn and the dogs from behind him that had rushed forward could not turn back. They met the full force of his powerful forelegs with their widely extended talons. Two quick blows and two more dogs were torn asunder. One of them tried to drag itself away, but its nearness to the tiger tempted him to make a false move that immediately offset the advantage he had just gained by his clever double-turn. He pounced upon the disembowelled wild dog and buried his fangs in its body.

The dogs from behind and both sides now fell upon him and covered his body, tearing out scraps of the living flesh. The tiger roared and roared again, but now there was a note of fear in each roar.

The huddle of tearing rending beasts disintegrated and the tiger had freed himself for the moment. There were now but six dogs around him and some of them were injured. But the tiger was bleeding profusely from the many wounds he had received. He gasped for breath. The dogs would not relax. From all sides they renewed the attack, yelping and snapping. The tiger roared again, but not nearly so loudly. The will to continue the fight was ebbing. He was definitely afraid.

Just then quite another sound could be heard above the pandemonium: the distant cries of answering wild dogs, not from one direction, but from several, all at once. Reinforcements.

The harassed tiger heard them too, and the fight went out of him. He turned tail and raced away with the six dogs, despite their wounds and exhaustion, after him.

Within a minute the reinforcements began to arrive. First three dogs, then another, and yet another. They halted a moment at the scene of battle and sniffed the blood-tainted grass and the three mangled dogs. This roused them to a fury and they growled and snarled. Then they raced in the wake of the fleeing tiger and his six pursuers.

Soon a larger pack of about a dozen dogs arrived on the scene. In a few seconds they had taken stock of the situation and followed the five that had preceded them. The fate of that tiger was sealed, for by now there were two dozen wild dogs on his trail. They would not relax their pursuit till they had caught him and torn him to shreds.

The sounds of the chase died away in the distance as I stepped from behind the tamarind tree to look at the three dead dogs and the scene of battle. The sambar stag that the tiger had slain lay untouched a few feet away. After disposing off the tiger, no doubt the surviving dogs would return and eat their fill.

Tiny had returned by the time I arrived and Merwan showed up soon after. Neither of them had seen or heard anything. It was quite late when Donald returned. He had met the tracks of a panther and not long after had passed a cave. Associating the two, Donald had thrown stones into the cave, expecting and hoping the panther would emerge. Instead, a sloth bear had dashed forth with two cubs riding on her back. She was greatly annoyed at being disturbed and Donald would have been compelled to shoot her in self-defence, had she seen him. Fortunately, this did not happen. The bear rushed blindly forward into the jungle, and that was the end of that. No panther could have shared a cave with a family of bears, and so Donald passed on.

Strangely enough, none of the party had heard the shots I had fired to frighten off the elephant and everyone was greatly interested in my account of the fight between the tiger and the wild dogs.

This time we all helped in gathering wood for the camp fire and arranged to take watch-turns of two hours, each. Then came an early dinner, followed by a smoke and a chat. Eventually the conversation began to die as, one by one, we became sleepy. It was only nine o'clock but time to turn in. We had chosen Thangavelu to be on watch for the first two hours. We did this deliberately, for later on he was bound to fall asleep anyhow. Merwan came next, followed by myself, Donald and Tiny. Merwan had tried hard to exchange turns with Tiny, but the big man was too clever for him.

As I fell asleep, a tiger began to roar somewhere over the hill, where I had been that day. I thought to myself that it must be the mate of the animal that the wild dogs had pursued and surely slain.

When Thangavelu called Merwan at eleven o'clock, he would not wake and the ensuing argument disturbed me. I told Thangavelu to throw cold water over him, but the former felt that such conduct by a servant might be misunderstood. So I had to get up and throw the water myself. Merwan sat up with a jerk and was very annoyed, but he took his revenge at 1 a.m., when the time came to wake me, for he did so with cold water. Merwan is like that!

He told me that he had heard a panther sawing a few minutes after midnight, apparently on the hill behind us and pretty far away. Then he told me something that was very important indeed. Only a few minutes before he woke me, a bird, which he thought must have been a jungle fowl, had clucked a noisy alarm and flapped away heavily. This had been quite close. Merwan remarked that he had almost forgotten to mention the incident; he thought it was a matter of no consequence anyhow!

I said nothing in reply as he covered himself up before falling asleep, but I knew the matter was of great consequence indeed. Why should a jungle fowl be so alarmed that it had cried out and left the secure place where it had sat to roost the evening before, to risk changing its perch and a flight in darkness? They don't do that unless some potential danger has passed very close. Perhaps it was a python searching for food. Perhaps a wildcat or a tree-civet. Perhaps even a panther.

The more I thought about it, the more I felt that here was the animal we were seeking, that it had returned to our camp with the deliberate intention of stalking and killing one or more of us. I arranged another log on the fire to make more light to see by. Then I changed my position so that I sat with my back to the nearest *muthee* tree, that grew a few feet from the water. This enabled me to face the jungle, with my companions a little before me and to the right, while I was safe from an attack from the rear. Then I settled down to listen and watch intently.

Nothing happened till after two o'clock. The gurgling sound of the river as it cascaded over the rocks prevented me from hearing the more subtle noises of the forest. A fish plopped loudly in the water, followed by a yet greater splash, perhaps a bigger fish, or even a crocodile in pursuit of the first fish. On the opposite bank of the river a night heron raised a wailing, plaintive cry, and a dark shadow caught my eye against the lighter hue of the star-studded sky: a giant horned-owl, a species confined to the forests and feeding on the smaller mammals, including rabbits.

Just then I heard a faint hissing, rasping sound. I could scarcely distinguish it because of the murmur of the rushing water. It stopped and then was repeated, quite close at hand, from near a clump of bushes a little beyond my sleeping companions, where the jungle grew thickest and was pitch-black. I had heard that sound before and recognized it at once.

I knew then that the pantheress was hiding in the thicket that was closest to the spot where Don and the others were sleeping, and that she was working up her courage for an attack. In a few seconds she would reach the point of springing upon them.

I could not see her. Only the blackness of the thicket. If I shone my torch on that blackness now, it might reveal the pantheress or it might not—according to whether or not she was sheltering behind some bush or shrub. Should the latter be the case, I knew full well she would disappear as soon as she saw the light. So I decided to wait a little longer.

But the pantheress decided to wait no more. She acted.

Voicing the short, sharp roars made by her kind when they charge, she sprang clear of the thicket to land a few feet from the sleeping men. With the next bound she would be amongst them.

I was waiting for this and it was fortunate that I had the rifle to my shoulder with my thumb on the light switch.

The torch-beam cut through the darkness like a knife and reflected the blazing eyes of the pantheress. She hesitated a second, taken completely by surprise and dazzled by the light. I was about to press the trigger when there was a shattering explosion, followed quickly by a second shot.

'Beat you to it, dad!' yelled Don, as he sprang to his feet, having wakened and fired his two shots while still lying on the ground.

Then the other sleepers awoke, and their surprise was indeed comical. Thangavelu just yelled. Tiny sat bolt upright and remarked, half asleep, 'Mother dear!' But Merwan surpassed them; he rolled about as if he'd been shot himself.

Then they saw the dead pantheress, or almost dead, I should say. For she was gasping and twitching still, while life faded slowly from eyes that were held in my torch-beam. They died to a cold, watery blue and became still. Then I knew that the pantheress was dead.

We gathered around and examined her. A fine specimen of a female. Truly my heart had not been in that night's work and I regretted every part I played in hunting her from the time we heard her story. I consoled myself with the thought that what had to be done had been done, and I left it at that, but my congratulations to Don on his prowess were more heartfelt than he ever suspected.

5

Sher Khan and the Bettamugalam Man-Eater*

Many years ago a retired British administrator, popularly known as the Collector in those days, had acquired for himself 300 acres of jungle land on the northern slopes of the Gutherayan range of hills in the district of Salem, where he built an incredible bungalow. He built it all of stone and to the pattern of a castle.

This man loved the jungle and he preserved it at a tremendous expense to himself by engaging an army of coolies to hack away the thorny undergrowth and the lantana plants which, in those years, were just beginning to envelop the forests of southern India.

Since then the lantana has grown apace and now covers thousands of acres of Reserved Forest land. Various government departments, including the forest department, have tried and are trying in vain to eradicate this scourge. Spraying with a poisonous solution can obviously be done only on a very limited scale. A white bug has been found which multiplies in millions; it covers the lantana bushes, blackens the stem, branches, all leaves, and kills all the lantana in perhaps an acre or two of land. Then something happens to the bugs themselves: they die within a few days, from some poison absorbed from the lantana itself, which thus gains the ultimate victory.

Jungle fires rage periodically, particularly during the hot weather. The lantana is burnt to the ground, only to spring up again and flourish with the coming of the rains, fertilized by its own ashes.

*For map, see Chapter 1.

Incidentally, the juice from a few freshly crushed leaves of this plant, rubbed Upon a scratch or an abrasion on the skin, will assist the wound to heal completely. It is as effective as tincture of iodine, with the added advantage that it does not irritate.

But to return to the British Collector and his 300 acres: he called his place Bettamugalam Estate, after the name given to the local sub-taluk area, and his stone house he called 'Jungly Castle.' Cleaned of the strangling lantana, the natural forest grew apace. The grass that flourished in the glades between the trees attracted bison and deer, which in their turn brought their natural foes, tigers, panthers, and the still more voracious wild dogs.

Conditions then began to change. The British Collector died and Bettamugalam Estate, with Jungly Castle, was bought by an Anglo-Indian who did not have the means to keep the place up to the standard of the former owner. Once more the lantana started to encroach upon the grassy glades, and as a consequence the bison and deer decreased in numbers. But the carnivores remained and they grew hungry.

Then the Anglo-Indian died in his turn, and no legal owner came forward. Jungly Castle fell into disrepair. Villagers came on moonlit nights in bullock carts and stole the cut granite blocks, pulling down the walls to get them. For these stones, especially when they could be obtained free, offered first-class material with which to construct the walls of their own huts.

The bison had by this time vanished, and the herds or deer had almost disappeared. The tigers, panthers and wild dogs that congregated to eat the deer followed them. Only the jungle fowl, spurfowl and peafowl remained to increase in numbers, for the heavy undergrowth of lantana gave ideal cover. Otherwise, the whole area assumed a forlorn appearance. Now and again an odd tiger or panther would pass that way, hoping but generally in vain, for a stray spotted deer or jungle-sheep to break his fast. He was generally very hungry but there was nothing to be got.

Now, in the village of Aiyur, a little over four miles away, lived a man of about twenty-five years, whose name was Gurappa. Gurappa had married very late in life for one of his caste and status, the usual age being around seventeen to eighteen years for a boy and thirteen to fourteen years for a girl. But Gurappa's father could not get his son married earlier, for they were a poor family, and the parents of every prospective bride turned down the marriage of their daughter to a mere yokel, the son moreover of such a poor father. But a girl was found at last. I was told that she was very deaf and had walked with a limp from birth. Very likely these impediments had caused her parents to agree to the marriage with Gurappa, who was so poor.

Now another problem presented itself. The bridegroom had no house. His father had sold the hut the family had lived in. Not even in India can a bridegroom bring his bride home on their wedding day to no house!

So Gurappa decided to build one in a hurry. True, he had no money, but fortunately a good number of stones still remained of Jungly Castle, although the best and largest of them had already been pilfered.

Scorning to wait for a moonlight night, the would-be bridegroom begged the village headman to lend him his cart. With a long-term policy in view of extracting free labour from Gurappa in return when the harvest came around, the village *patel* consented.

It is safer if there are no witnesses when one sets out to commit a felony. Gurappa knew this, so he set out alone after his midday meal, intending to collect the stones and be back by sundown. Working single-handed is invariably a back-breaking job, as he soon found out. To lever the stones out of the crumbling walls with the short crowbar he had brought for the purpose, and to carry each stone and load it on to the bullock cart, took much energy and time, calling for a fair number of resting periods. The sun had dipped behind the hills to the west and the nightjars were already calling from the sandy track along which the cart had come, when Gurappa decided to call it a day and bring away the first load. Tomorrow he would borrow somebody else's cart and fetch a second load.

So he beat the bony bulls with a piece of broken bamboo. They started to walk dejectedly homewards, for this strange man, who was not their owner, had not bothered to feed or water them all day. Gurappa followed behind leisurely, his mind at peace for the moment. Up to now there had been nothing to disturb the bridegroom. No sound had he heard to cause him any uneasiness.

The waiting tiger that had seen him must have been very hungry indeed, if not on the verge of starvation, to act as he did. Perhaps he was sick or wounded and had been disabled from hunting his natural prey. Certainly he was not a regular man-eater, for nobody had been killed in this area by a tiger for quite a time.

The bulls hauled the cart past a *babul* tree, the lower half of which was smothered in lantana. The tiger must have been hiding within that lantana, for that was where he sprang from. When I came to the spot with a Forest Range Officer, several guards, the sub-inspector of police and a constable, just twenty-four hours later, some of the stems still bent down by the weight of the animal as he had lain in wait for Gurappa.

Probably Gurappa had never known what happened till he found himself being carried away by a tiger. Then he must have struggled and screamed loudly, for the bulls took fright and bolted, hauling the heavily laden cart behind them. They did not get very far, for there was a curve in the track ahead, where it skirted some lower ground. In turning, the cart went off the track and down the *khud*, taking the bullocks with it.

Miracles often happen, even with bullock carts. While the vehicle was considerably damaged, there was no injury to either bull. Freed from the restraining yoke, they found their way back to Aiyur, terrified but unhurt, long after the sun had set.

Adjacent to the village of Aiyur is a Forestry department school where officials already working in the department, along with students who have passed the required examination, undergo practical instruction in field forestry. A Range Officer is stationed at the school, along with two or three senior foresters and a number of guards and watchers, who look after the nurseries and departmental buildings.

The headman, alarmed by the fact that his build had returned without the cart, assumed that an elephant had attacked and smashed it, and had accounted for Gurappa in the process. With half the village trailing behind him, he sought the cooperation of the Range Officer for permission to send out a search party into the jungle. Permission was readily given, but there was a marked lack of enthusiasm among the villagers to volunteer. Finally four of five persons were persuaded to offer their services, but by this time darkness had already fallen. Even in broad daylight a wild elephant that has killed a man is something no villager will face. In pitch-darkness an encounter of this nature is not to be thought of. So the search was postponed till the next morning. The headman must have spent a sleepless night thinking of his cart, while cursing Gurappa for being the cause of his misfortune.

Early next day the search party set out. It did not take them long to find the cart at the bottom of the *khud*, but of Gurappa there was no sign. The tracks of the cart wheels and the bullocks, made in the soft sand, showed that the animals had taken the corner at a gallop; hence the accident. What had caused them to do that?

Still suspecting that an elephant was to blame, the villagers backtracked and soon found the real cause. The whole story was written in the dry, soft sand of the track. There was blood, the pug-marks of a tiger, and a distinct drag-mark, left by some part of the victim that had trailed along the ground. Fear fell upon them then. It was dangerous enough to encounter a possible rogue elephant. But they were many in number and an elephant might be expected to hesitate before attacking such a large party. Not a man-eating tiger. He might reappear at any moment, from anywhere, with disastrous results.

Without further delay the group returned to Aiyur. Gurappa was dead beyond doubt. What could be gained by searching for him?

By chance, I happened to be camping at Sivanipalli that day. This little village lies about five miles to the west of Aiyur. It is a favourite spot of mine, and being just over fifty miles from Bangalore, I often go there at weekends. Incidentally, it marks the scene of the shooting of the only black panther that has ever been known in this region, the details of which adventure have been related in another story.*

The forest guard of Sivanipalli, who had gone to Aiyur to meet his superior, the Range Officer, returned at about noon to tell me what had happened to the unfortunate bridegroom, Gurappa. Carrying a torch and my sweater, with a pocketful of dry biscuits and a flask of tea for dinner in case I was delayed, I set out for Aiyur within fifteen minutes of hearing the news.

A report had already been made to the Forest department headquarters at Denkanikota, a small town eight miles to the north, by the Range Officer, so that shortly after my arrival the sub-inspector of police turned up on his motorcycle, with a constable on the pillion seat. Thus it came about that the two police officials, the Range Officer, a retinue of guards and myself came to the lantana thicket at the foot of the babul tree from which the tiger had sprung, almost twenty-four hours earlier, upon the unfortunate Gurappa as he had walked behind the bullock cart that was laden with stolen stones. The prologue of this story, as I have told it, had already been pieced together by me from scraps of conversation with the two officers and their assistants. The sub-inspector of police, who was a Brahman and a fatalist, remarked more than once on the connection in the web spun by fate between the old British Collector, long dead and gone, who had owned Bettamugalam Estate and Jungly Castle, and the modern bridegroom, Gurappa, who had no house at all and had been striving to build one. Not quite seeing the point, I quipped that there might also be

---

*See *The Black Panther of Sivanipalli*.

something in the thought that fate may have taken a dim view of the general situation and decided to punish someone who was in the act of robbing the dead. I meant this as a joke, but was surprised at the manner in which my suggestion caught on. The superstitious Brahman and the somewhat nervous Range Officer accepted my point completely.

Nobody was keen on looking for what was left of Gurappa.

As I have said, I found the spot in the lantana where the tiger had been hiding before it sprang upon its victim. The drag-mark was still faintly visible, although much of it had been obliterated during the night by the action of the wind upon the sand, grass and leaves, and the movements of ants and other insects.

However, we were able to follow for a hundred yards or so when, quite unexpectedly, our search ended. An 'aeroplane' tree was growing here—known thus by the local Tamil inhabitants because it sheds its seeds by a wonderfully clever and novel device. Each seed is situated at the junction of two three-inch-long leaf-like blades exactly resembling in miniature the twin propellers of an aeroplane. These blades fall from the parent tree and are spun and carried by the breeze, along with the seed, to incredible distances before they tumble to the ground. In the shade of this tree the grass was still green, and protruding from this grass, as if beckoning to us, was a human arm and hand, the five fingers spread and pointing upwards.

We had found Gurappa at last—what was left of him!

Peculiarly enough, the upper parts of his body, from breast to head, had been untouched. While one arm stretched upwards, the fingers of the other hand were stuffed into the mouth as if to stifle a scream. The eye sockets were empty, because the black ants had already eaten away the eyeballs. Then red ants had come, and these now swarmed over the face and skin. In many places the black outer skin had been devoured, exposing patches of white and red flesh, now rotting underneath. The reason why hyaenas and jackals had up to now not touched these toothsome portions was simple to guess. Red ants are notorious for their aggressive nature and painful stings.

But there was hardly anything left of Gurappa's body below his chest. The tiger had eaten his fill, while the scavengers of the night had removed the rest.

The foliage of the 'aeroplane' tree had hidden from the vultures what the tiger and the others had left, for had these birds arrived before us, nothing at all would have remained.

The stench of death and putrefaction hung heavily in the still evening air. Flies squatted in myriads on the stems of the surrounding grass, prevented from settling on the rotting flesh by the army of red ants that had already driven away their cousins. A terrific battle appeared to have been waged between the two species, as large numbers of dead, of both varieties, strewed the ground for a yard around Gurappa's head and arms. Now and again a sorely-wounded member of one of the opposing armies tried to drag itself away.

The tiger would certainly not return to eat the little that remained. Why he had left it in the first place was unaccountable; but he would anyway give the red ants a wide berth.

The sub-inspector ordered his underling to arrange for the removal of the remains. Then he wrote an unnecessarily verbose statement which I was asked to sign as a witness. It was getting dark when we returned to the Forest Rest House at Aiyur. The Range Officer offered me accommodation at his bungalow for the night, but the thought of the dry biscuits in my pocket made me decide to return to my camp at Sivanipalli and the corned meat that awaited me there. I had my torch, and after all the tiger might not be a confirmed man-eater.

So I started out to the dismay of the two officers, who shouted a warning behind me that I might never reach Sivanipalli. The path wound downhill mostly, between lantana, scrub and scattered *babul* saplings till, as a lower level was reached, the trees became loftier and clumps of heavy bamboo grew in among them. The darkness became intense, through which the beam from my torch cut only a narrow pencil of light.

Suddenly a feeling of great uneasiness came over me—rather, a feeling of mortal fear. Why, I could not imagine. I had heard no sound, nor had I caught any audible cries of alarm from the deer and other creatures in the jungle to warn me of danger. Complete silence reigned on every side. There was only the soft crunch of my own rubber-soled boots on the ground, and the occasional crack of a twig or crackle of a leaf as I trod upon it.

I halted abruptly and spun around, fully expecting to see the tiger stalking me from behind. But there was nothing to be seen, not even the glimmer of a firefly. There was nothing to be heard; not even the chirping of a friendly cricket.

Then I knew why I was so afraid: it was the idea of absolute loneliness. There was no living creature nearby to witness what happened to me. Nothing, and nobody to help. And, although I could not see him in the gloom, or hear him, even in that absolute silence, I was as certain of the presence of the tiger there as I was of my own.

I have found that at times of great peril in the jungle, the human reflexes act in one of two ways. The trumpeting scream of a charging rogue elephant, or the guttural roar of an attacking tiger or panther, sometimes galvanizes the victim into precipitate flight, or else he is so paralysed by fear that he is rooted to the spot and quite incapable of movement. It is rare, indeed, that the victim can think at all, much less think clearly, of what he should, or rather could, do in the circumstance. There is no time for thinking.

But in this case there was no screaming elephant before me, nor a roaring tiger for that matter. Only silence, and the certain knowledge that the man-eater was there. And the reflex that came to me was to run, and to run fast, as fast as I could, away from that dreadful spot. I had the greatest difficulty in restraining myself, for I knew that if I started to run it would be just what the tiger would like me to do. For then he would attack. All tigers, including man-eaters, know that every other creature is afraid of them. They are accustomed to striking terror into the hearts and minds of their prey, and with that knowledge comes the greater confidence that enables them to hunt so successfully.

I knew at that moment that the only thing that could save me from the tiger would be to act otherwise. He was lurking somewhere, watching and waiting for me. Perhaps he was behind, perhaps ahead, or may be to one side or the other, waiting and watching for an opportunity to spring upon me. He would have done so long before had it not been for my torch and the bright beam of light that was cutting through the darkness. This had worried him. If I wanted him to attack, all I had to do was extinguish the torch and start running. Then he would come.

I thought quickly. And I kept on walking at a measured pace, flashing the torch behind me, to both sides and then in front. The *path* was narrow, not more than six feet wide at the most.

The track turned a corner and ahead of me the light revealed a rock, standing to the left and about a hundred yards away. It was a sloping rock and appeared to be about six to eight feet high. I felt that I could run up and on to it without difficulty, provided I had a sufficiently long start. For I had had an idea. Here was a suitable place at which to try to tempt the man-eater to show himself.

As I turned the idea over in my mind, I continued to walk forward. Those hundred yards were far too long to risk a show-down. The speed of a charging tiger is something fantastic and has to be seen to be believed. But when the rock was fifty yards away, I decided to take the chance.

Making certain my rifle was cocked, and fixing the location of the rock clearly in my mind, I suddenly extinguished the torch and ran and fix its location before putting out the torch and ran as fast and as hard as I could.

The darkness, when the torch went out, was intense. I could not see a thing. That was why I had taken care to face the rock and fix its location before putting out the torch and starting to run.

It took quite a few seconds for the tiger to gather his wits and realize that his victim had actually done what he had been waiting for. As I ran, I was just beginning to think that perhaps there was no tiger at all and that my nerves had made a fool of me, when there was a shattering roar from behind and the man-eater launched his attack. I heard that roar, but I could run no faster anyway.

I was only a few feet ahead of the tiger when I reached the rock and ran up the slope. Then I whirled around, raised the rifle to my shoulder and pressed the torch-switch with my left thumb all simultaneously. The man-eater had reached the base of the rock and was crouched for the spring that would carry him to the top when the rifle went off, almost at point-blank range. With the crash of the explosion he somersaulted backwards while I worked the underlever of the .405 to place the second round in the breach. Then I pressed the trigger.

Nothing happened.

A moment later, with a loud snarl the tiger leaped to its left and disappeared into the long grass that grew there. Working the underlever again, I ejected the cartridge that had misfired and fired the next round at the spot where the tiger had just vanished.

I had been too frightened when I fired the first shot, but I distinctly remember hearing the echo of the second one reverberating against the slopes of Gulhatti hill, which I could not see in the darkness but which is within a mile of the rock I stood upon.

The growling had ceased. Had my second bullet found its mark? Had the tiger collapsed from the effect of my first shot? Perhaps both had taken effect. Or had I missed entirely? Worse still, perhaps I had only wounded the brute.

With the torch still shining upon the bushes where the tiger had vanished, I sat down on the rock to collect my scattered wits and control my breathing. Mostly, to try to think. Only then did I realize how narrow an escape I had had. Had the tiger been closer behind me, or to either side or ahead, he might have cut me off before I could reach the rock. Moreover, had the cartridge that had misfired been one ahead in the magazine of my rifle, it would have failed at the crucial moment and the man-eater would certainly have completed his spring.

When I grew a little calmer I began to wonder what had happened to the man-eater. It seemed inconceivable that I could have missed him at point-blank range. Then I remembered I had been running fast and had rushed up the rock at the last moment. Fear, excitement and exertion had made me breathe hard and this had evidently caused me to press the trigger unconsciously, causing me to miss entirely or perhaps just wound the beast.

It was impossible for me to follow up in that darkness. If I had missed him, he would have been scared away entirely. If he was wounded, it was very unlikely that the man-eater would resume the pursuit if I continued on my way to Sivanipalli. So after a few moments I decided to do that and return the next morning to take up the trail.

I reached Sivanipalli without event and lay down in my little tent, still thinking of what should be done the next day. Then the dried biscuits in my pocket reminded me that I was hungry and I got up to make tea and open the tin of meat that had been the cause of the whole incident.

There are no poojarees or aboriginal trackers at Sivanipalli, but there was Sher Khan, a character who had led a colourful existence and must at the time have been about forty years old. He was a Muslim, a poacher of game, a timber thief, and the suspected author of several dacoities on a minor scale, when bullock carts carrying sacks of grain to the villages of Denkanikota and Anchetty had been held up and robbed at night. The method of dacoity had been as simple as it had been effective.

The carts used to travel by night in order to save time. Generally, half-a-dozen of them would move, one behind the other for company and for protection from wild animals, particularly elephants, and of course the evil spirits that are said to be everywhere. Highway robbery, up to that time, was unheard of.

The first case reported to the police was by five cartmen who had been behind one another from Anchetty to Denkanikota. They were on the ghat road when it had happened, nine miles from their destination. The time was 1 a.m. and the bulls strained at their loads on the steep gradient. Each driver sat in his cart, more than half asleep. Suddenly a voice hailed them from the darkness of the roadside. It was harsh and loud. They saw no man, but the voice said that a gang of dacoits was hiding by the wayside. They had loaded muskets and all would be well if they followed orders. Then followed the orders. They were very simple.

'Get down from your carts, all five of you, and walk back for a full mile. When you reach the tenth milestone, you may sit dawn. Light a fire and wait there till morning. When daylight comes, you may return to your carts. Remember, some of us will follow and keep a watch over you till dawn. If any one of you dares to disobey, he will be shot without further warning. Remember also that we promise we shall not harm your carts or animals. You are poor men and we do not want to hurt you. It is the rich men's belongings, carried in your carts, that we want.'

The cartmen obeyed. They were thankful they had been spared. Early next morning they found their carts, standing where they had been left. Some of the foodstuff had been stolen, but not all if it. Only the more valuable items. The gang could not have been a very large one after all, or they would have taken everything.

This happened two or three times more, on other roads and tracks leading to Denkanikota and Anchetty, before the carts stopped moving at night and police patrols took their place. Several suspects were rounded up, including Sher Khan. They were beaten and locked up. But all of them always affirmed complete innocence and all of them had alibis.

That was how I first met Sher Khan. He was returning to Sivanipalli after one such beating and complained aloud of the injustice that was rampant in this world. But there was a mischievous twinkle of insincerity in his eye as he spoke.

As I said, he was a Muslim, and the literal translation of his name is 'Chief among Tigers'. He was a ruffian, but a very likeable one, and that is how he became my friend. I would never fail, when at Sivanipalli, to visit his little house and drink tea with him, and he would never fail to return my call.

So I went to Sher Khan early in the morning after my adventure, and asked him to assist me. For I was confident that I had not missed the tiger when I had fired at point-blank range. I knew I must have hit it. That meant following up a wounded tiger in the jungle, and to do that there must be two persons. Following a blood trail through bushes, over leaves and on hard and stony ground requires concentration of eyesight and mind. One must look here, there and everywhere, for a speck of blood or a mere smear of the underside of a leaf, or against a stem or rock. While you are engaged in so looking, the wounded tiger might be just ahead, waiting for you, or he may be lying to the right or the left, concealed behind a tuft of grass, a clump of bamboo, a tree-trunk or a termite-hill, waiting till you come within springing distance. There is a third possibility, and that is he may be stalking you from behind even while you are looking for him. But you are blissfully unaware of his presence, because your attention is concentrated on the ground, following his trail. On the other hand, if you try to keep an effective lookout for the wounded beast, you will soon find you have lost the trail. You just cannot do both jobs effectively, and so a second person is essential. One of you concentrates on following the tiger's blood spoor and tracks, while the other keeps a sharp lookout ahead, to the right, left and also behind. In the hands of this second person lies not only his own life, but the life of his companion.

Sher Khan volunteered to help without hesitation, but insisted that I drink the customary cup of tea with him before we set out. A clap of his hands and one of his four wives responded. He told her to make: 'Attcha-cha-first class!' for the *sahib*.

Being a Muslim, he was allowed to have four legal wives—and

he had them. Most of us find it a problem to manage one, but he managed all four with ease! And this is how he did it.

Sher Khan showed no preference towards any one of his four spouses—either to the youngest or the most recent or the prettiest. They were all kept strictly *gosha*—that is to say, they were compelled to cover their faces with a *bourkha* when they went out in public. No man was allowed to look upon them. I, as a very particular friend, had the privilege of seeing their faces, and even of speaking to them—but very sparingly, mind you—when I visited his house.

Sher Khan made it a practice to divide the household duties among his four wives on a weekly-roster basis. For a week one of them would be responsible for the cooking of all the food, with a second to assist her; the third would be responsible for washing all the utensils; the fourth for the household work such as sweeping, mending, washing of clothes, etc. The following week, the roster would change, and so on week by week thereby dividing all the work very equitably among all four. Sher Khan himself would not lift a finger to do any household work. He did the marketing—if his rather nefarious activities could be so described—and brought home the earning, or the money, whichever you my prefer to call it. The wife who did the hardest work for that particular week, namely the cook, he would sleep with two days in the week, the remaining three women one day each. Fridays and Sundays were 'off days' from that sort of thing. 'Days of rest' as he called them.

They were a poor family, but disciplined, happy and contented. The women never quarrelled with him and hardly ever among themselves. For if they did, a beating would be administered; fairly, equitably and impartially, each recalcitrant wife receiving an equal number of blows or cuffs according to the nature of the offence. And in spite of the often undeniably pressing demands made upon him, he had no children.

As soon as we had drunk our tea we were off. Sher Khan announced that he had no gun and brought a rusty sword with him instead. He remarked that it had belonged to his father, and to his father's father's father's father, who was a soldier serving under the great Tipu Sultan, the tiger of Mysore. The mathematics involved in the problem of checking whether this man's great-great-grandfather could have lived in Tipu's lifetime are rather too involved for me. In the meanwhile, we had walked out of earshot of all his wives and I raised an impersonal question, addressed perhaps to the air: 'A voice comes out of the darkness and threatens to shoot many cartmen. Yet there is no gun. How can that be, Sher Khan?'

The silence for a moment is complete. Then he replied. 'You may call me a liar if you wish, sahib. But that is exactly what happened. There was no gun at that time, nor any other. I never possessed one and still don't have a gun. And the gang consisted of myself and three of the wives, *sahib*. The fourth is too old. But she had the brains, and it was all her idea.'

And, I believed him.

We were nearly at our destination. There stood the sloping rock from which I had fired at the man-eater the previous night. This time it was to my right. We approached in silence and looked at the ground. No blood was to be seen and the earth was too dry and hard for tracks. Without speaking, I pointed to the bushes bordering the *path* where the tiger disappeared from view.

I took the lead for the moment, with my Muslim friend directly behind. In spite of the prevailing dryness all around, it was evident that a heavy body had recently passed through. A couple of broken stems hung loosely, still joined to their parent-branch by the outer skins. A yard or two further and we saw it almost simultaneously: blood!

There was a splash of bright red on the carpet of dry, brown leaves that covered the ground. I touched it with my forefinger and rubbed it against my thumb. It was thick and coagulated, and by that I knew that my bullet of the night before had inflicted more than a mere surface wound. It had penetrated deeply.

We changed places now, and I put Sher Khan ahead of me. He would concentrate all his attention on following the blood trail, while I would cover him and myself in all four directions.

The Muslim was no born tracker, but what he lacked in ability as an aborigine he made up for in intelligence. He fussed and fumbled around, taking far more time than would a member of any of the jungle tribes in following such a trail, but he found one blood spot after another. The tiger had bled far more freely now. The exertions caused by his wounds had no doubt opened the wound. Splashes and pools of blood lay all along the trail, making it easy to follow.

I caught sight of a slight movement ahead and lightly touched Sher Khan with my hand. He halted at the prearranged signal and froze. With rifle to shoulder, I watched the spot from whence the movement came. I also watched on both sides and even glanced behind us. For wounded tigers are notoriously clever in lying in ambush or in creeping upon their enemies from behind.

The movement came again. A small branch swayed ominously a few feet ahead of us. I prepared for the attack. Stretching out my hand, I gripped Sher Khan by the shoulder and pulled him unceremoniously behind me.

The branch swayed again. I stared at it for a minute. And then I relaxed. A false alarm. I noticed the leaves on the swaying branch were all upside down. That is because it had been broken by an elephant and was hanging suspended to the place from which it was broken by the stems of some creepers that were strong enough to bear its weight.

There must be no talking whatever in a situation like the present, so I reached backwards, gripped Sher Khan, and once again placed him in the lead. Then I nodded my head as a signal for him to press on. We proceeded slowly and passed the suspended branch.

Under a bush we noticed that the dried grass had been dyed deeply with blood. It seemed to be all over the place, on the leaves and stems of the bush as well. The tiger must have lain down here. Perhaps he rolled on the ground. Perhaps he covered his injured face with his paws and got them all covered with gore too. That would account for the blood, spread so widely under the bush before us.

I touched Sher Khan again to halt him, and we listened for a full five minutes. But we heard not a sound. As carefully and silently as we were moving the two of us would necessarily have made some noise in the undergrowth over that dry terrain. If the tiger was nearby, he must surely have heard us. Then he would either growl in warning, attack, or slink away silently. But nothing of the kind happened.

The blood trail now unexpectedly veered to the left and we knew that the tiger was making for a small stream that skirted the foothills. The wound must have been taking effect, and thirst had driven him there for water. At that time of the year the stream was dry except for a few isolated pools here and there. The tiger was making for one of these pools and the chances were that when he reached it he would lie up in the vicinity till he recovered from his wound or died of it, a lingering, starving, horrible death.

I hate wounding an animal and spare no pains, when I have done so, to follow it up and put it out of its misery. From the amount and nature of the blood lost by the tiger it looked as if my bullet had inflicted a severe wound from which there was little chance of recovery. Once more I thought of the dreadful lingering death that was in store for this animal unless I succeeded in finding it.

I stopped Sher Khan and we conferred in whispers for a few minutes. I knew of a pool on the riverbed which I judged to be at least two miles away, but Sher Khan said there was a closer one, smaller but which held water throughout the year, higher up the stream and less than a mile from where we now stood. So we continued to follow the blood trail, and as the Muslim predicted, after a short distance it veered to the left and made for the smaller pool, now directly ahead.

The ground sloped as we approached the streambed and I was made aware of its nearness by the repeated cries of jungle fowl that sheltered in the thick belt of trees and undergrowth that lined both banks, sustained in summertime by the water that was hidden from sight but still flowed beneath the dry sand. In a few minutes the short dry grass, withered by the sun, was replaced by long green stems, the heat and sight of the sun was shut out by a canopy of trees, and I knew we had reached the rivulet.

The blood trail went straight ahead; we were in sight of the dry sands of the streambed, stretching to right and left. I can imagine the agony of the wounded beast that came here last night or in the early hours of this morning in search of water to allay its burning thirst, only to be confronted by this waterless stretch.

But Sher Khan whispered that the pool was just around the corner to our left, now a stone's throw away, and unerringly the trail led in that direction. Once again I changed places with my friend and took the lead. Tracking was unnecessary now, as clearly the wounded tiger was making for the pool and I felt we would find it there. We turned a corner but I could see no pool. I stopped in silent perplexity, when Sher Khan came up from behind to point to an outcrop of flat rock which could just be seen above the sand of the stream and within a few feet of the further bank.

A plover rose into the air from the rock, crying 'Did-you-do-it! Did-you-do-it! Did-you-do-it!', and I knew that water lay hidden from my view in a hollow of that rock. The stream had narrowed there and both banks had come very close to each other. The undergrowth was dense, and the forest loomed menacingly around and above us from the ground that dipped down to the bed of the rivulet.

We halted again. There was silence and no indication of the tiger's presence. I looked down and could see no blood trail. Evidently it did not approach across the sandy bed, but kept to the cover of the undergrowth bordering the banks.

Forward we went once more. We were there at last, and what a sad story revealed itself in the water of the tiny pool and the sloping rock that led down to it! For the water was red with blood, and the rock was sticky with it, where the tiger had evidently lain in agony with his head in the water to assuage his thirst and to lessen the pain of his wound. His pug-marks were visible on the rock in several places, steeped in his own blood. Finally he had gone to the shelter of the bank and I knew that was where I would find him; laying in the cool of the undergrowth like all stricken animals, he would await his end with patience.

Then I remembered that this animal had been responsible for killing a human being, as far as could be made out for no apparent reason. If not brought to book, he would no doubt in time have became a confirmed man-eater. Motioning to Sher Khan to stay where he was, I advanced to meet him and finish him off.

I heard a slight sound behind me and looked around. Sher Khan was following. Perhaps he wanted to be present to witness the last scene in this drama. Perhaps he was just nervous at being left alone. We advanced into the dense undergrowth beneath the canopy of trees and were lost to sight.

The silence that had reigned all this while was then broken by a shattering roar that seemed to come from the very ground at my feet, and things began to happen very fast. Momentarily the undergrowth was agitated violently and then a mighty form launched itself past, and almost over me, on to Sher Khan who was not two feet behind.

The Muslim yelled and swiped wildly his rusty sword. The blunt edge met the bulk of the springing tiger and the impetus of both objects caused the blade to bite into the flank of the animal. Sher Khan went down, still screaming, and the tiger fell on top him.

Fortunately, Sher Khan had the presence of mind to cover his head and face with his two arms as the tiger sought to bite him. Leaning forward, I placed the rifle behind its neck, ensuring the bullet would not endanger my friend, and pressed the trigger.

I fired once again while Sher Khan scrambled to his feet and leaped out of range of the dying creature's claws. Then the drama was over.

Strangely enough, my friend was practically unhurt except for a few scratches, and the reason was that my bullet of the night before had gone into his upper palate and come out above his nose. The whole frontal or nasal bone hung loosely by the flesh, a truly ghastly wound from which the poor beast could never have recovered.

It was fortunate that the blow my friend aimed at the tiger with his ancestor's rusty sword had met its mark for I was directly in line with it. Had he missed, Tipu, the Tiger of Mysore and his henchman of long ago, Sher Khan's ancestor, would have claimed one more victim! I would have been decapitated by the force of that blow.

Sher Khan laughed afterwards when I told him this. He said I had my own revenge when my bullet, fired into the tiger's neck, had passed but a few inches above his head. He asked me if he might have the skin of the animal as a memento of our encounter and I gladly gave it to him. For, despite his many faults and his rascality, Sher Khan is a brave man and a most likeable fellow. Above all, I admire the way in which he manages his four wives. Long may they be spared to him, and he to them.

We sat by the camp fire before I left him and swapped yarns. He told me some of his adventures while I smoked my pipe and listened. Beyond the leaves all was lost in the darkness of the jungle night. Now and again a burst of sparks soared skywards as one of us threw a fresh log on to the fire to keep it brightly burning.

From behind his hut came suddenly the jungle chorus of the jackal pack: 'Oooo-ooo-ooh; Ooo-where? Ooo-where? Here! Here! Heere! Hee-yeah! Heeee-yeah! Yah! Yah! Yah!'

After that there was an abrupt hush. A heavy, all-pervading silence. You can hear it, you feel it, you know it. It is the silence that heralds the unexpected. As complete as if a switch had been turned.

Then, far away across the hill the second came rolling down to us, permeating the jungle and riding across the tops of the trees in the valley below.

'Oo-o-o-n-o-o-n!   A-oongh-gah!   A-oongh-gah!   Oo—ugh! Oo-Ugh!'

A tiger roaring.

Jungles Long Ago

1

A Night in Spider Valley

Eric Newcombe, who figures so largely in this story, was at school with me. We were great friends, and one of the reasons for this was that Eric had a very pretty sister.

Unfortunately, he was one of those people occasionally encountered who have an inevitable attraction for trouble. To make my meaning clear, if you were with Eric you could surely expect something unfortunate to happen. It was almost a certainty.

Sometime, as boys, we raided orchards, or we raided the girls' school at night, dressed as ghosts or Red Indians, or the dormitories of the convent, running the gauntlet of the nuns a dozen times; yet we always escaped, except when Eric was with us. For we tried it all again with him in the party. Dressed as 'yoemen' of old—Eric was 'Guy Fawkes', I remember—we had once terrified the girls in their beds at the convent and were making good our escape, pursued by various nuns with umbrellas, but vaulting over the wall to freedom, at whose feet do you think we fell? None other than our own headmaster, returning from a late night about which he was careful not to speak.

Eric was such a bumpkin that, not content with falling in love with a girl whose parents strongly disapproved, he had to fall off the wall he had climbed over in order to see her and to break his arm in the process. And when we were in pursuit of 'The Killer of Jalahalli', a panther that had been wounded, whose story I have already told* Eric, who was with me, had to go and get himself

---

*See: *Nine Man-Eaters and One Rogue*.

mauled. Not long afterwards we visited a circus and Eric conceived the idea of stroking a panther in its cage. As might have been expected, the panther resented this familiarity and badly clawed his hand. I might mention that for both of these catastrophies I got all the blame from his wife, for he had married that girl some years after falling off the wall.

Then one night we went to shoot wild pig at Gulhatti. It poured with rain. We were sitting in a field for the pig, but I decided to give up and return to the forest bungalow. But not Eric. What was a little rain after all, he asked? He would bag a pig regardless. He got pneumonia instead, and his wife blamed me even for that!

I have told you about these incidents so that you might appreciate that I was not overenthusiastic when this Jonah suggested we do a night jaunt into the jungle in search of adventure. To ensure we met with excitement in some shape or form, he stressed we should go unarmed but should carry torches and a supply of food. That was something at least. He was such a crazy character that I would not have been surprised in the least had he made it mandatory that we went torchless and foodless as well.

Eric was very likeable, extremely persuasive, very fond of nature and the wild, quite unassuming and altogether irresponsible. He was quite unaware of the possible trouble that some of his actions could bring to him and his unfortunate companions. I am always game for an adventure, but when I realised it was to be in the company of this amiable character, I do confess I felt a considerable degree of doubt.

Those of you who have read of my adventures with the tiger I have called 'The Novice of Manchi'* and my earlier story about 'The Marauder of Kempekarai',** will remember the valley I have described in those stories and which I called 'Spider Valley'. It is a deep and densely forested valley in the district of Salem, extending

*See: *The Tiger Roars.*
**See: *Man-Eaters and Jungle Killers.*

southward for about twenty miles from a little hamlet named Aiyur and enclosed between two lofty mountain ranges.

This valley is the bed of a stream, and a narrow footpath accompanies the stream, crossing it every now and then as the stream turns to right and left in an attempt to shorten the overall distance. The mountain ranges to west and east tower above the valley bottom, sometimes oppressively close, giving the traveller the impression that he is in a leafy tunnel. A delightful forest lodge, known as the Kodekarai bungalow, on the slopes of the Gutherayan peak at a height of over 4,000 feet, and to the east of the valley, overlooks the scene as the stream and the valley struggle onward to their ultimate junction ten miles away with the Chinar river, itself a tributary of the great Cauvery river, which is the biggest in south India.

We chose 'Spider Valley' for *ghoom* (a Hindustani word signifying to 'wander' or 'stroll') for a variety of reasons. It was a very densely forested area and abounded in those days with elephant, bison, tiger, panther and bear. Sambar and jungle-sheep, rather than spotted deer, were plentiful because of the hilly terrain and adjacent mountain ranges. Rock snakes, commonly termed pythons, were said to be present in numbers, and smaller animal life was abundant. The tall, waving bamboos and the damp undergrowth were the home of millions of fireflies as well as of a luminiscent beetle and three varieties of 'glow-worm'. Finally, I knew it to be the only area in Salem district where, by virtue of the dampness of the evergreen jungle, a hamadryad (king cobra) might be encountered.

In those early days I owned a fleet of Model T Fords, thirteen of them at one time in fact and all in running order. Purchased at various military auctions as scrap at prices ranging from Rs. 50/-to Rs.250 (£2.50 to £12.50), I tinkered with them and put them back upon the road for use on my trips to the jungle. The cheapest buy was an engine on its chassis and wheels for Rs.12 (about 60p.). Upon this chassis I fixed a body consisting of a dual-purpose box *machan* that could be rigged up on a tree or placed over a hole dug in the earth. Handles helped to fix this *machan* to a tree, while loopholes in the sides provided apertures for firing when it was employed to cover a pit dug in the ground. The whole contraption, as I have indicated, was clamped to the chassis of the model to form an inverted compartment in which to carry my tools, food, water and bedding. A comfortable cane chair, secured over the petrol tank, made a fine driving-seat. As for mudguards, there were none. Nor a windshield. A pair of dark glasses served to keep the grit out of my eyes.

It is true I was covered with dust by journey's end, or bespattered with mud on a rainy day, but this added to the fun. A companion, if there was one, would be seated on a similar cane chair to my left, and I would delight in driving the left front wheel of this vehicle very skilfully through pools of rainwater or heaps of cowdung, and laugh when he was showered with mud or worse.

Eric had a great liking for this vehicle which he called 'Sudden Death' and was adamant that we should make our journey in it, or rather on it, which would be a truer term, in preference to any of the other Model Ts.

I must tell you that it was, and still is, against the law to travel about on a chassis as a regular means of transport. The law requires that there must be a regular body of some sort on any vehicle. The question of registering 'Sudden Death' and obtaining a number for it had therefore to be solved. You will remember it was sold as scrap and had no number at the time. So I removed the numberplate from one of my other Model Ts and drove that vehicle down to the registration office for the needful action. On the application form that had to be filled in was entered both the engine number and chassis number of 'Sudden Death'. The engine and chassis numbers of the vehicle used as a substitute were doctored with a coating of shellac which made them indecipherable; it could be removed later by scraping and a few drops of petrol. 'Sudden Death' was duly registered and given a new number. That, too, under its very own engine and chassis serial numbers. The law was powerless after that to prosecute me for driving about on a chassis that did not have a regular body, for the portable *machan* could not officially be regarded as such. The car that had been presented in its place resumed its own identity when its own number was put back after the shellac coating had been removed.

There were two other features about 'Sudden Death' which I have still to record. The first was that I have fitted it with a special carburettor—also picked up as scrap—which enabled me to start the engine on petrol, and switch to kerosene when it had heated up. A Model T. covered about twenty-four miles to the gallon. Petrol in those days cost fourteen *annas* per gallon (about £0.05), and kerosene 8 *annas* a gallon, or about half the price. So motoring on kerosene was economical indeed. Engine oil was 3½ Rs. or £0.20 a gallon, while brand new tyres were around Rs. 15 or £0.70 each.

The other feature of 'Sudden Death' was a Ruxtel back axle. This provided a very low and a very high gear, in addition to the two transmission gears operated by pedal on every Model T. 'Sudden Death' could, therefore, because of her 22 hp engine and light weight almost climb a wall, and on the flat she could nip along under kerosene at a speed that made many a new car look like a tortoise. As for a failing spark plug, I never bothered to carry a spare. Pending cleaning it when I had the time to do so, all that was required was removal from the cylinder head, for 'Sudden Death' would then snort along on three cylinders as if she had never had a fourth!

As we would be on the move all night, we planned to wear the lightest clothing, the proverbial khaki, while I donned the pair of knee-length, alpaca-lined, rubber-soled boots that I generally wore on such prowls. They are light, noiseless and soft, but thick enough to absorb the fangs of any Russell's viper or a cobra that might be lurking in the undergrowth and inadvertently stamped upon. Eric wore rubber-soled boots with the ends of his pants tucked into them. Snakes offer the greatest hazard at night, far greater than that of running into an elephant or a bear. Tigers and panthers, unless man-eaters, wounded or in the act of mating, offer practically no danger at all.

'Sudden Death' took us to the Aiyur Forest Lodge without incident. Here we had dinner. Then, carrying our food and a change of clothing in haversacks upon our backs, and a bag of spare torch-cells each, we set forth for Spider Valley, the best part of three miles away. I had a five-cell torch hanging in a cloth case at my side while I used a three-cell torch, handier for spotting. Eric carried a pair of three-cell torches.

There is a fire-line leading through the forest in a southeasterly direction from the lodge. After nearly a mile this traverses the edge of a water hole, then changes direction westwards and after some time meets a track leading up a hill to another forest lodge at a place named Gulhatti.

At this water hole we had our first adventure. Our torches revealed a row of twin-pointed green lights on the opposite bank of the pool which kept bobbing up and down restlessly in an attempt to escape the unwinking stare of our torch-beams. A herd of spotted deer had been caught in the act of drinking!

I sank to my haunches to watch them, but Eric left the path we were following and moved down towards the water. This was a mistake, for his clothing got caught in the wait-a-bit thorns that clustered around the pool. Apart from scratching himself, he made quite a lot of noise and made yet another mistake. He moved into the beam from my torch, thereby revealing to the deer that the bright objects they had been staring at all this while, but could not quite identify, were connected with their deadliest enemy—man. With a drumming of hooves the herd disappeared like magic. But a far more ominous sound took its place.

'Woof! Woof! Woof!' A bear had come down to drink. And he, too, had done the unexpected thing.

He must have been moving along the very pathway we had been following and had decided to drink. So he went down to the pool just ahead of Eric. Being hard of hearing and poor of sight, the bear did not hear us at first, nor notice our torch-beams. Maybe he had his head down and was drinking. But when Eric began to crash about and show himself in my light, and the spotted deer thundered away in alarm, the bear realised that something was cooking and that something was directly behind him.

Like all his kind when they get alarmed, he did not wait to think. It did not even occur to him to run away. Instead, he rushed headlong at the intruder. Time enough for him to find out the nature of the intruder later. So he charged straight at Eric at top speed, and Eric at the moment was caught in the wait-a-bit thorns!

What did he do at this critical moment! He hurled his three-cell torch straight at the oncoming bear, then only a few feet away. Only he could have done such a thing.

Here was a bear coming hell for leather at the light when—behold!—the light came hell for leather at him! By luck the torch struck Bruin somewhere in the face, with the result that, as quickly as he had made up his mind to charge, he now made up his mind to run away. Veering to his left he disappeared in a crashing of bushes and loud 'Woofs!' Eric left the thorns with some of his clothing adhering there, rushed to where I stood rooted to the spot, and exclaimed 'A bear!'

I remained silent.

We turned due west for some time and then south along a much narrower track, which was the pathway we were to follow for twenty miles till it met the Chinar river. It led downhill and we entered Spider Valley. The vegetation grew densely on all sides; the lantana bushes, with their clusters of red, pink and orange-coloured flowers, visible in our torch-beams, were rapidly giving away to increasingly dense clumps of bamboo.

Then we heard the sound of elephants: a crash as one of these monsters tore down a culm of bamboo, followed by a curious 'wheenk' as the tender upper leaves and outer skins of which elephants are very fond were peeled off. Finally the thicker base stem was cast away. Truly wasteful creatures they are; for the sake of a basketful of tender leaves and skin, a whole massive culm had been destroyed.

Was this animal alone, or was there a whole herd grazing at the head of the valley for which we were making? We squatted on the ground to await further evidence, and for a while there was absolute silence. Then we heard the swishing as the elephant beat upon the ground a bunch of leaves that he had gathered at the end of his trunk preparatory to stuffing the whole lot into his mouth.

Then silence again, but not for long: 'Phutt! Phutt! Phutt! Phutt!', followed by a prolonged 'whooshing' sound.

He was closer to us than we had thought for these sounds revealed that he was answering the call of nature. It was also becoming apparent that he was probably alone.

He was directly ahead of us and the breeze was blowing from us in his direction, so that it could only be a matter of minutes, if not seconds, before he caught our scent. Then one of three things might happen.

Normally he should just have melted away into the jungle as elephants have a habit of doing, regardless of their great bulk, when they get scent of man. On the other hand he might stand absolutely still, as motionless as a rock, hoping that we might either pass him by without noticing his presence, or if he was on mischief bent, to allow us to come close enough to enable him to charge down upon us devastatingly. The third, but most improbable alternative, was to charge us without further ado. Elephants, even when in *musth* or in any other irritable mood, are unlikely to do this. The majority think things over for a minute or two before acting.

I was about to grab Eric and move off to the left to start a long detour in order to avoid the creature when a fresh sound came to our ears: 'Quink! Quink! Quink!' The sound of a baby elephant nuzzling up to its mother.

We now knew we were in far less danger: unless one gets too close to such a baby, a herd will generally avoid human beings. It is the solitary elephant one has to be careful of.

At least, that was the way things ought to have gone.

But there were other factors. For one thing, it was night; for another, the beams from our torches would frighten the elephants, even annoy them. We had deliberately chosen a dark night, for although the jungle looks pleasantly ethereal in the moonlight, to move about in such light gives one's position away far sooner than in real darkness. Further, our torch-beams would not carry very far in moonlight and the reflection of the eyes of an animal would be far weaker than in pitch darkness.

We had already agreed to talk as little as possible, so I extinguished my torch and with my free hand reached out to grasp and turn off Eric's too. For a moment the darkness was intense, then as our eyes became accustomed to the gloom, the darkness softened and the glitter of the stars added considerable illumination to our surroundings.

The silence continued to be intense. It became oppressive. It got on our nerves. Eventually it became ominous as we began to feel we were being watched.

A low and continued rumbling like distant thunder came from our right. But the sky was clear and star-spangled, so the noise could not possibly herald rain. Where did it come from?

Eric was staring hard to the right as we heard the rumbling again. I could see he was a little alarmed. Finally he put his lips to my ear and asked in a whisper, 'Do you hear that? Can it be a tiger?'

I raised my finger to my mouth to enjoin silence, rubbed my stomach with my other hand, and stabbed my forefinger in the direction where we had first heard the elephants. The starlight was bright enough for us to see each other and Eric recognised my action. I was trying to tell him that the rumbling sound came from the digestive processes of an elephant's stomach.

There are five fundamental lessons a night-prowler should learn if he hopes to prowl with success, whether 'ghooming' like ourselves or reconnoitring the front lines of an 'enemy'. The first is not to talk, or even whisper, on any account. The second is to 'freeze' at sight or sound of an animal or an enemy as the case may be. The third is to keep to the shadows and avoid crossing open spaces. The fourth is to be careful where you place your foot, for even if it is too dark to see, taking a false step into thorns or causing the dried leaves to rustle, will give away your position. You must cultivate the habit on these occasions of moving each foot forward in the manner of soldiers on a ceremonial slow-step parade rather than raising the knee and bringing the foot downwards, as in normal walking. Of course, this requires a little practice, but more than that it needs conscious forethought, remembering to use the 'glide-step' in a night-time ghoom rather than lapsing forgetfully into your ordinary walk.

The fifth and least thing to remember at all times, especially when you 'freeze', is to 'freeze' literally and not keep fidgeting about, slapping at mosquitoes, scratching, raising your hands to your face, and such-like actions.

You should never forget that the faintest whisper becomes audible in the still night air, while the slightest motion attracts the attention of an alert animal, or an enemy, as the case may be, and will give you away. Bear these five tips in mind always if you have occasion to go out on a night 'ghoom', or under different circumstances if you don't want to invite an enemy bullet in your direction. Eric had broken the very first of them by whispering to me and the nearest elephant had heard him.

An instant later there came an earth-shaking 'Tri-aa-ank! Tri-aa-ank'—the alarm cry of a frightened female.

These huge creatures are almost unpredictable. You can never say how they may react even under exactly similar circumstances, though with a wide experience of them in the wild, I can say that usually, under certain conditions, you may expect one of them to behave in this way or that.

After that alarm call, pandemonium reigned for a short time. Then followed a chorus of cries from all around us: 'Kakk!

Kakk! Kakk!' as mothers summoned their young peremptorily, accompanied by 'Quink! Quink! Quink!' as a dozen baby-elephants hurried to shelter beneath their mothers' bellies. What was more frightening was a prolonged roar from the streambed now only a few yards in front of us.

'Ahha-a-a-a-ah!Ahha-a-a-a-a-ah!' A bull-elephant, probably the master of the herd, had herd the alarm signal of his mates; he cried his reassurance as he hurried to their aid, while another male, this time to our left but further off also answered with a roar. Then the first bull, coming headlong toward us, splashed through the water. We heard the squelching as he hurried across the stream, roaring as he came.

We were unarmed, remember, and on foot. I grabbed Eric by the elbow. We turned and scurried back along the path. No time, now, for cautious walking. Rather, we broke into a jog trot.

Meanwhile the bull behind us, still roaring, rejoined the females who had raised the first alarm. He had stopped roaring now. Only the squeals and squeaks of the young and the coughing 'Kakk! Kakk!' calls of summoning mothers could be heard. The second bull, who had also been roaring, had probably joined them as well, for his roars stopped too.

If either or both the bulls decided to chase us now, as likely as not they would start off in silence and only give vent to the shrieking trumpet-sound of attack when they actually saw or scented us. This would be quite different in timbre from the shrill cry of fear and alarm first voiced by the frightened cow. The attacking note is pitched higher and is more prolonged. There is no mistaking the quality of hatred, anger and menace that is put into such a sound, while the alarm-cry is lower-pitched and of shorter, quicker duration, rarely voiced more than twice in succession.

Instead, we heard crashing sounds which seemed to be receding behind us. The 'quicks' of the young had stopped. Evidently the leader had decided that discretion was the better part of valour and was taking his charges away. Now numerous splashings announced that the animals were crossing the stream. We stopped running and sat down to listen.

A few moments later complete silence reigned except for a distant 'Ponk! Ponk! Ponk!' as a sambar doe, high up on a hillside to our right, who had heard all the commotion below, decided some danger might be afoot and voiced her own alarm.

Eric brought his lips to my ear again and whispered 'what now?'

I shrugged, held up the palm of a hand to signify we should wait a little and then, by pointing my forefinger down into the valley, indicated that we would continue our journey. Eric saw my point. Having started, we were not going back just for the sake of a few elephants.

We waited perhaps fifteen minutes to allow the herd to move out of the way. Then we got up and continued our cautious progress down the valley. Very soon we reached the stream. It was perhaps twenty yards wide at this spot. The water reached almost from bank to bank, which accounted for the great amount of splashing we heard when the elephants crossed over, but it was barely knee-deep, as we found out for ourselves when we followed the *path* which cut across the stream for the first time.

The undergrowth on the farther bank was very dense. There was less lantana here and a great deal of *vellari* shrubbery in its place, while mighty trees with trunks of great girth met overhead, their branches crowding and completely obscuring the starlight. Bamboos in profusion grew in massive clumps on both banks of the stream.

The darkness was stygian and a high breeze, which had just risen, blowing down the valley from behind us, caused the bamboos to creak and groan and their culms to bend and thrash wildly against one another. This breeze was unfortunate; we did not like it at all. Coming from behind, it would spread our scent far and wide and warn the animals ahead of our approach. Carnivora have a very poor sense of smell, so it hardly mattered as far as they were concerned, but deer and elephant would know we were coming long in advance of our arrival. We would not see many of the former, while the latter, unless on mischief bent, would give us a wide berth. At the same time, the noise made by the breeze filled the air and prevented us from hearing anything else.

I walked ahead, flashing my three-cell, while Eric followed closely. I had cautioned him not to use his torch, as its beams would fall upon myself and advertise my presence. Further, the light of a second torch from behind is very distracting to the person in front, for various reasons.

The elephant herd had taken itself off in some other direction, and for the time being, at least, there was neither sight nor sound of them, although we found ample evidence of their recent presence in the valley in the form of broken branches, chewed fragments of bamboo, and huge balls of dung all over the pathway.

A moment later something sticky and clammy clung to my face. I could not see it although my torch was lit. Then I recognised what it was: I had walked into the web of one of those enormous spiders that live in large numbers in this valley, and for which reason I had called it 'Spider Valley'. These spiders are huge, often measuring as much as ten inches from leg-tip to leg-tip across the body. This one was not great in bulk, however; it was perhaps the size of a large marble. The abdomen and thorax were black with vivid stripes of yellow running around and across. The eyes were large and blood-red and reflected torchlight as if two large rubies were hanging side by side in midair. The legs were long, hairless, black and powerful, as if made of wire.

I had watched these creatures spinning their webs in daylight. They climb to a high branch and from there they let themselves drop, emitting a thread behind them. When they judge they have fallen far enough, they control any further fall by the simple expedient of not emitting further thread. In this position, head downwards, they hang till a gust of breeze blows the thread close enough to some leaf or branch, to which they immediately cling and attach the thread. If no breeze comes within an appreciable time, the spider climbs up the line of web thread by which it has descended, and tries all over again from a more advantageous position.

Having secured the first line of its thread as a sort of bridgehead, it climbs to the top of this second tree and repeats the action by dropping itself from there while adjusting the length of thread emitted from its abdomen till it meets the first line of web, to which it attaches this new strand. Waiting for the breeze again, it drops lower to reach some point a few feet off the ground and a little distance from the first tree from which it began its operation.

The spider has now spun a huge X, extending some fifteen to twenty feet across. It now returns to the point it had started from and begins to connect all four corners of the letter X to each other by running up and down the arms of the letter X until it has made a huge rectangle with the X in the centre.

The rest is simple; the spider moves around and around, weaving strands of web in parallel lines all around, and perhaps half-an-inch from each other. All this is mighty hard work, but the spider I watched one morning, just starting work on its web as I walked down this valley, had finished by the time I returned that way late the same evening: a wonderful exhibition of precision engineering for an insect of its size.

These creatures will devour anything that gets caught in their webs, butterflies, moths, beetles, and even the smaller species of birds whose blood it consumes. The strands of its webs, although no thicker than the finest thread are very elastic and incredibly strong. Even a single strand will not break easily under strain. Moreover, the substance that forms this strand is very sticky.

Once the work is done, the spider takes up its position in the centre of the web with its legs outstretched. In this position, due to its colouring, it looks like some leaf-stem or other insignificant object suspended in midair. It hangs motionless, but entirely alert. As soon as some creature flies inadvertently against the web, the sticky substance of which the strands are made adhere to it. The creature flutters and struggles, thus fouling other sticky strands.

Immediately, the spider in the middle of the web comes to life.

It scurries towards its prey and scampers swiftly round and round it, emitting an endless flow of threads until the prey is entirely encased and enmeshed.

Then comes the final sad scene. The spider approaches its helpless victim, bites it and starts sucking out all its blood and body-juices, growing fatter and fatter itself in the process till frequently it more than doubles its own size. The prey, on the other hand, collapses as an empty bag of outer skin or as an empty shell, should the victim happen to be a beetle. When all is over, the spider repairs the damage done to its web in the struggle; it does this at once, without postponing the work till some future opportunity. Then it returns to its position in the centre, pending the arrival of its next victim. Spiders are voracious and seem to possess an insatiable appetite.

This spider is very pugnacious and will fight to the death against any one of its own kind who attempts to trespass into its web. I witnessed this for myself years ago, when I deliberately placed, one of these spiders upon the web of a companion of the same species. A battle royal ensued, in the process of which legs were quickly torn off each combatant. The trespasser lost in the end, after five of its legs had been bitten off by the spider who owned the web and who had lost two of its own legs in the battle. Those that remained, however, were enough to enmesh the trespasser securely in a ball of webbing, then came the *coup de grace*, the blood-sucking process, at which stage I ended my observations.

I brushed the web from my face and continued on our way. The *path* became narrower and the forest on both sides became dense. My torch-beam danced from one grey tree-trunk to the next; the moss and lichens that covered them looked like the beards of thousands of old men hanging to the ground.

Suddenly a stillness fell upon the jungle, a hush that could be felt as well as heard. Eric observed it, too, and quickened his steps. His toes kicked against my heels and he involuntarily touched my elbow. I halted in my tracks and he bumped into me. I extinguished the torch and sank down upon my haunches. In a jungle, the closer one can get to the ground, the better one can hear. For a moment Eric wondered where I was and groped with his hands in the darkness about me. Then he whispered 'Scotchie?'

It is a nickname by which I was known at school, though I rarely hear it today. My old schoolpals have practically disappeared. Many have gone abroad, while a large number have made the last journey we all must make. The thought makes me feel lonely at times.

I wondered what could be the cause of that hush, that almost palpable silence that hung so heavily about us. Reason told me there might be many explanations. The sudden cutting-off of the breeze that was blowing all this while from behind us by some hilly spur that we had circumvented in the darkness; an opposing breeze, blowing northwards up the great rift yawned before us in the night; a hush before a storm, a moment when all Nature appears to hold her breath in preparation for the fast approaching tempest.

The darkness was intense and there was no break in the gloom, even when I gazed upwards the tree-tops were lost in obscurity and the stars that until a few moment ago were visible here and there through the canopy of leaves were now completely obliterated. That was when I came to know the reason for the strange silence that had fallen all around us. Indeed, a storm was approaching!

To witness such a phenomenon in the tropics is unforgettable, whether on land or at sea; but to have to undergo it upon the ground in a dense forest is hardly an enviable prospect. People sometimes run under a tree to shelter from the rain, but that is not the kind of rain we have in India, particularly in the jungles, and it certainly was no safe place when the tree itself might be split in two by lightning or torn up by the roots in the wind.

A moment later came a vivid flash overhead. It seemed to rend the canopy of the tree-tops and scatter the darkness with a single blaze of ethereal light. The heart of the storm was so close that it seemed but a fraction of a second before the thunderclap followed in an outrageous, monstrous roar, as of thousand cannon firing in unison. The earth upon which we stood shuddered and the overhanging foliage quivered with the resonance of the thunder; the very universe seemed to tremble.

There was nothing to do but crouch close to the ground. To remain standing is to invite injury from falling branches. Together we scrambled towards the trunk of a nearby tree. I made certain it was one of medium height and not one of the greater specimens whose top would reach to the upper trellises of the jungle, for the loftier the tree the more it would present itself as a target for the lightning which, in violent electrical storms of this kind, can be expected to strike at any moment.

The hush and the darkness returned, but not for long. There was another, more intense flash, followed by an even louder clap of thunder. The third flash was not a flash at all. Like a great serpent of fire from the sky, the lightning struck a giant tree somewhere in the jungle and the thunder that followed seemed to burst our eardrums and numb us with its intensity.

The next moment we heard a mighty, rushing uproar approaching towards us up the valley, like a hundred breakers in unison dashing upon a rocky beach. This was the wind and as it came closer one gained the impression that the trees of the forest were bracing themselves for the onslaught.

It was almost upon us now, and together with this fearsome, roaring sound we heard the staccato reports of hundreds of branches as they snapped like matchwood in the irresistible squall. Above the rushing of the wind we heard the louder thudding and crashing of falling branches and trees, and the creaking, tearing, and rending of timber. Here and there, trees of outstanding height or bulk, by reason of their top-weight and resistance to the wind, were uprooted from the earth and fell with resounding crashes, bringing down a host of minor trees and saplings that were unlucky enough to be sheltering below.

The gale continued for a few minutes only then passed as suddenly as it had begun. The trees lifted themselves again, many of them bereft of half their foliage. All was quiet for a short while except for the diminishing roar of the wind as it receded up the valley.

A new sound soon became audible, growing rapidly in intensity as it drew nearer: a continuous, hissing noise like escaping steam. The rain.

Now it was upon us. What was dry ground and foliage a moment earlier was in the twinkling of an eye converted into a sodden morass of mud and greenery. The best of umbrellas and raincoats would be of no avail in a downpour of this intensity, and we were carrying no umbrellas or raincoats anyway. Not only were we soaked to the skin, but the little equipment and food on our backs was equally saturated. Water poured down our bodies and flowed down our pants, filling our shoes, including my prized alpaca-lined boots, to the brim. This footwear was sold under a guarantee of being waterproof. It now proved the merit of that advertisement, but in an inverse manner. The water that had filled it remained where it was and refused to leak out.

The rain went on and on.

The little stream which was wont to purl and ripple over smooth, mossy stones as it meandered hither and thither, gliding down its course, did none of these nice things any longer. It dashed, lashed and smashed against the rocks in its course, accompanied by a thudding and grinding of torn branches and tree-trunks that were swept down by the flood. The water rose higher and covered the rocks and boulders that obstructed its *path* it became a raging, unbroken flow, crested by the flotsam and jetsam that was whirled and tossed helplessly in the mad grip of the swirling flood.

The ground upon which we were standing was a foot deep in mud and there was not the slightest indication of the rain abating. But it lasted only a little more than an hour, and then it passed as swiftly as its precursor, the wind.

There were a million noises around us now, the dripping from the leaves, the gurgling rush of the stream, the frequent 'plop' from its banks as large section of earth, soaked by the rain and undermined by the raging torrent, collapsed into the flood.

We felt very miserable indeed. Unspoken thoughts turned to home, the comfort of bed and warm blankets, a steaming cup of tea, a relaxing pipe and a good book. What insane idea ever impelled us to start on a trip like this and place ourselves in such a predicament? Then recriminations passed. We forced ourselves to smile and begin to think what we should do next. We could only go back or press on. And who would think seriously of going back?

One thing was certain: we could not continue in our sodden clothing. As evaporation set in, our garments would grow colder and colder upon our bodies. Without clothes we could feel cold, admittedly, but at least we would not grow colder. However logical or illogical this argument might seem, we divested ourselves entirely, poured the water from our boots and put them on again. Our wet clothes we secured to pieces of bamboo, which we shouldered in addition to our kit.

Now we were ready to continue but far from comfortable, I can assure you. The bamboo dug itself into the flesh and the straps of our kitbags dug in too; thorns scraped our skins and our bare feet flopped about loosely in our boots; moreover, it was midnight and very cold.

Soon another hazard presented itself. We found ourselves slipping and slithering in the mud and ooze. The noise we were making by floundering along the soaked pathway and against the undergrowth on both sides of it would advertise our movements in the jungle for a furlong around. In any event, few animals would be on the move after the heavy downpour. Even the elephants would be inclined to call it a day—or rather, a night—and huddle together in some sheltered spot. Every creature would lie quiet; that is, every creature but the snakes! They would be up and about, hunting and gorging themselves upon the frogs that were making this night an occasion for rejoicing.

All around us we could hear these creatures croaking, particularly along the banks of the swollen stream. 'Korr! Korr! Korr! Quacker! Quacker! Quacker!' came the sound from a thousand bull-frog throats. The air droned with the noise. It vibrated and pulsated to the chorus of joy voiced by what was obviously the whole frog-population of the Spider Valley.

For this was mating time, and the forest floor was littered with squashy, lovemaking couples upon which we could not avoid treading in the darkness.

For a moment I caught a glimpse of something white in the middle of the *path*. Then it was gone. Again it appeared briefly and then disappeared once more. I could see the ground where it vanished and got the impression of movement, although I could not recognise what it was.

I came to a stop and directed the torch-beam steadily upon the movement. Eric halted behind me. For a few seconds I could not make out what lay on the pathway, then I knew what it was: a snake!

I increased my pace, motioning to Eric to remain where he was. Snakes have no ears, but they make up for lack of hearing by an acute sense of feeling. Through the scale upon their bellies that rest against the ground they are able to sense danger from anything that moves by detecting the vibration caused by that movement.

The boots I was wearing had soft rubber soles and I was able to approach relatively undetected. The beam of my torch was directed upon the reptile but it did not appear to be disturbed. Coming from behind, the source of the torchlight was beyond the range of the snake's vision. Snakes' eyes are lidless and fixed, and cannot turn sideways or backwards. Nor did my approach register itself upon the reptile's brain which, at the moment, was completely engrossed upon the work in hand, the swallowing of a very large bull-frog in one piece.

I was close enough now to make out the details. The snake's jaws, not being hinged together, were distended grotesquely and the gullet swollen out of all proportion. The head and one foreleg of the unfortunate frog had already disappeared down this passage, while the other three legs and the body hung limply outside. Normally, the creature should be kicking and struggling desperately to escape, but this frog was quite dead, and the reason was apparent. The snake was a cobra. The venom had killed the frog in a few seconds.

The cobra had not raised its hood in either alarm or anger, for it was still unaware of my approach, but the bulk of the bull-frog already in its gullet had sufficiently expanded the skin in the region to show up the characteristic V-mark. I was an ardent collector of snakes at that time, and the specimen before me was of outsize dimensions. I decided to catch it.

Unfortunately, the thick cloth bag I had brought for just such a purpose was with the kitbag on my back. I had to lay down the bamboo and my wet clothes before I could remove the kitbag from my back, and in all this movement the cobra became aware of our presence. It ejected the, frog it had half-swallowed, turned around to face me and raised its hood, trembling with fury.

It was a magnificent specimen, but it would slither away in another second if I failed to put it into a fighting mood, so to do this I stamped my foot heavily upon the ground a couple of feet away. The cobra responded by raising itself still higher and then struck the ground at the spot where my foot had been but a moment before.

Meanwhile I was working feverishly to get the kitbag off my shoulders, unfasten the zip and grope with my hand amongst the many miscellaneous items in search of that snake-bag. The operation took a long time. The outside of the bag was soaking wet for one thing and I was working with one hand, unable to look for the bag as I had to keep my eyes fixed upon the cobra.

At last I found it, pulled it out quickly and advanced towards the snake, which turned itself fully around to face me.

Catching a cobra is really very easy once you rivet its attention. It is only when the reptile is in rapid motion that the operation becomes difficult and entails considerable risk. In this instance, I stretched out my right hand, holding the cloth bag by its handle close to the snake's head. It quivered with fury, hissed loudly, and lunged at the bag. That is when I withdrew the bag so that the cobra, with hood fully distended, struck its head upon the ground for the second time.

One has to be quick at this moment, but there is really nothing to it. The quickness of action comes with practice. The length of bamboo on which I had slung my wet clothes was in my left hand. It came in handy now. I quickly pressed down upon the snake's neck, behind its head and above the hood, with the end of this bamboo about six inches from its tip. The ground was wet, so I had to be careful not to allow the head to slip free. Eric was to be of no assistance to me. I saw that he had retired a good ten yards away. I called to him urgently to come and hold my torch. He advanced reluctantly and took it from me.

'Hold the light steady,' I admonished. Then I stooped down, dropped the cloth bag and grasped the snake behind its neck with the thumb and forefinger of my right hand. Then I removed the bamboo. The snake coiled itself around my hand and forearm, but I uncoiled it with my left hand while urging Eric to pick up the bag.

He hesitated and I repeated, 'Hurry up; pick it up and open it.'

It seemed to me as if Eric was taking a terribly long time to do just this, but eventually the bag was held in position and I forced the coils of the snake into it. Lastly I thrust the head inside, keeping the fingers of my left hand around the neck of the bag, released the snake's head and jerked my right hand out of the bag very quickly. Almost in one motion, I closed the neck of the bag with the fingers and thumb of my left hand.

That is all there is to catching a cobra. Some people have told me that it calls for nerve. Don't you believe that. In my opinion, it is just the opposite. There should be 'no nerve', or as few as possible. For if there are nerves, the snake-catcher may not be able to catch his snake. Worse still, he may hesitate in the middle of the operation, and that would be just too bad for him! The snake would catch him then with a bite upon his finger or hand.

I took care to tie up the neck of the bag very firmly and then thrust it back into my kitbag. A few minutes later we were on our way again.

For the next thirty minutes or so our discomfort increased because of the wet and cold. It would have been nice to stop and light a fire to dry our clothing and ourselves, but the whole jungle was sodden and such an operation was out of the question. However we were young and ardently keen upon adventure. Mind conquers such obstacles and we pressed on forgetful of our physical discomfort. Except for encountering the elephants at the head of the valley, we had had no fun and we were longing for something to happen.

The stream began to flow rapidly now among steep rocks; the ground became hard and the trees and bamboos were shorter and more sparse. Larger expanses of sky were visible, and we noticed that the clouds had cleared. Myriads of stars hung over us and shone brightly.

The parallel ranges of mountains to the right and left of us, as we walked southwards, corresponded respectively to the western and eastern banks of the stream. Now we observed that they seemed to be converging upon each other while the valley narrowed to the proportions of a ravine. We could see the dark, unbroken outline of ridges and mountaintops on both sides as they towered upwards into the star-bedecked sky.

'Ayngh! Aa-u-ung! Oo-ooo ngh! Oo-ooo-ngh! Ooo-ooo-ooongh!'

We stopped in our tracks as we recognised that awesome sound. The canyon in which we were standing reverberated.

It was the call of the tiger! The animal was to our left and close ahead. It had come down the eastern range and was about to cross the stream. We extinguished our torches and hurried forwards to try to intercept it.

'Ugh! Ugh! Ugha! Ugha! Oooo-h! Ooo-h! Ooo-ooo-nigh! Aungh-ha! Ugh! Ugh'!

The call was almost continuous now. The tiger was being very noisy. Was this a sign of impatience? I seemed to detect an imperious note. Then remembered that this was the month of February. Rather late in February, admittedly, but nevertheless February still—the mating season or the tail end of it!

Here was the explanation of the prolonged semi-roars we were hearing. The beast was no tiger but a tigress. She was calling for a mate, and a tigress in this mood is not a very desirable creature to meet when unarmed.

As I have mentioned on many occasions, tigers are generally quite safe to meet, even when one is unarmed, with three exceptions—a man-eater, a wounded tiger, or a tiger in the mood for mating or in the act of mating. None of these conditions were literally fulfilled at that moment, but the third condition was very near.

The tigress continued her calling. She was but a short distance ahead now and still on our side of the stream. We were hurrying along that same bank. The stream was to our right. The flood water caused by the recent storm had abated considerably, but the stream must have been three or four feet deep at least. It the tigress intended to cross, she would have to swim.

As a rule tigers like water. Particularly in the hotter forests of Andhra Pradesh, I have come across them lying in shady pools to cool themselves when the temperature had reached over 110 degrees in the shade. But it was rather doubtful if this tigress would trust herself to cross the stream which was still foaming and frothing with the extra water fed to it from a myriad trickles reaching it from the forest on both sides.

At that moment my conjectures were interrupted by a fresh sound: 'Wrr-ung!Ar-ung! Arr-ungh! Oo-ooon!'

It was louder by far than the noise made by the tigress and the roar of water besides.

A tiger! He had heard and answered the call of a mate. The tigress heard it too. She answered with a loud 'Ugh! Ahha-ha-ha-ha!' of delight.

We were still in darkness. To flash our torches now would make our presence known. Most probably both tigers would disappear, unless they actively resented our company. Things would not be so pleasant then. But if we remained in darkness our presence would probably not be detected, as tigers have no sense of smell, while the noise of the stream would muffle any noise we might inadvertently make.

Our eyes had accustomed themselves to the starlight as we came to a halt and stood behind a tree that bordered the track. A few feet to our right was the bank of the stream. Beyond that and to our left, the jungle was a wall of darkness lit by a thousand flickering, moving lights, the fireflies that dart to and fro in ceaseless motion. The tumbling waters reflected countless stars, and here and there we could make out the darker forms of bushes or clumps of coarse grass on the bank. Of movement of any kind, we could see nothing.

Both tigers had now stopped calling. For them to meet, one or the other would have to ford the stream that lay between. The question was, which would be the one to cross? If the tigress crossed, we would be safe. If the tiger came over, both animals would be very close to us and would certainly resent our presence if they detected us.

The tigress clinched the matter by calling once more. This time she was almost mewing, like a very gruff and hoarse cat. Like all females in her circumstances, she was revelling in her position of advantage and was enticing the male to come to her; she would not condescend to go to him. Would the tiger be able to resist such a temptation?

He roared and roared again. It was a roar of defiance and challenge at the same time. Clearly he was warning all other tigers to keep away from his newly-founded mate. The tigress, still on our bank, continued her enticing mewing.

As I expected, the tiger could resist no longer. A long, dark silhouette emerged from the black wall of forest on the other bank, hesitated for a few seconds and then slid into the water of the stream.

I have already said that this watercourse is neither broad nor deep and it took him a very short time to cross. The silhouette became a solid grey form as he waded and then walked ashore, perhaps some fifty yards away.

All this while the tigress had not revealed herself. She now broke cover with a bound, herself another grey shape, leaped forward to meet the tiger with a loud growl and reared up on her hind legs to slap him across his neck. The mock-fighting in which mating tigers indulge was about to begin. Neither animal intends to hurt the other, but frequently during this fighting, through excitement or a stray bite or scratch, tempers run high and the tigress invariably gets really rough. The tiger tolerates a lot until she at last goes too far. Then he loses his temper and sets about her in real earnest.

Both animals can be badly scratched and bitten and bleed freely by the time the repeated mating is over, but both animals appear to revel in the routine, soon forget their differences and cling together as a couple till the cubs are about to be born, at which time the tigress will separate herself from her lord for a while through fear that he might devour the cubs. Thereafter they will rejoin for maybe a year, along with their cubs, when they will part to seek fresh mates with the next season, approximately two years after the last, although the cubs sometimes remain with their mother for a few months more.

We had lost our chance of beating a retreat while the going was good before the tiger crossed the stream. Now that he was only a few yards away, and moreover because the tigress was with him, the slightest movement on our part would betray our presence to one or both the animals. If that should happen, our extinction was more than probable as both the felines, and particularly the male would not tolerate our eavesdropping on their lovemaking. It is equally likely that the tigress, in the excitement of mating, would resent our presence. It was too late now, anyway, to do anything about it. The only course open to us was to sink down to earth behind the tree-trunk that hid us and hope that the mating animals would not move in our direction.

For the next hour we were compelled to listen to a pandemonium of grunts, snarls, roars, prolonged mewing and a medley of other noises as the two animals pursued their lovemaking, the sounds differing in accordance with their mood and temper at each moment. As the mating progressed to reach climax, the loveplay became rougher and rougher, until it reached a point when they were almost fighting each other tooth and nail. In mating the tiger bites the female in the neck and literally holds her down. They then separate a while and rest before starting all over again.

Several times, in the course of their gambols and struggles, they dashed hither and thither, on more than one occasion coming within ten yards of us. Occasionally, we thought we were discovered and prepared to make a dash for it, although we knew such a step would only hasten our destruction. The tree that hid us was too thick to climb, and the next was twenty feet away, but we could not climb it together. The first to reach it might possibly escape, provided the tigers did not follow him up, but the second man would be doomed. So we stayed where we were.

Finally the two felines tired of their efforts. The tigress curled up to rest like a cat, while the tiger sat on his haunches beside her to recuperate. And we wondered if they would never go away.

The placid scene was broken by a roar from the further bank. Another tiger, a male, had heard the sounds of revel and had come to see if there was chance to join in. The first tiger at once sprang to his feet to give an answering roar in challenge to the newcomer. The tigress uncurled herself, stood on her four legs twitched her tail from side to side, and then settled down on her haunches. Clearly she was enjoying the situation, no doubt extremely pleased with herself at the prospect of two males about to engage in a titanic contest on her account.

The tiger on the further bank answered the challenge with roars of his own. Then he broke cover and stood revealed. Now the two males faced each other, the stream between them. The tigress, upon her haunches still, snarled mildly, mewed and almost purred in glee. It was obvious she was enjoying herself. This provoked the first tiger beyond endurance. Coughing a loud 'Whoff! Whoff! Whoff!,' he entered the stream and rushed at his rival. The level of the water appeared to have dropped appreciably, for this time he was able to wade the whole distance.

The challenger awaited his coming, coughing and roaring. The first tiger reached the other bank, crouched low for a moment, and then hurled himself at his rival.

But something quite unexpected happened at the last moment. All this while the newcomer had given every indication that he was prepared to stand and do battle for the handsome female across the stream, but as her first lover crouched for his final spring, his courage turned to water. He whirled around and bolted for dear life. Seeing this and gathering momentum the first tiger charged after him with a series of victorious roars.

The female on our bank, disappointed that there was not going to be a fight for her favours, but anxious now to endear herself to her lord, coughed once and galloped across the stream to follow the two males that had vanished into the blackness of the jungle.

At that Eric and I lost no time. We raced away to get out of the vicinity of the three tigers and leave them to settle their lovemaking problems. We stumbled along through the gloom for the best part of half a mile before we risked switching on our torches again, for we did not dare to attract the attention of the three animals who had gone up the rising ground across the stream and might return at any moment.

From the contours of the surrounding mountains as silhouetted against the sky, I knew we were approaching the hamlet of Kempekarai. It was here that I shot the tiger I called the 'Novice of Manchi'. At this point the pathway we were following crossed the stream and we waded through the water which now reached just above our knees. The track leads up a slope to the hamlet, and we followed it till we reached the mud-wattle huts of Kempekarai.

A cur barked but none of the inmates bothered to stir, and it was only after repeated calling that a very tousled and sleepy head was thrust from a slightly-opened doorway. The half-closed eyes blinked in the glare of my torch. The head and eyes were those of my old friend Byra the Poojaree, of whom I have told you in other stories. For the greater part of the year this man lived with his wife and children almost stark naked in a burrow called 'gavvies' excavated in the steep banks of the Chinar river. When the rains came and the Chinar rose and the earth of the 'gavvies' turned too soft and was liable to collapse and close the burrow in which they lived, the whole family took service as cattle-grazers under some rich agriculturist, who sent his herd of cattle into the reserved forests to graze upon the long grass that spring up after the rains.

The agriculturist had to pay in licence to the government for grazing his cattle. In those days this fee was four *annas* (a fraction below four pence) per head for the whole period of five months grazing. The usual procedure was to buy a licence for about fifty head of cattle, paying the government twelve-and-a-half rupees as grazing fee (at the rate of sixteen *annas* to the rupee), but to drive anything up to 200 head—or even more—into the forest. A small gratuity of five rupees to the forest guard would cover the grazing fee for the remaining 150 unlicensed animals.

To look after these 200 beasts, Byra and his family would have to build what was called a *patti*, which was nothing more than a small clearing in the jungle. A smaller circular fence of thorns was constructed within this clearing for actually sheltering the cattle from wild animals at night. It was in the style of the African 'boma', with the difference that, as there are no lions in south India, the thorn fence would not be more than a yard in height and not very thick either. Tigers and panthers are not given to vaulting over thorn fences and carrying off their prey, as are the more daring lions of Africa that hunt in groups.

The hamlet of Kempekarai was nothing more than a multiple cattle *patti*, accommodating not only Byra and his family but a number of other families as well, all of them engaged in looking after different herds of cattle belonging to different owners. As a result, the animals actually in residence at any of these multiple *pattis* exceeded, by at least five times, the stipulated number of cattle permitted to graze in that area under licence from the forest department; the government got less than one-fifth of the revenue in cattle-licences that it should have collected; the forest guard received an amount in bribes at least equal to, if not more than, his official salary; the owners of the herds had made a good arrangement; the grass, shrubs and the saplings of certain varieties of succulent trees were eaten down and destroyed over a large area of forest; the deer suffered by losing that amount of grazing; 'foot-and-mouth' disease, rife among village cattle, spread and decimated the deer, bison and wild boar in the jungle; and everybody was happy, including the tigers and panthers in the area, who with easier hunting got a good deal more to eat, preying upon the domestic herds. Happiest of all were the jackals, hyaenas and vultures that ate the cattle that died, whether by disease or by being killed by other wild animals.

This is indeed a true picture of the state of affairs in those good old days till a certain deadly poison was introduced as an insecticide by the government and made available to farmers, almost free of charge, to protect the crops from insect pests.

Some peasant then discovered that the insecticide, intended to kill caterpillars, beetles and other such pests, would also kill tigers and panthers that preyed upon the domestic herds and, far more important, unwanted mothers-in-law, brother-in-law, in fact all 'in-laws' of both sexes and all ages with happy impartiality, not to mention secret lovers, rivals, elder brothers who were so inconsiderate as to inherit the property when father died, and a whole host of other unwanted characters into the bargain. To put it in a nutshell, opportunity was rife for those who were disgruntled in one way or another.

The carcasses of cattle killed by tigers and panthers were systematically doctored with the result that the felines died in hundreds and have been almost wiped out in southern India. Along with them jackals, hyaenas and vultures, who shared these kills, perished in still larger numbers. There was also a sharp rise in the number of in-laws and other inconvenient people who began to succumb, suddenly, mysteriously and in increasing numbers, to violent stomachache and other alarming symptoms. Life is cheap and nobody worried unduly, while the statisticians were compensated slightly in the other graph they were maintaining with regard to the vexatious problem of 'Population Explosion and Family Planning' which happened to coincide with the advent of the poison.

To this day, unlicensed still exceed the licensed cattle by many times. The owners save that much money in license fees, the forest guards draw more than their salary now, the government loses much more, and everyone is still happy. The only difference from the old days is that there are now no tigers, panthers, hyaenas, jackals or even vultures to join in the general rejoicing. Nearly all are dead—poisoned.

Incidentally, the villagers were not taking very kindly to the family-planning programmes. In fact, the greater number of them were distinctly annoyed about the whole thing. On the one hand, they were being urged to mechanise their farming methods and give up the old-fashioned, cattle-drawn wooden ploughs of their forefathers. At the same time, the cost of living and the prices of all commodities were rising day by day. The monsoon had a knack of not arriving when it should and of coming when it should not. Either way their crops failed. Landlords were more grasping and so were the moneylenders. The government had tried to help all it could by distributing land, oxen and ploughs free of cost to any family in order to assist farmers who preferred to stick to the old style; but money, that root of all evil, was a temptation, and the oxen and ploughs were sold or mortgaged shortly after they were distributed. The land would have followed suit as well, but that was rather too great a risk to take, being immovable property.

Finally, the price of kerosene was increasing by leaps and bounds. One could not afford to burn the midnight oil. An early dinner and early to bed became the golden rule.

In the midst of all these troubles, the poor ryot had but one consolation left to him—his cherished and beloved wife. At least she belonged to him, to do with as he wanted. What with rising costs, no kerosene, an early dinner and early to bed, he had at least some opportunity here. She was the one solid item that was entirely his own. But at this stage along came these Family Planning people with their ridiculous advice, offering strange devices their forefathers had never heard of and begrudging the poor farmer the one and only pleasure and recreation available to him in these hard days.

So the statisticians were worried at the still steadily rising curve of population, although a trifle relieved that here and there would appear a slight kink in it, caused by the untimely demise of some in-laws and others who had succumbed to a sudden unaccountable and unbearable stomach pain that had come on immediately after dinner.

All of which brings us back to Byra the poojaree, my old friend of the jungle. Byra was very happy when he discovered that the visitor arriving at such an unearthly hour was none other than myself. He crawled out of the narrow doorway of his hut and offered the accustomed greeting of the poojarees by touching his forehead to the ground before me. Then we sat down for a chat and I told him the reason for our presence.

The jungle man was surprised and not a little concerned at the fact that we were unarmed. He thought that we were taking too great a risk, especially with elephants, and gave us the disconcerting news that there was a particularly 'bad' elephant roaming that part of the valley we had yet to negotiate. Whereas this elephant had not yet been proclaimed a 'rogue', inasmuch as it had not actually killed anybody; it was an animal that charged on sight and only the fleetness of foot and jungle-cunning of the poojarees of Kempekarai had saved them, at least so far. Byra doubted that we had that fleetness or cunning and advised us not to continue our journey that night.

'Wait for daylight,' he advised. 'At least, then you will be able to see where you are running when he chases you, although I doubt that will do you much good.'

The other reason why Byra was annoyed by the fact that we were not carrying firearms was his hope that he might have persuaded one or other of us to shoot a sambar or spotted deer for his family and himself to eat. This was Byra's only weakness, his craving for meat. Every time we met it was the same thing. He would pester me to shoot a deer or sambar, and just as steadfastly I refused. Money I was ready to give him, but I had explained a hundred times that I do not like killing deer and sambar. Although he has never succeeded in his efforts to break me down on this point, Byra never fails to try and try again. Possibly he thinks that he will wear me down eventually, and so must have our preliminary struggle every time we meet.

Eric and I decided to eat and bring out our sandwiches. Unfortunately they contained beef, an ingredient that is forbidden to nearly all south Indians, including the humblest forest folk. The cow is sacred, and to eat its flesh is outrageously and unthinkably sinful. So although we did not make the mistake of offering him any, there was a distinct look of disapproval on Byra's simple face. Eating beef was one of two things that he held against me; of the other I have just spoken. On all other matters he felt we were buddies or, to use a slang expression, 'as thick as thieves'.

Considering he had never been to school, this man, aborigine as he was, was an authority on jungle medicines obtained from flowers, fruits, leaves, roots and barks of various trees and herbs. He was the 'doctor' of the surrounding poojaree community and had been summoned in emergencies to cure all sorts of illnesses.

He had a secret remedy for snakebite, and had not lost a single case, or so he said. I know for a fact he cured two cases of cholera when that dreaded epidemic spread to his community, and, as I have mentioned in one of my books, he delivered his own wife when she was having her baby.

I have witnessed this and his method was very simple. He prepared a shallow hollow in the sands of the nearest stream, and into this hollow he put a thick layer of green leaves. In this hollow his wife lay down on her back. Next he got a torn piece of saree cloth and tied one end to the soles of her feet. This cloth was only long enough to reach to her knees. Byra gave this end to hold with both hands, and to do so the woman had to part her thighs and knees, which she raised off the ground. Byra then instructed her to pull hard upon the end, whereupon, with hardly a whisper, the baby was born and Byra welcomed it into this world by raising it by the heels and slapping it on the back. He had no scissors, so the sharp end of a stone or mussel-shell (which could be found along the banks of most steams), operating against a flat stone, served to sever the cord.

Within half an hour of the appearance of the placenta, the wife rose, suckled her infant and walked away. Byra then shovelled the sand into the hollow until it was entirely filled.

Knowing my weakness for tea Byra had already made a fire, and on this I placed my canteen filled with water from the stream. It was very muddy and the resultant brew was rather substandard. I told the poojaree of our encounter with the three tigers not far upstream, and he said that these three were the only ones in residence there at that moment. There had been another female, but she had wandered away some months earlier and had not returned. He went on to say that frequently one or other of the three tigers would attack the herds while the cattle were grazing in the forest and kill one of the cows.

The tigress had been calling quite a lot recently, he confirmed. The poojarees in the hamlet had heard her only two nights earlier.

All three animals were cattle-lifters, but none of them had shown any inclination to attack the graziers, who had frequently driven them away from their kills to salvage the hides for drying and sale. He added that there was also a pair of panthers living on the other side of the stream that occasionally killed a stray cow if opportunity allowed. A month earlier, one of these panthers had pulled down a calf and was killing it when one of the tigers rushed out of the undergrowth, put the panther to flight and carried the calf away, slung across its back.

We stood up to leave, when Byra once again remonstrated about the great risk we were running with the 'bad' elephant. However, to remain in shelter at the *patti* for the rest of the night was not jungle 'ghooming', and ghooming was the purpose of the trip. We explained this to the poojaree and shouldered our loads, but not before I checked to make certain that the cobra was still safely secured.

'Very well then; I will go with you', the little man announced. 'When the sun rises I will return. Till then, I shall remain with you and offer what protection lies in my power. I don't think you realise the danger you will be in if you happen to meet the elephant in this darkness', he stressed, 'for the beast will be upon you before you know where you are and crush you to a pulp.'

With these ominous words in our ears we left Kempekarai and headed downhill to the stream. I led, shining the torch; Byra followed me, while Eric brought up the rear. We reached and crossed the water and followed the narrow *path* before us into the labyrinths of the jungle. It was distinctly chilly and a junglecock, crowing among the bamboos, reminded us it was two in the morning. Like their cousins, the domestic roosters, wild cocks follow the same habits in the jungles that are not unduly disturbed by men or too many wild cats. They crow at two and at four in the morning, and just after the false dawn, usually before six o'clock.

We might have covered a half-mile when Byra stepped up from behind and halted me with his hand upon my arm. He reached forward to extinguish the torch. Eric half-asleep now collided with us before he realised we had stopped. I strained my ears, but heard no sound. The junglecock had passed out of hearing range.

The stars cast a sheen over the forest that was quite different from moonlight. It was a soft and ethereal light that just succeeded in making itself felt in the darkness without breaking its dominion. The forest that surrounded us was as black as a bottomless pit, the starlight being enough only to see each other and the few yards around us.

I looked at Byra inquiringly. He touched his nose with the forefinger and thumb of his left hand, at the same time swinging his right arm, from elbow downwards, to right and left before him.

The elephant! Byra could smell it! It must be very close indeed, or the poojaree would have whispered his message in my ear.

I wrinkled my nose in an effort to catch the scent. At the same time I turned my head sideways, one cheek in the direction we were moving and the other in the direction whence we had come. I fancied I could detect a peculiar odour which within a few seconds I began to associate with the presence of an elephant. These animals smell strongly when they are close. But perhaps it was a figment of my imagination.

My cheeks told me there was hardly a breeze blowing from any direction, a fact that was neither good nor bad. Had the breeze been blowing from behind us, the elephant—provided there was one ahead—would have scented us by now. Had the breeze been blowing from him to us, we might have been able, exercising the greatest caution, to creep past him undetected. As matters stood, with practically no breeze in any direction, our situation was one of stalemate. The elephant—supposing there was one ahead—had not so far detected our presence. But he was bound to do so if we moved any closer. Even if he did not scent us, he would certainly hear us in that deathly silence.

Byra had come to the same conclusion much earlier. He raised his right palm at waist level. The signal was plain as if he had spoken:

'Wait!' Tensely we stood quite motionless.

The moments dragged by. We heard no sound. I could smell the strange odour still, but I could not associate it with an elephant. Perhaps Byra was wrong after all and there was no elephant before us.

Then the silence was broken. We heard a rustling sound, growing louder and heavier and moving along the pathway on which we were standing. Byra had been right. There was an elephant ahead, and he was moving through the undergrowth in our direction. It was only a matter of seconds before he would emerge upon the pathway.

Byra signalled to us to retreat and gave the lead by turning around and walking on tiptoe down the track along which we had just come. Eric followed, and I brought up the rear.

At that moment the breeze decided to take a hand. A gust blew strongly down the valley, passing over us and directly towards the elephant. The cat was now out of the bag!

The elephant scented us and in the next instant was crashing through the rest of the undergrowth. He came out upon the track behind me. Still retreating, all three of us turned around. We could see his colossal black bulk now, like a great big black rock astride the track. Two long streaks of white stood out against that blackness. His tusks!

A moment later and we knew, indeed, that this was the 'bad' elephant about which Byra had warned us. For no sooner did the beast set eyes upon us than he recognised us for his avowed enemies—men. He trumpeted his shriek of hate and came charging towards us, looking blacker and bigger at every instant.

To run away would be hopeless. At so short a distance no man can escape a charging elephant. Either Eric or myself, encumbered as we both were with our loads, would fall a prey to this monster. He would smash to a jelly whichever one of us he caught first. To try to dodge into the bushes either to right or left was equally hopeless because of the darkness. It looked as if only Byra would live to tell the tale.

I did the only thing possible in the circumstances. I took a very flimsy chance. I stopped, turned around. At the same time I yelled with all my might.

The bright beam fell fully upon the monster, scarcely ten feet away. In a peculiarly detached and interested fashion, I noticed that the animal had curled in his trunk, that his head was raised, showing a half-opened mouth, and that the points of his tusks were in line with his small, gleaming, wicked eyes. He lowered his head to bring those tusks into line with me and thus let the torchlight fully into his eyes. The next instant a cloud of dust hid the ground and the elephant's legs.

I was still screaming when I realised that the brute had come to a halt. Braking suddenly, by planting his four great feet in the ground, was the cause of the dust.

I did not know it then, but seeing the peril I was in made Byra stop, turn around and come to my assistance. He was screaming too, I suddenly realised; words of ludicrous, vile abuse to the elephant, all of its kind and its ancestors. Eric had dashed past him and was still in full flight. He did not mean to desert me but had not realised that the elephant was so close as to compel me to turn around and face him.

The next few moments were electric. What was going to happen next was a matter of life or death. Would the pachyderm press his attack home, or would Byra and I succeed in turning him?

With sinking heart I remembered Byra's words of warning, uttered but a short while earlier. Once it charged, nothing would stop this elephant.

The monster shook his head from right to left and back again several times, with the purpose of avoiding the piercing beam of my torch that shone fully into his eyes. But I followed his movements with my torch, still shouting lustily.

The brute stood his ground. Then I took the last chance left. Yelling like a maniac, I stepped forward sharply, directing the beam fully into those small, wicked eyes. Then his courage broke, he turned half around so that his huge bulk, facing broadside on, straddled the narrow track.

Without speaking to each other, Byra and I knew that it was now or never. With concerted shouts, we rushed towards the monster, my torch still shining directly upon its head. The elephant was unnerved. Like all big bullies, he was accustomed to attack and see his enemies scatter like chaff before the wind. Never before had any puny creature dared to attack him.

That was exactly what was happening now. He could not get that glaring light out of his eyes and our discordant screams were unnerving him. So he lumbered up the pathway away from us, Byra and I behind him, still shouting at the top of our voices. To shake us off, he swerved sharply to the left and crashed through the undergrowth.

Byra and I came to a stop. We had accomplished his rout. Now we had to get away as quickly as possible. Turning once again we walked back the way we had come. It would not do for us to run, for that might bring the elephant back. We could find no traces of Eric!

It was but half-a-mile to the spot where we had to cross the stream to return to Kempekarai, but Eric did not know the place. Probably he had passed it and continued along the track beyond.

Byra broke into a trot to try overtake him, while I walked rapidly on. I was not feeling so good. In fact, I was feeling awfully sick and I noticed that I was shaking as if in fever and did not seem to be able to stop. Also I was soaking wet—perspiration no doubt, although I did not remember perspiring so much. I toyed with the idea of sitting down for a few moments but the thought came to me that the black devil might change its mind and return to the attack. So I walked all the faster. Very soon I reached the ford leading to Kempekarai, and there was no sign of Eric or Byra.

I splashed through the stream and climbed the winding *path* to the hamlet. Reaching the huts I threw myself on the ground to get rid of the nausea that had not yet passed away.

It was some time before Byra arrived with Eric. The poojaree told me that my friend was a good runner. He had to follow for almost two miles before he succeeded in overtaking Eric. Eric's version was that when he glanced back, but could see neither Byra nor myself, he concluded that the elephant had got both of us. This had made him run all the faster.

Byra seemed quite unperturbed by our recent adventure. To him it was part of everyday forest existence. He suggested we brew some tea. If there was one thing Byra had a weakness for, it was tea. So have I, but for once I did not feel up to drinking any. Throwing down my haversack, I told him and Eric to help themselves. Then I lay down on the bare earth and fell asleep.

The sun was shining brightly when I awoke. Eric was sleeping soundly close by, lying neatly on his groundsheet, covered with a light blanket. Byra was coiled almost into a ball by the side of a small fire that had long gone out. His head was touching his knees.

My teeth were chattering with the cold. Lying on the ground with no covering had made matters worse. In the chill of the morning, when enthusiasm is usually at an ebb, I wondered if the risks we had taken the previous night were justified. I remembered reading in an article somewhere or the other, that it is at such a time—when one first awakens—that the influence of the subconscious mind is at its strongest, and the impressions one receives at the moment conveyed the wisest and best advice. It went on to say that, should the recipient follow this advice, he would prosper and avoid the pitfalls of living. But these few moments of good sense pass all too swiftly, the article continued, to give place to the individual's own individuality and way of thinking, and he then relapses into his own fixed ideas.

I fear this is what happened to me, for those minutes of common sense were put aside. I aroused Eric and Byra, and while the latter relit the fire to brew our tea, Eric and I went down to the stream for a cold bath and brush-up. It is wonderful what a bath in a mountain stream will do for the cobwebs in one's brain, and for muscles that ache and eyes that are still heavy from insufficient sleep.

By the time we returned, Byra had not only boiled the water and made the tea, but had drunk more than half of it himself. He offered a ready excuse for this by saying that he felt the fever coming on, and as the *dorai* knew very well, plenty of tea is the only prescription for averting fever. I replied that the *dorai* had never known this but would bear it in mind by dishing out less of the ingredients that go to make the beverage the next time. Then Eric and I finished what was left.

A cold breakfast, followed by a smoke and some desultory chat, led Byra to ask what we intended doing next. I replied that we would sleep for most of that day and start again with nightfall to finish our journey at the point where the stream joins the Chinar river. This we expected to reach about midnight. After another short rest, we would start to return, accomplishing the trip this time by daylight. We hoped to get to Aiyur by dusk the following evening, when 'Sudden Death' ought to get us back to Bangalore in time for dinner.

The poojaree was not happy to learn our plans. He implied, by indirect comparison with a donkey which, in spite of being repeatedly beaten yet refuses to go forward, that we had failed to learn our lesson at the hands of the elephant, by wanting to pass through his domain once again after darkness. He suggested we start about two in the afternoon instead, when all pachyderms take, or should take, their siestas by standing asleep in the shelter of some thick clump of tress, so that by nightfall we should be well away from the places where *pisachee* (devil) usually hung out. Of course, if our luck was bad, he might have gone further afield, in which case we might still run into him, but at least that risk was not as great as would be the case by starting after dark. Byra also insisted upon accompanying us as far as the Chinar River and back again, saying he would not leave us till we were at least five miles on the return journey between Kempekarai and Aiyur, where we had left the car.

We discussed the matter and wiser, if less adventurous, counsel prevailed. We decided to follow Byra's plan and, as there was nothing better to do, we fell asleep. Soon after midday we ate a cold lunch, followed by more tea, and at exactly two o'clock were on our way again, retracing our steps on the narrow pathway along which we had so precipitously bolted the night before. But this time we could look about us and take all possible precautions by testing the wind and keeping a sharp lookout for signs of the elephant.

We were unlucky from the start. A strong wind was blowing from north to south, that is, down the stream from behind us and in the direction we were going. It would inform the rogue of our approach should he be anywhere ahead.

Plainly, on the damp earth of the narrow pathway, we could see our own footmarks: the blurred impressions of Eric's rubber shoes, the larger marks made by my own alpaca-lined boots, Byra's bare footsteps, and imposed upon them all the ponderous, almost dish-sized tracks left by the elephant that had chased us the night before.

Byra was in front. Every now and then he stopped to test the wind by plucking a few blades of grass from the ground and dropping them from shoulder-height. Imperceptibly, they fell to earth at a slight angle ahead of us. The wind was still blowing from behind.

Byra stopped to listen. We halted and listened too. The forest was athrob with life. Birds twittered all round. We could hear their more distant calls from the hillsides to right and left. Cicadas and crickets of all varieties chirped in different cadences. The single, shrill resonance of the plains-cicada is here mixed with the rising and falling sonority of the hill variety, smaller in size than its cousin of lower-lying areas but capable of emitting a far louder sound. Then a myriad crickets of all sizes, ensconced beneath leaves or hidden under rotting logs of wood, joined in the general vibration of insect vociferation, filling the air with the sound of throbbing, omnipresent life.

Far ahead of us a barking-deer learned of our approach. The wind blowing down the valley told him. 'Kharr!' he cried, and again and again 'Kharr! Kharr!'

The langur monkeys, high up on both hillsides, heard him. 'Whoomp! Whoomp! Whoomp!' they shouted in sheer glee, leaping from branch to branch and rock to rock. But the little barking-deer continued his alarm-cry.

This worried the langurs. Their whoomps of joy died down. Now they were silent. I could picture the langur-watchman, seated on tree-top, peering hard into the valley below, trying to discover the nature of the danger that had alarmed the little deer. The shaggy brows in his round black face must be beetled with worry and uncertainty; his large, round, black eyes must be searching the streambed far below and such game-paths as were visible to him from that height, in an effort to see the foe. He was responsible for the safety and lives of the numerous she-monkeys and babies of the tribe gambolling in innocence around him. Should he fail in his duty, by failing to give the alarm, one of them would die. No doubt he thought that at any moment he would see the stripes of a tiger or the spotted coat of a panther slinking from bush to bush.

He saw nothing, for we were yet too far away.

Nevertheless the little deer, whose keen sense of smell had told him of something the langur could not see, announced our approach by continuing to bark and bark, 'Kharr! Kharr! Kharr!'

The langur-watchman became increasingly uneasy. What kind of foe was this, approaching but invisible?

At last he could stand the tension of uncertainty no longer. He had to warn the tribe. 'Harr! Ha!' he shouted gutturally, and again in quick succession, 'Harr! Ha! Harr! Ha!'

The alarm had its effect at once. Although we could not see or hear them, there followed a hundred thuds as langur-mothers clutched their babies to their breasts and leapt prodigious distances to safety in the loftiest tree-tops. Others scampered up rocks or ran up the hillside. A hundred black faces turned in anxiety to their watchman. What enemy had he seen? His next action would tell them.

If a tiger or panther were approaching, the watchman would, surely leap from his tree-top to another. He would stand on his two feet, with long tail erect to keep his balance, look downwards and abuse the enemy in langur-language.

The watchman did none of these things. He still had not seen us. So he continued his alarm, 'Harr! Ha!' and again 'Harr! Ha!' A sambar stag, resting on a bed of high grasses somewhere up the mountainside to our left, heard the commotion. He sprang to his feet and cried 'Dhank! Dhank! Honk!' These signals of alarm from the different denizens of the forest had not sounded in vain. They were heard by listening and understanding ears. Ponderous ears, indeed. For at that precise moment the elephant struck again.

Decades old, and wise in the ways of the jungle, he had been hearkening and hiding in motionless silence. He had heard the alarm-cry of the barking-deer, the calls of the langur-watchman and the belling of the disturbed sambar stag. Undoubtedly he had smelt us, too, for he was standing much nearer and knew that it was the hated human foe who had come again.

He made up his mind quickly. This time he was not going to fail in his purpose. His purpose was to destroy one of the hated, two-legged foes. He would wait in silence till we walked right up to him. Then and then only would he charge. By this means he was sure to catch one of us.

We knew nothing of his presence or what was passing in his evil mind. Despite his size, he remained hidden by a rock to our left behind which he had taken up his position. For once Byra, man of the forests as he was and versed in jungle-lore from childhood, and with unnumbered generations of jungle-ancestors before him, was deceived. Walking warily in the lead, with Eric and myself following light-footed behind, he moved forward step by step.

Byra saw the big rock to his left and halted to study it carefully. We saw it, too, and stopped to look. It was a large, high, loaf-shaped rock, almost black in colour except for two large patches of grey lichen growing upon its surface. A fig tree clung to one side of it. We noticed that some of the roots of this tree had run over the rock. One root strayed down the side, resembling a long, thick, light-coloured snake going into the ground.

All this we saw. But we did not see the elephant hiding behind that rock, because he made neither sound nor movement.

Byra was satisfied that there was no danger and that it was safe to proceed. He walked forwards slowly. We followed.

Now we stood abreast to the rock. Now we began to pass it. The elephant knew then that in another second we would see him. He also knew that now we were so close that he must be able to catch at least one of us. He made up his mind.

An ear-splitting scream rent the silence: 'Tri-aa-aa-ank!'

Then he was upon us. He meant business this time for he did not utter another sound. From behind the rock his black form emerged. The great trunk was coiled inwards like a giant snake, behind high-thrown head and flattened ear. His mouth was half-open.

Eric, in front of me, turned and ran. So did I. Instinctively, Byra knew that if he followed he would be caught, as he would be a third man running behind two others, who would baulk him. He decided to swerve and try to escape by running downhill and across the stream which flowed parallel to the pathway we were following.

He had no chance. The elephant was upon him. It uttered a short and muffled half-scream, above which I heard Byra's shriek of despair. There was 'whoosh' followed by a thud.

The elephant then gave vent to his rage by trumpeting repeatedly: 'Tri-aaa-ank! Tri-aaa-ank! Tri-aa-ank!'

I was running as fast as my clumsy boots would let me. Eric younger in years, lighter in build, and wearing soft shoes, overtook me and disappeared ahead. I am ashamed to say that I continued to run. I know I should have stopped and gone to Byra's aid. Of small consolation was the thought that unarmed as I was, there was nothing I could do, and as the elephant was thoroughly enraged my shouts would not deter him. The night before, my torch beam in the darkness had confused him. Now he would finish me off as well.

The elephant had stopped. I could hear him screaming still. He was probably trampling poor Byra to pulp.

I reached the crossing. Eric was on the other side of the stream. A short distance higher lay Kempekarai and safety. As hurriedly as possible we recruited all the poojarees in the hamlet. Torches of wood and grasses were made. Embers to light them were carried in broken pots. Two dozen in number, we recrossed the stream, set the torches alight, and with the whole party shouting at the top of their voices, we set forth to gather what remained of my poor friend.

The elephant was silent, although we expected him to show at any moment. Would he charge our party?

I did not think so. We were two dozen strong and we were making a terrific noise.

The next moment we saw him. He was standing squarely upon the pathway. Irritably, he was shaking his head from side to side, his great trunk wagging along with the motion. His ears were flapping forwards. We could see his bloodshot little eyes staring at us. Clearly he was undecided as to whether to charge or beat a retreat.

Each member of our party excelled himself that day. Every one was shouting louder still, if that were possible. The elephant continued to hesitate. Then his nerve failed. He turned about; then he faced around again. Unexpectedly, he made off up the hill to our left. We advanced cautiously, continuing to yell.

At each moment we expected to come across the remains of the luckless Byra, squashed to a pulp. I could picture the little man before me, his grin spreading from ear to ear, and two jet-black little eyes gleaming with laughter. The vision choked me. I could join in the shouting no longer. The little man had sacrificed his life to save us. Had he escaped, the elephant would have followed and got one of us. Eric, walking beside me, looked grim, although he continued to yell with the rest.

But we could not find the remains of what had once been Byra, although we searched everywhere. Could he have escaped?

We spread out to search in an ever-widening circle, but still there was no sign. Hope began to dawn in each of us. Just then, I heard what sounded like a faint groan. A couple of the poojarees near me had heard it too. We stopped to listen, but there was no other sound.

My companions, always superstitious, began to grow afraid. Three of us had clearly heard that groan. Some spirit must have made the sound. Maybe Byra's spirit. The two who heard cast fearful glances at me. A few moments more and perhaps they would take off.

Then I clearly heard the word '*Dorai*'. It came very faintly, but there was no doubt about it. But from where? There was nothing in sight but grass and trees—and the big black rock.

The solution came in a flash. Byra was alive, and he was on top of that rock. How did he get there? Why, the elephant threw him there, of course!

I told my two companions the good news. In a trice they had clambered up the steep sides of the rock, and then we heard their joyful shouts: 'He's alive! Byra is alive!'

All of us grouped around the rock while the two men on top called out that Byra had said the elephant had thrown him up in the air. Luckily, he had fallen on top of the rock, where the beast could not get at him again. Had he fallen back to the ground, he would certainly have been crushed.

Then came bad news: 'His leg is broken, *Dorai*. Broken at the thigh.' Removing my clumsy boots, I managed to get up the rock aided by my two companions pulling from above and others pushing from below. I found Byra with his thigh broken, but he was still smiling!

Possibly the elephant had seized him by the leg and broken the bone when it threw him. Perhaps falling on the hard rock was the cause. However, the all-important fact was that Byra was still alive. We made a stretcher out of branches, jungle-vines and soft, green leaves.

As tenderly as we could, we moved him on to this. Meanwhile I sent for ropes from Kempekarai. Fastening these to the ends of the rough stretcher, we lowered him off the rock as gently as possible. Then we carried him back to the hamlet.

I had a difficult task to persuade Byra to let me take him to a hospital in Bangalore. He wanted to remain at Kempekarai until the ends of his broken thighbone joined.

Many jungle medicines and leaves possess marvellous healing properties. No doubt the end of the broken bone would unite. But would they join straight? Would Byra be able to walk normally again? I stressed these things and urged him to let me take him to hospital, but it was nightfall before I got his consent. The people of the forest are very afraid of our hospitals.

We set forth for Aiyur at break of day, willing hands bearing the stretcher, but it was very difficult to fasten the stretcher across the open box-machan that formed the body of 'Sudden Death,' my Model T Ford. At last it was done and by slow driving, avoiding the many potholes, it still took us a long time to reach the hospital at Bangalore.

There we created a sensation. Every doctor, nurse and ward-boy present, and every patient who could hobble and was not at death's door turned out to see the strange sight. It is not often that one comes across a car without a body, with no mudguards or driving seat, but with only an open box tied to it behind, and balancing precariously upon that open box a fragile stretcher of jungle wood, vines and leaves holding a small man, practically naked, with a broken thigh.

In four months Byra could walk as well as ever. The broken thighbone joined perfectly. The doctor said he had been a good patient. I know that the only thoughts that had sustained him throughout this period of pain and adversity were visions of his beloved jungles, and their mountains and streams.

It was a glad day when I took him back by car to Aiyur and walked with him to Kempekarai. We had to do it in slow stages. This time you may be sure I did not take Eric. For one I did not want to tempt the jinx that seemed to accompany this friend of my schooldays.

I almost forgot to relate that I was compelled to release the cobra I had caught two nights earlier when we were carrying Byra to the car. It would have been an added burden and a nuisance on the journey.

2

Some Indian Game Sanctuaries

I have had the privilege of visiting five of the game sanctuaries of northern India. These five, and a number of others, have been created by the government in a last minute attempt to save some of the noblest animals of the subcontinent from extinction. Among these creatures are the Asian lion that is found only in the Gir forest of Gujarat state, the one-horned rhinoceros that lives in the northeastern extremity of the country in the state of Assam and in Nepal, the Indian wild buffalo found roughly in the same localities as the one-horned rhino, and the swamp deer, sometimes called the *barasingha* (meaning 'twelve-horned deer'), because of the twelve tines that adorn this magnificent animal, six upon either antler.

I began a tour of five sanctuaries in the company of two American friends and a Canadian, and as I maintained a day-to-day record of all that happened, I had better present the facts as they occurred. As far as I was concerned, the journey started when I left the airport of Bangalore for Bombay on the morning of March 3, 1970. It was a smooth fast flight, with nothing much of interest to see. We flew over Belgaum and soon saw smoke rising from several forest fires that were raging on the ghats between Poona and Bombay.

In exactly one and a half hours we touched down at the Santa Cruz airport at Bombay, whence I went by taxi to the Nataraj Hotel, which was the arranged rendezvous with the other members of the party, whose plane, however, arrived only after a fifteen-hour delay.

Eventually we started one morning for the small airport of Keshod in Gujarat state, from which point air-passengers are conveyed to the heart of the Gir forest, where we had booked rooms in the spacious forest lodge, where travellers are generally accommodated. The plane—a Dakota magnificently dolled up and in excellent flying condition—carried us across the small strip of the Arabian Sea which separates the city of Bombay from the peninsula of Saurashtra, which forms the western portion of Gujarat state. We flew over several steamers and noticed shoals of dolphins leaping from the waves.

The airport of Keshod is a few miles inland. There we were met by the van that was to convey us to the settlement of Sasan Gir, fifty-five miles distant, in the heart of the forest of the lions. En route we passed the port of Veraval with its ancient Somnath temple. There is a legend here that when the Mohammedan invader, Mohammed of Ghazni, planned to destroy this edifice in 1026, two thousand Brahmins poured holy water, brought all the way from the Ganges river, upon the idols, and strewed flowers over them night and day, to win the grace of the Gods and avert disaster. Mohammed of Ghazni never destroyed the temple.

The road was dry and dusty and the forest, when we reached it, was equally dry, rather open, sprinkled with *babul* trees and interspersed with dwarf teak and not too many thorns. Except for the teak, the scenery was reminiscent of Africa.

The 'Guest House', which is the grandiloquent name given to the forest lodge, was comfortably furnished and the *khansama* (cook-butler-tableboy) laid out a welcoming meal. We found the officials of the Forestry department most obliging and cooperative.

What is popularly called the 'lion show' had been arranged for five o'clock that evening. A live buffalo-bait had been tied up about eight miles away and the pride of lions that had been located in the vicinity actually 'called' to the spot by the junior forest officials, corresponding in rank to the forest guards of southern India, but known in Gir as *shikarees* or *chowkidars*. Many of them are quite old, and have been in the employment of the Forestry department when the Gir forest belonged to Junagadh state and ruled by a

Muslim prince. This prince flew to Pakistan when India annexed his territories, and that was how the Gir forest became part of the province of Saurashtra in the Indian state of Gujarat. The *shikarees* and *chowkidars* were transferred to service in the government of Gujarat, but many of them still proudly display the letters J. F. (for Junagadh Forests) in polished brass on their tunics.

Incidentally, no visitor is allowed to watch the actual killing of the buffalo-bait by lions. The authorities consider that this might encourage the taking of life. But there is no objection to watching the lions feeding once that bait has been killed by them. The bait costs the visitor Rs. 150, and there is also a fee for using still or cine cameras.

It is interesting to watch the *shikarees* and *chowkidars* actually calling the wild lions. There are generally two of these men present, and they make a 'Khik! Khik! Khik!' sound with their mouths, followed by a 'Kroo! Kroo! Kroo!' noise with their lips. The wild lions appear to respond to these calls, if they do not recognize the persons who are making them and actually approach quite close to the caller.

To be on the safe side, the guards are armed with single-barrelled guns of .12 bore, loaded with buckshot. I examined the weapons carried by the men who had called the lions and found them to be as ancient as the men themselves assuredly hailing from the days of the old Junagadh forests. I then questioned the men as to why they carried these weapons, and the older of the two replied that sometimes, although very rarely, a young lion in his prime would resent the presence of onlookers in numbers, armed with cameras big and small, who keep moving around while he and the other members of the pride are eating. This animal then becomes aggressive, begins to growl and excites the rest of the pride. Then anything might happen.

'I have been dealing with lions since I was a boy, *sahib*,' he confided in Hindustani, 'and my father before me, and his father, and his father before that. Always watch the tail, *sahib*, then the eyes. And listen to any noise the animal might make. When the tail begins to twitch and rise above his back, when those large green eyes lose their roundness and start to half-close, when the whining sound he is making—or perhaps he is making no sound at all, or maybe he is just grunting—changes to a rumbling growl, he is about to charge you. Run for your life then, if you think you can. Actually it will be useless, for you won't run very far. Should none of these things happen, you are safe, although it might only be for the moment. Never can you tell when these *shaitan log* (devil people) suddenly become angry. You should always watch, watch, watch. The tail *sahib*, and those big green eyes!'

Apparently the purpose of the ancient gun and its load of buckshot was to fire in the air if necessity arose, rather than at the offending animal should it begin to evince signs of rising excitement. My informer said that the noise of the shot invariably had the effect of calming it down. Personally, I think the main purpose of the old guns was to boost the courage of those who carried them.

There was a pride of six lions on the kill when we arrived shortly after five o'clock. It consisted of two full-grown lionesses and four half-grown cubs, two cubs belonging apparently to each lioness. Unlike tigers and most other animals, all the lions seemed to be on friendly terms with each other and there were no signs of quarrelling.

As we grew bolder, we went closer and closer, till we were within thirty feet of the feasting animals. My friends, who were equipped with cameras, were taking photographs as fast as they were able. At one stage one of the lionesses, possibly disgusted at our close presence, seized the kill by a hind leg and pulled so hard at it as to break the tethering rope. She started to drag the dead buffalo away.

Then an amazing thing happened. The two chowkidars ran forward, caught hold of the dead animal by a foreleg, and started to pull in the opposite direction. It was an incredible spectacle. A tug of war between two human beings and a wild lioness, with five other lions looking on and a crowd of human spectators. I would never have believed it had anyone told me. The foresters were no match for the lioness, who started dragging them along with the kill. Then, amazingly, they let go of the leg they were pulling and ran forward towards the lioness, shouting in unison at the pitch of their lungs. The lioness released her hold, leaped backwards, and stood erect to look at the two men wistfully.

The other five lions were watching the scene with interest. We continued to regard it with amazement. Hastily, and not without considerable effort, the two men dragged the bait back to the tree to which it had been secured, and re-tethered it. I then lost my regard for the ferocity of the lions of Gir. As if nothing whatsoever had happened, all the lions returned to their meal, and in less than an hour there was not much left of the buffalo but bones.

The cubs, now replete with meat, began to take an interest in us. Their mothers, also full, rolled on to their sides and went to sleep. The sun was low in the western horizon.

Seeing themselves free of parental interference for once, two of the youngsters bounded playfully towards us, making guttural, mewing noises. Clearly they were purring as lion cubs usually do.

'Get back, *sahib!* Get back!' cautioned the elder chowkidar in a low voice, at the same time motioning urgently with his hand for us to retreat. Rather surprised at his unexpected concern at the approach of the cubs we nevertheless obeyed.

'If the mother wakes up and sees them near you,' he said by way of explanation, 'she will think you are going to harm them. Then all hell will break loose. You will come to know what the *shaitan log* are really like.'

Very soon the two lionesses awoke and returned to the remains of the kill which, as I have said, now consisted mainly of bones. One of the spectators, a professional photographer from Austria, got the *chowkidars* to drive the lionesses back for a moment while he hung a microphone from a branch of the tree beneath which the bones lay. Then he photographed the lionesses teasing the bones while he tape recorded the sounds.

Just about this time one of the lionesses had a small fracas with a cub that was worrying her. The Austrian recorded this too. Then he played the tape back. It was amusing to observe the expressions on the lion's faces when they heard their own growl and snarls.

Suddenly the pride stopped feeding. With one accord all heads, including those of the cubs, were turned away towards a *nullah* a few yards distant. We could see nothing. We heard nothing. The next moment, silently, from between the stems of teak and *babul*, a magnificent lion in his prime stepped forth, his mane was only slightly less heavy than that of his African cousin. Even at this distance and in the fading light, we could see the tufts of hair protruding from the elbows of his forelegs.

Our *chowkidars* became perturbed. They backed away from the pride and motioned to us to follow. We did so, retreating the fifty yards to where the van awaited us. We got inside.

'It is the bad lion, *sahib*,' said the older forester. 'When he turns up, the lion show must come to an end at once. For he brooks no spectators and is no respector of cars or persons. See even the other lions fear him.'

We turned to see the pride of six scatter in all directions. There came a thundering growl as the newcomer walked up to the bones, sniffed at them, and raised his head to regard us balefully.

The light was bad, but the photographers in the party wanted to stay to photograph the lion. The two *chowkidars*, however, were obdurate. To remain would be to court trouble, if not tragedy. They urged the driver to start the vehicle and drive away. When we complained the older man replied, 'Sahib, we are responsible for the safety of all of you. That animal is a *shaitan* personified. If he had made up his mind to charge, these ancient weapons we carry would not stop him. Allah himself knows whether the cartridges would go off, for they are very old. We give him a wide berth when he appears. So also do the other lions, as you can see for yourself.'

It was dusk when we left the bad lion in undisputed control of the situation and began the return journey. We passed a few spotted deer, some late peafowl and a four-horned antelope a mile or so further and then, just as it was getting too dark to see, we heard a lion roaring a few paces from the track.

The elder *chowkidar* motioned to the driver of the van to stop, then banged the metal door with his hand while making the 'Khik-Khik!' sound with his mouth and the 'Kroo-Kroo!' noise with his lips. Within a few minutes a half-grown lion stepped out of the gloom, halted and gazed at the van expectantly. Clearly, he was hoping for something to eat in the way of live bait. We watched him for some minutes, then stepped out of the vehicle, whereupon the lion melted away into the shadows.

More excitement awaited us upon our return to the Guest House. Not content with the lion show, the enterprising Range Officer in charge had laid on a panther show as well. After dinner we were invited to attend this exhibition by following a pathway which led from the bungalow through scrub-jungle to a spot scarcely 300 yards away. A goat had been tied up to a post earlier in the evening and killed by a panther which was, apparently, a regular visitor to the spot, as he got an easy meal almost every second day in order to allow visitors to watch him eat. As with the buffalo-bait and the lions, spectators were not permitted to see the actual killing but there was apparently no harm in watching the panther eat once it had killed the goat. Incidentally, that goat cost us about Rs. 60.

All was ready. The panther had killed the goat—a black one—earlier, and then been driven off, being held at bay by a *chowkidar* with a big stick, squatting beside the dead goat. As darkness had fallen already, the scene was faintly illumined by concealed floodlights. The path we followed led into a big, circular iron-barred cage similar to what one sees at a circus but with this difference. At the circus the animals are in the cage and the spectators outside. Here, we were in the cage and the panther, outside.

Once we had assembled, the *chowkidar* with the big stick who had been keeping the panther off the kill, left his post, bringing his stick with him, and entered the iron cage with us. Then he secured the door behind him.

The panther had been watching and waiting for this moment. Obviously he was well practised in the procedure and may often have wondered to himself what it was all about. Perhaps he was wiser and wondered how stupid human beings were to go to all this trouble just to watch him eat.

Up he trotted within a few moments and fell with gusto upon the goat. The floodlights were gradually increased in intensity until, in about ten minutes, the scene was brightly lit. The panther became aware of this and must have felt uncomfortable, for he made one or two attempts to drag the goat away. But the tethering rope held fast, and the panther eventually resigned himself to tucking-in to meal under brilliant floodlight.

What might have been a rather unexciting exhibition was fortunately ended by the unexpected arrival of a hyaena. Perhaps this animal thought that he should also be given an opportunity to show himself. He sneaked up from behind, but the panther discovered him. With a snarl the panther left the kill to chase the hyaena away. The hyaena bolted, with the panther behind him, and the lights were dimmed.

Soon the panther returned, and a little later the hyaena too. Another loud snarl and another chase. Back came the panther followed by the hyaena who, growing bolder, showed himself. This time there was much snarling and growling on the part of the panther, and shrieking by the hyaena, but they never came to actual grips. Clearly the panther was not going to have everything his own way.

In the meantime the *chowkidar*, a young man this time, who had been through it all many times before and was manifestly bored, remembered that he had a young wife at home and felt that she would be in need of him. He coughed vigorously and clapped his hands. At the same time the floodlights were put out.

The panther show had come to its end. In the darkness we

could scarcely find the exit from the iron cage, but eventually we got back to the luxurious forest lodge and the foam-rubber mattresses and pillows on its beds.

At midnight I went out on the verandah. My companions were sound asleep. In the distance a lion roared. From the low hills on the opposite side came a chorus of roars in answer: 'Aaauuungh! Aaauuungh! Aauungh! Aauungh! Aungh! Aungh! Aungh! Aung! Aung!' The bewitching sounds died away into silence. I wondered if the 'bad' lion was calling to the frightened pride.

Before six o'clock the following morning we were on our way in the van to a jungle lake half-a-dozen miles away and reached it in time to glimpse a lovely sunrise over the jungle-clad hills to the east. The morning was pleasantly chilly in spite of the fact that we were in midsummer and in one of the arid areas of India.

A spotted stag brayed his challenge by the lakeside and in a few moments we saw him break cover and approach the water to drink, a dark silhouette against the golden path laid by the rays of the risen sun across the limpid water. A bevy of peafowl, quite twenty birds in all, followed one another to within a hundred yards of where the spotted stag was still drinking, and at that moment a magical sound rent the air. A lion roared in a low valley beyond the roadside and another answered from a short distance further off.

A sambar-stag, hearing those roars, belled his alarm from a distant hill-top. I was excited, perhaps even more than my three friends from overseas. For I am familiar with the habits of tigers which are quite different from those of lions, and the calls of the lions enthralled me. I tore down the hill in the direction of the sounds and my friends followed closely behind.

Soon we arrived at a sandy stream. Impressed freshly upon the soft earth of the further bank were huge pug-marks. And they had not been made by a tiger—for there are no tigers in the Gir forest. They were the pug-marks of a lion.

We hastened onwards and were in time to catch a glimpse of the animal leap into the undergrowth and vanish. Clearly it had known that we were strangers and not the *chowkidars* to whom it was undoubtedly accustomed. We could not see much of his mane in the few moments the lion gave us. It was probably a young animal; certainly not the 'bad' lion, which was just as well.

The sun had risen by the time we got back to the car. The road circumvented a hillside and we were able to look down upon a vast sheet of water. Floating upon it in several places were what appeared to be logs of wood, but which I recognised as crocodiles. Then we began the return journey, passing more spotted deer and peafowl on the way. Also a small sounder of wild pigs.

The jungle-track passed several hamlets occupied by Maldharis, the name given to a pastoral sect of people who live in this area and bring their cattle into the Gir forest for grazing. They are a colourful race. The men wear loosely-gathered jackets and voluminous trousers, a turban or headband of coloured cloth, a metal necklace with large ornaments, sometimes bangles of bone, and inevitably carry wooden staves. The women dress rather like the Indian gypsies, with ample brightly-hued sarees, tight-fitting jackets that reveal wonderful figures no Western woman could hope to approach, necklaces, bangles, ear-rings of silver, beads and imitation ivory. They are most handsome. The children look like miniatures of their elders but are even more brightly clothed.

In days past there was an abundance of water and grass in the Gir jungle. Animals were plentiful too. The lions had their natural prey and were not much interested in eating the livestock owned by the Maldharis, a species of buffalo, large and with curved, looping horns, which the peasants were mostly able to protect successfully.

The Maldharis were poor but happy in the forest with their buffaloes, whose milk and milk products they sold to the local *sahukars* or moneylenders to whom they were in debt. But with the passing of the old Junagadh state came unexpected problems. More and more cattle from all over Saurashtra and Kutch were driven into the forest, their numbers estimated at about 48,000 a year, in addition to the 21,000 stock owned by the resident

Maldharis, who inhabit 129 *nesses*, or hamlets, corresponding to the cattle *pattis* in the jungles of southern India. The Gir forest then became a vast cattle camp, which created an acute shortage of water and grazing, for which the Maldhari now has to travel a long distance. With the continuous increase in cattle came cattle diseases that spread to the wild fauna. The shortage of grazing also cut the wild fauna down in numbers, and so did the increase in promiscuous poaching.

All these changes affected the lions; they began to kill the cattle and buffaloes of the Maldharis in greater numbers. The Maldharis became poorer with the rising cost of living; they could not afford to purchase cottonseed and groundnut cake to feed their herds. Municipal taxes made the sale of their milk products difficult and they were denied the benefits extended by welfare schemes in the towns for the sale of butter and ghee for the reason that they were not urban folk.

In desperation the Maldharis, who were generally not able to procure firearms, began to poison the lions that killed their stock by poisoning the flesh of the cattle that had been killed. When the lions returned for a second meal, they ate the poison and died in agony.

This is the same sort of thing that has led to the almost complete extinction of tiger, panthers and even hyaenas in southern India. But the position is even worse in the Gir; for whereas tigers and panthers almost always hunt alone and are therefore poisoned one at a time, the Gir lions, like their African cousins, hunt and feed in prides and are thus poisoned in numbers. We were told that nine lions had been poisoned in this manner very recently. This was shocking news, considering the fact that the lions of Gir are the only representatives of their species in the whole of Asia.

The Gir itself has also been intruded upon by cultivation around its perimeter, so that the area now comprising this forest is but 1,300 square kilometers or 576 square miles in extent. A census of the lions remaining in this jungle, conducted in 1955 by measuring and counting footprints, indicated about 247 animals. The next census in 1968 showed only 177 lions, a decrease of about forty per cent. The fate of the Gir lion is, indeed, hanging by a thread.

A century ago, the forests of Gir covered three times the present area. Recent statistics reveal that sixty-three per cent of the land surrounding the Sanctuary is under cultivation. With the felling of the forest and advent of more and more cattle, together with the presence of poachers and the poisoning of kills, the noble lion of Gir seems doomed to extinction.

The Sanctuary is now estimated to support a wildlife population of less than twenty-five per cent of its original strength, compelling the lions to rely almost solely on the buffaloes of the Maldharis for food. Their ability to get enough to eat is severely taxed. Although this animal is by nature a nocturnal hunter, existing conditions compel it to hunt by day because the Maldharis corral their stock at sundown.

The Maldhari settlements past which we drove in the van that morning proved to be small mud huts, thatched with sticks and leaves. Allowing a vacant space for the cattle, the whole area of each ness is enclosed by a strong, tall thorn fence, very reminiscent of the thorn bomas of African herdsmen, or in some instance by rock-and-mud walls. Indeed, the whole scenery in the forest is much like that of the thorny scrub-jungles of Africa except for the occasional stunted teak tree growing in between.

Should a lion succeed in jumping one of these fences or walls and killing a buffalo, his effort is vain, since he cannot get his kill over the obstruction to freedom. Should a lion succeed in killing one of the herd in the jungle, he generally loses most of the meat when the Maldhari herdsmen combine to drive him away to salvage the hide.

Incidentally, this also happens in southern India when the herdsmen drive a tiger or panther off the cow it has just killed. Occasionally the feline resents this intrusion and attacks a herdsman, mauling him, even occasionally killing him. That, in turn, has often led to the tiger or panther becoming a man-eater. I was told that the same thing has happened in Gir, although infrequently. Now and then a lion has taken to killing men and eating them; it has then had to be shot.

It is estimated that of the domestic stock killed within the Sanctuary fifty per cent are taken by lions and outside the Sanctuary, up to eighty per cent. Panthers account for the remaining kills. As I have said before, there are no tigers in the area.

Because he is mostly deprived of his victim, either as soon as he kills or when he returns to the carcass to find the hide removed by the owners, the lion is of necessity compelled to kill more often than would be the case if he were allowed to gorge his fill. Statistics show that twenty-three per cent of the kills are not eaten at all, while the lions are barely able to consume ten kilograms of meat from a further twenty per cent of kills.

This cycle of unfortunate circumstances has brought the lions of Gir forest into conflict with the Maldharis who occupy the 129 *nesses* they have established all over the Sanctuary, as well as the owners of thousands of visiting cattle. Enraged herdsmen do not hesitate to shoot or poison such lions as they are able to if they will not be detected.

The government pays compensation to the owner whose animal has been killed by a lion outside the Sanctuary, but not when it has been killed within. This is not good enough. The Sanctuary, which was primarily created for the protection of these Asiatic lions, is not being allowed to function as it should and fulfil the purpose for which it was instituted.

Of the natural wild fauna three-quarters have disappeared. Most of the fertile valleys in the Sanctuary have been cultivated and a continuous strip of cultivation has already cut the Sanctuary almost in two. The felling of trees—mainly teak—continues, while the hordes of domestic livestock prevent saplings from replacing them. Nearly two million kilograms of grass fodder are removed from the Sanctuary every year. The Sanctuary has been reduced to an impoverished, artificial and heavily-exploited zone. The presence of the few remaining Asiatic lions alone has aroused worldwide interest, but only the government of India can save the situation at this last-minute stage.

I am glad to be able to record that the Central government has risen to the occasion and has entrusted the state government of Gujarat with a scheme called The Gir Lion Sanctuary Project, which started in January 1972. The Governor of Gujarat, Shri Shriman Narayan, envisaged a twofold target, the first object of which was to protect the lions of Gir in particular, as well as other wildlife, from poaching, poisoning and dangerous diseases. The second object is the socioeconomic improvement of the Maldharis' condition.

Many meetings were held and resolutions passed, resulting in formal orders being issued by the government of Gujarat to: (1) Close the Sanctuary permanently to grazing by migrant cattle. (2) Enclose the whole area with an effective physical barrier. (3) Allot land outside the Sanctuary to the Maldharis at present inhabiting 129 *nesses* inside it, and to shift them, with their families and livestock, out of the Sanctuary in a phased programme. It remains to be seen how far these aims are carried out. One fact is certain. Should the programme fail to be executed, the Gir lion is doomed to extinction within the next decade. Any number of meetings and resolutions, stacks of orders that exist on paper, speeches by the highest officials, drawings, plans and schemes supported by statistical data will not save the lion. What is required is action, and that quickly.

It is discouraging to learn that, after the passage of a whole year, the Maldharis were still where they have always been, in their nesses within the Sanctuary.

After breakfast, at about ten o'clock, we left the forest lodge in the van to motor the dusty roads to the capital of the old Muslim ruler, a town named Junagadh, which is filled with ancient Muslim tombs and mosques. A quick lunch at the Circuit House and we were away again, this time bound for the royal palace of Wankaner, where we were to spend a night and day as guests of His Highness the Maharajah and the Prince Yuvaraj of Wankaner. The distance from Sasan Gir to the palace is 105 miles by road.

Petrol trouble delayed us, but we were more or less on schedule when we reached the palace at 5.30 p.m. where the Maharajah and the Prince greeted us with old-world courtesy, garlanding us to the particular delight of my friends.

Next morning the Prince took us out in a tourist cart to his father's private jungle of some 3,800 acres, situated about six miles away. The country consisted of low, rolling hills; the soil was very dry and clothed with dwarf *babul*. The Yuvarajah complained that the townspeople from Wankaner made inroads into his father's forest, cutting the sparse timber for firewood and poaching, if they got the chance.

We came to a palisaded house where the private salaried range officer and two forest guards in the employment of the Maharajah resided. These turned out and gave the Yuvarajah—and ourselves—a big salute.

Picking up one of the guards, we motored along the rough tracks winding around the hills and sometimes across them, if the ground permitted, meeting sixteen blue bulls, the colloquial name for Nilgai, in small batches, the largest consisting of five members, all male. We also disturbed two chinkara, a species of antelope smaller in size than blackbuck, a lone fox, and numerous sand grouse. The Yuvarajah told us that black partridge and sand grouse visited the area in large numbers during the monsoons, but went away with the approach of summer. The estate was covered with porcupine diggings and burrows.

The Yuvarajah invited us to stop over another day and motor with him to see the famous 'wild asses of Kutch.' These animals, of the donkey family but standing almost as high as mules, live in an area of this dry land somewhat over a hundred miles to the north of Wankaner. Unfortunately we were bound to a tight programme and just could not spare the time. Returning to the palace, we were struck by the large numbers of wild peafowl that strutted about and called to each other. Even the extensive grounds of the palace were full of them. Nobody shoots these beautiful birds in Gujarat. 'Pea-or! Pea-or!', their cries echoed from all around.

The Yuvarajah, who had appointed himself as our guide, took us next to his private farm, situated on the outskirts of the township of Wankaner, where we were shown around a lovely guest house that he was remodelling, with excellent furniture and, of all things, an up-to-date swimming pool, something unheard of in this arid land.

Close by was an ancient well, with steps of pure marble leading down to two terraces built into the sides of the well. From the centre of the well spouted a fountain of water that reached up to the higher terrace and then splashed down to cover everything, including part of the lower terrace, with a fine mist. We felt delightfully cool, as if we were standing on an air-conditioned verandah.

After lunch we left to motor to the capital city of Ahmedabad, 140 miles distant. I felt as if I were in another world, the countryside being totally different from that of southern India. It was a parched area, semi-desert, and this fact was emphasised by the strings of camels we passed on the road, their numbers sometimes assuming the proportions of a caravan. Seated on these animals were wild-looking men and women in curious array. Other camels carried their household effects, string-cots, all sizes of pots and pans, immense heaps of clothing tied into bundles, and miscellaneous other articles that could scarcely be identified. The afternoon was exceedingly hot. As we approached Ahmedabad, the country became slightly greener. It was evening when we reached our destination.

Part of our programme the following morning was to visit the Nal Sarovar lake, a bird sanctuary and a bird-watchers' paradise, but this had to be dropped. Due to two very severe summers in succession when the monsoons had failed, the lake had dried up completely. So we visited the local zoo instead, where we saw a large variety of animals and a collection of birds from all over the world that is really excellent. I was particularly interested in the snake-pit with its jet black cobras. No doubt owing to the colour of the local soil, which is very dark and known in these regions as 'black cotton-soil', nature has arranged that the creatures that live upon it should also be dark in colour to prevent them from being conspicuous, which would otherwise be the case.

Amidst a collection of tigers and panthers, and a pair of lions from Africa, were a Gir lion and two lionesses. This lion we discovered to be far fiercer than any of the wild lions we had met at Gir, even putting the 'bad lion' to shame. He repeatedly charged at his keeper and us, stopping only at the bars of his cage. Even the African lion was unfriendly. Assuredly, the big felines are far more docile in their wild condition.

That afternoon we took off by plane for the city of Udaipur, where we landed after a very bumpy flight of fifty-five minutes, due perhaps to flying over heated, almost desert land, barren, rocky and unfriendly to look down upon. From the airport we motored to the edge of a large and magnificent lake, boarded a motor-launch and chugged across to one of a series of islands that dotted the water. But this island was different from the rest, for upon it has been built a beautiful hotel, known as the Lake Palace Hotel, with sixty-five rooms that, for the most part, directly overlook the water. The building encloses an open-air garden, abounding with trees and flowering shrubs. It is the private property of the Maharana of Udaipur, till recently one of the important ruling princes of India. He has converted it into a tourist hotel and is running it himself.

In the evening we went by launch to visit one of the neighbouring islands, where the Maharana has a palace which is also being converted into a twenty-room guest house with a magnificent swimming pool. Some of the carving we saw in this palace were wonderful, being old Moghul and Rajput work of ancient origin. The Maharana has a huge palace on the mainland, too, and yet another on the top of a neighbouring hill. From where we stood, the hill-top palace seemed almost inaccessible, perched like an eagle's nest upon rocks at summit, it gleamed a pale pink in the rays of the setting sun.

The Prince also owns a number of shooting boxes scattered about the low scrub jungle of rolling hills that surrounds the lake. Around the city of Udaipur itself are the remains of a continuous wall, once built to protect it against the invading Muslim hordes of the great Moghul conquerors.

When the sun began to set behind the western hills and cast a rippling red-gold pathway across the waters of the lake, we heard raucous voices and saw a strange sight. Thousands upon thousands of green parakeets flocked across the lake from every direction to roost upon the huge trees that grew on the island. It is estimated that over 10,000 birds fly here to roost each evening, coming from areas over fifty miles distant. Each morning they fly back again to feed, but return punctually once more the following evening. This has been going on for centuries, as on the orders of successive Maharanas no one may molest the parakeets; this protection makes it possible for them to increase in numbers every year.

Packs of jackals could be heard that night, howling on the mainland: familiar and welcome sound, it brought back a hundred memories of nights spent in jungles, now far away in the south. The packs called and answered each other from shore to shore: 'Here! Here! Here! Heee-hah! Hee-yah! Hee-yah! Hee-yah! Yah! Yah!'

Then the following morning we took the launch for the shore, where a car conveyed us to the Maharana's main palace, a wonderful structure of white and black marble, with coloured glass windows, amazing carvings, and a rare collection of old armour and swords. Nearby was an ancient temple. And in the afternoon we set out for Jaisamal lake and game sanctuary, thirty-five miles away, passing through dry jungle in hilly country enroute.

In a little over an hour we arrived at the lake, an immense expanse of water. The Maharana has yet another two palaces here, on opposite shores. The lake appeared to be well-stocked with fish, and we could see them leaping out of the water and falling back again. The evening was bright and sunny.

We motored five miles into the heart of the adjacent, Jaisamal game Sanctuary to view a 'Panther show' of a different sort. The jungle was fairly heavy, but very dry. We passed two herds of spotted deer by the wayside, some of the stags carrying exceptionally fine heads. Our destination was an abandoned watchtower, constructed by a bygone Maharana and converted by his descendant into a shooting box. It was built of stone and was three floors high, and the walls were filled with loopholes presumably for firing through. It looked like a miniature fort, and overlooked a narrow, shelving valley, through the middle of which passed a dry streambed. On the further side of this valley was a gentle, sloping hillside. There were small glades clearly visible to us between the trees and low bushes.

About fifty yards beyond the shooting box a wooden platform, roughly five feet high, had been erected. It stood upon four legs and was a more or less permanent structure. The unfortunate goat, this time a brown one, was tethered on top of it and beneath was a trough, filled with water.

We were invited to enter the stone tower, where four cars were already parked, through a low doorway at its foot and to climb a narrow stairway to the third floor. There we found a full house of people assembled; they were seated in chairs before all the available loopholes that overlooked the platform and its goat. In this gathering were a film star and her friends. All of them were chattering, smoking, moving about and hailing each other in very audible voices.

It soon became clear that, so great was the audience, if we wanted to see anything we would have to go down to the floor below. This we did and chose four loopholes before any more people came along.

I could not resist the temptation of asking the agreeable Forest Range Officer (F.R.O.) in charge of the operations whether the authorities felt any harm was being done by allowing us to watch the panther kill the goat, telling him that in the Gir we had not been allowed to see either the lions kill the buffalo or the panther kill the goat prior to the 'show', as that was considered as encouraging the taking of life. The F. R. O. smiled disdainfully. 'We are Rajputs', he vouchsafed by way of explanation. 'Those fellows are Gujaratis.'

He then went up the stairway to where the film star and her friends were gathered, and soon the chattering ceased. He must have impressed on the party that this was no rehearsal.

Staring through the loophole, I glimpsed a single spotted doe across the dry stream in the mid-distance, soon followed by bevy of after bevy of peafowl. Then dark forms filtered through the undergrowth: a sounder of wild pigs. Then a slight movement behind a bush in the foreground caught my eye. I stared hard. A panther crouched close to the ground. I had not seen him arrive. No one had. It was 6.15 p.m. The panther remained where he lay without moving. Obviously he was aware of people watching and preferred the greater darkness before he showed himself.

At 6.30 p.m. he moved slightly, but still did not risk an attack. It was seven o'clock and getting quite dark when the panther could contain its hunger no longer. From where it was crouching, the spotted cat leaped neatly on to the platform, walked calmly up to the goat that had turned around to face its attacker and was straining backwards at its leash, and almost unconcernedly seized it by the throat. The goat bleated once and kicked feebly. Then the feline pressed the head of its prey to the platform and held it there for a long time, till life was extinct.

It was getting more and more difficult for us to see anything in the increasing darkness when the Ranger pressed the switch that was to bring the spotlight into play, but there was no response. The current had failed.

We could barely see the panther tearing at the goat's throat to suck the blood from the jugular vein. A few minutes later it leaped down from the platform and drank deeply at the trough of water. Clearly this panther had been through the performance very often before and knew exactly what to do. Then it became too dark to see more.

The film star gave us a winning smile as she brushed ahead on the narrow stairway in the ground, and soon we were heading for Udaipur.

The next day was idle till the afternoon, when we left for the airport. We were bound for the distant city of Nagpur, from where we were scheduled to motor to the Kanha National Park. But there were many delays on the way, due partly to bad weather and partly to an argument at Delhi between the pilot and a passenger who turned up after the engines had been started, so it was not until early next morning that we landed at Nagpur. Rain was still falling.

But we had to be up again at seven o'clock to set off on a journey of 210 miles by car. Our entourage was of two vehicles: a car for travelling and a Land Rover for our use in the sanctuary, where some of the tracks, up and around steep hills, cannot be negotiated by an ordinary car. Meanwhile the Land Rover was hauling the trailer tightly packed with camping kit, a cook, a butler, a table-boy, and all manner of food for our use while we were 'in camp'. Also any number of bottles of Coca-Cola for my American friends. These stood upon ice in large ice-box, in rows like soldiers on parade. Nagpur is situated in Maharashtra state, while Kanha is in Madhya Pradesh. Thus we had to cross an interstate frontier and in doing so were required to sign a form. Our kit and foodstuffs were also examined with awe. It is not clear what the searchers were looking for, but what they saw must have puzzled them beyond belief. They passed us on without further argument.

Forty miles short of our destination the car became stuck in the mud. It had been raining heavily an hour or so earlier and the road was a morass. We got out to help and discovered we also had a flat tyre. To jack the car in that mud was a problem. There seemed nothing to do but wait for the Land Rover to catch us up.

Luckily it appeared fairly soon. We climbed aboard, changing places with the cook and the other two servants whom we transferred to the car. We left them to help the driver in his struggle in the mud.

The road was in a terrible condition due to the recent heavy rain and it was a difficult journey, even for the Land Rover, encumbered as it was with the heavy trailer behind. We passed through three forest *chowkies*, or checkposts, in succession, at each of which were displayed numerous notice boards with warnings against poaching and other offences. At every one of these a fee or tax of some sort was collected from us. At last we arrived at the guest houses, for there were quite a number of them.

When, as we unloaded the trailer, I saw all the food that had been provided for us, I was lost in amazement. How different was this fare from what I took on my own trips in the south! There, after the second day, my diet invariably consisted of dried *chappati*, often without butter. Roast beef was the luxury, but only on the first day. Thereafter there were *chappaties* only, and of course lots of tea. Here we had turkey, duck, chicken, mutton, fish, fruits of every sort. Not one *chappati* could I see anywhere, nor any sign of beef!

So we set off for the jungle in the Land Rover, a forest guard seated beside the driver to direct him. Within a furlong we met herd after herd of spotted deer, some of the stags carrying amazing horns. Grazing along with these animals, and sometimes by themselves, were herds of blackbuck. Now and again we could pick out the almost black form of a mature stag with its white belly, but for the most part the males were young. Does, along with their fawns, were quite numerous. Peafowl were plentiful, and we saw two red junglecocks. One flew across the track ahead of us while the other ran along the roadside for a while before dodging into cover.

The red jungle fowl of central and northern India is quite different from the silver-hackled bird of the south. Neither species changes its habitat: the central and northern bird is slightly smaller, dark in colour with rusty red wing feathers, and crows somewhat like a domestic cock. The southern bird is larger, with a silver-grey hackle, and wing feathers that look as if they have been painted with heavy oil-colours in a very dark brown border with dark spots. Feathers of the same kind adorn the hackle in addition to those of silver-grey. It has a very distinctive call: 'Wheew! Kuck! Ky'a! Ky'a! Khuckhm!' It is by far the more beautiful of the two varieties.

We returned to the guest house at sunset to find that the cook had performed a miracle and our supper was ready. The dining-room lay just off the verandah, so that while we ate we were able to listen to all the sounds of the jungle. Soon we heard a series of strange sounds, the like of which I had never heard before. Loud, trumpet-like cries, somewhat like the braying of a spotted stag, but with much more of the brassy resonance of a male sambar's note of alarm: 'Aa-hh-harmm! Aa-hh-harmm! Aa-hh-harmm! Aa-hh-harmm!'.

This was the call of a male *barasingha!* It is rather difficult to imitate that memorable sound on paper, but when you hear it, it is distinctive. And it is sad to think that in a few more years it will be heard no more. The barasingha, or twelve-horned deer, derives its name from its magnificent head of twelve tines, six upon either side, the word 'bara' signifying twelve in Hindi, Urdu and Hindustani. It is only very slightly smaller in size than a sambar, but is dark brown as distinct from the brownish grey of the sambar. Like the sambar, the stags have coarse, long hair on their flanks and around the neck and throat, where it almost resembles a mane. They are far larger than spotted deer.

Unfortunately, these creatures seem to be rather silly, lacking the alertness of both sambar and spotted deer. They move slowly, heavily and sedately, and are slow to take alarm, slow to react, slow to run away. Nor can they run as fast as sambar, although the latter is bigger.

The stags have the same habit as the nilgai or blue bull: they congregate in small herds of half-a-dozen without a single doe.

These characteristics have led to their downfall, inasmuch as they fall easy prey to the poacher, their principal enemy, in addition to marauding tigers and panthers, as well as wild dogs and even hyaenas. Barasingha, once plentiful in India, are now almost extinct.

The Kanha Sanctuary, designed for their protection especially, holds but fifty-five of these beautiful animals. Kaziranga, and a few other sanctuaries, have rather more; but everywhere they are alarmingly scarce. Their future in India, together with the lion of Gir and the one-horned rhinoceros of Kaziranga in the northeast, is very bleak indeed.

I had not yet fallen asleep that night when I heard a tiger roaring. He must have been half a mile from the guest house. How good it was to hear that memorable sound again: 'Oo-oongh! Aa-oo-oongh! Aungh! Oo-oo-ongh!'.

We were away by six-thirty the next morning and very soon found the group of barasingha that had been calling the night before: five stags, all in a bunch together. Hardly a mile further on we encountered four doe barasingha, these also in a group by themselves. Not far from them we passed three groups of blackbuck and many herds of spotted deer, one of them comprising over a hundred animals. Bevy after bevy of peahens, and some isolated cock birds, scattered to right and left of us. It was a peaceful scene until we observed two jackals slinking through the grass close by, silent reminders of the sudden death that can overtake the creatures of the jungle at any moment.

Leaving the park-like country that is the abode of the deer, the Land Rover took us into the low hills that surrounded it. Soon we saw a pair of bison staring at us from under the tall *sal* trees. The jungles of Kanha are very different from those of southern India. Stately *sal* trees clothe the former, tall and straight and beautifully green. The absence of lantana undergrowth is noticeable, also of the 'wait-a-bit' or *Segai* thorn, both of which make wandering in the south very difficult at times. This, and the absence of wild tuskers, which are dangerous and a positive hazard for the unwary hunter or greenhorn naturalist on foot, make Kanha a paradise for 'ghooming', the Hindi name for wandering about. On the whole, I would say the Kanha jungles are about the best for this purpose that I have ever visited.

The next morning we drove through heavy forests, covering over thirty miles or so of rising, hilly country to a high ridge where the natural teak opened on to an extensive maidan or expanse of low grassland, entirely surrounded by the jungle.

We were agreeably surprised to be told that the government of India tourist department plans to convert this area into a landing-ground sufficiently large to operate a Dakota plane service from Nagpur for the convenience of foreign tourists and local sightseers, thus obviating the long car-journey of 210 miles from Nagpur.

This plateau overlooks a famous former shooting block, the Bandla Block, which still goes by the same name. Many old hunters who have spent their early years in Madhya Pradesh, which was previously known as the Central Provinces, will remember this area with nostalgic affection as one that produced some of the most magnificent tigers, for which these forests were world-renowned. On the return journey we encountered as many as seven sambar together, quite an exceptional number for creatures that generally graze in solitude; also many families of langur monkeys and any number of red jungle fowl, and the small barking-deer or muntjac. Returning to the low, and the country, we passed the usual families of spotted deer and blackbuck.

In the morning we were back again in the Land Rover, meeting once again large herds of spotted deer and blackbuck, any number of peafowl and a few *barasingha*. In desperation the authorities are now planning to enclose the *barasingha* within a high wire-fencing of fairly close mesh, covering an area of a few square miles, to protect them against their natural enemies, tiger, panther and wild dog, and of course poachers. It is to be hoped this succeeds, although by its adoption these animals could hardly hereafter be classed as living in a truly wild state. Still, I suppose that fifty *barasingha* within a fence are better than no fence and no *barasingha*!

By this time we were tired of driving about in the Land Rover. Three elephants, belonging to the forest department, were obtainable on hire, so we changed over to the backs of a couple of pachyderms and went searching the borders of some *nullahs* in the hopes of seeing a tiger or panther. But we saw only the usual *barasingha* and blackbuck.

At about four o'clock we took the Land Rover again to look for tigers, but we saw only spotted deer, peafowl, red jungle fowl and langur monkeys. A couple from New Zealand, who had booked elephants for that evening, were more lucky. They had gone separately on their respective mounts, and while Jack Doon, the husband, was returning he came across a spotted stag struggling on its back. A few yards distant crouched the panther that had attacked it, caught in the act of slinking away. The stag was evidently badly mauled and its spine had been broken. The elephant Jack was riding upon had only recently come to Kanha. A nervous female, it bolted twice upon seeing the stag and its assailant. When the mahout finally succeeded in controlling and bringing it back, Jack discovered the panther again and took pictures of it for nearly thirty minutes, during which time it climbed up a tree, jumped down again and then went up a low rock. Margaret Doon, while returning on the other elephant, came across a dead spotted fawn. For some reason its killer had abandoned the meal and now the fawn was being devoured by a pack of jackals.

That night an official who had arrived at the guest house insisted that we go out with him at nine o'clock and use his spotlight to try to see bison or a tiger. As a matter of fact, such journeys in vehicles with spotlights are strictly disallowed in Kanha, but being the boss himself, and for our sakes, he made an exception. We found a very large bull-bison, followed by a cow a few paces behind, but no tiger ; and when returning met the usual herds of spotted deer and blackbuck and, close to the bungalow, a couple of sambar.

At dawn the following morning the official took us out again, this time using our own Land Rover and driving it himself. We went to a natural salt lick, where a tower had been constructed, with a ladder reaching to a covered platform. This tower overlooked a large jungle pool in which the water was partly covered with beautiful pink-petalled lotus flowers. Within a few yards of this pool was the salt lick in a hollow in the ground. A sambar stag that had been at the salt lick thundered away at out approach, while from the pool came the flapping of a myriad wings and swarms of spot-bill and brahmini ducks arose, spiralling into the air with a whir of wings. As they flew round and round they uttered sharp cries of alarm.

We also disturbed other creatures: a herd of about fifteen adult bison with half-a-dozen calves, all of them led by a huge master-bull. They had been drinking at a smaller pond opposite the watchtower and we had not seen them at first. This pond was to the west of the track we were motoring down, and in the park-like section of the country, while the watchtower and the lake and salt lick, surrounded by forest, were to the east. Thus the track formed a sort of natural boundary between the two types of country. The master-bull, with his following, saw us and attempted to cross the track to get back into the forest. We prevented them from doing this by racing the Land Rover ahead, or in reverse when the need justified it, so that the bison always found our vehicle between them and the jungle.

Maybe a dozen times we drove forwards or backwards at express speed, by which time we could see that the herd was becoming restive and the master-bull distinctly annoyed. The bison were within thirty yards and less of us; they made attempt after attempt to cross the track. Then the bull uttered a shrill, whistling sound and pawed the ground, shaking his monstrous horns at our driver with increasing anger. Then we let him pass. The herd presented an imposing sight when it finally thundered across.

The morning mists had not yet lifted when, little further on, we came upon a sambar stag grazing in the open, and still further two *barasingha* stags wanted to do just the opposite—cross over the open country.

In both our cases our official followed the same tactics, driving the Land Rover backwards and forwards to prevent them. This allowed my companions to take some good photographs. Finally we drove on and allowed the stags to go where they wished.

The usual herds of spotted deer and blackbuck were everywhere, accompanied by families of peafowl, and we were all in high spirits that morning by the time we got back for breakfast. At lunch our friend had a pleasant surprise for us. He announced that a tiger had killed a buffalo-bait he had ordered to be tied up the previous day. So our official inquired if we would like to accompany him on elephant back to try to see the tiger, and of course we all agreed. Thereupon he ordered all three elephants to be got ready, one for ourselves, one for another party of visitors who had arrived that morning, and the third for a young German and his wife who had also just turned up.

We sent the elephants ahead and followed in half an hour in our Land Rover, with two jeeps from the Forestry department carrying the other people. We found the elephants awaiting us in a shady section of jungle and transhipped. Our official rode with us on the largest. Following each other in single file, the three elephants approached the buffalo kill.

As is the case very often, the carcass was not where it should have been, and where it had been lying a couple of hours earlier when the scout for the forestry department had spotted it and come to report its death. In all probability, the tiger had spotted the scout in turn, and no sooner had the man departed than the tiger had succeeded in breaking the buffalo's tethering rope and dragging the dead animal away. The ground was thickly covered with dried leaves, but from my perch upon the elephant I could detect no signs of a drag-mark. It looked as if the tiger had not dragged his victim away after all, but had shifted it bodily by carrying the kill across its back.

Some tigers adopt this strategy when they want to be particularly secretive, so leaving no drag-marks behind. Others prefer it as being more convenient than a kill that is dragged along the ground and gets caught by bushes and thorns. In the former case instinct appears to tell them that its is more difficult to trace a kill that has been carried away rather than one that has been dragged, while in the latter case it is entirely a matter of convenience.

As there were no thorns and scarcely any bushes at this spot, its was apparent the tiger had carried its kill away to prevent it from being traced by the scout whom he had seen snooping around. There was also another possible reason: the disquieting fact that there were hide-hunters in the Kanha Sanctuary (just as there were at Gir), who remove the hides of animals killed by carnivora in order to sell them. Perhaps this tiger had already lost some of his kills in this way and was taking no chances.

The practice of removing natural kills can have disastrous consequences. When the killer is frightened away, he does not return to his kill. Thus he is getting less food than normal and he is forced to kill some other jungle animal unnecessarily, or a domestic animal (as so frequently happens in Gir), which enrages the owner and leads to retaliation against the carnivore. Moreover, after the skin has been removed, it is a strong temptation to the skinner to poison the raw carcass lying exposed in the jungle. Deadly poison—in the form of Folidol—is very easy to obtain on the explanation that it is required as preventive against crop pests, for which purpose it is supplied plentifully by the government. Also, it is so very cheap. The owner of the cow reasons that his beast has cost time and a great deal of money, and that after consuming the poison the killer will not be able to wander far and will soon die. Then the grazer will take the. tiger skin, too, and the money obtained for it will help to defray the loss sustained by the death of the milch cow.

Anyway, to carry its kill particularly a buffalo, this particular tiger must have been a large and powerful specimen. No cub, and very few tigresses, could accomplish such a task.

I dismounted from the elephant to examine the ground. A freshly broken leaf above waist-level and, a little further, a snapped green twig at about the same height, confirmed that the tiger had indeed carried the buffalo away bodily. There being a thick carpet of dried leaves on the grounds, no pug-marks were discernible; had the tiger dragged away its kill the dried leaves would have revealed it.

The tiger had headed directly downhill. The official whispered that a small stream, holding water in places, wound around the base of the hillock where we now stood. It was about a furlong away. With little doubt, the tiger had made for the stream.

I remounted the elephant, and spreading out to a distance of a hundred yards from one another, the three elephants with their parties now moved slowly downhill in line. The elephant on which my friend and I were riding was in the centre; the German and his wife were to our right, and the other party to our left. A belt of thick-growing green trees revealed the presence of the stream, and as we reached the high bank overlooking it we heard a low growl to our right and were just in time to see the hindquarters of a tiger in full flight with its tail. The German couple heard the growl too, and from their position to our right had a clear view of the tiger as it came bounding along the streambed. The next instant it saw them, changed direction abruptly, and scrambled up the further bank of the *nullah*, to vanish from sight.

Down below us lay the half-eaten remains of the dead buffalo within a foot of a pool of water trapped in the drying bed of the stream. Of the tiger we heard or saw no more. Much disappointed, we returned to where we had left the Land Rover and the two jeeps, changed into them, and were soon back at the guest house. In the afternoon we were on our way back to Nagpur.

On our journey we came to a large tank that was on the verge of drying up. Although there had been rain at Nagpur and Kanha, the area midway appeared to be suffering from drought. The entire village population had turned out and men, women and children of all ages were a foot deep in water, scooping the helpless fish into their baskets. Some of these were quite big, weighing four to five pounds each.

It was two in the morning when in drizzling rain we caught the plane from Nagpur to Calcutta. We were not scheduled to spend any time in Calcutta on this stage of our journey; we were to catch the next flight to Jorhat, a town in northeastern Assam, in an area known as the North-East Frontier Agency, from where we would have to drive by car to India's greatest game sanctuary, Kaziranga, to see the famous one-horned rhinoceros in its wild state, in addition to wild buffalo, barasingha, tiger and elephant.

I approached the booking-clerk to verify our seats on this plane and book our luggage, when he blandly told me that the official concerned would attend to this work only at 6.15 a.m. The flight to Jorhat was scheduled for 7.05 a.m.

The one thing passable about the Calcutta airport is its dining-room. We had tea there and waited till the clerk arrived. He scanned a list and said our names were not among those of the passengers on the Jorhat flight. He admitted we had been 'booked', but that was not enough; our names had not been 'confirmed'. Mere booking was not enough, he said. Any clerk could 'book' your name. But the airline authorities had to 'confirm' that there was a place for you on the plane. For us this had not been done. And the plane was already full.

He advised us to wait another fifteen minutes or so. The airline coach would be coming from the city, which was nine miles away, bringing the passengers for this flight. Our luck might be good. Maybe four persons had cancelled their flights, in which case there would be room for us.

The coach turned up at 6.30 a.m. What was more wonderful, four seats were available! Then an official asked to see our 'permits'.

'What permits?' we asked in unison.

'What permits?' he repeated. 'Don't you know that you are all foreigners? Foreigners are not allowed to enter the N.E.F.A. area without a permit signed by an official of the government of India as represented by the Assamese office in Calcutta, because Jorhat is close to the Nagaland border, where foreigners are not allowed.'

We did not know, and said so with some heat. We wanted to go to Kaziranga to look at rhinos, and were not bothered about N.E.F.A. or Nagaland. He shrugged and said we could not board the plane. Then he turned away.

Joe, one of our American friends, was a professional photographer. He had made the journey to India to take pictures and publish them in a series of articles about animals. Every moment was of consequence to him in terms of money. He really blew his top at the news. The airline official merely smiled. 'You will not be able to go to the Assamese office in the city today,' he added. 'You see, there is a general strike in progress and you will not be able to get a taxi. All motor traffic is off the road.'

'You might walk the nine miles,' he went on, 'but the office is certain to be closed, due to the strike.'

Yet, in spite of the gloomy picture he had painted we had a little luck. We succeeded in finding a conveyance to the city. It took us to one of the largest and best hotels in Calcutta, where we were fortunate to find accommodation. The strike that had been threatened did not materialize, but a *hartal* (which amounts to the same thing) was in progress. We managed to get a taxi and went posthaste to the office of the representative of the Assamese government for our permits. Here our passport numbers were noted and questions asked. We were told it would take a day or two for counterchecks to be made before the required permits could be given. Joe again blew his top. We just managed to get him out of the office in time. A few seconds more, and we would never have got those permits.

We decided to fill in the time while waiting by seeing as much as we could of Calcutta. Then it would not be necessary for us to stop over when returning from Jorhat.

We visited the zoo first. There we saw the three famous white tigers and their three half-grown white cubs. Light grey almost white in colour, they are certainly unique. One of the tigers is a beast of outsize proportions. Each of the six animals is housed in separated quarters. Then there is a *gayal*, a large animal with the body of a bison but with straight horns. It comes from eastern Assam and the Burmese border. Also, of course, the Indian rhino and a number of Gir and African lions. A feature of the zoo is a large lake within its boundaries to which great numbers of wild-duck of all varieties, migrants from beyond the Himalayas, find their way and spend four months of the year.

For the time being Joe was happy and seemed to have got over his irritation at the delay in reaching Kaziranga. But his pleasure was short-lived, for when we got back to the hotel at 5.30 p.m. we received the bad news that Indian Airlines had suspended all their flights to and from Calcutta owing to another hartal, called with immediate effect, due to the resignation of the West Bengal government.

The news made Joe furious. He wanted to charter a special plane to Kaziranga or go by car. Since neither of these things could be done, he became grumpy and sulky. The situation grew rather unpleasant.

All this happened on Monday, March 16, 1970. The last we heard before dinner was that, if the local government could sort itself out, we might be able to fly to Jorhat on the 7.05 a.m. flight on Wednesday, the 18th—if the permits came by then.

Tuesday (the 17th) was an uneventful day. We did some sightseeing by taxi in the morning and called at a few shops. By afternoon, however, the political situation had deteriorated; taxis were off the road and were replaced by truckloads of armed policemen patrolling the streets. We were warned not to attempt to step out of the hotel. Calcutta is crammed with over a million-and-a-half homeless people who dwell on the pavements. They cook and eat there, sleep there, and of course hardly ever get the opportunity to wash. It is unsafe for anybody to go out on the streets on foot during periods of political trouble of any sort, for these pavement-dwellers are not slow to take advantage of the first opportunity that comes their way, and when law and order go awry, to knife a passer-by in the back. They have no interest in the contesting political factions.

The only ray of hope that reached us that afternoon was in the form of our four permits. Frankly, I had not expected these to arrive for a long time. We ate our dinner early and retired, to wake up before 5 a.m. and get ready for the air journey we hoped to make at seven.

I had to carry my own suitcase and airbag down the stairway from the third floor, as the lift was not working. Nor were the servants willing to be helpful in this hotel, because of the rule that they must not be tipped. The airlines office was a bedlam. Nobody would pay us the least attention and it was impossible to find out whether we could proceed on the 7.05 a.m. plane, or even if that plane was taking off. The airport was another bedlam. Nobody knew if our names were on the list of passengers.

Seven o'clock, then eight and finally three in the afternoon. We were still firmly upon mother earth. None of us had lunch and we were all exhausted—what with Joe wanting to do this thing and that, claim a refund in court, send a telegram to the President of India with copies to the Prime Minister and the American Consulate, and the incessant chattering of the Bengalis around us, which reminded me of the noise made by the thousands of mynah-birds when they return in the evenings to roost on the tall trees surrounding my home at Bangalore. It was a nerve-wracking experience.

Nobody could say at what time our flight to Jorhat would take place; indeed, nobody knew whether the plane would fly or not. To make matters worse, the officials suddenly received instructions from their union to go on a 'work to rule strike', while the porters were told to go on 'total strike'.

At last, at 3.15 p.m., the loudspeaker crackled, somebody coughed, and prepared to speak flight no. 211 was cancelled! We were lucky to find a taxi to take us back and drop us at the hotel from which we had started early that morning.

Being of a stubborn sort, I made a jaunt on my own to the

airlines office the same evening, to find that our luck had changed at last. All four of us were booked on flight no. 249 at 6.10 the following morning, Thursday the 19th. Returning to the hotel in triumph, I found I had lost my old room; someone else had already taken it.

We left at 4.45 a.m. the following morning to find Dum Dum Airport in the same state of strike and confusion. The fate of flight no. 249 was greatly in the balance. However, with the use of much animal cunning, elbow grease and some surreptitious *baksheesh*, we managed to work a transfer to a combined flight of nos. 205 and 249 in a Viscount aircraft which, seemingly to the surprise of the airport officials themselves, and most assuredly to our own, took off at last at 9.30 a.m. None of us glanced earthwards at Calcutta as we left the city behind.

3

The Anaibiddahalla Tigress

'Anaibiddahalla' literally means in the vernacular 'the hollow into which the elephant fell.'

A stream winds downwards in southerly direction, having its source quite close to the forest hamlet of Kempekarai in the mountainous jungle stretch to the north of the town of Pennagram in the district of Salem in Tamilnadu—formerly the Madras Presidency. This stream drops sharply at one point. It is a fall of about two hundred feet and it occurs in the region of granite rocks, so that the water has worn a deep hollow through striking the streambed over a period of perhaps thousands of years.

In the rainy season the water fills this hollow and rushes madly onwards in its course, but in summer, when the stream ceases to flow, a deep pool of still, dark and forbidding water fills the hole. Nobody knows its exact depth. Probably it is well over thirty feet. As summer advances and the heat increases, the level of the pool descends, leaving a sheer, circular wall of smooth rock all around, covered with slime and moss, up which nothing that has fallen into the pool can ever hope to climb back to safety.

That is what gave the place its name. For an elephant came along one hot season in search of water. The animal came to the pool and must have extended its trunk to suck up some of the water. Probably the water was just out of reach. The elephant extended too far, slipped on the slimy sides skidding down into the pool.

Elephants are excellent swimmers, but nothing and no one except a fish can continue swimming for ever. Some cartmen who were travelling along the nearby road to Muttur heard the elephant's screams and gurgles of fear and suffocation. They left their carts, seated themselves on the rocks, around the pool and gloated over the drowning beast's efforts to escape.

It is said that the elephant made prodigious but vain efforts to get a foothold on these slimy rocks. It slipped back each time.

The cartmen were so interested that they lit fires on the rocks and camped there the whole night. The elephant finally disappeared beneath the surface with a last shriek and gurgle in the early hours of the morning. It took over a fortnight before sufficient gas could collect in the stomach to float the carcass to the top. By this time the stench was awful, and it grew worse and worse as the thick hide and flesh fell apart in decomposition to expose huge chunks of rotting meat.

After that no creature came near that pool for a very long time. That is, not for at least thirty years, when a tiger that had been roaming the area and had started to prey upon men repeated the whole act by slipping into the pool itself. But that's another story.

Tigers rarely remained in this area for long, yet it was in fact the bend in a regular 'tiger beat' that resembled a rather wide letter U if laid upon its left side, that is with the opening facing left. The lower side represents the bed of the Chinar river, from the point where it empties itself into the larger Cauvery and for a little over seven miles up its course. At what point the stream from the north, along whose course lies the deep pool of Anaibiddahalla, empties itself into the Chinar.

Tigers were occasionally in the habit of swimming across the Cauvery and wending a leisurely way up the course of the Chinar, killing what spotted deer, sambar or pig they could find, and an occasional heifer or buffalo at the cattle pattis at Panapatti and Muttur along the way, to turn northwards up the course of the Anaibiddahalla stream, skirting the big pool and climbing the hill above it. They then continued another seven miles as the crow flies till they reached the bed of another stream, euphemistically known as the 'Talavadi river' although it is really little more than a deep and rocky nullah, flowing westwards for perhaps fifteen miles to empty itself into the Cauvery river at a point maybe seven miles above where the Chinar river itself joins the Cauvery. The Talavadi stream, of course, is represented by the upper side of the letter U lying on its left side.

As I have related, these wandering tigers from across the Cauvery would stroll eastwards up the Chinar river, then turn northwards up the Anaibiddahalla stream and finally return westwards down the Talavadi *nullah* to reach the Cauvery and swim across it once more to the Kollegal bank on the opposite side.

It was interesting to note that the tigers always followed this course and never came in the opposite direction—that is, from the Talavadi to the Anaibiddahalla stream down to the Chinar and back to the Cauvery. I wandered across this area for many years and found it always so. I even questioned the poojarees who have spent all their lives in these forests, and they said the same thing. It is one of those jungle mysteries that appears to defy explanation.

These feline hunters had always been harmless, confining themselves to hit and run raids on the cattle *pattis* that lay along the beat if they were not lucky enough to find wild game.

What came in time to be called the 'Anaibiddahalla Tiger' was no exception. In fact it was no tiger, but a tigress. She would follow this beat approximately every four months. At times the interval would be longer. From what people living in the mud-and-wattle huts along the Cauvery told me, she would take a month to six weeks to complete the journey. Then they would find her pug-marks coming down the rocky Talavadi watercourse, taking advantage of the cooler sandy stretches that skirted the edges of the stream where the rushes grew, and the tall clumps of the 'orchid' or 'muthur' grass, till once again she had reached the banks of the Cauvery. Here, as her pugs indicated, she had spent no time hesitating. They led to the water's edge where, whether the season was dry and the water low, or the monsoons had broken and the Cauvery in flood, they would disappear from sight. The tigress must have been a strong swimmer.

Clearly, she had her home on the Kollegal bank of the river, probably in some cave at some lonely spot on one of the lofty mountains that rose abruptly in tiers from the river bank. Very definitely her mate was there too, for suddenly she failed to return to her old beat and a whole year passed. Even more than a year, in fact.

Then the tigress returned. Once more her familiar tracks were seen on the sands of the Chinar river as it wound past the cattle *patti* of Panapatti and this time she was not alone. Two sets of pugs accompanied her, one upon each side. They were small pugs, about the size of the tracks that would have been made by large Alsatian dogs. The tigress had brought her two cubs along.

It was most unfortunate that she had done this, for it brought trouble to the cattle, the herdsmen that attended them and finally to the tigress herself and her cubs.

The cattle that had been killed hitherto by passing carnivore, both tigers and panthers, had been few, and the herdsmen who attended them had not taken the matter very seriously. They could always get away with an occasional lie by telling the owner that the animal had died of a sudden sickness, or slipped and fallen down a *khud* or steep *nullah* and broken its neck.

But this tigress, finding the cattle many in number and comparatively sleek in condition, decided to settle down in the area with her two cubs. It was so much easier to kill and to feed her cubs upon fat heifer or buffalo calf than have to wander for miles in search of food and then perhaps find none: she would have to go to sleep on an empty stomach and, worse still, so would her cubs. She knew from experience that when they were in that condition, as large as they had grown, they would still persist in trying to drink milk from her and that was a very painful experience. For the cubs had long and sharp claws that would tear into the fur and skin of her belly, and they had grown sharp and strong teeth that bit into her udders.

Kills began to take place in quick succession now, on almost every third day, for the cubs had keen appetites. No longer could the excuse of sickness or an accident be put forward to account for missing animals. They became far too many. So the poojarees and other low-caste villagers, who comprised the herdsmen that attended on the large assortment of cattle and buffalo kraaled at Panapatti, sent out a call for help to my *shikari* and camp-follower, Ranga by name who lives at the small town of Pennagram, about eight miles away.

I have told you something about Ranga in other stories. He and a poojaree named Byra and I had wandered in these forests, mile upon mile, for many years, and there was hardly a corner of any of them that was unknown to one or all of us. Byra had been a poacher, and he remained one till he died. Ranga was a far more versatile fellow. Starting as a poacher, he had climbed the ladder of status to that of cartman, *shikari*, cultivator, and finally to that of a miniature landlord. He had attempted to kill his first wife and gone to jail for it, because he made the mistake of getting caught. Profiting from this experience, he had murdered his second wife after making sure he would not get caught by leaving a complicated lead to her uncle. Thereafter, realising it would be far too much of a risk to attempt a hat-trick by murdering his third, he had solved the problem by marrying a fourth, leaving the two women as a check upon one another while he got tied up with a fifth.

Leaving this place of many marriages for the moment and returning to the subject of the tigress, Ranga received the call for help and took it very seriously. He had an old muzzle-loader in those days. But it was a good weapon, inasmuch as it had laid low many a sambar hind that Ranga had ambushed over a water hole in summer, many a spotted deer, doe or fawn that had come to drink at the same water hole, and many a wild pig that had been so daring as to wander into the sugarcane fields near Pennagram on a moonlit night. Ranga was certain that he could account for the tigress with his trusty firearm without any trouble at all.

He sent word by the men who had come to summon him

that the herdsmen should carefully conceal the remains of the next cow or buffalo killed by the tigress with branches of trees so that vultures would not find and finish it, and then to call him immediately. He would come at once, keep watch over the carcass and finish off the tigress as soon as she had returned for a, second meal.

The plan worked well up to a point. The tigress killed a buffalo and with her two cubs ate nearly half of it. The herdsmen concealed the remains under branches cut from nearby trees and sent for Ranga. Ranga came without delay, bringing his trusty matchlock.

The only fly in the ointment was that there was no convenient branch close enough to the carcass for him to build a *machan* upon which to sit up for the tigress. There had been one and only one, and it had been just in the right place. But the foolish herdsmen of Panapatti had lopped it down just to get at its leaves and smaller branches to cover the cadaver! Could they not have brought the leaves from somewhere else? The whole jungle lay before them for this purpose. They had been far too lazy. Why walk so far when a convenient bough was to be found so close at hand?

So Ranga had to look for another site for his *machan*. He found it. There was another branch on another tree. But it was from eighty to hundred yards away. The range was rather too far for a muzzle-loader, particularly at night when everything appears so distorted. Some of these old blunderbusses are wonderfully effective at impossible ranges for a shotgun to be of any good. But on a dark night, when it would be difficult to bring off a good shot even with the aid of torchlight the odds were stacked against Ranga.

The tigress came along with her cubs. Ranga had heard them coming. Soon he knew the tigress had started her meal; he could hear the growls made by the mother and her offspring as they quarrelled over the meat.

That was when he pressed the button of the electric torch he had tied with string to the barrels of his muzzle-loader. The cells were probably half-exhausted, for Ranga said he could hardly pick up the eyes that shone back a whitish red in his direction. Trusting to luck he pressed the trigger.

There was the usual roar of the explosion, the bright flash of the ignited black gunpowder, and the heavy pall of smoke that covered the whole branch upon which he was seated. Ranga knew he had not missed. He could hear the tigress roaring loudly and angrily.

To reload the muzzle-loader in the darkness, balanced precariously on a hastily constructed and unstable platform, was not easy, but he managed it at last. The roaring had ceased when he timidly depressed the switch of the flashlight a second time, but now he saw nothing beyond the dim, dark blur of the carcass lying upon the ground. Of tigress or cubs there was no sign.

When daylight came, my henchman and the herdsmen, who had heard the shot at night and came from their huts, saw that the tigress must have been hit. There were drops of blood upon the ground, and later, by dint of careful stalking, they found the trail with smears and spots of blood on the grass and upon the leaves. It led downhill and across the Chinar, which at this time of the year carried running water hardly a foot in depth.

On reaching the further bank, a heavy outcrop of orchid-grass showed where the tigress and her two cubs had passed. More smears of blood upon the green stems indicated that the tigress had been hit somewhere in the right flank. There was no evidence that her right shoulder or thigh had been damaged, as the pug-marks she had left in the soft sand showed no signs of a limp, nor did the wound appear to be a serious one, as the blood trail was comparatively light. After the clump of orchid-grass, the tigress and her family had crossed a low thorny hill, on the further side of which the trail had petered out. Either the wound had gradually ceased to bleed, or a layer of fat or hide had worked itself across the cavity to stop the bleeding.

In the usual optimistic fashion of the Indians, Ranga and his companions congratulated each other that between them they had got rid of this troublesome animal. No doubt it would die of its wounds somewhere in the jungle or be drowned when it tried to swim back across the Cauvery in its weakened state. Of the fate of its two cubs they never thought or cared.

It was a dark night, just over two months later, when a string of bullock carts bumped and jangled down the three sharp hairpin bends in the track that led from the higher-levels of the hill above the Anaibiddahalla pool to the lush valley through which the little stream purled on its way to the Chinar. The vegetation was dense in this valley, and elephants and sloth bear, sambar and jungle-sheep abounded. The felines and spotted deer kept for the most part to the more open forest slightly higher up; the deer because they disliked getting into heavy vegetation where they could be easily ambushed by carnivore and the even more dangerous wild dogs, and the felines because the valley was full of insect pests and they hated the big ticks, the mosquitoes and, strangely enough, the tiny fleas that were a feature of this forest.

The leading bullock-cart carried a dimly burning lantern hanging from the yoke securing the two buffaloes that drew it; it hung just behind their hindquarters. There was a reason for this. The domestic buffalo is an abnormally stupid animal. If the lantern had been suspended anywhere near its neck or face, it would refuse to draw the cart. Nobody knew just why. Maybe the beasts that drew the cart thought that they were home, so why go further? With the light behind them and darkness ahead, they thought they had still to go on. Rather illogical reasoning, I admit, but maybe buffaloes are illogical creatures. The cartmen had to use them in preference to the usual bulls, for the loads of cut bamboos were unusually heavy and the track stoney and steep. Buffaloes have more strength than bulls.

Admittedly, to hang the light behind rather than in front had the obvious disadvantage. Nobody, not even the buffaloes, could see what lay ahead. And when there was only one lantern to the whole convoy of a dozen carts, it did not help. But perhaps it was better not to see too much, on the principle that to see no evil was to know no evil. What I mean is, an elephant might be standing just around the corner or just off the track. Ordinarily, he would not be visible at night. Also, ordinarily, unless he was a 'bad' elephant, he would take no notice of a string of bullock-carts passing by. So why see him unnecessarily and become unnerved?

However, this did not always work. If perchance the elephant was not so good, or even slightly bad, he might not relish this disturbance of his privacy. Yet there was nothing the cartmen could do about it anyway. They certainly could not turn back. Try turning a bullock cart around hurriedly on a narrow track on a pitch-black night, with eleven more carts and eleven friends driving them behind you. Of course they could all come to a halt instead; at least the leader could. Number two would bump into him and stop. Number three would bump into the number two and so on. Would it help? Better to keep going. If the beastly elephant comes too close, beat the empty kerosene tin in the cart behind you, kept there for just that purpose. That should stop him. And if it does not? Jump out of the cart and leg it down the line of carts behind you. But do not lose your head and run into the jungle; there may be another elephant there. By the time the elephant smashes up your cart, throws one or both your buffaloes into the air in his exhilaration and then turns his attention to cart number two, you have enough time to be well out of the way. Besides, there are eleven other fellows behind you. By the time they wake up and realise all is not well, the elephant will have had a roaring time. The main thing is to save your own skin.

But what about snake? Poisonous snakes crossing the road? One of the buffaloes might step upon one; in which case, within two hours there would be only one buffalo less.

The cartman should always ride in his cart, not walk behind it for fear of elephants. One such cartman never kept to this rule. He had met a herd of elephants on this very track, but about seven miles further on. It had been evening and he had been alone in his cart; so he had returned to the camp of the bamboo-cutters, to set forth before dawn the next morning. This time he walked behind the cart, so that if he bumped into the elephant he could fade away without being spotted.

However, the buffaloes escaped treading on a cobra in the track, but one of the cartwheels broke its back. The next thing the cobra saw was the man's foot. So he bit it. The cartman walked another mile or so, reaching the Muttur forest bungalow, where I was encamped, at break of day. I cut the wound to bleed it, and walked him about vigorously.

All to no avail. The poor fellow died in about two hours, and the police gave me no end of trouble for two days. Apparently, the fact that I had cut his foot with a knife to cause bleeding was highly suspicious. Perhaps if I had done it with some blunt instrument and concealed the blood things would have been okay. I just could not get them to understand the reason. I think I have told this story somewhere else, but it suffers repetition as it has direct bearing on bullock-carts that travel through jungles by night.

However, no elephant ambushed this particular convoy. But a very hungry tigress did, accompanied by two equally hungry cubs. They let the convoy pass, that is all but one. They attacked the last cart.

The driver was sound asleep when it happened, hunched up over the scraps of rope he used as reins, and rolled up in a coarse black blanket. He awoke with a start, to the sensation of falling through space, as the cart toppled down into a *nullah* bordering the road. He could hear deafening sounds; growls, snarls and the bellowing of his own two buffaloes. He did not know it just then but riding on the back of one of them, with her fangs embedded in its throat, was a tigress. A cub, slightly less than half-grown, but ineffectually into its side, while another clung to the hindquarter of the other buffalo.

The cart and all the creatures involved in this melee landed with a crash at the bottom of the *nullah*, which was luckily not deep. The cartman was thrown free, while the yoke holding the buffaloes snapped. The buffalo that had been attacked by one of the cubs broke away and bolted down the *nullah*, leaving the bewildered cub to join its mother and the other cub that were attacking the remaining buffalo. In another two minutes it was dead.

The cartman, hastily extricating himself from the entangling blanket, saw struggling black forms and heard frightful noises. By the light of the stars he scrambled up the side of the *nullah* to regain the track the convoy had been following. Away in the distance he heard the jangling and thumping of the other carts as they raced away from the scene. Those of the drivers who had been awake and heard the pandemonium that had broken out behind them had guessed that something terrible was happening to their companion behind. Exactly to which companion they did not care nor stop to find out; the buffaloes yoked to the carts needed no goading to speed their pace. They knew the roars of a tiger when they heard them! Galloping behind each other in a jagged line, the convoy bounced and thudded down the precarious track, while running for his life, the luckless driver whose cart had been attacked ran behind to catch them up.

News of this event spread far and wide and the bullock-carts ceased to travel by night. This did not help the tigress, who became more hungry, and she had to feed her cubs besides herself. Nobody knew it then, but her right shoulder had been badly hurt; in fact, the bone was split by the lead ball from an old, old musket. It was Ranga's musket that had done the damage.

Driven by hunger, the tigress started to attack cattle by daylight. In this she was joined by her cubs, who were rapidly learning the art of killing, though the methods were crude and amateurish as befitted their inexperience. Their mother could not do much better, handicapped as she was by a smashed shoulder. Thus it transpired that each kill made by this trio of animals presented a nasty spectacle of mangled living flesh and torn hide and bone, a victim that had been partly eaten alive. It was all so different from the kill made by a normal tiger; a neat job in which the neck of the prey is neatly broken with a minimum of bloodshed.

These attacks continued for the best part of six months, during which time the cubs grew apace. They now required no help, but could kill expertly by themselves. Curiously, they remained with their maimed mother instead of breaking away and fending for themselves as cubs begin to do when about a year old. The killings of cattle and buffaloes increased as the cubs grew older and larger and their appetites increased.

Probably nothing more exciting would have happened had not Mariappa, the cowherd, instead of running away as fast as he could, as did all wise cowherds, rushed to defend his milch-cow when the three tigers attacked it at the edge of his field. He might have succeeded had the attacker been a single beast, but numbers bring courage, both to human being and to tigers.

If you should be 'ghooming' in a jungle—that is wandering about with the hope of seeing what animals you come across— or should you meet a pair of tigers or a tigress with cubs (both of which are today most unlikely to happen, I might tell you), halt and above all do not move. Do not start to run away, for that will attract the attention of the tigers which, just like your dog, love to chase things that run away from them. Take cover, by all means, if you know how, without floundering about and advertising your presence. Above all, remain absolutely motionless. And never, I strongly advise you, start to follow them to see where they are going. There is a fair chance that you can do this in perfect safety with a single tiger, or even with a pair of panthers. But when a pair of tigers are involved, or a mother with cubs, the chances are small. Tigers do not like their family privacy disturbed for one thing, while numbers definitely bolster their courage. With elephants it is quite the opposite. Leave 'Jumbo' alone if he is by himself, and avoid a female with a calf, though you can drive a herd of thirty like cattle almost with impunity, even if you are all by yourself.

Mariappa committed the grave error of rushing towards three

tigers lying over the lovely cow which they had just killed. I suppose he thought he would be able to save it. Very brave of him, but equally foolish. The next instant he was dead. Which of the three 'felines killed him nobody knows.

4

In a Jungle Long Ago

It all happened at Panapatti many years ago. *Patti*, as I have explained in earlier stories, signifies 'a cattle-camp', and Panapatti was one such camp. It is situated on the southern bank of the Chinar river, about three miles and a half from its confluence with the Cauvery, which is the largest river in southern India. The Chinar holds water only in the monsoons, and possibly a couple of months after that. For the remaining six months of the year it is a dry *nullah*, although both banks for a dozen mile or more from where it empties itself into the great river are clothed with heavy jungle, acres of bamboo, with *muthee*, tamarind and *jumlum* trees and other varieties in between.

When the monsoons end vegetation dries quickly in India. As a consequence the grass and the stalks of *cholam*, *ragi* and rice, harvested from the fields and given to the cattle after the ears of grain have been removed, becomes exhausted too and there is nothing for the domestic herds to eat. That is when the owners of the herds turn covetous eyes upon the forests, where the grass still grows and certain varieties of leaves and shrubs provide grazing.

Grazing licences are purchased from the forest department, and thousands of domestic cattle are driven into the jungle, where they are kept till the advent of the next monsoons, when they are driven back to the village again once local grazing becomes possible as the grass and crops spring up. As this is an annual performance regular campsites have grown up in all the forests where the cattle are kraaled during the summer months. These sites in the south are the '*pattis*'.

Panapatti is in the district of Salem of what is now Tamil Nadu state and was formerly the Presidency of Madras; hardly anybody outside a radius of twenty miles knew or heard of its existence. To my knowledge on only two occasions did excitement in any form come to Panapatti. The first of these was with the advent of an elephant that killed a few people, including a hunter that had come after it. This animal came to be known as 'The Rogue Elephant of Panapatti'. I have told the story in an earlier book.*

There was a lull of several years after that. Then notoriety visited the little camp for the second time with the advent of 'The Avenging Spirit', which I am going to tell you about. Let me hasten to add that this spirit was not a human phantom but a tiger that appeared suddenly from nowhere, earned a ghostly fame, and then disappeared as mysteriously as it had come.

The owners of most of the herds kraaled at Panapatti were rich landlords inhabiting the large town of Dharmapuri, about twenty-eight miles away as the crow flies. Three or four, of lesser importance, hailed from the smaller town of Pennagram situated just ten miles distant. The herdsmen to whom the cattle were entrusted during their stay at *patti*, were the lowest caste of villagers from Pennagram, augmented by a few 'poojarees', who were jungle-men belonging to an aboriginal tribe, living in the forest all the year round, sheltered in little thatched huts or in *gavvies* or hollows dug into the banks of the Chinar river at spots where that stream ran through hilly country and the banks were steep and high. This protected the inmates from elephants that crossed the Cauvery and walked up the bed of the Chinar river in the dark hours of the night.

Such a poojaree was Kaiyara. He had been one of the graziers regularly employed for quite a number of years in looking after the herds that came to Panapatti during the summer months. On an average the cattle remained in this camp for about six months

---

*See: *Nine Man-Eaters and One Rogue*.

in the year, and Kaiyara's wage was ten rupees (about 50p) for the entire period, plus a weekly allowance of rice or *cholam* or *ragi*. Not all together, mind you, for that would be gross over-payment. Say about ten pounds in weight per week, whichever grain was the cheapest available in the market at that time.

When Kaiyara had first taken service several years ago, he had had his wife with him and an only child, a daughter named Mardee. Then the krait came. It had been a very hot night and the slim, jet black snake with the infrequent white notches across its neck and back, had slithered into the grass-thatched hut occupied by the little family and coiled itself around the base of the dark earthen pot in which the drinking water was kept. No doubt the reptile was feeling the heat, too, and relished the cool of the pot.

Kaiyara's wife had very long hair. When she lay on the floor of the hut at night, it had a habit of getting knotted or falling across her face and disturbing her. So on that occasion she had decided to tie it up with the strip of black rag that she kept for the purpose.

But where was that rag? By the water-pot. Talking to her husband as she did so, the woman stooped and her fingers closed around what she thought was the rag. Unfortunately it was the krait she had grasped.

The snake struck at what it thought was an enemy, burying its small fangs just above her wrist. Then it disengaged itself, slithered behind the water-pot and passed through the wattle hut wall into the jungle outside.

The woman hardly saw what had bitten her. Something cold and black, she knew, and then it was gone. She called to her husband and held out her arm for his inspection. Kaiyara looked and saw two tiny drops of red blood on her back skin. They were hardly half-an-inch apart. The poojaree recognized the marks for what they were, punctures inflicted by the fangs of a venomous snake.

He got busy. There was no doctor, no anti-venom injection, no hospital within twenty-eight miles. Only his dirty cloth bag, containing some powdered herbs and roots, could help.

Kaiyara knew nothing about lancing the wound and bleeding it. So he stepped outside, picked up some soft cow-dung, made a mixture of it with some of the powder from his bag, and smeared the paste thickly over the wound. Then he started muttering a mantra, over and over again.

Within thirty minutes his wife complained of great pain in her wrist. Also shooting pains in her abdomen. She said she was beginning to feel giddy. After another thirty minutes she could not speak. The last she had said was that she had great pains in her stomach. Saliva was pouring from the corners of her mouth. Her breathing was heavy. Yet another thirty minutes later there was hardly any sign of breathing. The woman was cold and limp. Her eyes had rolled back in their sockets. A few minutes more and she was dead. Kaiyara was left alone with his little girl, Mardee, to look after.

The years passed. Mardee was now a comely lass. She had grown into full womanhood, mature and well developed in body. Handsome, too for a poojaree aboriginal. She was her father's mainstay and looked after him well, cooking all the meals and doing the chores in their tiny household. She also went out with the cattle at dawn and grazed them till sunset, returning with the herds of beasts as they ambled home in the evenings when the sun sank behind the jagged hillocks to the west on the bank of the Chinar.

Many of the poor herdsmen and a number of the poojarees coveted her and came to Kaiyara with proposals of marriage. To strengthen their suits, some were prepared to forego the usual dowry which every father had to pay the bridegroom and his family before a daughter could be married. Mardee spurned all her suitors. Young as she was, the girl was of a determined nature; she would have nothing to do with common herdsmen or poojarees.

Then one day, Sathynarayan came to Panapatti. He was the eldest son of his father, Gopalswamy of Dharmapuri, a rich landlord and merchant who owned over two hundred head of cattle grazing at Panapatti. Sathynarayan was also married and had a wife and young son. But they stayed behind at Dharmapuri when he came to Panapatti to inspect his father's herd. Sathynarayan arrived at a comfortable time of the morning when the herds had already been taken out for graze: about nine o' clock. The cattle had been driven out as the sun's rays were just rising above the Muttur Ridge, four miles to the east, to melt away the heavy mists that clothed the valley of the Chinar and the sloping land on both its banks, and to send the wild elephants into the dense bamboos for shelter, and the sambar into the hills.

He left his car on the main road with his chauffeur and walked the two miles of jungle track that brought him to the *patti*. It was a filthy track, Sathynarayan thought; the earth was several inches deep in layers of cow-dung, deposited year after year by successive herds of cattle and buffaloes. He stepped delicately, avoiding the more recent patches of dung for fear of soiling his shoes.

Soon he stood at the doorway of Kaiyara's hut and coughed loudly; then he spat. It was utterly beneath his dignity to call the inmate by name. The poojaree had watched his employer's son approaching. He crawled through the low doorway and prostrated himself on hands and knees, touching his forehead to the ground, the customary salutation of a poojaree in the old days.

'What news?' inquired the young man curtly.

'All is well, *Swamy*,' replied the poojaree regaining his feet. 'By the grace of the gods, none of your revered father's cattle have been taken away by the ferocious wild beasts that fill this forest nor stricken by the cursed foot-and-mouth sickness. I give thanks daily to the gods for their mercy. The animals have been driven out to graze under the care of my unworthy daughter.'

'So that is how you earn your keep?' asked Sathynarayan pointedly.

'By sending the cattle out in charge of a girl while you sleep in your hut. What can she do if a wild animal should attack?'

The father was silent, then he thought of a brilliant excuse: 'I was sick of the fever, with pains in my stomach and diarrhoea all last night, your honour, else I would have gone with the herd myself.'

'You lie!' accused the landlord's son. 'However, as I have come to see the animals for myself, you must now guide me to where your daughter has driven them.'

Thus it came about that Sathynarayan saw Mardee for the first time and lusted after her greatly. He could not speak to her straightaway. That would have been beneath his status, particularly with her father looking on. He would have to look for some better opportunity.

The young man took a great interest in his father's herd after that day. His parent was rather surprised suddenly to discover that his son-and-heir, who had hitherto shown little liking for his business and none whatever for cattle, had developed an unexpected thirst for knowledge. So he smiled indulgently and decided to encourage his son. Probably it was just a passing fad and would soon wear off, when the boy would become as useless as before. Of course Sathynarayan's wife could not comment. Women in India are not permitted to question the comings and going of their men.

Sathynarayan timed his visits to a later hour, when he knew the animals would be grazing in the forest. Moreover, he avoided the *patti* and went directly to the grazing ground. Thus he met Mardee for the second time, and third and fourth time, and many times thereafter.

Although she was still a child, her woman's instinct told the poojaree girl that the young man had fallen in love with her, a sentiment which he was not slow to encourage with small gifts of money. Mardee had always aimed high, far above the local cattleboys and poojarees, and here was the answer to her dreams. A very rich young man; her employer's only son to boot!

Sathynarayan lost no time in seducing her. The jungle offered plenty of scope for that and Mardee became pregnant. Of course, the lovers thought that nobody knew of their clandestine affair. Actually everybody in the *patti* knew about it. The herd-boys had seen from a distance. The poojarees had gone one better: they had stalked the lovers and peeped on their most intimate moments at close range. Then they had run back and told Kaiyara.

The old man was astounded. Such a thing was unheard of; it had never happened before. His employer's son was a Brahmin of the highest caste. Moreover, he had his own wife and son. Mardee, his own daughter, as a poojaree was of the lowest caste! How could this thing be? If he should dare to question the young man, the matter would be reported, and his employer, the father, would undoubtedly throw Kaiyara out of his job. So he kept the matter to himself for five months until it was evident his daughter was going to have a baby. He questioned the girl. To his dismay, she appeared to be not in the least ashamed. She admitted that Sathynarayan was the father and declared he was in love with her and had promised to marry her.

At the very next opportunity Kaiyara screwed up enough courage to question the young man.

Sathynarayan flew into a towering rage. 'What are you talking about?' he thundered. 'Would I defile myself with your daughter, a slut of the lowest caste, like yourself? Who told you this absurd tale?'

'She told me herself' answered the old man flatly.

Sathynarayan scowled, but said nothing in reply. He turned his back and walked away.

The next morning Mardee took the herd out again for grazing. It was clear she had not slept the night before. There were rings under her eyes and they were red. She had been crying. This could be understood, for her father had said that the young man had denied having touched her and had called her a low-class slut.

It was long past the sunset hour when the herd struggled back that evening. They came in twos and three, and a few of them did not come at all. And of Mardee there was no trace.

Darkness fell before Kaiyara fully realized what had happened. He begged the other men to come with him in search of his daughter. Some agreed. Others pleaded that they were indisposed.

There were no lanterns in the *patti*. Nor did anyone possess an electric torch. Each little hut had just one small oil-light of its own, a tiny taper of wick, floating in a little earthenware bowl of oil. There was no moonlight either, for it was time of *amavasa*, the darkest period of the month. Moreover, this is also the most inauspicious and dangerous period to be out at night, the time when devils of all kinds roam at will: evil spirits that sometimes appear as men and women, sometimes as elephants, tigers and other wild animals, and often as tall white pillars reaching to heaven. They would cackle and scream with unholy laughter when they came across defenceless mortals to kill.

In this atmosphere of terror the little party set forth, treading their way along the trails left by the cattle as they grazed in the forest. The only lights came from the stars that blinked down through the foliage. Inky darkness covered the ground. A demon might be anywhere, behind tree-trunk or bush, and might strike at any moment. A tiger or panther might lurk round any corner. Even an elephant could be three paces away and would be entirely hidden in that gloom. The men walked together, in a bunch, those at the sides making considerable noise as they brushed through the thorns bordering the pathways and getting their skins well lacerated in the process because nobody wanted to be the last man in line.

It was common knowledge that it was the last man who always fell prey to the attack of a tiger, a panther or an elephant. At least, if that happened, he would cry out and warn the others, who would have a chance to run away. But if a demon attacked him he would just disappear in silence. Nobody would know about it. Then the next last man would vanish, and the next, and so on. No one would know a thing till all had disappeared.

In this fashion the little party crept forward, faltered and then came to a stop. Each member had worked himself into a state of abject fear and the feeling was infectious. By mutual consent they came to a halt.

'Mardee', screamed her father in desperation. 'Mardee, Mardee, where are you my child?'

There was no answer but the sough of the jungle breeze as it began to blow down the valley. Far away a tiger roared. Just ahead an elephant heard the roar and trumpeted in challenge. A sambar stag on the further bank of the Chinar caught the scent of human beings and belled in alarm. Once, twice and many times. A langur monkey, higher up the hillside, woke to the disturbing noises and grated his repeated warning to the other members of his tribe.

The search party wavered no longer. They turned and hastened back to the *patti*. Indeed, they walked so fast it was impossible to do so in a bunch. Somebody had to be last. But this time the gods were good: no wild beasts attacked him, nor did a demon strike him down. They all got back to the *patti*, but without Mardee.

As the girl had vanished in broad daylight, everybody thought she had been taken by a tiger. Had an elephant killed her, or a panther for that matter, some trace of her would have been found. But although Kaiyara, and every other resident of the *patti*, combed the surrounding jungle for a week, not a trace of the missing girl did they come across.

Then there came a clue. A lone cartman, struggling to get his vehicle up the steep incline of the Muttur track leading through the jungle to Pennagram, remembered that he had been forced off the roadway into the ditch by a big car that had come up from behind and was trying to get ahead of him. Because of the gradient, all carts were hauled by buffaloes, as they were more sturdy than the customary bullocks, and more sure-footed. Unfortunately, they were also more stupid. When the car had come up from behind, the cartman had noticed that, strangely, the driver had not even once sounded his horn. Instead, he had attempted to overtake the cart in swift silence, with the result that the buffaloes had shied and run down into the steep ditch beside the road, capsizing the vehicle with its load of bamboos.

Luckily, the cartman had been thrown clear, and as he hit the ground he had looked up to see who was responsible for this callous behaviour.

The car was Sathynarayan's. The cartman knew it well by sight. Somebody else was driving but he recognized Sathynarayan in the back seat. He had been holding on to a woman. He had caught a glimpse of a red sari as the car lurched past at high speed. He said he did not know who the woman was. But Mardee had been wearing a red sari on the day she disappeared. Slowly the pieces of the puzzle came to fit together.

Normally, one could expect the Muttur track to be deserted in the early hours of the morning. The presence of the car-man was something unexpected. If a car were parked at a bend in the track where it wound around a stony hillock called Karadimedu (Bear's Mill), the owner could follow a short cut through the forest that would take him in about twenty minutes to the grazing ground where Mardee had driven the cattle.

The whole thing seemed to lead to a choice of two conclusions. Either the lovers had made an appointment which the rich young man had used as an opportunity to abduct her, perhaps with the intention of murdering her later; or unknown to her, he came upon her by stealth and had taken her away against her wish.

Kaiyara reasoned all this out in his mind aided by one or two of his companions whom he felt he could trust. He dared not speak of it openly. There were informers everywhere and none knew who could be trusted. Word would be carried to the young man, or his father, Gopalswamy. Kaiyara would then be sacked. That would be the least that could happen. He remembered he was up against moneyed people. They could pay *goondas* (ruffians) to beat him up, perhaps murder him. For that matter, they could bring a false charge against him of theft or something else. He would be locked up in the police station and be beaten up mercilessly. His cronies advised him to leave well alone. Treat the whole matter as the will of God, and forget about it.

But Kaiyara was a father. Further, he held a reputation at least among the herdsmen and his brother poojarees at Panapatti, of being a black magician who could cast powerful spells, and if he did nothing he would lose the reputation for good and all. He would be scorned as an imposter, a coward. His companions would say to each other: he called himself a black magician, but where is his magic now? If he were genuinely what he claimed to be, he would cast a spell upon the man who had committed this crime and that man would fall very sick and die. For everybody at the *patti* had reasoned out for himself what had happened, although none dared to speak of the matter openly.

A few days later, the night of *amavasa* came again, the darkest night of the month, when evil spirits are afoot and magicians cast their most potent spells. When the camp fire burned fitfully at Panapatti after the evening meal and the herdsmen sat around to chat for a few minutes before retiring to their huts for the night, Kaiyara stepped into their midst and addressed them. He had adorned himself for the occasion. Red and white marks changed his face into a fearsome sight. A silver armlet above his right elbow identified his status as a black magician. A necklace of the large serrated seeds of the *oudarrachamani* plant encircled his neck, and another of large, black, glass beads.

He cleared his throat and began to speak: 'Brothers, as you all know some evil man has beguiled my daughter. Not only has he done wrong, but he has taken her away and perhaps murdered her. The days are bad and we are poor people. There is none we can approach for help. None will stretch forth a finger to aid us, for we have no money, while the evil man who has done this thing is very, very rich. But I do have this power which neither he nor all his money, influence and friends can take away from me. It is the power to curse him and his family, from the realms of the living to those of the dead. I will go in search of my beloved daughter. Maybe I will find her, maybe not. Maybe, I myself will not return. Should any harm befall me at the hands of this evil man, I want you to bear witness that I now curse him and his family. His life, and the lives of his dear ones, will be swallowed up for the life of my beloved daughter and my own. I curse him! I curse him! I curse him! By this thrice repeated curse, it shall be as I say.'

Next morning Kaiyara went forth from the *patti*. Only his close companions knew he had gone to Dharmapuri boldly to announce to his employer, the rich businessman and cattle-owner, what Sathynarayan had done to his daughter.

Kaiyara never came back. He was never seen again! The herdsmen soon forgot about him and the words he had uttered. Possibly his special friends thought about it and felt sorry. The poojaree had been foolish enough to put his head into the tiger's mouth, so to say.

Six months passed. It was the festival of Pongal and everybody was enjoying themselves. In the village the bullocks' horns were gaudily painted, red, blue, green, bright yellow. Upon their foreheads were long red and white marks of ochre too. Games were arranged and sometimes mock fights between men and bulls.

Sathynarayan and his wife and son, accompanied by his father, motored from Dharmapuri through Pennagram to the point on the road where they had to leave the car in the care of the driver and walk the distance to Panapatti.

In fact this trip had been entirely the father's idea. Sathynarayan certainly did not want to go to Panapatti ever again. The place held too many awkward memories for him. That damned poojaree girl had taken him seriously. She had actually believed the silly stories he had spun that he was going to marry her and make a lady out of her. To make matters worse, the wretched girl had the misfortune to become pregnant, and to crown matters she had told her father all about it. The affair had cost him a thousand rupees, which he had to pay to the chauffeur, Das, to gain his silence about the day they had abducted the bitch. Luckily not even Das knew what he had done with her body. He had made the driver get out of the car so that there would be no witness.

As if that were not bad enough, the damned girl's father had had the temerity to come all the way to their family home at Dharmapuri to inquire about his daughter's whereabouts. By a stroke of good fortune, his father had gone to Madras the day before. That incident had cost him another thousand rupees. This time Das knew, for it had been Das who had taken the dead body late at night in the spare car. He and the driver had weighted it with stones and the latter had dragged it out of the car and thrown it into a large tank forty miles away, along the road to Salem.

But all this meant that Das knew too much. Last week the driver had approached him with a demand for five hundred rupees. Sathynarayan had started to refuse, but had stopped short when he saw the smirk upon the driver's face which told its own tale.

Then Sathynarayan made a plan. Immediately after Pongal he would go for a big shoot, and he would take Das with him. There would be a shooting accident and the driver would be killed! Of course, a lot of awkward questions would be asked by the police, but he knew that his father would come forth with bags of money and the questioners would fall silent.

Now why, of all place, did his father want to visit Panapatti for the Pongal festival? Sathynarayan had tried to put the old man off. But as everybody knows, old people are very stubborn. His parent had got quite hot about it. He had even chided the young man with the disappointment he had felt when the latter's sudden interest in the cattle herd at Panapatti had as suddenly ended. And so the four of them were trudging through the jungle to Panapatti, having left Das to look after the car. The Chauffeur had worn another of his nasty smirks as he caught his eye before parting. Sathynarayan resolved that he would have to stage that hunting trip and the accident that was to go with it, without further delay. Das was becoming far too dangerous.

The four visitors reached the *patti* where the herdsmen and the few poojarees had made ready to welcome them. As the august patrons were of the highest caste no refreshments of any sort could be prepared by them or pass through their defiled hands before being presented. Thus the gifts took the form of green coconuts, which had to be broken before the water could be drunk, and huge sweet-limes called 'sathgoodies', from which the outer skin had to be removed to get at the pulp. Gifts of this sort would be readily accepted, as there was no chance of the ingredients being contaminated.

The painted and gaudily decorated cattle were displayed and a couple of mock-fights between men and bulls were staged. As the animals were roped and held in restraint by half-a-dozen men on each side, these encounters were farcical and excited nobody except perhaps those who took part in them. The evening closed with the usual felicitations and, after consuming more coconut water, the visitors prepared to depart. They had taken care to ascertain from the herdsmen that there were no elephants in the vicinity and so they dawdled till a later hour than they would otherwise have done. Once again the sun was sinking behind the jagged hills across the western bank of the Chinar, but with normal walking they would reach the main road where the car awaited them before dusk.

It happened somewhere midway between the *patti* and the main road. Sathynarayan and his father were walking ahead together, probably discussing a business deal of some sort. The young man's wife, as behoves all respectable and dutiful Indian married women, was obliged to walk a few paces to the rear. This she was doing, leading her small boy by the hand. The child was tired and bored to death by the whole proceeding. He was crying.

It is not good for the young of any creature to cry in the forest. The jungle recognizes no law of pity for the young and helpless, only the rule of the survival of the fittest, which certainly does not include the young. There was a sudden snarl; at the same time a great tawny body with black stripes materialized from nowhere to seize the crying child in its jaws. The mother saw this and instinctively hurled herself at the beast's head to save her child. The two men in front heard the snarl and swung around. They saw the tiger with the child in its mouth rear up and strike the mother with its front paws. They waited to see no more.

Sathynarayan, who was younger, ran faster and reached the car first. His father fell from exhaustion several times before he also made it. Then Das drove the car at breakneck speed to Pennagram to get help. No help was forthcoming at that hour, for the shades of night had already fallen. The next morning a vast concourse of people armed to the teeth, retracted the steps of the fleeing men and came upon the tragedy.

Mother and the son lay a yard apart. The tiger's great teeth had bitten through and through the little boy. His mother had been killed by the two great blows that had been dealt to her. Not a morsel of flesh had been eaten from either victim. Upon the hard ground were no traces of pug-marks.

As may be imagined, pandemonium reigned at Pennagram and in the nearby villages and forest *pattis*. No man-eating tiger or panther had been heard of for a hundred miles around. As a matter of fact, at this particular time the herdsmen of Panapatti and the fishermen at Uttaimalai and Hogenaikal and the other hamlets on the other banks of the great Cauvery river confirmed that there was a distinct lack of carnivores of any sort in the area. Being the dry season, and this year a particularly hot one, the sambar had taken themselves to the mountains and the spotted deer had gone to less dry area. Such carnivore as had existed, and these were few, had gone with them.

Where the killer had come from, nobody could tell. Why he had killed and then not eaten was a still greater mystery.

I had been on a visit to my land at Anchetty, a hamlet in the same forest but about twenty miles to the north when all this happened, but no news had reached Anchetty yet. I had later left Anchetty, walked to another *patti* named Gundalam, and then sixteen miles down the course of a stream I have called the 'Secret river' to its confluence with Cauvery river. From there I had come another ten miles to Uttaimalai, where the fishermen were very excited at having heard of the happenings near Panapatti.

There is a short cut across the foothills which brought me to the bed of the Chinar river two furlongs below Panapatti. I found the herdsmen and poojarees gathered under a tree discussing the recent event. They had not driven the herds of cattle into the forest for grazing for the last two mornings for fear the killer might attack either the animals or themselves—that is, the one or two herdsmen who felt that such a thing might happen, and they were in the minority.

All the poojarees, without exception, and the rest of the herdsmen were of the opinion that they and the herds were quite safe. The tiger that had killed was not a man-eater, for it had not touched the bodies of the woman and child it had slain! Nor was it a game-killer, for they had come across no bones or carcases of sambar or spotted deer. The vultures had not soared in the sky nor quarrelled over the remains of a kill for a long time.

In fact, this was not a tiger or a panther at all—at least, not one of flesh and blood! It was the spirit of Kaiyara, the poojaree, who had avenged the murder of his only daughter and of himself. The poojaree had assumed the form of a tiger to fulfil the curses he had placed upon the braggart Sathynarayan.

'Nor is this the end, *dorai*,' the eldest of the poojarees at the *patti*, and one who had been a particular crony of Kaiyara's, confided to me in an undertone. 'Not by a long chalk. It is but one half of the curse. The lesser half, in fact. The two really guilty ones have yet to die, the murderous Sathynarayan and the rascally car-driver who helped him.'

It is a rare thing for an Indian to confide his innermost thoughts to a man of Western origin. An unwritten and unspoken proscription exists against persons of another race and colour, to whom it is considered most unwise to impart secret information of any importance. There is a general belief that Westerners are extremely foolish, very callous, most disbelieving and, in fact, grossly ignorant of all matters not directly involving the five material senses. This prejudice is everywhere in the land and perhaps strongest in the minds of simple folk from the villages and jungles. It took me more than two hours of subtle and adroit questioning before I could wheedle from the old man the facts which I have already set forth in this story. Considering moreover, that I have mixed with jungle folk and villagers from the time I—and they—could walk and talk, I consider myself extremely lucky to have been able to get all the facts I eventually collected.

To me, of course, all this was but jungle-talk, the sort of thing one could expect to hear from superstitious folk. In my opinion, the tiger was just a tiger and nothing more. Perhaps it was a wounded animal and in pain when it saw the woman and child and attacked them in sheer rage. Maybe the crying of the child attracted and enticed it, perhaps even annoyed it. Maybe a hundred other reasons, but it was only a flesh-and-blood tiger. From this followed the next thought that, although for some unaccountable reason it had not eaten either of its victims, it might attack again at any time. Accordingly I made arrangements to try to shoot it. At that time I was not working, so the time factor did not count and I was in not hurry to return to city life.

As I have related in other books, most man-eaters follow a regular 'beat' in the territory where they operate. By this I mean that they follow a definite itinerary in moving from one jungle area to another, past particular villages, up the beds of or across certain streams, or along certain game-trails and fire-lines, in moving from one locality to another. Having moved this way once and killed and eaten a human or two here and there, they come back along the same trails and routes after a certain period of time, and do this over and over again. So, with patience and care, it is possible to map out the 'beat' followed by such a man-eater and to forecast with considerable accuracy when and where to wait for him in ambush, or try to entice him with a bait or by some other means.

All this did not apply in the present case. This animal had not killed any other human being anywhere for miles around. As

I have said, it had not even attacked a single cow in any of the herds, nor had it killed a deer or pig as far as was known.

I enlisted the aid of the poojarees and herdsmen in the *patti* and scoured the bed of the Chinar river, both up and down, for several miles in each direction in order to find its pug-marks and ascertain if it was a male or female. Search as we did, we found no pug-marks anywhere.

This tiger must have come from the east, therefore, where lay comparatively open country, scrub jungle which petered out into cultivation for miles around. No tiger could live, or conceal itself, in such conditions. It had to come from the forest. Tigers do not live in fields!

I prevailed upon the herdsmen to lend me four cattle from the herd that belonged to Sathynarayan's father, promising to pay for any one that was killed. I knew that the owner would not object under the circumstances, but nonetheless sent one of the herdsmen to Dharmapuri to inform the owner of what I was doing.

I found the poojarees in the *patti* disinclined to be cooperative in the proceedings from this point onwards. The ancient one among them told me, flatly that I could not expect him and his clan-members to help me to lay a trap for their dead companion when he turned up in the form of a tiger—not that he would be so foolish as to kill any of the baits I had tied up, or allow himself to be shot at. It was well known that no bullet made of lead could penetrate a spirit. Nevertheless, it was the motive of their actions in helping me by which they would be judged. They could not, and would not assist me in trying to shoot this tiger.

Money talks and so I was able to entice the herdsmen who were not poojarees to aid me. After much inquiring and tramping up and down, I chose four places as being the most likely for a tiger to turn up. All that I could do now was to wait complacently till one of the baits was taken.

Rather than be idle meanwhile, I scoured the forest from dawn to dusk searching for the pugs of the tiger up and down the banks of the Chinar river. As the herdsmen and poojarees at Panapatti were not keen on helping me, I sent for my old friend Byra, himself a poojaree, who lived at Anaibiddahalla, another *patti* about fifteen miles distant, and for Ranga who had accompanied me on many adventures. Both these men were expert trackers and knew the area for miles around. But the three of us searched in vain: not a single tiger-pug did we find. The killer had disappeared as silently and as suddenly as he had come.

Time ran out on me and the day came to go back to Bangalore. I returned the four baits I had borrowed together with a small gratuity. Normally, it is not possible to come to an arrangement of this sort and the hunter is compelled to purchase his baits outright. But this case was an exception because they knew for certain that none of the baits would be harmed. How could they, when there was no tiger to harm them?

About two months elapsed and Das, the driver, was returning alone to Dharmapuri in the big family car from the city of Salem, sixty-five miles away, where he had taken Sathynarayan's father for admission to hospital for removal of a cataract. Das had left the old man there and was hurrying back for dinner. He had forty miles to go to reach his home in Dharmapuri. The road narrowed down to traverse the winding bund of a large deep tank. There appeared to be no traffic in sight and Das accelerated.

Then something must have happened to the steering, or may be a front tyre blew out. Nobody knows for certain. The only witnesses were two villagers hurrying homewards who saw the whole incident. The car left the roadway suddenly at a point where the road turned left, crashed through the thin brick wall bordering the bund directly ahead and plunged headlong into the tank.

Das had closed the windows. He was trapped in the car and his body was recovered a week later when the vehicle was hauled out by the police.

Was it coincidence that he was drowned in the very tank into which he had thrown the body of Kaiyara after his master and he had murdered the poojaree and weighted the body with a stone? Sathynarayan heard the news and madness fell upon him. First, his only son, then his wife. Now the chauffeur, Das.

Sathynarayan remembered the murder of the old poojaree and his daughter before him. Tales had been carried to him about the curse the old man had uttered against him and he became convinced it was his turn next. At that moment, Sathynarayan realized he must die. Thus his mind gave way. His father returned from hospital to find his son a lunatic. The old man did not spare expense. He took Sathynarayan to Salem and consulted the best of doctors. The boy kept repeating the names of Kaiyara and Mardee in his raving but the doctors could do nothing to cure him.

Sathynarayan was then taken to Madras, and admitted to a mental home. The psychiatrist discovered that the mania arose from some connection in the madman's mind with the two persons whose names he kept muttering. However, no treatment was effective and the father became reconciled to the fact that his son and heir was permanently insane. The young man was brought home, where he was given two male attendants to look after him night and day. His father hoped that he would improve with time.

In this he was doomed to disappointment. His son became worse and grew violent, whereas before he had been but a gibbering maniac. The old man reluctantly decided that he would have to put him into the asylum at Madras as a permanent inmate. But this was not to be, for the curse of Kaiyara had yet to exact its full toll—or so people said!

Sathynarayan was missing from his room when his attendant brought his breakfast early one morning. He had been there the evening before. A search was made all over the town but nobody remembered to have seen him anywhere. They young man was well known and somebody would have noticed his movements. It was four days later when vultures spiralled the sky above the track that leads from the main road to the cattle kraal at Panapatti. They flew in wide circles, which narrowed as the birds of prey rapidly increased in numbers. Then, one after another, they plummeted to earth, their wing-feathers emitting a loud rattling noise as they tore through the air.

Byra saw the vultures and heard the sound. He had taken employment that year among the graziers at Panapatti and was driving a herd of cattle to the forest for grazing. He knew the vultures had spotted a 'kill', and being a hunter from childhood he went to investigate. Perhaps there might be some meat for him to eat.

The kill was easy to find. The discordant screeching noise made by the vultures led him to it unerringly. The birds were gathered round in a circle and had not yet begun to feed. For they were afraid!

The reason for that fear lay in the fact that dead thing they were contemplating was a human body. It was Sathynarayan, and he had been killed by a tiger. But no part of his flesh had been eaten.

Byra told me, the next time we met, that he and the other poojarees and herdsmen had searched the whole area thoroughly for pug-marks, but they had found none. Then he shrugged: 'How could we *dorai*?' he asked. 'For it was no tiger that killed that swine! Kaiyara made a good job of it.'

www.ingramcontent.com/pod-product-compliance
Lightning Source LLC
Chambersburg PA
CBHW030633030726
47497CB00006B/1761